# +HE LAS+ DAYS

Andrew Masterson is a Melbourne-based writer. He has contributed extensively to newspapers and magazines, often writing about music and popular culture. He lives with his girlfriend, his cat, and a fluctuating population of European crested newts. This is his first novel.

# THE LAST DAYS

## ANDREW MASTERSON

### THE APOCRYPHON OF JOE PANTHER

PICADOR

First published 1998 by Pan Macmillan Australia Pty Ltd

First published in Great Britain 1999 by Picador

This edition published 2000 by Picador
an imprint of Macmillan Publishers Ltd
25 Eccleston Place, London SW1W 9NF
Basingstoke and Oxford
Associated companies throughout the world
www.macmillan.co.uk

ISBN 0 330 37562 8

Acknowledgements are due to the following authors and publishers
for permission to reprint material from:
Jorge Luis Borges epigraph © The Estate of Jorge Luis Borges. All rights reserved.
'Wandering Star', words and music by Geoff Barrow and Beth Gibbons, © 1994 Chrysalis Music
'Heartattack and Vine' by Tom Waits, © Fifth Floor Music.
Reprinted by permission of Rondor Music (Australia) Pty Ltd
Reprinted with the permission of Pocket Books a division of Simon & Schuster from
*Beyond the Chains* by Eric Fromm. Copyright © 1962 by Pocket Books.

1 3 5 7 9 8 6 4 2

A CIP catalogue record for this book is available from
the British Library.

Printed and bound in Great Britain by
Mackays of Chatham plc, Chatham, Kent

*For Sahm*

*The song is finished.*

# ACKNOWLEDGEMENTS

This novel contains many quotations, half-quotations and paraphrases drawn from historical sources. Some of these are credited in the text, but many are not. Accordingly, the author here acknowledges the work of ancient writers known and unknown, including Tertullian, Augustine, Origen, the authors of the Old and New Testaments, and the Gnostic Gospels of Nag Hammadi.

The author also wishes to thank his agents, Jane Burridge and Alison Urquhart of The Other Woman, for their encouragement and humour. Nikki Christer of Picador also deserves many thanks for having the courage to take a punt on what was then a barely started manuscript, as does Virginia Lloyd who had to deal with it once it was finished. Designers Mary Callahan and Dominic O'Brien both did great stuff with the cover image.

Special thanks must go to Adele Lang, columnist, author and friend, for being the generous catalyst who got the whole show on the road. Endless patience and encouragement have come from many sources, particularly Ilana Rose, Stuart Milke, Carolyn Logan, Andrew Penney, Fiona Brindle and Monica Butler. And deepest gratitude is owed to Sahm Keily, who has coped with the author's manifest anxieties rather better than the author has himself.

My suspicion is that in Heaven the Blessed are of the opinion that the advantages of that locale have been overrated by theologians who were never actually there. Perhaps even in Hell the damned are not always satisfied.

Jorge Luis Borges


You can be a gambler, who never drew a hand,
You can be a sailor, who never left dry land,
You can be Lord Jesus, all the world will understand,
Down where the drunkards roll.

Richard Thompson


Other sayings in this collection criticise common Christian beliefs, such as the virgin birth or bodily resurrection, as naive misunderstandings. Bound together with these gospels is the 'Apocryphon (literally, 'secret book') of John', which opens with an offer to reveal 'the mysteries [and the] things hidden in silence which Jesus taught to his disciple John'.

Professor Elaine Pagels, *The Gnostic Gospels*

# 1

Thus do things reduce.

Not so long back it had been a girl, a young woman, blessed and flawed, frail and tough, weak and strong, a sinner pursuing ragged redemption through the lamentations of the street.

Part of a young girl, anyway.

Now it was a severed head, cradled, eyes open toward the sky, by the granite curb and bluestone gutter, black hair drifting Pre-Raphaelite in the run-off from the rain, tangling with journeying tram tickets, twigs and the last redundant elm leaves of winter.

Her lipstick was smudged left across her lower cheek, like she'd turned away from a forceful and unwanted kiss.

Except she hadn't.

'Ach,' said Father Corrigan, 'and she looked so pretty when she came out of the box. Like a doll. Like the Mother herself.'

I turned away and put the breeze to my back, lit a Dunhill, cupping the match like it was the holy flame of St Brigid. The sky was white, smudged with dirty grey. The drizzle, for the moment, stopped. It was another featureless day in a featureless season, a winter cold and uniform, a mean and bureaucratic purging that chilled without challenging, morose, bland and passionless, with neither storm nor hail for weeks on end to relieve the gnawing tedium. This was not a winter of myth, a winter you survived. This was a winter you simply bore; you simply lived through, trying not to notice.

Some of us at least.

I let the current pull smoke and foggy breath from my mouth and lash it away, dashing it, exorcised, against the front of the church. My throat stung. I'd give it up if there was a point to it.

I turned back and looked once more at the opaque and smeared imperfection that not too long before had been the uppermost anatomy of Shelagh Jane Purdey, seventeen, troubled recidivist of the parish of St Cuthbert in the shadowed and littered Melbourne inner-city suburb of Fitzroy. The lipstick was a violent cerise, polluting now, in its disarray, the thick white pancake which coated her face, but not quite reaching the russet blooms that marked each cheek. The mascara had run like the tears of a mourner beneath the dappling of the rain and the traffic of the gutter. The eye shadow was cheap and blue.

The police photographer was lying on his belly in

the road, adjusting his lens for maximum depth-of-field, trying, perhaps, to capture her profile in the foreground, the mottled pavement, path and pockmarked steps diminishing through the scrubby front lawn to the church behind, the whole framed by the blue-black solidity of the building itself, Father Corrigan and I neatly placed, smoking and wet in front of the doors, the alabaster Virgin ignorant and serene in its alcove above.

'The Mother, eh?' I said.

The priest nodded, didn't turn his head. 'The Mother.'

'For, surely,' I lowered my tone half an octave for the effect, 'those women sin against God who anoint their faces with creams, stain their cheeks with rouge, or lengthen their eyebrows with antimony.'

He turned his head then, stared at me like all of a sudden I was a stranger, an unpleasant and dangerous stranger. He'd known me for years.

'Tertullian,' I said.

He turned back to face the obscenity outside his gate. 'Shelagh never wore much make-up,' he whispered. 'And Tertullian was a bitter old bastard.'

He turned again, right around, and walked through the doors to where the rest of the horror was waiting.

✝

All in all, the feast day of St James the Great, son of

3

Zebedee and brother of John, had not begun well for Father Brendan Pearce Corrigan, self-styled radical priest and guardian of the little-frequented church of St Cuthbert.

Truth be told, the priest probably was only distantly aware that on that uncharitable morning in July others of his faith in naves and sacristies around the globe were in the process of commemorating the death of the first apostolic martyr, witness to the agony in Gethsemene, at the sword of King Herod Agrippa. It wasn't his style and, anyway, his hagiographic learning had been progressively eroded since he graduated from the seminary thirty years back. His saintly cosmology had been worn smooth and featureless by the same force which etched his face with crags and shadow: a life of exposure to the grinding, unforgiving poverty of his parishioners, the welcome erasure of whisky and the creeping amnesia of a battle deep and fiercely unacknowledged.

Hardly surprising, really, the Jimmy business. I barely recall it myself. Was he the first to die? Or was that Stephen, under a hail of rocks? It doesn't really matter, in the end. Memories fade, even the memories of friends, given time and the determination of strangers. By the Middle Ages, conjuring Stephen was the bee's knees when it came to curing headaches. Much later, his cult was surpassed by a small colony of pin mould.

So there's Corrigan, local identity, crops up regularly in the local press, saying this, saying that, railing against the latest uncaring side-effect of monetarist social policy. Every Sunday he did the business, said the prayers, broke the wafers, heard the confessions of the two dozen or so old codgers who hove into the pews mistaking the comfort of ritual for the blessing of heaven. There was no choir, of course, not in Fitzroy, and the candles came by the box from a Vietnamese clearance store two blocks away in Smith Street. It was more low-rent than High Church, but hell, it came with the territory.

The rest of the week he did what he considered to be his *real* work. After unlocking the church each morning he'd do his rounds, walking the streets, lanes and alleys of the parish, talking to the young men and women who stalked therein, living lives, he considered, short, dark and brutish, abandoned by society and God alike.

These, he said, were his true flock and the object of his ministry, whether they sought the love of the Lord or no: the street kids, the wards of state, the sex workers, the abusers of junk, drinkers of methadone, blasters of speed, the rackers, the steamers, the incest escapees, the illiterate, the drunk, the paranoid, the deluded, the heads of grease, the faces blasphemed by acne and filth, the boys and girls with blush on their faces, cum in their mouths and eyes like the widows of massacre.

Blessed are they that have been persecuted for right-eousness' sake: for theirs is the kingdom of heaven.

Sure as shit, Father.

He carried condoms in his pockets, clean syringes in his bag. Like a battered Ford Falcon, he was loved a little, used a lot. He welcomed the misbegotten to his nearby modest house any time of the day or night, left the doors of the holy bosom unclasped until mid-evening each day in the vain but resilient hope that once, just once, he might return from his wanderings to find perhaps one of his charges there within, seeking salvation.

It never happened. Until the feast of St James. But by then salvation was way off the menu for Shelagh Jane Purdey.

Or already granted. I couldn't rightly say.

When he walked up the steps to the front doors in the eight o'clock drizzle that morning, he saw the hatbox—featureless, thick brown cardboard—resting on the iron grid which served in place of the oft-stolen doormat, protected from the weather by the eaves. It contained, he assumed, as he bent to pick it up, some form of donation to the charities of the church: old clothes for the op shop perhaps, books for the jumble, or cakes for distribution to the doddery.

Holding it with one arm to his chest, he lifted off the lid, not overly curious. Resting inside, lavishly and carefully coated in cosmetics, was the dull-eyed head of the girl. It was a head familiar to him, a head which only the day before had asked him for condoms, for lube and a clean fit, a head which had promised yet again to abandon turning tricks just as soon as it turned eighteen and qualified for the adult dole. A head for which, not twenty-four hours before, he had harboured hope.

The familiar is rendered hideous in death, more so when the mask of the soul's passing is desecrated by the application of coloured wax and oils. Something mysterious, ancient and beyond the will smote Father Corrigan from deep within at that point, causing him to throw his arms wide, step backwards and gasp like a heretic impaled by the Inquisition.

The hatbox, also obeying something mysterious and ancient and beyond thought, fell to the ground, landing on its side. Given added momentum by its unsecured and weighty cargo, it rolled, as Father Corrigan watched immobile, off the top step and, gathering speed, careened down the remaining six to the gently sloping path, continuing its journey, like the boulder of Sisyphus, through the gate, rocking and yawing as it collided with and leaped over the foot of an elderly woman hobbling along the pavement. Airborne, thus, and turning, it deposited its grisly and now smudged cargo with a smallish splash into the choking gutter.

The old woman screamed, first in surprise, then in fright, then in disbelieving numb horror, each outburst rising up—Father Corrigan noted in his own frozen unreality—like a chorus from 'Oh Come All Ye Faithful'.

The noise, however, jolted him out of inaction. He moved neither to retrieve the head nor comfort its stricken witness, but away, through the doors and into the church, heading, he later worked out, for the telephone.

As he entered, the view which greeted him as

7

always—as always every day for three decades—was that of the darkling, thin, triangular perspective caused by the aisle between the pews, leading to the modest blackwood altar and its cut-price weeping candles, above which, in glory and in sadness, hung a life-size sculpted replica, painted in peeling gold, of Christ suffering on the cross.

Except that this time it was different. Christ was not alone.

Nailed, hand of flesh upon hand of wood, ankles of blue-grey crossed in front of ankles of blood-smeared gilt, dipping at the shoulders like the Saviour from the burden of its own self, was the naked body that had, until so recently, been harmoniously and vibrantly attached to the foulness which was hampering the drainage outside.

Father Corrigan would later admit he possessed no recollection of the next twenty minutes of his life. Effects, however, often dictate causes, and it was subsequently possible to reconstruct the probable geometry of the time. He went to the telephone in the back office. He made three calls. Then he opened his desk draw, pulled out his cosily hidden bottle of Jamesons— his Sunday strength-giver—walked back through the church, up the aisle, out of the door, put the bottle to his lips, sat on the topmost stair, fixed his gaze on the cranial remains of Ms Purdey, offered no prayer to God, and waited.

He had called an ambulance for the old woman.
He had called the police.

And he had called me. Joe Panther.

I got there first.

✝

The thin-lipped, middle-aged and distinctly rectangular features of Detective Senior Sergeant John Gordon looked none too pleased when he noticed me, as he would no doubt later put it in his semi-literate report, already present at the scene. His driver and offsider, a surly and overweight knuckle-crunching careerist named Detective Constable Antonio Pordelli, showed no reaction at all. This was probably because the little cognition he possessed was entirely occupied by the process of pulling up, somewhat too leisurely, at the front of St Cuthbert's.

Gordon's initial discomfit, however, increased markedly when I yelled at him to park on the other side of the street.

He wound down the passenger-side window of the unmarked car, which Pordelli was trying to nudge closer to the curve, and scowled. 'This your new job, Panther? Parking inspector?'

'Correct,' I said. 'I am the father, the son, and the grey ghost. Let not my nature be divided.'

A young male cyclist, clad in the body-hugging embarrassment of his type, slowed in his progress down the opposite side of the road, and sat up in his seat, curious, perhaps, as to why a man in black jeans, eroded leather jacket and a Smashing Pumpkins tee-shirt was shouting at the occupants of what was clearly a cop car.

I waved to him, trotted down the steps and squatted by the creeping vehicle. I felt like grinning but controlled myself. In this line of work, appropriate behaviour at appropriate times is everything. It's all theatre, in the end. All of it.

'If your chum,' I began, 'Pordelli, isn't it?'

'*Detective Constable* Pordelli to you, Panther—'

'—if Pordelli keeps moving your car on the trajectory he seems to intend to keep moving it on, *Detective Senior Sergeant* Gordon, you will find that you have (a) polluted a crime scene, (b) committed an act of uncommon desecration and (c) clogged the tread on your nearside front tyre with a nasty and persistent amalgam of hair, bone and brain.'

Gordon looked at me in much the same way a moray eel looks at a crippled herring. I paid no heed, and turned my head slowly around and down in the direction of the gutter. Something stirred within his cortex, some dim recognition of the need to interpret non-verbal communication. His head mirrored mine, gradually craning out of the window to permit the required angle of vision.

He saw it. He saw, too, the shadow cast by the car's bumper bar fall gently upon the upturned forehead.

'Jesus Christ!' he squealed. Then turned to Pordelli and screamed, 'Back up! Back up! Park across the road, man! *Backwards! Now*, for Christ's sake.'

Pordelli, characteristically reflexive in his reactions, did as he was told, sending the car in a graceful, wheel-spinning, reverse curve, colliding heavily with the cyclist in the process. The bicycle and rider ended up on the pavement, both in a state of considerable disarray.

The entropic surge, thus begun, accelerated along woefully predictable lines. Both officers sprung from the vehicle. Pordelli went to the aid of the bruised and understandably abusive rider, palms raised in hasty and unconvincing supplication. Gordon attempted to sprint across the road—presumably to check on the welfare of Shelagh Purdey's head—while simultaneously trying to radio for back-up, for traffic control, for forensic and for a bloody morgue van. Two paces into his advance he lost his footing on the slippery blacktop and heaved over, his hip and ribcage taking the brunt of the scraping fall. His call to base was thus punctuated with a sound chillingly reminiscent of a Hereford cow being unexpectedly mounted from behind by a determined Hereford bull.

Regaining his feet, he had but a split second to continue his advance and instructions before the ambulance, under lights and sirens, spun around the corner and began to pull to a stop, its path laid directly for the head. Gordon bellowed. Pordelli, turning for a moment from the still protesting cyclist, saw the object of his superior's panic. Leaving the cyclist mid-accusation he bolted across the road and slammed himself, shoulder-first, into the ambulance driver's door, yelling, echoing, '*Back up! Back up!*', before submitting to his own reverberating momentum and falling backwards heavily, twisting his leg beneath him and landing on his arse in a shallow puddle.

'Fucking circus,' said a voice beside me. Father Corrigan, bottle in hand, had come down the steps, woken from his post-traumatic stupor by the slapstick in the street.

In the ten minutes since I'd arrived he had said nothing, managing to nod when I asked whether he'd called both cops and ambulance, but nothing more. He had simply stood, stiller than the Virgin herself, just in front of the open doors, not quite staring at the first discovered partial remains of his slaughtered lamb which, in turn, were not quite staring back at him.

'Into their hands,' I murmured, 'you commend your spirit.'

'Fucking circus,' he repeated, and took a violent slug of Ireland's finest.

'Give me,' I said, prising the bottle from his fingers. I took a solid swallow from the contents and handed it back. 'Why did you call me?'

'This is your job,' he said, voice flat.

'Wrong, Corrigan. It's the cops' job.'

The good father spat on the pavement. 'She was a street girl, and I'm a troublemaker.'

'Will somebody rid me of this troublesome—'

'Will you stop quoting the fucking classics at me, bastard,' he snapped.

Gordon and Pordelli were both now on their feet, Pordelli limping, trying to cadge a couple of pain killers from the ambulance driver. Gordon and the other

12

ambo were crouched either side of the pale and hyper-ventilating old lady at the base of the church's wrought-iron fence, the paramedic trying to manoeuvre her into a standing position, the cop telling her, gently, that he would have to take a statement from her, asking her address.

The cyclist was out of the picture, and knew it. He limped off, carrying his newly bent conveyance, glancing back over his shoulder until the streetscape intervened.

Sirens sounded not too far away.

In a couple of minutes, administrative chaos would again assert itself, the priest would be monopolised, and I would be asked to depart.

Which I would. In due course.

'So listen, good father,' I said. 'I take it this is the gig. You want to know who chopped up little Shelagh—'

He winced. I ignored it.

'—and turned her into an Easter decoration. You think the cops won't bother all that much, unless they can nab someone quickly from the Rent-A-Kook register, so you want me to do it.'

He nodded.

'How much money you got?'

He looked at me, aghast. 'For the love of God, Panther, a girl has been murdered ... mutilated, mocked ... and a church defiled.'

'Do you think the girl cares?'

'Panther ... I ... God cares. He must.'

13

'God, if he's around, presumably already knows the answer. He probably set the question. And not a few scholars over the centuries would be forced to conclude that God himself, ultimately, was the one what done it, officer.'

'A woman is dead, and you play cod–theology. Fuck you, man.'

'Cod is on my side,' I said.

'Shit, man. I'm pleading with you, Panther. Shelagh Purdey gave me her trust. I owe her.'

'You'll owe me. More than usual.'

'This is a poor parish.'

'It is not meet to take food from the mouths of babes, and cast it to the dogs.'

Corrigan spat again. The wind whipped his spittle back across his face. He stuck a stubby knuckle in his eye and wiped. 'So it's Mark he vomits up now,' he sighed. 'Ach, you'll get your bloody cash, hard man.'

'You own your house, or the Church?'

He glared at me, and then nodded. 'All these years . . .'

'Sell it,' I said. 'Sell it to the middle class.'

'You'd turn me homeless?'

'So the flock, so the shepherd.'

He said nothing, hit the bottle, turned away.

I nodded. I had maybe just a couple of minutes to take a good look at the cargo on the crucifix before the crime scene tape came out. I pushed open the doors.

'Panther.' The priest's voice behind me.

I looked over my shoulder. His face wore the sorrow and misery of the martyrs, the millennia filled by terror received and returned, the constant reminder of evil unexplained and undefeated.

'Did you unlock these doors?'

He thought for a moment, then gave up. He shook his head, shrugged, waved the bottle.

'Damn you for this,' he said.

I stared at him for a moment. I saw a good man, a decent man, a man whose broad, pale Celtic face bore the pinking web-marks of too many whiskies taken in sadness. The furrows which traced his cheeks, eyes and forehead were not the lines of wind erosion, not the poetry of age. They were the scars of too many nights in silence and pain, the creaking, inexorable collapse of a hopeful mind forced to bear the weight of other people's unfathomable inhumanity. He lived in peaceful times but his pastel-green eyes were those of a trench soldier, up against an enemy as unknowable as the God which commanded him to fight it. A good man, salty, a good man now betrayed. He thought me a friend. I shared neither his goodness nor his decency. Couldn't share it. Ever. Not now.

He didn't know shit.

For a second there I wanted to tell him, tell that good man lots of things he really had a right to know.

Tell him probably the only things which at that moment could have made him regard the death of Shelagh Purdey as the triviality it really was.

But I didn't. Like I knew I wouldn't.

For I am weak and wretched, in courage failing and with purpose none.

'It's already been done,' I said, and walked into the darkness.

✝

I've often wanted to tell people things, Father Brendan Pearce Corrigan more so than most.

He'd been a client of mine—if that's the right word—for more than half a decade. Casual, like. I'd met him one Saturday night in the strip-lit saloon of the Bradford hotel. He was sitting at the bar, his dog collar visible above the neck of his tattered green jumper, hacking back the Jamesons like he was on a mission from God.

And he was, so he thought.

I pulled up a stool next to him. He wasn't a regular. Neither was I, not daily anyway, but I'd been there often enough to figure out the dozen or so crumpled lonely men who were. Also, he wasn't playing on the bingo machine, or watching the football replay on the television above the menu blackboard. He was not, therefore, an arriviste, attempting to curry favour. Acceptance was not the issue; squirt was.

'Drunkenness is a sin, holy father,' I said.

I like doing that sort of thing. Annoying people.

I signalled the barmaid to bring me another pot of beer and a fresh scotch. He didn't shift his gaze from

16

the sodden bar-towel in front of him. 'Bollocks,' he mumbled.

'No, it is,' I continued. 'I read it somewhere.'

The drinks arrived. He gulped his with neither pause nor acknowledgement, then belched. 'And I read somewhere that Christ turned water into wine, and I'll let no man tell me he didn't do that in order to get smashed on a hot afternoon.'

'Probably right. What else was there to do in Galilee?'

'What else is there to do when the booze runs out at a piss-up? Another?'

We got to talking. Turned out the priest was worried, hence his decision to seek the silent company of strangers instead of drinking alone in his house, his usual custom. He'd done a funeral that afternoon and then returned to his quarters to meet one of the local kids, a teenager, strange and estranged, due in court two days later to face his umpteenth shoplifting charge. A charming lad, and stupid with it.

Corrigan had agreed to stand character witness for him, in a probably vain attempt to keep him out of a youth training centre. The late afternoon appointment had been for the purposes of getting the story right and grilling the little fucker not to present himself before the magistrate clad in anything unwashed or distasteful.

It had been a no-show. Nothing unusual in that, said the priest. Except that this time the gig was serious. The kid had done youth time before, and hadn't enjoyed being beaten and raped one little bit. Since then, his only ambition in an otherwise directionless life had been to stay on the easy side of the wire.

Something must have happened, he reckoned. Something bad.

I told him I was pretty good at finding people. It was my job. One of my jobs. I told him I lived in the area, knew most of the street population in a casual, nodding sort of way, knew people who asked questions, who heard things. Not much, I said, in answer to his next question, not much and strictly cash. If he had it on him, I could most likely locate the little tyke in a couple of hours, tops.

He handed over the notes. Where was he going to be, I asked, later on?

'What time this pub shut?' he asked.

I drained my glass and left.

I found the kid half an hour later. He was in the back yard of one of the two-storey pay-by-the-night dormitory boarding houses on Gertrude Street, lying behind the rubbish skip. His lips were blue, his faded Megadeth tee-shirt up across his thin and pimpled chest, his right arm bent up behind his back from where someone—a couple of the other dorm people, probably—had dropped him after heaving him outside, doing a pathetically botched job of concealment.

At least he'd not be doing time. Time had done him.

Job done. Money earned. It hadn't been too tricky at all. Which was hardly surprising, considering.

Ten minutes later I was back at the Bradford, telling Corrigan that his parishioner had been freed of the

18

burden of flesh through the unfortunate mainlining of a tad too much smack. He took it quite well, with the assistance of a couple more shots of slosh.

He was silent for a few minutes, his eyes closed and his lips moving a bit. Offering up a prayer from the sanctity of the front bar, I guessed. I liked his style.

'Ach,' he said, after finishing. 'And no confession . . .'

'Never mind,' I replied. 'It was only an intravenal sin.'

I thought he was going to hit me for a second, but he didn't. Pity. It would have been fun. Instead, he gave a sort of rueful smile, the smile of the sad fellow-traveller, and asked me my name again.

'Joe Panther.'

'Joe. Joseph?'

'Joshua. Joshua Ben Panther.'

'How old are you?'

'Thirty-three.'

'Stick to Joe.'

✝

After that, the priest turned out to be a handy little earner. Not huge, but handy. At least once a month, on average, he'd call me up and set me after one of his self-defined flock—a kid gone missing here, a boy skipped bail, a girl skipped home, a new face on an old corner, an old face in new trouble. He didn't meddle

19

much, just liked to keep tabs, be around if he was needed.

I never had any problems running the missing to earth. Sometimes they were dead, of course, or locked up in concrete cells or rubber rooms, about to disappear down the slathering maw of institutional purgatory, but I found them.

I got to know the local cops pretty well too. I never reported a murder, or a suspicious death, but I was often nearby when someone else did. They couldn't measure me, so didn't like me one tiny bit. No respect, they reckoned.

They accused me once of working as an investigator *sans* licence. It was a hobby, I said. Just a hobby. They ran a check on me anyway. Found zip. No licences, no fines, no tickets, not even a defaulted electricity account. There are two ways to be a model citizen. The first is to pay on time. The second is never to write your name.

They knew I knew the priest, the boozy old preacher who was forever asking them tricky questions, mounting bail and, so they alleged (correctly, of course), harbouring runaways, whores, petty thieves and junkies.

That first evening, he never asked me how I found the kid so fast. Not that I would have told him, but the subject never arose. That set the pattern.

Priests can be an admirably pragmatic bunch, as long as you ignore obvious irrationalities such as their quaint insistence that the Messiah is a biscuit. Take the evangelists of the sixth and seventh centuries, for instance, faced with the problem of the locals preferring to worship sacred trees instead of some invisible, irrepressibly nosy deity best known for inflicting plagues of boils and suchlike. Did they organise the holy militia to whip, beat, torture and burn them into submission? No. That was a strategy still several hundred years in the future. Instead, they chopped down said trees and built churches out of them. The locals came in droves.

But were they worshipping the new god or the old trees?

It didn't matter, not in the end. And never has. The destroyers became saints. Such is the value of carpentry.

So Corrigan never asked me how I did it. He simply had faith that I would.

And I did.

That first lad had been a matter of childishly simple deduction. He had been living at the boarding house two days before, on bail, when I had sold him the scag. He wasn't going to go far.

Everyone has a weakness, a nagging empty place deep within them, an existential pain that hurts so much precisely because there is nothing there to hurt, a spiritual colander that demands constant filling. Some people try to fill it with work or religion or love or booze or bigotry. Others try heroin, speed, acid, or book a ticket on the benzodiazepene bus.

I like to help out where I can. The good which I would, I do not; but the evil which I would not, that I practise.

The priest would have condemned me in body and

21

in law if he knew. But he didn't. Didn't want to. Faith is like that. Blind and dangerous.

That was one of the two things I wished I could tell him as I walked into church to view the body of Shelagh Purdey.

The other, for him, would have been much, much worse.

One day, on his deathbed, if I'm still around, I might.

I might then.

For I knoweth our frame.

I remembereth that we are dust.

✝

By the time the paperwork had been done and the Police Media Liaison office given the bare details by Homicide, it was too late for the Sunday papers to pick up the story.

The Monday editions, however, had a ball. Corrigan might have been correct in his assumption that the cops would search for evil in but a few well-lit places and then give up. If so, both he and they had reckoned without media and myth. The word 'Satan', or derivatives thereof, appeared on the front page of that day's broadsheet and tabloid.

The reasoning beneath the speculation of the crime reporters ran thus: Shelagh Purdey was found naked, beheaded and for the most part nailed to a crucifix above the altar of a church, *ergo* she had been sacrificed by Satanists.

In the circular manner of what passes for police and media cooperation, Detective Gordon, seconded to the murder squad because of his local knowledge, was quoted as saying 'The possibility of some form of black magical involvement has not yet been discounted.'

I discounted it immediately. I'd never even contemplated it.

Tried telling somebody, once. Look, Brother Francesco, try to think it *through*. Put the tongs down and . . .

But that's another story. Later, maybe.

The bare findings of the investigators and the forensics people were presented, albeit buried. I was glad of this, because there was no way Gordon or Pordelli would have told me squat if I'd rung them for goss.

The meat, then.

Shelagh Jane Purdey had been killed by precise, clean and speedy decapitation some time on Friday evening. The lack of significant blood–deposits in the church, the church grounds and the hatbox indicated she had died elsewhere, and then been rearranged *post mortem*.

An axe, then, I figured, maybe a guillotine (plenty of *those* about), strength, skill, and transport.

There was no evidence of vaginal, anal or oral trauma, nor any traces of sperm. Traces of vaginal lubricant, however, were present in the appropriate orifice. There were no signs of bruising, abrasions or ligature

23

marks, indicating she had met her death passively, if not willingly.

There were traces of heroin in her bloodstream, along with alcohol, cannabis and lingering echoes of Rohypnol. None of these, however, individually or in combination, was thought to have been enough to produce unconsciousness.

It was assumed that more than one person was involved, due to the inordinate difficulty a loner would have encountered in crucifying her body. For pretty much the same reason, not to mention the breathtakingly obvious, suicide had been ruled out.

Neither Father Corrigan nor any other officer of the Church in any diocese had received any communication referring to her death. Nevertheless, added Gordon, it could have been meant as a warning, or a revenge attack.

(Revenge attack? I thought. A shadowy body called the Saracen Liberation Front, still angry that the bishops failed to keep the crusaders under control, perhaps?)

Purdey's parents: ditto. Said to be distraught and deeply shocked.

Inquiries continuing.

Funeral Wednesday, a private affair in the outer suburbs, handled by the mother and father. Memorial service on Saturday at St Cuthbert's, handled by Corrigan.

Second of August. Feast day of St Sidwell, the virgin beheaded. And Stephen, poor Stephen. Dead, ugly and in vain. Paul's doing, like all of it.

The next day, boasted the local tabloid, would be revealed the results of an exclusive investigation into the secret satanic cults sacrificing the helpless young of Melbourne.

It all matched pretty well with my own observations and reasoning.

Most of it anyway.

I didn't bother to read the rest of the papers. It all gets a bit samey after a while.

It was 10.30am. I had finished my ritual two cups of strong coffee. The sky was grey, yet again, and the rain falling like an unskilled factory job.

I needed to talk to John the Baptist.

✝

'Come on in, son,' said John, answering my knock. 'Find yourself a space. Mind the Pekinese.'

I knew he'd be in. John the Baptist never went out before midday, when he'd start his daily wobble to any one of the three pubs in the immediate square mile that still offered a two-buck pensioner lunch.

Sometime in the sixties the city planners, gripped by a vision long on theory and short on smarts, erected enormous brown and white prefab concrete towers around the inner city, therein, they said, to house the homeless and destitute in conditions bright and airy.

The four Fitzroy towers, like their forty-one equivalents in the other suburbs, had become dark legends in the bitter corners of the public imagination. Far from cut-price utopias, they had become a sort of high-rise Hades, crammed with thousands of refugees, the old, the infirm, tight-packed with the deluded, the danger-ous, the drunk and the damaged, shabby Babels as tense as the Golan Heights, confounded and polyglot, where the stairwells stank of human waste and the gardens rang, on bad nights, with the groans of the robbed and the silence of the raped.

John lived on the eighteenth floor, had done for years. Going on for sixty-five, bent, skinny, dipsoma-niac, dyspeptic and diabetic, he was what was known, in the imprecise lexicon of social work, as a raving loon. He had gone away to Vietnam, the locals said, and when he returned he was never quite the same. He had faced tribulation in the wilderness and returned transformed, his past a silent stranger.

Just who first dubbed him the Baptist was a matter lost in local lore. It wasn't me, I know that. Wish it had been. The explanation for the moniker, however, was quite clear. Every day, after his pub lunch and pot, old John would spend a few hours walking the streets, hobbling and limping on limbs long ulcerated and fouled. He carried with him a glass borrowed from the bar, full of water. Holy water, he claimed.

And it might have been. It might have been. Generic brand holy water, perhaps.

He went looking for toddlers. When he found one—and there were many to be found—he would dip his fingers in the water and reverently describe a dripping cross on its forehead, intoning a blessing halitoid, slurred, and not conforming to any known liturgical canon.

'Mercifully hear our prayers, O Lord,' he would mumble and slur, 'and graciously accept this oblation which we Thy servants make to Thee. You are the Source and the Silence, the Mind and the Truth, the Logos and the Life. Your cruelty is our glory, for ever and ever. Amen.'

It brought back memories—dim, distant and scarred with distaste—the first time I heard this addled offering. I asked him where he found it. 'It just come to me,' he'd said. 'One night in Saigon. It felt like the good oil.'

Some parents objected, scared and invaded, but most didn't care, as long as he didn't make junior cry. They knew him from around, after all, and adjudged him harmless.

And harmless he was.

Unless you happened to be a small dog.

John the Baptist loved small dogs. He loved to take them home and entertain them for a couple of days. And then he loved to twist their cute little necks to breaking, hack their heads off and boil the flesh from their skulls on the top of his black and greasy gas stove. He hung the results on his living room wall.

Dogs were his link, his touchstone, his ticket to ride.

'What's its name?' I asked, as the little pooch snuffled

at my feet and wiggled its arse in dumb doggish pleasure.

'Don't know, son,' said John. 'One more day, I reckon.'

'Call him Tuesday, then.'

John beamed a gappy grin. 'Good thinking, son. Then I can collect the set.'

I glanced around the room. At least fifty little skulls bared their teeth, hanging lopsided from nails whacked in through the pale green dirty paintwork. Several of the eye sockets were providing long-term accommodation for various species of spider. The new collection would have to hang about knee-height just to fit.

Time for business, I decided.

'You haven't expanded your operations, have you, John? Haven't started doing a bit of big-game hunting?'

He stared at me blankly for a second, a cigarette paper hanging from his crusted lower lip, temporarily forgotten. Then he got the drift, chuckled and shook his head.

'Oh, you mean the woman, the girl—'

'Shelagh Purdey. You know her?'

'In the church, yeah?'

I nodded.

He followed suit. 'I seen her around. Corner girl, yeah? Needler. Nice tits, son. Yeah, I seen her.'

'But did you chop her head off and nail her to the crucifix?'

He looked at me, water suddenly brimming in his crimson-cloudy eyes. 'Joe, son, you hurt me. That'd be killing. You think I'm a killer, son, eh? Think I'm a killer?'

I bent down and chucked the Pekinese behind its ear. It was falling in love with me, I could tell.

'You kill dogs,' I whispered.

'Only when they ask me to, son. Only helping out.'

'You killed in Vietnam.'

He said nothing. He never spoke of the war. When he'd done his time and returned he'd built a door in his memory and locked it. He knew where the key was, but convinced himself he didn't. In that contradiction, he sought what peace he could.

I pushed the mutt away. It wouldn't take the hint. John the Baptist didn't kill Shelagh Purdey. I just needed to put him on edge. He worked better that way. In contentment lies bog-all of use. In fear ... well ... whoever made a difference to this world not out of terror?

It was working. He finished rolling his racehorse cigarette, arthritic fingers struggling with the dexterity required. He fired it and coughed, a sound which gradually turned into a rough chuckle.

'Anyway,' he said, 'I would have thought that was more your style, son. Nailed to the cross, eh?'

I ignored it. John the Baptist was the only person who knew who I really was.

The only one still alive, anyway.

Can't remember why I told him now. Must have been having a bad day. Another one. Pissed, probably. Every now and then, the need to confide becomes

29

overwhelming. Like a cobra's need to kiss. Or a shark's need to eat. My confidence is not a gift given lightly.

John the Baptist was away with the fairies, anyway, so it didn't matter too much. There was no danger he would tell anyone else (notwithstanding that he wouldn't be believed for a moment if he did). His mind, what there was of it, was both acquisitive and parsimonious. A lot went in, but not much came out. In his own skewed and filthy world he didn't miss much.

Anyway, he might have been mad, but he wasn't insane. That was what made him so useful.

The Peke peed on the paper-thin carpet. It was a bitch.

'Who did, John?' I asked, fixing him with my eyes, like I do. 'What do you know?'

'Know nothing, son,' he wheezed. 'Knowing's your department.'

'So they say.'

'They say a lot, son.'

'Like what?'

'Like knowing's your department.'

I fired up a Dunhill, dropped the match, still flaming, on the back of the dog. She yelped and ran across the room, falling over as she tried to lick the sting.

John swore at me, told me not to hurt the little thing. I lit another match, flicked it through the air at her. Then another. Then another. The third made contact. Another yelp, and a hissing sound.

As well as he could, John lurched towards me, arms

30

outstretched, an obscenity sharing his lip with his fag-end. I struck him hard, palm first, on his birdcage chest, sending him back, toppling over and landing in his one threadbare armchair. Too easy. His eyes clouded again—the fear rising anew—his lungs heaving as he fought for air.

Never let go of his smoke though.

'Do violence to no man, neither exact anything wrongfully,' I said. 'And be content with your wages.'

He struggled to speak, still sucking in air. 'Who said that?' he managed to whisper.

'You did,' I replied. 'Look, John, this is getting tedious. I'm on a good earner here, but I want to figure it out quickly. There isn't a day rate. Just tell me. What?'

He didn't get up. Looked at me.

'I'm not long to go,' he mumbled.

'Longer if you tell me something.'

'Don't be like that, son. Not like that. Will you put in a good word for me, son? Will you do that for old Johnno?'

I nodded. Stupid fuck. Belief isn't reason. Belief is deep vein terror.

'Pass me the dog,' he said.

The bitch was cringing in the far corner. I walked over to it. It tried to wriggle away. No chance. I hefted her by her belly—no pain, now—and dropped her in his skinny lap. He hugged her like a letter from a lost lover, started stroking her back rhythmically. His eyes glazed. He started to sway slightly, back and forwards.

When he spoke, it was in a monotone. The dog lay immobile, scarcely breathing.

'And she came in trust ... she came before the light of the father ... came ... and she saw into the light, both lit and blinded ... saw the light contained her darkness ... and laid her head to rest ... in waking sleep ... The light ... where before there was no light ... shining its warning of love in her eyes ... all is calm and no surprise ... the light of the father ... shining and sharp ... the light behind the door ... now there, now gone, now there again ... the hungry light and the father who would eat his own—'

'Okay, John, I've got the gist. Shut up now,' I said. 'All the bloody same, you mystics. Mad as coots.'

The old man didn't hear. He was well gaga, wobbling around in some impenetrable shell-shocked vision, talking salad. The dog was wheezing, little back feet pedalling impotently in the air. It was clear she was going to end up being called Monday.

He'd keyed in on the girl's passivity, which was a start. There was no newspaper in the flat to give him a clue. The father bit might have been merely a reference to the church. Then again, maybe not. I decided to try again later, maybe after the shifting sands of his brain had been cemented by lamb chops, two veg and a pot of piss.

I had my hand on the handle when I heard his tone change. I glanced back. He was still rocking, staring now at the Peke, which was quivering, twitching, arching convulsively. His gnarled old hand grasped its

32

head. He twisted it hard, snuffing the yelp in its throat.

'The Son of Man came . . . eating and drinking, and they say . . . Look, a glutton and a drunkard . . . a friend of tax collectors and sinners . . .'

I could have sworn the bastard smiled.

I slammed the door on the way out.

✝

Who I am, yeah?

Joe Panther.

Joshua Panther.

Joshua Ben Panther.

Anglicised to buggery. For the present.

From the Aramaic. Yeshu ben Pantera. Yoshu. Take your pick.

Jesus, son of Pantera.

It was all true.

And all wrong.

But later.

You won't thank me.

✝

# 2

I HATE SUBURBS, ALWAYS HAVE. Suburbs don't echo. The skin isn't taut enough.

The house, when I found it, was monstrous in its banality. It was a two-storey number, grey brick, and fashioned at several removes on the Georgian. It must have been all of a decade old, but looked younger, its facade sand-blasted and scrubbed, rendered sterile and mossless, its expression blank as a coma. The garden was a neat, ordered amalgam of bordering hibiscus and bottlebrush, hemming in two rectangles of cropped grass split by a path of wan concrete slabs.

There was one car in the double garage, a blue Honda Something, late model. A small oil patch marked the roost of its partner.

Good work, Panther. Simple really. Now get on with it.

I pushed open the gate and walked up the path, hoping I wasn't about to violate the territorial rights of

34

some large dog. I thought not, though. The area was comfortably middle-class, grudgingly upward in its mobility, the sort of burg which favoured alarms over Dobermans. Micro-dogs, terriers for the kids, maybe, but not slathering killers.

Maybe I should bring John the Baptist next time, I thought. I hadn't gone back for a post-lunch visit. I knew him too well. He'd be in his guilt phase now, bloodied and at the stove, asking forgiveness from the soul of Monday. I wasn't up to it. Mess and stench were bad enough. Theological absurdity was beyond the pale.

'Good afternoon,' I said, when she opened the door. 'Sorry to disturb you. My name is Joe Panther, from the parish of St Cuthbert in Fitzroy. Are you Mrs Purdey?'

The woman before me said nothing. She was shorter than me, about forty, I guessed, thin and mousy with it. Hair cut to just above the collar line, lightly permed. A little dab of rouge on the cheeks (or was she blushing?), a thin phrase of pinkish lipstick. Laura Ashley dress, floral, to below the knees, unstockinged feet in cheap, black kung-fu slippers. Her fingers knotted in front of her crotch. One ring, barely there.

The top of her head was level with my chest. As she looked up, the light from behind me illuminated her face. Pale green eyes, squinting, faintly rimmed by red.

I tried again, gently, gently. 'Mrs Purdey?'

She nodded, quickly, as if giving away a secret. Then a spark of fear. 'Is it about Shelagh?' Her voice was little more than a whisper.

In bed, I thought to myself, this woman would never

grunt and scream in passion. This woman would squeak, then head for the shower. I tried to imagine her naked. I couldn't.

I was working on the size of her nipples when she repeated her question. I pulled myself together.

'My deepest condolences, Mrs Purdey.' Was that right? Was that the thing to say?

She nodded, like she was supposed to. Said nothing.

'I am a grief counsellor from the church,' I said. 'If it's not too much to ask, I wondered if I might have a word?'

She stiffened a little, fingers gripping each other more tightly. I tried to imagine her arching her back. Couldn't.

'We don't need any help, thank you,' she said, like she was talking to a Mormon. 'We're not . . . well . . .'

I smiled my indulgent all-embracing smile. 'I'm glad to hear that, Mrs Purdey. Actually, it's Father Corrigan I'm counselling. He was the one who, you know, I thought, perhaps . . .'

She relaxed a bit. 'We don't blame him, you know. He didn't . . .'

I did the smile bit again. 'Bless you,' I said.

Oral sex? Never. 'I just thought that if I could talk to you, I might in some way be able to better lighten his load. He's a good man, Father Corrigan. He feels his sadness keenly and . . .'

No reaction. This was not a person accustomed to making decisions. I cut to it. 'Might I come inside, Mrs Purdey?'

The fear sparked again. 'Have you any . . . have you any . . . identification?'

Progress, I thought. I'm not a Mormon any more. I'm a telephone repairman.

'Of course.' I smiled, and patted ineffectually at the pockets of my Salvo op-shop black suit. 'Oh dear,' I did a sort of sad and goofy I'm-a-harmless-dolt grin, 'I seem to have forgotten it. I'm sure if you rang Father Corrigan at the church he would—'

That did it. She would react, this woman, but never initiate. Strictly eyes closed, I thought, strictly missionary. 'No, no,' she said quickly. 'I'm sure it's all right. Please, come in.'

She turned and walked up the hallway. It was coated in beige carpet. A repro Queen Anne telephone table, framed still-life print, something Victorian, minor, and passionless. I followed, staring at her buttocks beneath the dress. Parting would be such sweet sorrow, I thought.

She led me to the lounge room, speaking without turning around, her voice a little louder now that she was back inside her safe zone and with a clearly defined role to play.

'How did you find us? Did the police—'

'No, no,' I replied quickly. 'The police are far too busy to be bothered by the likes of me.'

Did the shoulders tighten then, just a bit?

'Then how?'

'A little bit of detective work of my own, Mrs Purdey,' chuckling like a self-effacing coot. 'Actually, I noted where the, um, funeral will be held, and then checked the phone book for Purdeys in the general area. You're the only ones, you know. Not a very common name, Purdey.'

What a nice old duffer I am.

She turned to face me, right arm lifted, listlessly displaying the room.

'That's all right, then. Please, make yourself comfortable. Can I offer you a cup of tea or coffee . . . Father? I'm sorry, should I call you Father? Are you a Father?'

'No,' I replied, 'I'm a son. Please just call me Joe, and a cup of tea would be very nice, thank you.'

'Take a seat, then. I won't be a minute.' She disappeared through a door at the other end of the room, leaving it ajar.

I was hanging for a cup of coffee, but knew better. I have not accumulated wisdom in my time. I know very little. Immortality does not confer understanding. I know this, though: never accept a coffee in the suburbs. It's always instant, sometimes decaffeinated.

And decaffeinated coffee is an abomination in the sight of the Lord.

The room was much as I'd expected: vulgar, predictable and understated all at once. The three-piece lounge suite was grey leather, expensive, but common. The carpet was the same as the stuff in the hallway. The coffee table was pine, polished, and chunky, supporting two cork drink coasters and a copy of one of those celebrity gossip mags they sell at supermarket checkouts.

All of it was dust-free. There were several framed paintings and posters on the wall. Two of the paintings—anodyne landscapes in abstract—appeared to be originals, products of some Town Hall charity exhibition, the frames cheap. Then there was a Toulouse-Lautrec print (one of the Follies ones) and another of André Derain's portrait of Matisse. All very sexless and predictable, all very bland.

I sat on the sofa, listened to the clinkings and scrapes coming from the other side of the door.

Mrs Purdey re-entered carrying two green mugs, teabag tabs dangling. 'It's only Liptons,' she said apologetically. 'I hope that's all right.'

'That'll be lovely,' I replied, and glanced pointedly at the wall. 'I love the Fauves, don't you? So full of life.'

She looked at me without the slightest flicker of comprehension. I pointed to the print. 'The portrait. Wild animals, they called them.'

'Oh,' she said quickly, putting the mugs on the coasters and sitting in one of the armchairs. 'Yes, I suppose so. My husband chose that one. I don't know very much about art, I'm afraid.'

I tried to imagine her making love on the carpet, her husband ripping her dress in the savagery of lust. Couldn't.

'And where is your husband, Mrs Purdey?' I asked.

'Please,' she said, 'call me Elaine. He's at work, I'm afraid. Won't be back until . . .'

She petered out. She didn't have any idea when he'd be back.

'It must be very hard for him, having to go to work at a time like this.'

There ensued the briefest of pauses, as if she hadn't until then contemplated the proposition. 'Well, yes, but, you know . . .'

I nodded, sympathetically. 'Needs must, and all that. What does he do for work? Lovely tea, by the way.'

It wasn't, but sometimes you just have to lie. Most of the time, actually.

'He has his own business.' There was a note of pride in her voice. His own business. Dead posh. 'He's got an advertising agency. Nothing very big, but you've got to start somewhere, haven't you?'

'Ahh,' I nodded and smiled. 'Very worthy. Has he done anything I might have seen on television?'

She didn't have a clue. 'Yes, yes, I expect so. That sort of thing, yes.'

I nodded again. 'I have some friends just starting a new business. You never know, they might be able to put some work his way. Would you mind if I gave them his office address?'

'Image Makers. South Melbourne. I'm sorry, I forget the exact—'

'Lot of advertising places in South Melbourne. Seems to be the thing there.'

She didn't reply. Chitchat was not her forte. I changed tack. Ultra gentle now.

'Tell me about Shelagh. What sort of girl was she?'

Her fingers clenched again, resting in her lap. She

hadn't touched her tea. 'Did you know her yourself?' she asked.

I'd sold her scag once or twice a month for the past year and a half. I'd had a cup of coffee with her at a table on the pavement outside one of the cafes on Smith Street, neither of us talking much. I'd watched her beg money from locals and strangers alike, standing outside the pharmacy where she got her daily metha-done, claiming a bus to Geelong, a mugging, a theft, her sparkless eyes and persistence telling of other needs more urgent, fooling no one.

I'd watched from the shadow of an alley as she fellated a drunken businessman in a littered car park behind the Easter egg factory. She worked hard. I'd told her I'd only hold the deal for twenty minutes. I'd been to her flat a few times. Home delivery. Contra. Once, sitting in the littered kitchen, she'd asked me to shave her head with the set of electric clippers she'd acquired from some-where. Short hair was cool, she said. Also it stopped bas-tards grabbing your head in the final suck-off thrust. I saw the clippers in a pawn shop two days later. Her hair grew long, and bruised at the roots.

I slept with her three times, in her grimy bed, the mattress on the floor, the traffic spilling from the freeway to Alexandra Parade just metres below, her flatmate and sometime lover, Caroline, back in the lounge room trying not to hear above the inane bab-bling of the Letterman show, all business, all ritualistic small talk, a half-forgotten choreography of burlesque and trade. Corrigan didn't know it, of course, but the

41

love of the Lord had entered her, no help from him.

'A little,' I said. 'I believe Father Corrigan knew her better.'

'She was a strange girl.' Sadness crept into her voice. Regret too? 'I'm afraid she and Graeme didn't get on too well.'

I spoke quietly, treading light and slow. 'When did she leave home, Elaine?'

'About three years ago, must be.' She suddenly looked around the room, as if seeing it for the first time. 'We weren't living here then, of course. That was when we had the house in Carnegie, before we found this place.'

'This is a very nice house, Elaine.' It seemed appropriate. The cue had been obvious. She flicked her hand up in a quick dismissive wave, looked down at her knees, flushed slightly.

I tried to imagine her masturbating. Couldn't.

'Did Shelagh like it?'

Fear spark. A fraction pause. 'Like what?'

'This house.'

Glance back to the knees again. 'She, ahh, she never came here. Never saw it.'

I nodded knowingly. The young of today . . .

'What happened between Shelagh and your husband, Elaine?'

Her fingertips went white. Her lips contracted like salted slugs. Her eyes looked directly at me, without focus. Neck stiff. Spine rigid. She gave her head a tight little shake. Not a word came out.

I gave it a beat, tried again. 'What happened between Shelagh and your husband, Elaine?'

Again the little head shake. Her eyes started brimming. She ungrasped her hands, the right one darting out, grasping the mug, pushing it across the table maybe an inch, pulling it back again, back to clasp. Then the babble, sudden, automatic.

'Well, I'm really sorry Mr, ah, but I'm really *very* busy today. Very *busy*. Lots to do, you know, and I think so I *really* haven't the time to—all these things I have to—and I'm *very*—awfully sorry, but you really *will* have to go now. Perhaps another time you can— when my husband's—'

'Elaine Purdey.' I did the voice and the eyes bit. She stopped midstream, staring at me, very scared. Her fear stemmed only partly from me, though. Mostly, she could hear the padding feet of her own demons.

I kept the stare. 'Elaine Purdey,' soft now, 'close your eyes.'

She kept staring. I stared back. She closed her eyes as if she were standing before a firing squad.

I stood up and quietly walked around to the back of her chair. I placed my hands lightly on her shoulders. She jumped like I'd given her an electric shock, let out a little pre-verbal squeak. (Thought so, I thought.) I made shushing noises, low and long, and started to lightly work my thumbs into the taut knots along her shoulders.

'Relax, now, relax,' I crooned, doing my best therapist impersonation.

'Rel-a-a-a-x now. This is a terrible time for you, Elaine, terrible. You have so much to bear, such burdens, and all by yourself. Relax now, let those burdens fall away.'

She was still watch-spring tight, but not moving, broomstick straight. I worked my thumbs a little harder, round and round in easy circles, letting my index fingers weigh down on her shoulders, oscillating just a bit.

'You've been so *brave*, Elaine, so very, very brave. So *very* brave and good—'

She gave another little squeak. A different squeak.

'Oh, yes, so *very* good, with such terrible burdens to bear and bear in silence. God chose the weak things of the world, that he might put shame to the things that are strong, did you know that, Elaine? That he might put shame to the things that are strong . . .'

I pressed a little harder, my middle fingers joining my indexers, working away, crooning soft and baritone. I could have been reciting *Little Bo Peep*, would have made no difference. Tone is all, tone is the message. The mass is in Latin. The Assemblies of God talk in tongues. Her head tilted back, ever so slightly.

'That's good,' I murmured. 'Good girl, let that weight slip away, right away, right away, rest your head, let it lean, let it rest, let it all come flowing out . . .'

Her head sagged to the chair rest. I looked down at her face. The eyes were still closed, the lips loosening just a bit. I slipped my fingers and thumbs through the neck of her dress, started kneading her flesh. She squeaked again, a little lower.

'You are hungered; let me give you meat.'

Squeak.

'You are thirsty; let me give you drink.'

Squeak.

'I was a stranger and you took me in. You are naked; let me clothe you.'

Squeak, squeak.

'You are sick; I visit you. You are in prison; I come to you.'

Silence.

'Were there happy times, Elaine? Can you remember the happy times, the times in Carnegie before it all went wrong?'

She nodded, lifted her hands from her lap, placed them palms down on the arms of the chair.

'Tell me about them, Elaine. Tell me about the happy times. Quietly, now, so quietly.'

'He used to call her his little darling,' she said, little more than whispering. 'His little darling.'

'What sort of games did they play, he and his little darling?'

'All sorts. Oh yes, *all* sorts. He used to take her to the park all the time, play tennis with her, play volleyball at the beach. Used to have one of those little movie cameras, dress her up in my clothes, put make-up on her face, tell her to dance, tell her he was going to make her a movie star . . . Oh, she *loved* that one . . . My little darling, he used to call her, my little, little movie star . . .'

'My little darling, my little, little movie star,' I echoed, kneading harder, circles wider, working my thumbs around the base of her neck.

'His little, little movie star . . .'

'How old was the little, little movie star, Elaine?'

Dreamy now. 'Oh, twelve, thirteen, fourteen . . .'

'And did you like the little, little movie star, Elaine?'

'She was so cute . . . so gorgeous . . . a real little lady in her make-up and dresses . . . real little . . .'

'And did you make the movies with them, Elaine, with daddy and the little, little movie star?'

Harder now, fingers beneath her clavicles, thumbs running from shoulders to behind her ears. Her hands gripped and released the chair arms, gripped and released, gripped and released, gripped and released.

A pause, not tense.

'Sometimes . . .'

'When, Elaine?'

'Sometimes . . . twelve, thirteen . . .'

'And then . . .'

'Then not so often. Daddy said they didn't need an audience, that I'd be in the way, put his little, little movie star off her stride . . .'

'What were the movies about, Elaine, the movies Daddy made with the little, little movie star . . .'

'Only pretend, he said, only pretend movies, only playing . . .'

'Pretend, then, Elaine, only pretend.'

I slipped my hands down further inside her dress, circling my fingers, working them gently over her bra.

46

She squeaked, made a noise in her throat.

'Let's pretend to make a movie, Elaine . . .'

Mmm . . .'

I began to play with her nipples. Her mouth was open slightly, breathing shallow.

'I'll be Daddy, you be the little, little movie star.'

'Aha . . .'

'Am I doing it right, little, little movie star? Am I making a Daddy movie?'

'Aha . . .'

'What happens next, little, little movie star? What happens next in the movie?'

Eyes still shut. Her hands moved like robot arms from their resting place, moving to her knees. Slowly, easy, she grasped her Laura Ashley hem and bunched it up, bending her elbows, pulling the skirt up her skinny legs. She moved her knees apart.

Then she balled her fists tight into her crotch, arms rigid and ridged like high-tension cable, shoulders up, throat constricted. She screwed her eyes shut and growled, low, hard, angry, scared, breath coming in short, sharp gulps of panic.

'Wait, little, little movie star,' I said. 'Stay like that. Wait for Daddy. Daddy's got to get another reel of film.'

'No, Daddy . . . not . . . nnnhhh . . .' Voice different now. Deeper. Resisting. Holding it in.

'Shhhhh. Keep your eyes closed. Wait for Daddy. Hold that pose . . .'

I closed the front door behind me as quietly as I could.

Walked fast, lighting a Dunhill on the move, looking for a cab in the middle of desperate nowhere, rain flagellant and pious, the tea clagged and sordid on my tongue.

✝

It was dusk by the time the cabbie dropped me outside the Bradford. I went inside, ordered a pot and a neat Jamesons, lit a Dunhill and aimed to be out again by the time I hit the filter.

No one bothered me. It's not that sort of pub.

Anyway, I had a look on my face which said I'd likely ram my fist down the throat of any mouth that opened in my direction.

Blessed are the meek; for they have enough sense to stay out of pubs like the Bradford. Other than that, fuck them.

There was a time when I believed in it all. Like the book says. Really believed.

I was no godling (Sauly-Pauly came up with that one), but I was good. I was, in fact, *damn* good. I railed against the *Hasidim* and all their empty ritual. I gathered followers, spun my yarns. I worked for the sick and oppressed, against the Romans and the Temple Guard both. I wanted to uplift my people, reveal how *radical* was the love of God.

And I believed, at the end, my martyrdom was my message, and my route to reward. Into His hands I commended my spirit.

Then I woke up three days later lying on a slab of rock in darkness. Alone. Naked. Scabbed and septic.

Still fucking alive.

Do you have any idea what that sort of experience can do to a belief in blessed salvation hereafter?

At the journey's ragged end, when rest seems just a shuttered eye away, when the pain and the blood and the thorns and the spearhead and the heat and the horror, the cactus-prayers stubborn in the desert of my vinegared lips, seem suddenly not to matter, when the light of the welcome appears dim and approaching above the walls of the town, it all begins again.

No. Not begins. Continues, as before.

And not as before. The guts ripped out of it. I had accepted my death, dying, I knew, because my God was alive. Then I was a dead man walking, and God was silent as cholera's laugh.

Of course I'm thirty-three years old. Every school kid knows that. I have been thirty-three years old now for almost two millennia.

I cannot remember my birthday. Wasn't December, I remember that much.

I have never died, but I have been killed five times. I was stabbed by a Franciscan monk during the Black Plague. I was crushed as a heretic during the persecution of the Waldensians in the twelfth century. I was run through in Damascus during a Crusade. I was hanged by Judge Jeffreys in England in the seventeenth for stealing lead from a church roof. I was shot point-blank in Los Angeles by a Pentecostal who mistook me for an abortionist.

One begged my forgiveness as my eyes rolled back. Another demanded repentence. Two called me devil and the last called me liberal. All wore a crucifix and none was called to account.

Every time. Three days, I wake up again. Wounds healing, the fading stigmata of another pointless lifetime, not ended, just begun. Still thirty-three.

And then I move on, somewhere, anywhere, cash only and never give receipts. That is my predestination. I have walked among nations. Christ stopped at Eboli. And Croatia. And Japan and Texas and Glastonbury and everywhere in between. And then he buggered off again, leaving disbelief, madness and scorn to bloom in his footprints. People notice if you stay thrity-three for more than a decade.

Love is thus not possible. Neither is faith.

I was blind, but now I see.

So I keep moving, the Wandering Jew, lapsed, living longer, learning more, knowing less and less. That which I held self-evident in Jerusalem—that of God and passion and righteousness—I have long borne no regard.

So I don't know if God exists. I've never met him. Think on that, next time you worship me.

My journey has not been entirely without reward. I have learnt that which is true, the only things which are true, the only Absolutes in the whole fucking universe.

I am not, despite it all, a nihilist. I have a philosophy by which I live. It brooks no debate, because it asks no question.

You have it too.

You always have. It comes to you, an instant revelation soon forgotten, at the very moment the pressure on your head eases and you slip, choking and blue, onto a brightly lit sheet coated in blood, faeces and amniotic fluid, safe no more and utterly, irrevocably, unbidden, alone.

And it is this.

What's done is done. What is, is.

I decided to head for Corrigan's house, see how he was holding up. I wouldn't have to pay for the whisky there.

✝

'A fucking circus.'

His favourite phrase. He was in his study, a cramped room choked with books on dusty shelves, a small crucifix and two framed Renaissance maps on the walls. His desk, pitted and scratched, erupted in quasi-piles of manila folders containing documents, reports, discussion papers from welfare bodies, church councils, charitable agencies, government departments. The Jamesons bottle left a piss-coloured arc on the cover of a slim volume titled *A Christian Response To Poverty: An Ecumenical Perspective*.

A computer, its screen smeared with greasy finger-prints, sat on a side table, joined by a box of discs and a dusty modem. A fifties bakelite lamp provided the only light.

The good father clearly had not shaved since the morning of the discovery. Neither, apparently, had he changed his clothes, nor washed. He had spent most of Sunday in a foul-smelling interview room at police headquarters, alternately answering questions about the life of Shelagh Jane Purdey and asserting his innocence in the matter of her death. The church doors had remained locked, services cancelled for the first time in his career.

He had returned to the house around 8.00pm Sunday night, flicked on the lamp in the study, grabbed the bottle and gone nowhere except to the toilet since. He had drunk the first bottle, cracked the spare, and rendered himself grimly sober. The spirit was within him and its absence would intoxicate.

'A fucking, fucking circus.'

I lit a cigarette, looked round for an ashtray, couldn't find one, grabbed the whisky bottle, pressed the up-ended cap into service, and swigged from the neck.

'Many calls?'

Corrigan downed his shot, splashed in a refill. 'Shit, Panther, it's a fucking—'

'Circus, I know. What?'

'Newspapers first. Two from the tabloid: crime guy and some feature writer wanting my take on devil worship. Two from the broadsheet: crime guy and the

52

religious affairs roundsman doing a piece on the decline of the notion of church-as-sanctuary.'

'Tell him to ask Quasimodo.'

'I told him to fuck himself.'

'Not good politics.'

'Fuck politics. Then the television people: four news programs, three current affairs programs wanting interviews and the ABC religious department after a contribution to a documentary called "Mephistopheles in the Nineties".'

'That must have been tempting.'

'Then there was the bunch of born-agains insisting on holding an exorcism in my church, the New-Agers wanting to perform a Native American healing chant around the altar, the coven of white witches offering a purification ritual in the name of ecumenical cooperation, the bunch of black witches wanting to hold a Sabbat in the front garden, two psychics offering to solve the murder by touching the crucifix, and a guy into S&M who wants to turn the place into a nightclub.'

'Any calls from the Incest Survivors' Association?'

He looked at me blankly.

'No, well,' I continued, 'they wouldn't, I guess. She didn't.'

'Didn't what? Talk sense, Panther, or leave me be.'

'Survive.'

'You're—'

'Did you know about the incest?'

'I had a—'

'I'm pretty sure the father was slipping her. Three years maybe. That's why she left home.'

My detective work left him distinctly unimpressed.

'Panther, you're a naive bastard underneath it all. With the kids out around here, especially the junkies, it's rare to find one who isn't a victim of abuse. They've mostly all been raped ragged. Up the arse or in the head. Doesn't matter which, in the end. Parents, brothers, strangers, some bureaucracy or other, teachers, cops . . .'

'Even priests.'

He sighed, looked away.

'Even priests.' He folded his arms and glared at me. 'Why am I paying you to find out things I already know?'

I scrunched my cigarette butt into the whisky cap.

'As thou art going with thine adversary before the magistrate, on the way give diligence to be quit of him, lest haply he hale thee unto a judge, and the judge shall deliver thee to the officer, and the officer shall cast thee into prison.'

He said nothing, refilled his glass, passed me the bottle.

'The cops think you did it, don't they?' I asked.

Still nothing. A tear brimmed.

'Did you ever fuck Shelagh Purdey?'

He swung in his chair, leaned forward, spun a straight-arm fist at my face. Too old, too pissed, too angry. I didn't even need to dodge. His momentum and skewed axis tripped the legs of his chair and sent him and it crashing onto the floor. I put my foot on the side of his head, pressed it into the carpet.

'Did you?'

Quiet now, the fury having fled with his breath. 'No. No, never.'

I removed my foot, reached down, helped him up, righted his chair. He sat again. I poured him another slug.

'Then you'd better know all there is to know about this girl, Corrigan. Not supposition. Fact. Stick to what you know about her. Never mention what you *think* about her, what you assume about her, however obvious. People never die for what they do, only for the thoughts behind the doing.'

'I didn't do it, Panther.'

'I didn't do most of what people think I've done, either.' And done most of what people think I didn't, I could have added. 'It wouldn't make much of a defence if it ever came to it. It never has.'

It's true. They're still dusting for fingerprints, two thousand years later.

'Do something, Panther.' He pushed at the manila folders on his desk, sending a few toppling off the back. 'I'm not strong enough for this.'

'No one is, priest.'

He shook his head. 'God is.'

'You don't know God.'

'I know the idea of God.'

'Which one? There's been a few. The jealous one? The angry one? The righteous one? The loving one?

The immanent one? The transcendent—'

'Shut it, Panther, please. Just because you've read the works of the early theologians doesn't make you an expert. The *humble* one. The idea of God that says to be humble, to be less than the next man, to be not above. The idea of being open, vulnerable and flawed. To be the tax collector, not the Pharisee. To love the wretchedness of others, to recognise the weakness and sin of others as a man recognises his brother, not to offer guidance, but to offer love without question . . . or hope of love returned.'

Somewhere inside the gilded halls of the Vatican at that moment, no doubt, sat at least one learned cardinal who could have shown such views to be heretic. I could have told him that, but I figured he already knew. I called him an arrogant prick instead.

'As you wish,' he muttered. 'But that's my idea of God. Whatever thing God turns out to be when I die and meet Him on my knees isn't important, Panther. Not now. Not in this life. What's important is the idea of Him, the idea that keeps us looking up in wonder, not staring down, despising.' He was rambling now, drifting on a current of single malt, too tired to row against the horror and exhaustion. I let him go. 'And if God, when I meet Him, asks obscenity and pushes my face into the ground with His boot on my cheek, if He turns out to be a right cunt, Panther, if the next life turns out to be as big a circus as this one, I will still love Him. I will abase myself before the tyrant, Panther. Because to do otherwise would be to place myself

56

above Him, to put myself above the idea of Him—*my* idea of Him—above the world. Bugger it, man, there is no sin greater than that.' He paused, staring at something inside him, shook his head at it, coughed, pulled into shore and plunged into platitude. 'It's better to give than receive. There's a diamond beneath the dust for you.'

'And remember that when they bang you up in maximum security. Come morning, priest, do this: call the incest self-help groups, call the community welfare bodies, the sexual assault lines, ask about Shelagh Purdey. See if she ever confided, see what you can get. It'll be confidential, of course, but she's dead and, shit, you're a priest. Get everything you can. In writing.'

'And render indignities upon her even in death.'

'She doesn't give a shit, man. Think straight: the more you know about her, the clearer the picture. This is the gig. You don't need to find who killed her. You just need to point to better probabilities than you. We need to cast doubts, in the finest missionary tradition. That is, if you want to be on the right side of the Remand Centre by the time the memorial service rolls around.'

He nodded. 'You think the father killed her?'

'Way I see it, she was dead the day her mummy bought her a training bra.'

'Incest happens all the time, Panther, always has. People survive it, that's what it's all about, all these groups. It fucked her up, sure, but it hadn't killed her, not like that. She wasn't just a taker. She wasn't

57

without hope, man. She still had things to give.'

'But she did cast in all that she had, even all her living.'

I checked my watch. 11.00pm. I put my hand in my inside jacket pocket, felt the dozen little plastic sachets there within. I had some deliveries to make. One had been for Shelagh Purdey, but no matter. There'd be someone else, somewhere, not too far. Cashed up.

I stood up. 'Got to go. I'll come see you tomorrow night, see how you went. Get some sleep, Corrigan.'

He nodded again, looked up. 'I tried, Panther. I really tried with that girl.'

Three grams a week, I recalled. More when she was holding. Cocks in her mouth to put spikes in her arms to put cocks in her mouth.

'She was searching for oblivion, priest, and all you could offer was everlasting life.'

'Ach, she got what she wanted then.'

'Chalk one up for Mephistopheles.'

'Her? No. There is forgiveness.'

'You. And no. There isn't.'

✝

Tuesday started badly. It started badly with a knock on the door of my warehouse, halfway through the first cup of coffee, Patti Smith's *Horses* barely into *Gloria* on the stereo.

Coffee caught on in the seventeenth century, called

*kaveh*, courtesy of the Turks. I took to it immediately. The first taste was salvation, freedom from sluggishness, the sweet gift of alertness. The second was religion: bonded and ritual, the fear of its absence greater than the demands of its rule.

The knock was very bad indeed. Bad, first, because I simply refuse to communicate with another human being before two belts of caffeine. Bad, second, because no one knew where I lived.

I thought.

The place is invisible from the road. It used to be an artist's studio before I took it on. To reach it I have to walk up a blind cobbled alley, hang left into an undercover car park, duck between two cars into darkness, head up an unlit wooden dogleg fire escape and enter through the thick, unmarked door.

There are no deliveries—no couriers, no pizza, no wandering evangelists. No one has ever been there, bar the lost and the landlord once in a while, and he isn't local, and not of inquisitive mind. The house of the Lord was inviolate.

I ignored the knock.

It happened again, louder, faster, punctuating an unpleasantly familiar voice yelling, 'Open up Panther, or I'll crowbar the bloody lock off.'

I did as I was bidden.

DSS Gordon and DC Pordelli shoved their way past, the minion grabbing my shoulder as an afterthought and pulling me in the wake of law's unstoppable journey. Gordon, savouring his invasive triumph for a moment, stood still and moved his head, taking in the bare red-brick walls, stained by small clouds of spray-paint, the lightly cobwebbed rafters, and the particle board floor. He registered the single old sofa, the cast-off kitchen table, its three attendant directors' chairs, the cupboard, with its kettle, plunger, and almost empty biscuit packet on the top, the mattress up on the mezzanine. He noted the pile of books in the corner, my crack-spined and folded little library: Augustine, Tertullian, Origen, Suetonius, Bede, the *Compendium Maleficarum* (a favourite), books on theology, on comparative religion. I've never kept a diary. There seemed no need. He observed the neat rack of compact discs, my easily disposable companions: Patti Smith, Smashing Pumpkins, Nick Cave, Palestrina, others. One thing I've always been—and I think this point has been frequently overlooked—is cool. I live light. Possessions are meaningless when transience is fact and flight a constant possibility. There are other types of burdens.

'Yup,' I said. 'No family room. Then again, no family.'

'Shut it and sit, Panther,' growled Gordon. Pordelli made sure I complied. I offered no resistance. It's best to let them get on with it, I've found. Gordon walked to the CD player, hit the stop button.

They'd plonked me on the folding chair by the table, next to my half-cup of brew, which was a bit of a bonus. I picked it up, gulped it, shucked my shoulder to give Pordelli the hint that he could let go of it now and stand up straight. He did, next to his boss.

60

'You're a dirty little piece of work, Panther, aren't you?' said Gordon. 'I expected better from you, really. Not your style, I'd have thought.'

Pordelli chuckled, his belly wobbling from the effort. 'Filthy bastard.'

'What did you expect?' I asked. 'It's a warehouse. You get a bit of dust, a few cobwebs—'

Gordon leaned over, grabbed me by the throat. 'I've got you slap bang on attempted rape, mystery man.'

I contemplated this. It was not difficult to see where it was coming from. I chided myself. I never learn. I take people to the edge of the precipice. I get what I want, I walk away and leave them there. One day I'll remember either to push them off or pull them back. It's too big a decision to leave up to them, and some of them simply stay there, terrified to move, screaming into the wind.

Whatever, it was a nasty little situation that now presented itself and demanded resolution.

Not the matter of Elaine Purdey and her guilt, her sad notion of fidelity towards a man who clearly told her nothing of his own life and got his kicks cleaving unto his daughter. Not that. That was a matter of performance, no more. There was something rather more serious askew.

'How did you find me?' I asked.

By placing our mark so do we exist. I have no mark. I have never written my name, even on the first time around, with the distant screams of the Passover lambs ringing in my ears. A signature is a thumbtack in time, pinning a moment like a moth to a mounting board. You can have position or momentum, but never both. I prefer the latter. Last time I stood still, some bastard nailed me to a tree.

That means cash only and never give credit, even when it's due. To the telephone company I am Justin Sanderson, to the power company I am Malcolm Petrovski. To the real estate agent where I deliver my rent on the first of each month I am George Armitage, refereed by Justin Sanderson and Malcolm Petrovski. To my ageing Hungarian landlord who occasionally potters around tapping the plumbing and fixing the roof, I am Simon Stylites, just Simon, stand-offish, no trouble, good tenant.

I have never had a visitor. I have slept in the beds of women, but mine own is as barren as death.

Gordon was shaking his head. Pordelli was chuckling again. 'Mystery man,' he rumbled.

'Think you're so good, don't you, Panther?' said Gordon, visibly gloating. 'Think you're so awfully bloody good, sitting here in the middle of your web of lies, thinking no one can see you, no one can find you, that the sun don't shine in your crypt.'

'You're mixing your clichés, Gordon,' I replied. 'Be careful.'

Pordelli leant in close, doing the bad cop bit. '*You're* the one who should have been careful, mystery man,' he whispered, treating me to the nauseating fog of his last meal. 'Think you're the only one with contacts? Think you're the only one who can ask questions and get answers around here?'

I turned my head, thinking that maybe I should offer to make them both a coffee so at least I could have my second one.

'Never trust a junkie, Panther,' said Gordon. 'You should know that. Ten bucks here, ten bucks there, a fist in an alley, a strip-search in a cell, doesn't take much. The complaint was through to the station by nine o'clock last night. I wasn't on shift, mate, I do days, but D24 rang it through, thought I'd like to know.'

'See,' breathed Pordelli, 'we're hot for you, mystery man. You're a long-term project . . .'

Gordon again. This was a set-piece, I figured. 'So I left my hearth and family, Panther, left the warmth and comfort of my home, came down to Fitzroy and hit the streets. You think your clients don't know where you live, mate? Wrong. They know. They've watched you.'

Pordelli now. 'They just leave you alone here because they think you're a schmuck, mystery man, a merchant man, a trader, of no more interest than the fat guy who owns the pawn shop around the corner.'

'You'll damage my self-esteem, talking like that.'

Gordon snorted. 'I'll damage your ribcage, give me half a chance. I'd made this place by midnight, mate, but you weren't home—'

'You should have left a note. I would have called you.'

'Smart guy. So here we are this morning, fresh-faced and frisky, about to take you down.'

Pordelli started singing. '*Oh what a beautiful morning, Oh what a beautiful day, dum de dum, dum de dum.*'

I couldn't stand it any longer. 'Gentlemen,' I said, all polite, 'may I offer you both a cup of coffee?'

'No,' snapped Gordon.

'Then do you mind if I make myself one? I have a feeling you're about to ask me some potentially life-altering questions (Pordelli giggled at that one) and I'm sure I don't have to remind you of the international convention, to which Australia is a signatory, which guarantees that all suspects must be in a state of mental competence before interrogation begins.'

Gordon grinned. 'And which convention is that, Mr Expert?'

'The Second Council of Constantinople,' I said.

'Never heard of it.'

'You can bet the lawyers will have.'

It worked. A doubting dullness crossed his face and he nodded. I got out of my chair, walked to the other end of the room, Pordelli a lumbering shadow, fired up the electric kettle, drained the plunger and dropped in four heaped teaspoons of Lavazza.

Coffee thus made—Pordelli having accepted my second offer of a cup, Gordon still refusing—we sat around the table, much more civilised.

I recounted my visit to the Purdey household, explaining that I had been seeking information, any information, which might assuage the torment of the good Father Corrigan. They said nothing to that one. Mrs Purdey had been highly strung and emotional, I said, distraught over her loss, and I had simply rubbed her shoulders in a natural expression of compassion, attempting to calm her down, ease her terrible burden.

'Natural compassion?' sneered Gordon. 'Grabbing her breasts is natural compassion? Making her flash her panties is natural compassion? Sounds more like attempted sexual assault to me.'

I denied it, of course. I said she was upset, devastated, imagining things, living six inches left of reality, grief stricken and delusional, transferring guilt.

'She feels guilty about Shelagh's death?' Gordon asked, saying really, *Oh-yeah-so-what*?

I paused a moment. I hadn't thought about that. It needed working through for a second or two. 'No,' I replied. 'No, she doesn't. She feels guilty about her husband. He's been unfaithful to her.'

Pordelli's turn. He grunted, slurped at his coffee. 'What's that got to do with Shelagh?'

'Everything,' I said.

They both stared at me. I said nothing, kept my face poker, watched it slowly sink in. Gordon got there first.

'You mean . . . ?'

'Say it, Gordon,' I said calmly. 'Speak its name. Name the horror. You didn't know? How are *your* children, by the way?'

He lunged across the table toward me, face reddening. Pordelli pulled him back. Not again, I thought. All this macho stuff was getting really tedious. 'Hit yourself, Gordon,' I whispered. 'It's your demon, not mine.'

He sat still again. Didn't apologise, though. When

he spoke, his manner had changed. The interrogation, I sensed, was over. I had something he wanted.

'You're saying Graeme Purdey was fucking his own daughter?' He sounded like his tongue was coated in faeces.

I nodded. 'Persistently. That's why she left the family home at the tender age of fifteen. Whether it continued, I don't know. Yet.'

'And Elaine Purdey knew?'

'Yes.'

'And did nothing to stop it?'

'That bit of her didn't know. Didn't want to know.'

It was his turn to nod. We were professionals now, round-table consulting. 'Do you think Elaine Purdey was jealous of Shelagh Purdey?'

'Elaine Purdey doesn't have the passion to be jealous of anything. She's all gesture and ritual. I think she's fogged off her face on relaxants and probably has been for years.'

Gordon and Pordelli were silent. Pordelli looked at his empty coffee cup, wishing, maybe, that it would fill again. Time to take the lead, I thought. 'You didn't know, did you?' I asked.

That stung. 'We would have found out, Panther. Don't get smug. We would have found out in the end.'

'Without grabbing her titties,' grinned Pordelli. I didn't dignify him with a response.

'You've saved us a bit of time, is all,' continued Gordon. 'Now do us all a favour—mostly, do yourself a favour—and back off out of it.' He stood up, echoed by Pordelli, getting all serious again. Face-saving time, I thought. 'I mean it, Panther. Stay out of my face, stay away from the Purdeys, and stay away from the priest. You'll notice we do not have a search warrant, but if we have to come back, bucko, rest assured that we will have.'

Pordelli glanced around. 'Big space, this, Panther, plenty of nooks and crannies, cracks in the brickwork. Plenty of places to hide little baggies, little twists of aluminium foil, little folds of paper, little bits of whatnot.'

'I don't know what you mean, officer,' I said, letting them know I did, but didn't give a shit. 'And I must say, if this is what it leads to, I will never again venture into the charitable act of consoling a bereaved mother. It's simply not appreciated.'

They both laughed at that one, which was an unpleasant surprise. It was meant to annoy them.

'Think you're such hot little shit, don't you, Panther?' smirked Gordon. 'Such a hot shit little private eye. And you really haven't got a clue, have you? Not a bloody clue.' He laughed again, ugly. 'Go on a holiday or something, Panther. Read some paperbacks or something, you might learn a thing or two.'

Pordelli was having a right old guffaw.

'What's so fucking funny?' I snapped. I hate being on the back foot. There are times when I wish the omniscience rumours were true.

Not many, though.

'Basic,' said Pordelli. 'Basic research. You should try

it sometimes. It makes the world a bit easier to understand.'

'Not mother,' said Gordon. 'Stepmother. Graeme Purdey divorced when Shelagh was two, remarried a year later.'

Oops. 'But hang on,' I blurted, way off beam 'why didn't the real mother get custody?'

'She didn't want it.'

Even after this long, surprise is still possible. Will there never be relief?

Shit. 'Where can I find her?'

Gordon winked, headed for the door, Pordelli trailing along. 'Stay lucky, Panther,' he said. 'Stay lucky.'

Alone again, I fired up the kettle, ditto the CD player.

*'Jesus died for somebody's sins,'* drawled Patti, *'but not mine.'*

✝

The encounter fazed me. Too much to think about all at once. I went back to bed for a nap to recover. Nothing happened round my patch until midday, anyway.

I am away. I dream of St Brigid. Dear Brigid. What a girl.

I was close to her for a while during my time in Ireland, back in the sixth. The last lonely time of love. After Mary, the only time. Secret and silent, close to her. Brigid, who earned her sainthood by giving succour. Brigid, who was bathing in a pool at Uinmeras when there approached six wandering priests, cold, ragged, exhausted, raddled and delirious from thirst.

Brigid who seeing them rose from the water in her nakedness and commanded the wanderers drink, drink of the water which she turned to ale.

I was one of those priests. Blending in. Being no one in particular, black-cowled and silent. The others quivered. Some denounced her as devil, some as succubus. Others pronounced her phantasm, a glamour cast by an Irish witch, a conflagration in waiting.

They all drank her booze, though. Then blessed themselves forgiveness and damned her to desist. They left, cowls drawn against the drizzle, walking, their holy mission to perform.

I stayed. She was a passionate soul, and could murder a hogshead of ale when the spirit moved her.

After a while, I told her who I was. I think she believed me. She had been expecting me, she said. She became the bride of Christ, *de facto*, secret, blessed, outside the walls of her convent, moonlit and earthy.

I stayed. For a while. As long as I dared, until the light of revelation began to glint inside her eye, and the horror that it spawned began to shape.

I abandoned her to her nuns. No words. No explanations. It was the last action of mine that I remember that was wholly predicated on mercy.

Brigid is with me now. I am lying on my bed and she is on her hands and knees above me, brown eyes looking into mine, her face serene with her own completeness. Behind her the hooded nuns of Kildare stand in a circle, heads bowed, around the eternal flame of her shrine, breathing low and quiet lest they make it shudder.

Brigid rises on her knees, never taking her eyes away. She pulls the wide neck of her brown habit away from her slender neck and over her shoulders, letting it fall to reveal her holy glory. She bends down again, brushes her lips against mine, backs down the bed until her head is at my thighs.

'Not that which goeth into the mouth defileth a man,' she says, 'but that which cometh out of the mouth, this defileth a man.'

She lowers her head, taking me in. I am of one nature.

I hold her hair in my hands. I struggle to speak. 'Therefore there is one Christ, God and man,' I say. 'Of the same essence with the Father as touching his Godhead, and of the same essence with us as touching his manhood.'

The nuns begin to chant, low and lulling, lachrymose and longing. The flame rises and twists, same as it ever was, same as it ever was.

I feel myself lifting and pulsing, my whole being concentrating itself into one bright moment not yet arrived, the bright moment from which darkness extends and cradles, makes it all stop, makes it all go away. I am on the mountain. I am close to the kingdom.

I stretch my arms, clasp the head of Brigid gently, pull her towards me, open my eyes to see her beauty swell in my vision, watch her breasts kiss my chest, my nostrils eager for her smell.

Her head comes away in my hands, suddenly cold, without resistance. It is not her head. It is the head of Shelagh Purdey, make-up smudged, the thoughts of putrefaction dripping from her neck. Her body lies crooked between my knees.

The nuns laugh aloud, cackling and harsh, turn and run from the flame, which sears white now and snarls.

Shelagh's lips move. From somewhere behind them comes the voice of Paul.

'I see another law in my members warring against the law of my mind, and bringing me into captivity to the law of sin, which is in my members.'

There is a fear in me, an old and ancient fear. I stare at the dead eyes of Shelagh Purdey, watch the prattle of the salesman fall from her like maggots. I have been here before. It is I whom thou persecutest. Still. Is there no end to this?

I did not start it. Any of it. I did not walk to Damascus.

I tighten the grasp on the head. 'It is hard for thee to kick against the pricks,' I say.

I push it back, ram it down on my manhood, render it silent, and explode inside it.

The flame screams and goes out. Shelagh Purdey's head rolls aside, falls to the ground.

Then silence. Blackness. Absence.

I woke up feeling refreshed and replenished.

I knew what had to be done.

First, though, I headed for the shower, followed Pope Gregory's advice to Augustine, and washed my lust away with tears.

✝

Graeme Purdey's office seemed the logical place to start. First, though, a little damage limitation seemed advisable.

I walked round to John the Baptist's flat, knocked, but heard no answer. The stench of cooked meat wafted from under the door. It reminded me it was lunchtime.

I got lucky and found him in the nearest pub, the Champion, huddled at a tiny side table, worrying at roast beef surrounded by vegetables boiled into flaccid submission. I bought him a pot, a shot for myself. He greeted me volubly enough—his fear, like the remorse of a penitent at confession, was transitory—spilling gobbets of half-chewed food whence they came.

'What's the word, John?' I asked.

'The Word is the way, son.' He gave me a gappy smile. 'You of all people should know that.'

I let it go. 'Somebody hooked me to the cops. Last night. Gave them my address.'

He didn't react. John the Baptist knew all things. He was a seer but not a shaman. Interpretation, he reckoned, was someone else's business.

'Who, old man?'

He wedged another mouthful of dead cow in his gob, spoke thickly through its transformation.

'That would be telling, boy. Ask me to grass, makes me no better than the grasser.'

I didn't have time for it. Patience is the trademark of a saint, and the saints can have it. I am not a saint, and no one, in two thousand years, has ever suggested I was. It's about the only thing me and the Vatican agree on. That, and red wine.

'John,' I snapped, 'put your knife and fork down and look at me for a moment.'

He looked up, a trace of doubt flicking across his red-streaked eyes, did as he was told. Holding his gaze, I reached across and picked up his fork.

'That's better, my old friend,' I said, letting a smile curl my lips. 'Have you washed your hands before eating? Show me your palms.'

He laid his hands on the table, his wasted shoulders dropping a little as he chanced a smile.

I tried to judge the impact precisely. It was, after all, only a matter of foreshortening the process, a bit of a gee-up towards the inevitable end, nothing more. I have but the body of a man, however, when all is said and done. I am weak, fallible and, odd as it may sound, still coming to terms with the mysteries of the body I've inhabited since way before St Jude was clubbed to death in my honour.

The prongs of the fork thus pierced his skin, not dangerously deep, but deep enough to draw blood from the wound and a sharp obscenity swallowed by his involuntary in-rush of breath. He didn't try to pull his hand back, though. He was too brute-smart for that.

'This is one way to receive the stigmata,' I said. 'The other involves being a grossly deluded, self-mutilating virgin.'

He said nothing, breath coming in rapid snorts.

'Who, John?' I pressed a little harder.

'Watching last night from my window,' he said, the words spilling fast. 'I see two cops asking on the corner. Few of the youngsters standing there. Waiting a delivery, I reckon.'

I thought, shit, must have been just before I got there. Lucky. Very lucky.

'Who, John?'

'Son . . .'

I moved the fork, slowly, back and forth. He winced, swallowed his breath again. The barman probably knew something was going on. I didn't turn around to check. I figured he wouldn't interfere, anyway. John had already paid for his nosh.

'Young lad I saw, had him up against the fence. Landed him one in the belly, son, pushed his head against the wire. Then they took him down the road a bit. I couldn't see. Thought that was his lot, but five minutes later he's back. He don't look too upset, but he didn't hang around long. Gone by the time you got there, son.'

I leant down on the fork, twisted it sideways. He went pale. You learn a lot watching witch trials.

'I wasn't there, old man. I wasn't there. Remember that.'

'I remember, son, I remember.' His voice was up half an octave, cracking. He wanted to cough, but didn't dare. 'I remember. You wasn't there.'

'Good. The kid. Thin? Light brown hair, manky, past his shoulders? Bum fluff beard?'

He nodded. I removed the fork, smiled.

He rubbed his hand, eyes suddenly watery. 'What you going to do, son?' he asked, sounding like he really didn't want to hear the answer.

'Thy body was broken and thy blood shed for us,' I said. 'Grant that the commemoration of this holy mystery may obtain for us peace, and that those who receive it may find everlasting rest.'

I stood up to go, nodding thanks. The old man was staring at his plate. 'Here, son,' he said, chancing a whine. 'Me food's gone cold.'

'Stay there,' I replied. 'I'll order you a fresh meal. Fair's fair.'

I went to the bar, put some money on the runner. Ordered him a fresh pot, a fillet of battered cod and a bread roll.

✝

It took me fifteen minutes on foot to find Davey Parker, he of the bum fluff, snooping eyes and flapping jaw. I'd pretty much figured it had to be him, even before John's confirmation. He'd been the only one of my regulars not present at the drop-off.

Apart, of course, from Shelagh Purdey.

He was where I thought he'd be: at home in his littered room in the three-bedroom house he shared and rented with four of his mates. None of the others was in.

He was surprised to see me, fearful at first, but relaxing into the pathetic trust of a dog for a cruel master when I told him I had some new scag, different source, extra good, and wanted to give him a free sample because of his value to me as a customer.

He took me into his bedroom, produced a black-scarred spoon and yesterday's fit. I made him toss the spike aside, pulled a clean one from my jacket's inside pocket. 'Will you never learn, Davey?' I chided. 'You could die that way.'

He grinned like a fool, rolled up his sleeve and set the tourniquet.

He grinned even more when I slipped the needle beneath his scabby skin. I didn't bother to inform him of the nature of his transgression as I pumped one and a half grams into his arm.

'I am not your master, Davey,' I said. 'Because you have drunk, you have become drunk from the bubbling stream which I have measured out. He who will drink from my mouth will become as I am: I myself will become he, and the things that are hidden shall be revealed to him.'

He smiled at that, dimly, as the rush hit him. His

eyes rolled back, taking his head with them. It hit the filthy carpet with a percussive thud.

'*Ite missa est*,' I whispered. Go, you are dismissed. Send me a postcard. I'd love to know how you get on.

It would have been arrogant to give him a reason for his death. I figured, anyway, if there was an afterlife, as per the manual, someone up there would tell him.

Who am I to presuppose the moral code of God? What would I know?

'I'll find my own way out,' I said. I don't think he heard me.

✝

# 3

MY RIB, SAID THE OVERSTRESSED doctor at St Vincent's Hospital emergency, really wasn't broken, however much it felt like it. Neither was my ankle. The bruises would be up by morning, he predicted, blossoming into a blue-green floridity pretty much in inverse proportion to the decreasing swelling of my testicles.

It was gone 9.00pm by the time I left the place, some five long, sluggish, aching hours after I first walked gingerly in, four and three-quarters of them spent waiting for a doctor to see me.

I walked down the broad boulevard of Victoria Parade, slowly, splay-legged and limping, turned left into Smith Street, past the Seven-Eleven, intent on a couple of short, sharp anaesthetic belts of malt at the Bradford before heading back to the warehouse.

The warehouse. Another problem. It was known now, to Gordon and Pordelli, its location and their suspicions no doubt linked and flagged on the CIB database. I had to do something about that. More than I'd already done.

I must set at liberty them that are bruised. In this case, me. Again.

Progress and repetition. Sometimes hard to tell the difference, I find.

Smith Street was in its nightly transition phase. The discount shops, snack bars, struggling boutiques, pawn brokers and op shops that crowded the litter-strewn pavements were long shut; the cheap Vietnamese, Thai and Chinese restaurants doing good business; the yuppie bars not yet pumping out the sixties salsa and soft jazz that were the current fashion. Cars cruised slowly, looking for parking spots, however improbable. Trams roared and chimed in opposite directions, fanning the litter in brutish little whirlwinds. The wind was chill and begging; the rain, for once, at ease.

The pavements were busy and tense, as always. Groups of diners, still in the garb of their work, peered in restaurant windows, checking the menus. The locals strolled, heading for pubs, for poker machines, for home, the low-income earners of all nations hunched against the chill. A middle-aged hippie busker cawed out Dylan in the harsh light outside the 24-hour super-market. A woman, wide-eyed and chain-smoking, sat on a bench, talking to herself. A trio of men with prison tatts shared a brown paper bottle. In the doorways, people squatted, some on the nod, some of the cadge. Dealers dealt, thirsts were slaked, territories marked.

A couple of teenage boys, bottom-end smack-sellers, flop-fringed and baggy-trousered, hung about in the purple light outside one of the games arcades, smoking cigarettes and glancing round with the eyes of nervous hunters. They looked away when they saw me—too quickly, I noticed, to realise my fragile state.

That was good. The drugs trade on Smith, like everything else, was tight, many-tongued, competitive and quietly desperate. Customer loyalty was achieved more through fear than good service, and as Davey Parker had demonstrated to his cost, I had been getting a bit too lax of late.

For there are two names never to be spoken. The first is the name of God. The second is the name of your dealer. Only one of them matters.

Word would get around. Panther's getting slack. The teenagers would try to edge me out if I wasn't careful. I should have done Davey Parker public, I reflected, left him cold and stiffening in a side street. Feed the flock of slaughter, whose buyers slay them, and feel not guilty.

That's my problem. I don't think ahead. I never contemplate the consequences of my actions.

Never have. And look where it's got me.

I'll never amount to much now.

I stood at the bar in the Bradford. A stool would have hurt too much. Three, maybe four measures of Jamesons should kick in nicely with the pain-killers, I reckoned. I tuned out the waffle of the football replay on the television, let my mind wander where it would.

About Pantera. I don't know. It was a story going round when I was a kid in Nazareth. He was my father, said the story, a Roman centurion long gone, just another casual impregnation under military rule. I used the surname in my childhood, encouraged by Mary.

She was a sharp woman. Canny. A Roman surname was good cover, she said.

Cover for what, she never said.

Bethlehem, the star, the wise men and myrrh. I never heard about them, any of them, until after my death. If you could call it that.

I have met many wise men, calm and knowing and learning and content with no fear of the future. Most of them died unjust. The rest just died.

I went to Bethlehem once, later on, preaching, when the momentum was building and insurrection hung in the air. It was a dull little hill village full of dull little hill people. Much later, it developed a tourist trade.

Joseph was not my father, we all agree on that. I knew that, I think, from the first, before thought started, interfering with the wisdom of the newborn. I knew. The looks between him and Mary were cold. He was a quiet and resentful little man, conned into something he didn't understand.

We had that much in common, although it was never mentioned.

Joseph never laid a hand on the pungent breast of the Holy Mother, that I know. He was a cuckold, a patsy, more cover. A necessary pretence.

And most pretence is necessary, as my afternoon had

81

demonstrated rather painfully. I signalled for another glass, and shifted my focus from the distant to the immediate past.

✝

Image Makers, it turned out after due reference to the telephone directory and street map, was situated on the top floor of a two-storey, bland brown brick and steel, decade-old building in a South Melbourne side street. The ground floor was occupied by a firm of graphic artists. The identical building to its left housed a market research business and a company that did post-production for movies.

The car park between them held a dozen vehicles, three of them Saabs, the rest production-line Japanese pseudo-sports numbers. The company announced its presence at ground level by means of a modest brass plaque (san serif lower case text, little rhomboid logo). Double glass doors opened onto a shared foyer, graphic artists to the left, staircase dead ahead.

Two tram rides, one to the city, the second heading out across the river, had given me plenty of time to consider my approach, but no definite answers. Being Joe Panther was obviously out of the question. Elaine Purdey had clearly registered my name, despite my lack of written identification. Certainly, too, she would remember my face if she ever saw me again, although whether she would have been able to describe me accurately to her husband was a bit more unlikely.

I look, in fact, fairly much like you'd expect me to look: something under six foot, not overly muscled, dark brown hair cut to just below the collar line, largish nose and a smallish beard. Quite similar to the paintings, in fact. Funny thing, though: the image is so familiar to most people, and has been for so many centuries, that it's become simply a pattern, a geometry of faith, utterly anonymous. I hide, thus, in plain sight. If Bono and I went strolling through the city, it would be the singer who was asked for his autograph.

I was wearing my black suit, jacket open to reveal a white tee-shirt decorated with a large rendition of Andy Warhol's portrait of Marilyn Monroe. I carried a slim black briefcase, empty, but adding the proper businesslike effect. Suitably nondescript, I thought, but definitely inner-city. Appropriate.

The reception area at the top of the stairs was large, irregular in shape, and probably far too hot and bright in summer. The carpet was grey and crew-cut, the walls a dull salmon pink. Two padded chairs, minimalist in design and taste, sat either side of a black coffee table, plastic with pretensions. The place could have been a 24-hour medical clinic, a party-plan cosmetics operation, a computer software company—anything, in fact, started by the aspiring middle-class on a cheap bank loan during the eighties.

On the walls, where there was enough space between the aluminium-bordered windows, hung half a dozen large Cibachromes (cheap frames, like the ones at the Purdey house). They were campaign posters, or enlargements of magazine adverts. Image Makers' proudest moments, it appeared, involved the marketing of the tourist attractions of northern Victoria, a go-kart racing championship, a hairdressing salon called Prime Cuts, a potting mix, a range of painted ceramic plates, and a proprietary brand of kumquat.

DDB Needham the place wasn't.

There were two doors set in the far wall, neither marked. In front of them was a semicircular counter, also salmon pink. At it sat a receptionist, a short woman in her early twenties, with cropped black hair, green eyes, slim build and a tight pink tee-shirt bearing the legend UBERBABE. As I entered her domain, she was speaking with rote-mechanical brightness into a headset, tapping quietly at a computer keyboard.

'Good afternoon Image Makers Sophia speaking how can I help you?'

Pause.

'I'm sorry Mr Purdey is in a meeting right now may I take a message?'

Pause.

'No I don't I'm sorry may I take your name and number and have him call you back?'

Pause.

'Very well then bye-bye.'

She tapped a button on the phone, looked up and failed to smile all in one fluid motion. Her face was expressionless, but there was just a wisp of doubt in her eyes as they met mine. The business doesn't do much walk-up trade, I decided.

'Can I help you, sir?' she asked, restrained.

'Probably, darling, but you're working and I'm in a hurry,' I leered, stressing Australian pronunciation more than usual. I had decided my ploy—must have been at least thirty seconds before—and figured that given the nature of the business nothing less than total arsehole would be believed.

She stared at me, giving me a flat-eyed tight smile which left me in no doubt that my impersonation was working.

'Actually,' I plunged on, sauntering over to her and resting an elbow on the counter, 'I can probably help *you*. Or rather your boss. I'm in the import business. Got some product, you know, good stuff, very classy, in from Russia. Needs a good push—well, don't we all?—but selective. Niche, know what I mean, darling?'

I got a well-rehearsed reply. 'Sorry but we aren't in the market for new clients at the moment our schedule is very full.'

From the evidence on the walls, I didn't think so. 'Blessed are they that hunger and thirst after kumquats,' I said, mostly to myself. 'For they shall be filled with righteousness.'

Receptionist Sophia simply stared at me, unblinking, patient and dismissive, all at once.

I grinned, made a point of shifting my gaze between her eyes and her tiny breasts as I spoke. 'Oh, he'll want me, darling. This is about new material, new markets

85

opening up, moving with it, not your old Thai tat, sweetheart. The world's a changing place, girl, and a good business has to move with it. The old Soviet Union's the place now: cash rich, tooled up—if you know what I mean—and lots of people happy to do anything to make a few zlotnicks. Get my meaning?'

She stared at me, saying nothing.

The phone rang. She hit a button, never taking her eyes off me.

'Good afternoon Image Makers Sophia speaking could you hold please?'

She tapped the button again. Her silence was stiletto sharp.

'Listen, love, the boss in? Graeme Purdey, isn't it? Course it is. Course he is. I'm not some mug punter on the phone, darling. I do my research, you know. Matter of fact, his name was mentioned to me by a number of my suppliers. Truly. Got a good name in the business, has your boss. Good, I'll bet, because he never misses a trick. Do you ever miss a trick, darling?'

If she got the slur, she showed no evidence of it. During the time she stared at me entire species evolved, flourished and sank to extinction. The phone trilled again. 'Still busy I'm sorry.'

I winked and leered back. 'What are you doing after—'

'Who shall I say is calling?' she asked coldly, back in the gig.

'Nick,' I said. 'Nick Myra of Nicean Films. Name's Turkish. You got any Turkish in you?'

She shook her head.

'Would you like some?'

She hit the phone.

Nick Myra. Not bad for the spur of the moment. I almost smiled. Really. I met him once, Nick, or Nicholas, bishop of Myra as he then was. That would have been back in three-hundred-and-something. I was in Turkey, wandering, befuddled and numb, selling bits of the True Cross to Roman converts on the pilgrimage circuit.

Either that, or slitting their throats in the back streets.

Rendering unto God, whichever.

I met the bishop in a brothel, paying for a shag. They knew him by name. He was pissed.

And who could blame him? It was a heady time for the Christians. Constantine had converted. Overnight, it must have seemed, the Christian community went from being persecuted and tortured heretics to the chosen people. For the first time, their cause and their suffering were sanctified by the state. Their God was legit. Their beliefs were mainstream. Their expenses were tax deductible.

The bishops went batshit, drunk with power. Nicholas, for instance, was feted by the social and political elite, absorbed therein, lauded and loved. Abundance and vindication combined in a surge of almighty power.

More power than Almighty, in fact. The pattern was set.

He was paying the whores with bags of gold.

Check his hagiography today and the gold was meant to keep the women out of prostitution. No one believed that at the time, least of all the bruised and dead-eyed subjects of his lust.

Filthy old coot.

History is another of those necessary pretences. The cult of the Bishop spread far and wide over the next few centuries, a cult bought, paid for and spin-doctored by the gold of the emergent ruling faith.

One theory has him ending up as Father Christmas.

Enjoy his gifts, children, in the spirit in which they are offered.

'Films,' I told Graeme Purdey in answer to his question. 'Films for collectors.'

He was not entertaining me as a prospective client. He was checking out the source of a disturbance, just in case.

The father of Shelagh Jane Purdey was in his mid-forties and trying not to look it. His suit was maroon, cut well and thick, expensive, but not overly so. His collared shirt was a startling red, ironed, worn fully buttoned and bereft of tie. I couldn't see his shoes beneath his ordered, dark grey and white, metal and plastic desk. His hair was brown, styled, if that's the word, in a centre-part. (A sin insufficiently recognised, I've always felt.) His face was pale, like Shelagh's, a mean web of tiny capillaries struggling across his sharp nose, the eyes cold, pale blue and even, the lips on the thin side, set.

'I'm not looking for new clients, Mr Myra,' he said flatly. 'Sophia must have told you that.'

'A good girl, Sophia,' I replied. 'Very loyal. Does she do anything you ask?'

The silence stretched a good ten seconds. There was little of note in his lair: two more framed posters, repeated images from the outside office, two standard-issue guest chairs, computer, filing cabinet and a wood-veneer storage cupboard, doors closed. He glanced down at the large day-to-a-page diary on the right-hand side of his desk, flipped a page back and forth, sighed, and looked up again.

'I don't like you, Mr Myra,' he said, still calm. 'You have nothing I want, I know that. But let's do this by the book. Make your pitch, I'll turn you down, and then you can leave.'

I could have obliged him, bookwise. I could have told him that as a father pitieth his children, so the Lord pitieth them that fear him, but I doubted he would have clocked the reference, or the irony. Or the threat.

Was there anything I wanted from *him*? Not specifically. If his was the hand that had taken the life of his daughter, in a blood sense, asking him straight out would achieve nothing, even if an admission came forth. There was no evidence, nothing forensic to tie him to the scene and the body, otherwise Gordon and Pordelli would have already moved.

And this man, I knew, I could tell, knew the ways of lawyers.

I needed to take him to the precipice. Adjudge his actions.

To exact vengeance? No. I am past retribution.

Except when it's necessary. I felt no need to settle the debt of Shelagh's death. What is, is.

No. The salvation I sought was my own. My heart burned with desire: desire to build up evidence, build a case to clear the priest and thereby cause said priest to deliver unto me the profits of his house, and thereby fund my now urgent need to get the hell out. I had little money, not nearly enough to bankroll another major move, another new name, another phantom passport.

Same old shit. Cursed is the ground.

The priest would be all right if I cleared him. He wouldn't lie restless and shivering in the darkness of a doorway like so many of his flock. He would have a bed and a door inviolate. The Church always looks after its own.

I looked at Purdey. I could see him having sad sex with his wife, but it wasn't a pleasant sight. I didn't want to see him having sex with his daughter.

Does bereavement mark a man? It didn't seem to have marked Shelagh's dad.

'Mr Myra,' he prompted, without enthusiasm.

'Nick, mate,' I interrupted. 'Call me Nick, mate. Hate that Mr Myra shit. Policemen call me Mr Myra, tarts call me Sir, everyone else calls me Nick.'

His eyes narrowed slightly. He hadn't asked me to sit down. I did anyway.

'Do you see a lot of policemen, Mr Myra?'

'Nah, mate, nah. Only when I've had a few too many and try to drive the Porsche along the sidewalk.

I figure it's safer that way. Not so many drunks.' I laughed out loud, thinking, shit, even *I* don't like me.

He didn't so much as smile, not that I blamed him. He leant forward in his chair, placing his left hand firmly on the desk, palm down, taking control. The gold ring on his third finger was as robust as his wife's was frail.

'Sophia tells me you're in import.'

I nodded, but didn't get a chance to comment.

'And you tell me you're in films. I have to tell you, Mr Myra, I think you're wasting your time coming here. I don't know the nature of your product, but I think I have an idea. This is a small advertising agency. Small and *respectable*.'

He hit the last word like a warning. Continued.

'I started this business two years ago, after I left one of the big agencies. I work hard and I work clean. I have a small roster of clients and intend to keep it that way. This is a good business and I'm proud of it. I don't want to be rich, Mr Myra. I'm not the hungry type. It serves its purpose and feeds my family, and I will let nothing fuck it up.'

He didn't look like the sports car type. He wasn't that fast. One of the Saabs had to be his, and they don't come cheap. The office, for all its lack of luxury, was in an expensive area, not kind to fragile businesses. He was maybe half a klick from the casino complex, a huge, brash, new temple to Mammon. Temple precincts, nothing changes: you get lucky or you get out.

I wasn't born yesterday.

91

'Where can I buy the kumquats?' I asked.

He said nothing.

'I too am a specialist, Mr Purdey,' I said. 'I'm in the documentary business.'

He stared at me, still silent. Pitch time.

'I specialise in what you might call the new wave of Russian cinéma vérité,' I said. 'These are the type of films that wouldn't stand a cinema release, or a television slot. The community interest is not that broad, mate, but very, very deep. There are collectors, dotted about the country, South-East Asia, the Philippines. That's where the market lies. They have money, and they have high expectations. That's who I need to reach.

'They are discerning types, Mr Purdey, and cautious in their investments. They don't respond to tat. They respond to class. My films carry a heavy price tag because the market demands it. These collectors demand rarity. I need top quality copy, single page and catalogue, used in mail-out and placed in some very exclusive publications. It's an ongoing account. Good business for a man with discretion. Say, ten grand quarterly, on top of your expenses.'

He raised an eyebrow at the figure, didn't smile. Didn't speak, either.

'The filmmakers I represent believe in realism to the *nth* degree. They don't use actors. They use real people, mate. Everything you see is real.'

Purdey let out a dismissive snort. 'I don't do home movies.'

For a lazy forty grand a year, clear and black, he'd strip himself naked, kiss my arse and call me Satan if I asked. He was on the mountain, looking at a world of which he could be master.

I let my voice harden a bit, offended. 'Neither do I, mate. Give me some credit, shit.' Without asking, I lit up a Dunhill. I could see no ashtray, and Purdey made no attempt to produce one. 'My production values are top quality, mate. The best. This isn't spur-of-the-moment, wobbly–cam stuff. This is set up, lit, thirty-five mil, three camera, real time. The fathers are paid well for their efforts. They know to take it seriously.'

The eyebrow raised again, different this time. Lips thinned. 'Fathers?'

'Yes, mate, that's the kicker.' I grinned, let some ash hit the carpet. 'The beauty of a parent's love for a child. Fathers with daughters, fathers with sons, mothers, fathers and daughters together. Young ones, older ones, with hair, without. The most natural love there is. And good for the soul, too, Mr Purdey. Good for the soul. My makers put their people on royalties. The more we sell, the more they make. Life is tough in Russia these days, mate. If it wasn't for these docos, those kids would probably be swinging their arses outside the Kremlin or wherever.'

His face had gone red. The hand on the desk was tense, going pale at the knuckles. When he spoke, it was barely a whisper.

'Get out, shithead.'

I grinned again. 'You're a man of vision, mate. I don't have to tell you that incest films are the coming thing. Big money, mate, big—'

He was round the desk with surprising speed for a man of his bulk. He grabbed me by the jacket collar. I let him haul me up from the chair, dropping the Dunhill in the process. He started shoving me backwards towards the door, flat-palming my chest up close, speaking in a pressure cooker hiss.

'I don't know who you are or where you came from, shit, but I want you out of here now. I don't deal in filth. Got that? I. Don't. Deal. In. *Filth.*'

His face was about an inch from mine. His last word covered me in a thin shower of spittle. I could, I thought, turn the other cheek. There was a time when that would have been my counsel. But that was then. The man was bearing false witness. He was also wearing an offensive aftershave. I brought my forehead down sharply on the bridge of his nose.

He let go of me immediately, put his hands to his face, staggered backwards and sat heavily in the chair he had just forced me to vacate. He made a sort of moaning noise.

My cigarette was making the carpet smoulder. I stepped over and ground it out.

'Think about it, Mr Purdey,' I said, dropping the act. 'There's always a demand for little, little movie stars.'

He kept his hands cupping his nose. I was pretty sure I hadn't fractured it. He glared at me. Then his pupils widened, as if he'd just seen the New Jerusalem descend right behind me.

Turned out he hadn't.

The Doc Marten hit home like a revelation, coming from behind, a swinging, perfectly controlled round-house that caught me on its upward trajectory in my ribs, just below my right nipple. My eyes lost focus as the breath spat from my body and then tried to get back in, double quick. I spun around, not really feeling the pain yet, my arms operating on a confused and contradictory instinct that demanded both attack and defence of the wound.

I caught a flash of her, the Uberbabe—silhouetted by the door open in the background—standing easily with the weight balanced between her feet, body moving side-to-side, arms suggesting more than a passing acquaintance with tae kwon do or something similarly esoteric and lethal. Before I could fully process this information, she swung in, swept her right knee into my left thigh, whipped it front and around and back, brought her right calf sharply into the back of mine. I quarter-spun on my own wobbling axis and went down like a sack of onions, my kidneys bouncing painfully off the unforgiving edge of the desk.

My feet were wide apart when my back hit the carpet. I tried to roll onto my side, bunch up and curl away, but she was moving with the wrathful speed of a friar sensing loot in a foreign shrine. In a flash, she had planted her left foot between my knees and with the right broke from the traditional martial arts protocols and slammed the toe of her boot into my groin.

There was no scream inside me to come out, just a clenched teeth growl. It took every ounce of self-control I possessed to resist the autonomic urge to grab my balls in my hands and rock to and fro. I couldn't get up, not yet. I concentrated all my energy into my eyes, trying to stay alert and maintain half a hope of dodging the next attack.

It never came. The receptionist from hell was back in her ready-for-action stance, waiting, not hungry. Whatever she was, she was a professional at it. She had nullified the threat to her boss and had nothing else to prove.

Purdey was silent. I could hear his breathing somewhere behind and above me, bubbling gently through the blood in his nostrils.

Slowly, but as fast as I could, I climbed to my feet, the process an adventure in pain. Sophia never took her eyes from me, never even blinked. She didn't ask for instructions from Purdey and he didn't issue any.

I thought for a second that I was going to black out as I bent down to pick up my briefcase. I didn't, and managed to keep my face set in what must have been a pretty poor impression of a hard man. She flowed to one side, like high-viscosity oil, staying in fighting position all the time as I walked past her to the door. I kept my eyes locked on hers, didn't look at Purdey, although I could feel his stare drilling into the back of my neck.

There was face to save. An act to complete.

'Thanks for that, Sophia,' I said, as evenly as possible, which wasn't very. 'I think your boss would like you to hold his calls for an hour. Are your nipples pierced?'

Her stare was a scalpel, long, slow and without anaesthetic. I didn't see her lips move, but I saw her chin dip.

'Then come and see me some time.' I managed a crooked leer, concentrated on her legs, realised my eyes were leaking. 'Then shall you lay calves upon my altar.'

Pathetic. But enough to win a fractional upwards twitch of her mouth.

I made it outside, flagged a cab, sat in the back and said the name of the hospital through gritted teeth. The cabbie kept quiet, drove fast.

The fourth Jamesons was a dull fire in my throat. My brain was a vapid swirl of booze, paracetamol, pain, anger, embarrassment and confusion. The barman was pulling the sodden runners off the bar and wiping the veneer with a toxic sponge.

However I looked at it, it was time to go.

No deliveries tonight. The faithful would have to gnash their teeth. Or go elsewhere. Probably go elsewhere. Junkies have no king but Caesar.

No matter. They'd be back again tomorrow. Better the devil you know.

And what of tomorrow? I thought as I limped out into the whistling night. What to do, what to do?

It was the day of the funeral. I could go to that, stay back from the action, check out who said what to whom. Everyone would be there.

Which meant it would also be the perfect time to break into Purdey's office to see what I could find. I figured the place would be locked up with an appropriately black-bordered sign stuck to the front door. Sophia would go with the boss, I felt sure of that. Clearly she wasn't just his receptionist.

Or even mainly his receptionist.

Decisions, decisions. As I left the alley and turned into the echoing car park I figured the best thing to do was sit down on the sofa, roll up a large joint, calm the phasing maelstrom in my head and wait for revelation to come.

In the end it didn't matter. Waiting at the head of the stairs were four uniformed police officers. They took me down to the station, muttering something about a warrant.

✝

It was difficult to fathom, in the fullness of time, what the hurry was all about. They drove me to the Fitzroy Police Station, a modest and seedy building tucked in behind the old Town Hall, and made me empty my pockets beneath the yellowing glare of grime-caked fluorescent lights. For once there was nothing incriminating therein, just some loose change, pain-killers, half a packet of Dunhills and a string of pale blue plastic rosary beads I occasionally find useful for dropping through slightly open car windows and popping the push-down locks inside, radios and handbags there to remove. Even the undead have to earn a living, after all.

I signed a piece of paper identifying me as a prisoner. I used my real name (well, not my *real*, real name, obviously), because there seemed little point in pretending otherwise.

'Joshua,' sniggered the desk sergeant.

They took my photograph (I smiled serenely) and wanted to do the same with my fingerprints. I kicked up a fuss about that, refusing to do so until they informed me of what charges were being brought against me. The officers either could not or would not do that. The arrest was a CIB operation, they mumbled, and detectives would be along shortly to explain matters.

'Shortly', in this case, turned out to mean nine hours. I spent the intervening time locked in a stark-lit smudge-green cell, the amenities of which extended merely to a slim concrete slab, greasy and graffitied, a throat-clutching open toilet, and a fifty-year-old man in a grime-coated suit who lay on the floor alternately snoring, farting and ranting about families and Heaven. I sprawled on the slab and wondered.

Graeme Purdey or Davey Parker? The first, no problem; the second, major shit.

I was too sore to worry much. No matter how long a person lives there is a limit to intelligence, to learning and to wisdom. Experience is no guarantee against recognising mistakes, let alone the invention of new and unusual ones. In the end, whatever the scrapes and games and adventures and murders and lies, we remain dumb as house bricks, theories to the contrary notwithstanding.

For there is nothing covered that shall not be revealed; and hid that shall not be shown.

Bollocks. There is always something. That's what fucks you up.

I, of course, am not finite. Or perhaps I am. I appear to be infinite, at least if the past two thousand years afford any evidence. Yet I am finite in my infinity. I am thirty-three years old. What I don't know, though, among many other things, is whether I am thirty-three years old, period. Do I age at all? Am I, say, thirty-three years and one day old, progressing through to thirty-three years and three-hundred-and-sixty-four days old, then flipping back the next day to thirty-three years old on the button? Or am I, say, thirty-three years and seventy-four days old every day?

Progress and repetition, progress and repetition. Unstoppable movement, standing still. Perhaps I am in Limbo, frozen in time, a theological cryogen, just like Walt Disney only with better dress sense. I get pimples sometimes. That must mean something.

I have never had a tooth rot. Brother Francesco ripped a couple out with tongs back in the Waldensian days ('*Now* confess, heretic!' he raged, the dickhead), but they grew back over the next couple of years.

My foreskin has never grown back. That must mean something, too.

After two hours I was starting to straighten up, dry out and ache bad from the absence of fresh pain-killers. The truth of the situation, I decided, hinged on absence. I had not touched anything at Davey Parker's house, bar the fit and the spoon, both of which I had taken away with me, the first flushed out, both wiped, and dropped into a charity clothing bin.

The fact that such items were not present at the scene of an overdose death would lead even the most feeble of investigators to conclude that a second party must have been there at the time, and that, further-more, said second party must have had a reason for not leaving a calling card. That, however, did not neces-sarily, or even primarily, point towards me.

The timing would, but not half as enthusiastically as the toxicology report, which would clearly show a quantity and quality of heroin in Mr Parker's corpse far greater and far better than a coroner would expect to find in the average dole-dependent white trash junkie.

Stupid. Just stupid, Panther.

All of it, however, rested on an assumption that Davey's bloating remains had been discovered. This, surely, had to be a matter of some doubt, given what I knew of the lifestyles of his acquaintances.

Doubt is a very personal thing, I find. The doubts

which I possess may be the certainties of another. A promise as a virgin is a hopeless disappointment as a whore.

My companion had quietened somewhat. In his madness he was Everyman: tired, uncomfortable, only dimly aware of where he was, whimpering for his mother and for Jesus Christ. He writhed in his cack and piss-stiffened mismatched Good Samaritan suit.

He looked like a plague victim, which lifted my spirits a bit. I was there, you know. I saw. By the time the plague had spent itself, more than three-quarters of the monks and friars in France were dead. They fell, many of them, on their knees, offering a choking benediction through sore-swollen leaking lips, impotent messiahs, sure the Apocalypse had come. So many died, in fact, that in England the Bishop of Lincoln allowed every priest, even the lay, to offer absolution to the dying for any and all sins. Except debt. Debt is serious shit.

This was their chance, the monks, to call down the grace of God and raise up the sick. They failed, dying themselves without blessing or confession. And as they died, as their sunken eyes rolled back into their oozing heads, there was fear in them. They were about to discover, each knew with the clarity that only the end of breathing can bring, one of two things. Either there was no God, or God had abandoned Man as His instrument and chosen instead the flea on the back of a snarling street rat.

At its end, when the last of the corpses buried and

burned, only the old, the cowards and the apostate remained in the monasteries. They built anew.

I was there. I was immune. I could have helped. I didn't.

The man begged redemption, quietly. None came. I turned my face to the wall and slept the sleep of the just.

✝

By the time Gordon and Pordelli arrived to escort me to the interview room, somewhere around 10.00am, I had been awake three hours. My head throbbed. My ribs throbbed. My balls throbbed. I had consumed nothing more stimulating than a mug of pissweak sugarless tea, been denied medication and was desperate for a cigarette.

All of these factors no doubt contributed to why I greeted the pair by calling them a couple of dick-brained, dumb-as-shit, snot-sucking Neanderthals. This was a pity, because they seemed disinclined to consider mitigating circumstances, however valid. Gordon looked across at Pordelli, his expression a badly acted mixture of surprise, disappointment and mild shock. Pordelli shrugged his shoulders. 'The young of today,' he tutted. Then he pushed me hard in the chest and shoved me back into the holding cell, slamming the door shut. I heard their footsteps fade like faith in a drought.

Half an hour later, a uniformed cop came by and turned loose the schizoid. 'The hostels are all full still, Henry,' he said, loudly but not unkindly. 'Out now. St Mary's House of Welcome's doing breakfast up on Brunswick Street. Try not to be here tonight, eh, mate?'

The man just stared. Maybe he understood. Maybe he didn't want to.

'And *you*,' said the constable, turning to me. 'You just wait.'

'I need coffee, cigarettes and pain-killers,' I said, calmly and evenly.

'And I need a good shag from Elle Macpherson.' The bastard grinned. 'Reckon we've got about the same chance.'

'The sole key to unlock Paradise is your own life's blood.'

'You threatening me?'

'No. Quoting Tertullian.'

'Who's he sing with?'

'The angels.'

'Bit loud for me. Give me Bryan Adams any day.'

The door closed again. Forty minutes later, the bloke was back, bringing a mug of instant, a plastic beaker full of water, one cigarette and two tablets. 'Compliments of Detective Senior Sergeant Gordon.' He smirked and left again.

I relaxed a bit. That meant two things. First, Graeme Purdey was the only thing on the agenda. And second, Gordon wanted something from me.

It wasn't long before they came and got me. 'Feeling better now, mystery man?' asked Pordelli in a tone as pointed as the question was pointless.

I didn't answer. Nothing more was said until we were seated in the station's claustrophobic, windowless interview room. It contained three metal chairs, bolted to the floor in a trinity around a metal desk, similarly secured. On the desk sat a dual-cassette recorder encased in steel, also bolted down. Neither cop hit the switch before Gordon started his dull, turgid litany.

'Attempted fraud, dealing under the Obscene Publications Act, assault, affray, attempted murder, failure to render assistance.' He shook his head.

'Take your pick, Panther,' chimed in Pordelli. 'You're going down.'

'How about attempting to give away money by deception? It may have escaped your notice,' I said calmly, 'but *I'm* the one in pain here.'

Pordelli chuckled. Gordon grinned, referred to a type-written report in his manila folder.

'Hmmm. The work of one Sophia Ognenis, who, it says here, courtesy of our colleagues across the river, claims she entered the office of her employer, Graeme Purdey, upon hearing a disturbance, to find you, who had earlier identified yourself falsely as one Nick Mira—M-i-r-a or M-y-r-a or M-i-r-a-g-h, no written identification having been proffered—in the process of committing an act of violence on that very man, and who then, with a commendable absence of concern for

105

her own welfare, proceeded to intervene. It didn't take an Einstein to figure out it was you. The beard's a dead giveaway.'

'Lucky, that. It was a set-piece routine, Gordon,' I said. 'That woman is his bodyguard. If he's so innocuous, why does he need a bodyguard?'

'Very popular pastime, martial arts.'

'My brother used to do it, when he was at school,' added Pordelli. 'He did aikido, waved a big stick around.'

I am not a big fan of circumlocution. Particularly after only one cup of coffee, bitter instant at that.

'Charge me or let me go,' I said flatly.

Gordon grinned again, then snapped his face shut.

'Stay away from the Purdey family, Panther,' he growled. 'Well, well away.'

'Not much mourning from a man whose daughter's dead and decapitated.'

Gordon leaned over the table towards me, eyes steel. 'What do *you* know of death, Mr Expert?'

He had me there.

'What do you know of mourning, you, you solitary little prick, you man without friends, whose only human contacts extend to a cop-baiting priest and a bunch of godforsaken junkies? You're an arrogant fuck, Panther. What makes you think you can judge the reactions of others, judge the right responses to the loss of a loved one on a scale of one to ten? What lessons do you draw from your scum? What makes *you*, you of all people, you who have contributed jackshit in your life, you who live beneath a rock, the judge of other people?'

'Nothing,' I said. 'Nothing at all.' I never did find out who moved the rock. I suspect Joseph of Arimithea, back in the black hours for a spot more souvenir-hunting.

Glad he did, though. It looked like a heavy fucker.

Gordon was in his stride. 'We are not stupid, Panther. Get your hand off your dick and listen. Don't know why I'm telling you this.'

'Confession is good for the soul,' I said. Pordelli tried to push back his chair and raise his arm in a calculated threat, as per procedure. The chair, of course, didn't move. Gordon regarded him balefully for a moment, before returning his gaze to me.

'The Purdeys are clean,' he said. 'Of course we checked them out. You always check the family first. Always. The wife was at home asleep during the time Shelagh Purdey most likely met her death. The father, he was out all evening Friday. He left his office at six, had a business dinner with a client—'

'Kumquats?'

'—some regional tourism body, until 11.00pm, then went back to his office until approximately 2.30am—he made some calls to some American travel magazines—something out of his meeting, apparently—we have the number records from Telstra—then went to a brothel in North Melbourne until 4.00am, then drove home.'

I shook my head.

107

'Morality is not the issue here, hypocrite.' Pordelli's interjection was uncommonly vehement.

I shook my head again. It wasn't the time to get into that one.

'You accept the alibi of a whore?' I asked.

'He has his alibis,' replied Gordon. 'He also has his honour. We checked your allegations of incest. Nothing to them.'

I raised my eyebrows. My point was obvious, even to these guys.

'He *also*,' continued Gordon, suddenly sombre, 'has his burdens to bear. Had them long before his junkie daughter copped it. We checked the wife again. Though it pains me to admit it, your assessment of her was essentially correct. She's a loop, Panther. She has a history of paranoid delusions. She's on medication, has been for years, sees a shrink twice a month, once spent six weeks as an in-patient, private hospital, hush-hush.'

'Let me guess, around the same time Shelagh Purdey left home?'

'Spot on. It was her, not the father, who drove her away. Classic stepmother syndrome, jealous as hell of the daughter. They both cracked up.'

'Only one of them got help, though.'

'Only one of them asked for it.'

'We all have choices, Panther.' Pordelli again.

'Not if you believe Augustine.'

'Who?'

'Never mind. So whodunit, officers?'

This time they both grinned. 'You know who,' said Gordon.

'You think Corrigan.'

They said nothing.

I shook my head, added to the silence.

'She knew her attacker, or attackers, Panther,' said Gordon. 'There were no signs of struggle and she wasn't doped. That means more than *knew*; that means *trusted*. Who did she trust, Panther? Her father? Maybe, probably not, but he's clean anyway. Corrigan? Yes. He tried to help her, if you can call a man of God giving a juvenile junkie hooker the means to pursue her vices helping.'

'You, perhaps?' added Pordelli.

I didn't dignify the insinuation with a denial. It was a frivolous accusation, and I, I have been accused by *real* professionals in my time. An overweight detective constable didn't even rate.

'So charge him.'

Gordon smiled sadly. 'Not today,' he said. 'The charge for today is you.'

'I want another cup of coffee.'

'The Second Council of Constantinople defence won't work this time,' said Pordelli, looking evil. 'I checked. Our lawyers had never heard of it, so they checked, too. If there is a connection between an ancient meeting of bishops and the need for caffeine, I'd love to hear it.'

There is, but I didn't enlighten him. First you create fire, then you make the wheel, then you invent the

109

espresso machine. Thus is civilisation measured. Between the second stage and the third lie demons and superstitions, fear of the unknown and imprecision in thought. There has never been a coffee-drinking saint, and there is no saint of coffee drinkers. These things are not unrelated. If the bishops in Turkey had belted down a couple of stiff machiattos before they started, the whole gig would have ground to a halt by lunchtime.

Gordon did the serious bit again. 'Joshua Ben Panther, you are charged with one count of assault occasioning serious injury. I'll read you your rights when we do the paperwork. You will be released on bail. In due course. On the day of the hearing, the police prosecutor will inform the court that the charge is to be upgraded to one of attempted murder and any application for continuation of bail will be strenuously opposed.'

The old one-two. The correct response to a statement like Gordon's, I have learnt over the centuries, is neither to loudly protest your innocence nor accuse the police of victimisation. It is to say this: 'Unless?'

I used to wonder what might have happened had I had enough wit to do that the first time around. Would people now worship in the name of the Holy Compromise? For thine is the Kingdom, the power and the glory, for ever and ever, let me get back to you about that.

The *unless*, in this case, turned out to be a thick file, dog-eared and creased, secured with red ribbon held by an impressive but broken red wax seal. It was about two centimetres thick, loose leafed, the pages white, yellow, pale blue. Pordelli fetched it from somewhere up the corridor after a wink tipped by his boss. It landed on the table in front of me with a dull thud.

His burden thus cast, Pordelli turned to Gordon, his face serious, and mumbled something in his ear, hand before his face to prevent me lip-reading. Gordon mumbled something back. Pordelli replied. Gordon scowled, then tutted, then nodded. Pordelli left without saying goodbye.

'Patterns.' Gordon addressed me, attempting weighty authority. 'Everything is patterns. We think your scabrous priest did Shelagh Purdey but, as you've probably guessed, we don't have a witness, and we don't have anything forensic worth sixpence.'

'What *do* you have?'

'Well, we've got fingerprints, Panther, from here to breakfast—all over the church, all over the hatbox, all over his house.'

'That must've surprised you. Any on the corpse?'

'Shut it, prisoner. We also have suspicions, strong ones.'

'You have a score to settle.'

'We have fucking prior knowledge, smart man. We have a pattern.'

I said nothing. Gordon took a breath, came on all reasonable.

'We think he might have come close to doing this once before, Panther. Look, I can see where your

111

respect for him stems from. I can even see why you like the guy—'

I'd have bet he couldn't.

'—and although I'm sure you'd not believe me, I'm actually thankful that there are people out there who have a sense of justice, of helping maybe, different from the police, especially when they spend their time dealing with people more victim than perpetrator. Sometimes, you know, I wonder if there isn't a better way . . .'

Saul of Tarsus! I thought. The interrogator turned evangelist. You're an archetype, Pauly!

Gordon pulled himself together. 'But that's neither here nor there. What is, is that file in front of you. Your Corrigan's a dangerous man.'

I didn't look at it, kept my eyes on his.

'What's in it?'

'Not to leave the station. Shouldn't even be here. Take a few hours now to read it.' He grinned. 'There's not much else to do in the cell, anyway. There's a woman named in it. We can't find her and we need to. She sounds like just your cup of tea.'

The deal, if you could call it that, was already crystal clear, but the light shining through crystals can sometimes be deceiving. I reached over and hit the record button on the tape machine.

'And if I find this woman, like you're asking me, Detective Senior Sergeant Gordon, what will you do for me?'

He reached over, quick as electricity, hit stop, then

rewind. 'We drop the charge. We rip up the paperwork.'

'And if I don't?'

He smiled, turned, opened the door. 'A uniform will come to escort you to your cell in a minute. I'd do it myself, but I've got to go check something. Looks like one of your scaly mates has flipped out.'

I raised an eyebrow.

'Charming company you keep, Panther. A volunteer worker at St Vincent de Paul has just found a used syringe in a clothing donation bin. Could be some kind of threat.'

I shrugged. 'Or merely a pointed comment.'

He didn't hear me. The door was closed again.

✝

They must have rung Corrigan and told him where I was. It was the sort of irony which appealed to them. It was going on 6.00pm by the time he arrived to negotiate the paperwork of signing me out, bailed on my own cognisance. By that time, I had read the report through twice, some pages more than that, and had well and truly run out of cigarettes.

'My apologies for the time,' he said.

'Where the fuck have you been, priest?' I snapped. We were walking the few blocks back to St Cuthbert's, via the convenience store in the BP service station so I could stock up again on smokes. The wind cut sharp, cold and critical, but that wasn't why I kept my head down.

'Ach, man, the funeral. Methodists, would you credit? Very dull.'

I lit a Dunhill, stopped walking for a moment, enjoyed the sharp rush of smoke into my lungs. 'I never knew you, ye that work iniquity.'

Corrigan shook his head, his weathered face crinkling in pained amusement. 'That's not very nice, Panther. They may be pale and lifeless as American lager, but the Methos still preach the word of the Lord in their own way.'

It wasn't what I'd meant, but I was glad he hadn't realised. 'And you, priest, what do you do?'

'Me, I preach it in His way.' His laugh was as robust as the joke was old, his self-pity of two days before vanished, replaced by a new confidence sucked in by the slipstream of departing grief. Perhaps his pragmatism was born of the theory that since he had not yet been charged, whether innocent or guilty, he was unlikely now to be. Or maybe he just got a kick out of watching someone else conduct a funeral service for once, a sort of professional pride through comparison.

'Your spirits are up.'

'Ach,' he replied, suddenly downcast. 'He destroyeth the perfect and the wicked. He sees fit to test me, and I hope I'm equal to the task. I have a job to do, Panther, and feeling sorry for myself is just the sin of vanity in another robe. There's people need me, or so I like to think. Shelagh's with the Lord now, and I've

114

got others to bring to the fold. And as for the coppers, well, what happens, happens.'

'Something we agree on.'

He nodded, didn't have a clue to what I was referring. We turned the corner, the dark triangular outline of St Cuthbert's at the end of the street.

'Tell me though, priest, with the help you give.'

'Aye?'

'Do you give it for them, or for yourself? Whose soul are you saving, whose place in heaven securing?'

'I do it for God, Panther.'

'He doesn't need it. He owns the joint.'

He wasn't to be drawn. 'Spirits!' he said, clapping his hands together. 'I'll show you spirits. Amber ones, like the eyes of the prettiest Irish nun you ever saw. Come into the house, man, and have a drop. I've something to tell you.'

I grunted assent, and we walked the rest of the distance in a silence that he, no doubt, and with understandable misinterpretation, took to be amiable. I was deep in thought.

I could have been thinking about the eyes of the prettiest Irish nun I ever saw, so long now returned to dust, so resilient in memory. I wasn't, though. I was thinking about the report.

The crest on its cover had not been, as I was expecting, that of the Victoria Police, but of an archdiocese council. Its contents were only a decade old, but had the musty smell of papers long trapped in a filing cabinet, undisturbed and unregarded. They concerned

115

the alleged sexual proclivities of the nominally celibate Father Corrigan.

The Church, ever since it got its shit together back in the fourth century, has always looked after its own. Sometimes this has been a good thing, providing for the welfare of its parishioners and clergy alike. Often, however, its self-sufficiency has masked a deeper, less noble intent. The Church is, first and foremost, an organisation, a power base that will protect itself and its reputation with all the savage ferocity of a cornered bush pig.

And the value it protects above all others is its honesty. To maintain it, it will lie, cheat, vilify, rob, murder and condemn with neither thought nor mercy. It will invoke any deadly sin available, break any commandment deemed inexpedient. As medieval Christian communities like the Waldensians and the Fratricelli discovered to their pain and peril, it will attack and ruthlessly destroy even its own kind if the power structure is at risk— whether through arcane heresy or, often, a simple belief that accumulating vast wealth in the name of the Lord is a bit iffy, theologically speaking.

And it *is* a bit iffy, believe me. As long as they don't offer me a cut.

Control, of course, is central to this process. In particular, controlling the uncontrollable. *Who can control this when its appetite is aroused?* whined Augustine, looking down, possibly after an illicit knee-knocker in a narrow alley strewn with garbage and the gangrenous odour of beggardom. Who, indeed?

116

I never tried abstinence, myself. That, like all of it, came later.

Augustine, the old ass, reckoned the exercise of the will and the exercise of the willy had nothing in common. Ever since his bizarre ideas took hold, the Church has maintained this notion as a rigid paradox, denied and condemned without, acknowledged and forgiven within. I know this. In 1248 I shadowed Archbishop Odo of Rigaud to the region of St Just in France. He found seventeen priests and parsons—most of the roster—openly, as he put it, 'ill-famed' with women of the district, often married women, one with his daughter 'against synodal prohibition'.

They were none of them defrocked, however. The priests, that is. Most of the women, on the other hand, were defrocked thrice a week and twice on Tuesdays. Too often, the servants of the Lord, silence for the raped; protection for the rapers.

Theresa Mary Farndale discovered this in no uncertain terms when she tearfully confessed to Father Dominic Scopemi, the priest at St Peter's Church in nearby Clifton Hill, that for a period of several months she had been engaging in sexual intercourse with Brendan Pearce Corrigan. She, like Augustine, spoke of will. She had wanted at first the affections of the strong and gentle priest, she said, the only man in her troubled and scorned nineteen-year-old life who had believed in her and left no bruises.

But then it got weird, their secret, it got weird. Corrigan started to tie her wrists and ankles to his bed

117

before taking her with neither pity nor softness. Two, maybe three times a week. Somehow, he talked her out of her fears at the end of his lust each time. It was love, he said, and love in the eyes of the Lord. He was a priest, after all, and her faith was as ingrained and unthinking as the dye on the Shroud of Turin.

Then came the crucifix. Corrigan built a crude wooden cross, she told Scopemi, leant it up against the wall. He would tie her to that, arms outstretched, legs bound at the ankles, high off the floor, knees wide, and take her with force and brute thrusting. Often, the secret nature of his semen revealed, he would leave her there for hours—once even going off to perform a baptism in the church—before returning, taking her again, and then cutting her down with soft words and benedictions.

Theresa Mary Farndale told all this, in fear and humiliation. She wanted it to stop she said, so much, so much.

Father Scopemi told her he wanted to help. He gave her two options. To repent her sins, or to tell the church authorities and listen to them tell her to repent her sins.

She was strong, Ms Farndale, a character trait the bishops were later to term as vengeful. She went to the diocese, guided by her mentor, ready to repent, but only on condition something be done about Corrigan. Her religious education had done its job. She asked not for a punishment for the priest, but for help—and a repentance every bit as sincere as her own.

The archdiocese council, after due care and consideration, called her imaginative, destructive, self-destructive, vindictive and, by implication, vile. She was delusional, they said, smugly secure in the impression that sexually frustrated men who fervently believe in something invisible and nameless can judge the delusions of others. They ordered her to repent, or face excommunication.

They also ordered her to publicly apologise, in the body of St Cuthbert's, to her cruelly wronged confessor.

She never did. She disappeared.

Perhaps the council was right. It's been known. Perhaps she was mad. That's been known, too. Perhaps.

And perhaps I was about to take a glass of whisky from the foul hand of a fornicator, a hypocrite, a rapist and a cad.

And perhaps my name is Judas.

Perhaps it always has been.

'I found the mother,' said Corrigan, necking his glass and settling back in his brown leather desk chair. The desk itself was still confounded by its shifting topography of reports and documents. The computer on the table was switched on, the monitor casting a cold blue glow interrupted by the repeated sliding phrase of the screen-saver: *Bella premunt hostilia*. Our foes press in from every side.

'Found her at the funeral. Followed her home. Hoo, boy.'

I took the Jamesons in one gulp. Filled up, repeated

the process. I stared at him, trying to find revelation. It never came. It never does.

'Give me the address,' I said, emptying the glass and standing up.

Who I am bears heavily upon me. I feel my weakness keen.

✝

# 4

I HAVE NOTICED a flinty sympathy for the children of the rich and high, a pity laced with envy and scorn. We mock Tori Spelling, awkward in her father's bright mythologies, and then ask can we blame her. We close our eyes when Hemingway's descendants die in lonely hours and imagine, at hopeless remove, the weight of a name unasked. We giggle and point at the sons and daughters of rulers and kings, weak-chinned and cosseted, genetically condemned to madness and to power.

What price a wealthy father, we tut, what price the fame of the old on the hopes of the young. We'd never swap places, we know what's good for us. We watch and read and shake our heads and secretly covet the fun and dread the responsibility, free to riff on the fantasy.

Sweetlings, children, my old man makes Spelling look like a dwarf.

My father created the world, the universe, and all that shudders and weeps within it. My father is contemplation, the unmoved mover, the uncaused cause, the perfect nothing, the perfect all. My father is not aware of his creation. My father emanates.

Or maybe not. My father is El Shaddai, the warring god of Abraham. My father is Yahweh, Yahweh Saboath, the god of Moses, the blood-flecked volcano god of the Midians, intent on upping his profile. My father sends plagues. My father demands obedience. My father smites his enemies. My father takes what he gave, by the thousand, by the million, by locust and war and flood. My father abandoned Jacob and David and Esther.

Or maybe not. My father is a soldier, a filthy man, careerist brute, posted to heat and babble and foreigners, denied the sight of his own deities. My father is a rapist, a taker of women, a keeper of catamites, a plunderer of boys in imitation of his masters, a dumb product of power and ambition, wealthy and centred, blessed by warrior gods far distant.

Or maybe not.

My father never called.

I called my father. Guess he was busy.

I saw Caroline, Shelagh Purdey's flatmate, when I stood loitering with intent to sell hazardous substances that evening. She told me she'd just been diagnosed with hepatitis C.

I guess he's still busy.

She came by the telephone box in the shadow of

the tower block, across the road from the Speakeasy hotel, where the doors open at 7am and the carpet sweats and rots from its burden. I could hear Bruce Springsteen's 'Born To Run' pumping from its jukebox in the moments of silence between the cars and the trams down Gertrude Street.

She came at 9.00pm, checking it out, checking out the spot, seeing if I was there, open for business. I was, but seeking more than cash.

I kissed her on the mouth, feeling her hands wrap round my waist, drift towards my bum. My tongue flicked in moisture, not curious, guiding the tiny wrap of cellophane over her teeth into her cheek. I felt the notes, folded, pushed into my back pocket.

There was no mourning in her face for Shelagh, for her casual lover. 'I get comfort from women,' Shelagh had told me once in the frail repugnant silence that followed her servicing. 'I get income from men. I wank a lot. I fake it then, too.' At home, perhaps, in the flat, the late night television selling abdominal perfection in three easy payments, perhaps then Caroline had wept for the loss of friendship and chat. But not now, and not for long. Heroin demands no lovers but itself. It is a jealous god, cruel and fleeting.

I asked her about Theresa Mary Farndale. She didn't want to talk. No time, she said. It would take her twenty minutes to walk back to her flat. My guess was she'd end up brewing up long before that, in some scarred loading bay beside a warehouse, almost out of sight, unbothered anyway by the hastening steps of any who saw a glimpse of her shape, a flicker of a lighter, or streetlight glint off the barrel of the fit.

'Never heard of her,' she said.

'Ten years back, around here. I don't know. Bad background. Maybe on the game, maybe on the spike.'

'I would have been eight, Joe—'

'I would have been thirty-three. Point is, she might still be around. Settled down, maybe. Or gone. Maybe talking to someone you might come across. Find her, I'll see you right for a month.'

She looked at me, eyes up, the flashing pink neon on the front of the pub bathing a face boarded up like a building waiting destruction, closed off, alone with its past. She didn't believe me. Why should I be different?

Why, indeed?

She turned and walked away, her frayed trainers silent on the pavement. 'Ask anyway,' I called to her.

'You've aged well,' she called back, her head not turning.

The word travels on the streets. My arrest was common knowledge among my clients. The numbers had dropped. My casuals, men and women of reasonable dress and income, controlled users, content in their one taste a month, stayed away. No one knew of their vice but me—neither boss nor spouse—and a dealer marked by the law was bad news indeed.

They were consumers first, drug users second. They had freedom of choice in the market, and chose to exercise it.

No gratitude, some people.

Which left just the dozen or so regulars, scabbed and broke, for whom nothing else mattered. They came, snap-grinning, acid-washed, perfunctory and quivering. I asked them all, Spring-Head and Helen and Rashid and Faye, Tessa and Macca and Feeney and Shazz, Peter and Thomas and Simon and James. Some tried and some promised and some smiled and some shook. Feeney asked for credit and threatened betrayal. He knew about the cops, he said. He knew Davey Parker had tipped them off, too. He hadn't seen friend Davey in a while. Maybe he should go visit him, make sure he didn't have the sickness.

As he passed me his money, five short of the asking, I took his hand in mine, compassion and sorrow in my eyes.

Springsteen had finished. I could hear the Stones. A tram lurched slowly down the road, blocking the traffic, blocking the view.

When I snapped his finger, Feeney's eyes never left mine. His face went pale, though. 'Forgive us our debts,' I whispered, pressing the deal into his hand, folding his fingers, the whole and the wretched, around it, 'as we forgive our debtors.'

By the time the tram had passed, way before Keith Richards hit his solo, I was standing alone, not getting any satisfaction either.

✝

Sleep came hard that night, back in the warehouse. The joints I rolled and smoked to calm me down had, as they often do, the opposite effect, leaving me strung, churning and anxious. My sanctuary had been violated, and violation never heals. The intermittent footsteps of the drunks in the alley, stumbling on the bluestone cobbles, full of the pausing of the pissing, usually a comfort with me so safe on high, made me edgy now.

This could be the garden, and they could be the Temple Guard.

I had been followed back from Gertrude Street, I knew that.

By whom, why, that was another matter. Art thou he that should come, or do I look for another?

I flicked the television on. David Letterman gabbled. Every time he raised his right hand his studio audience screamed and clapped, a drum roll sounded. Wish I could do that.

I poured a scotch, tried to lay it out.

The priest was a suspect. If I could clear him, he would give me money, lots of it, enough to finance a move. I needed to move. Bad.

The priest was my master then.

The priest was a suspect. If I could nail him, the cops would refrain from charging me with attempted murder. Seven years in a cage had to be avoided at all costs. Maximum security is one rock that won't roll back. Things would be noticed. Questions would be asked.

The cops were my master then.

The priest was a suspect. If I nailed him, I'd still need money. Gordon's offer was predicated only on convenience. As soon as I was of no further use, he'd move in. Drugs, violence: it wouldn't take him long. Different charges, same result.

The priest was my master then.

Graeme Purdey was not a suspect. He had a bodyguard. He had something to hide. His daughter was dead. His wife was cracking up.

My movements were being monitored. On the street, rumours were blooming like algae. Theresa Farndale had disappeared. She was sought. There's a first time for everything.

The priest was a suspect.

Salvation lay with the priest.

The priest was my master. The cops were my master. No man can serve two masters.

But, ah! Am I a man?

There's the rub.

Sleep came, hesitant and merciful.

I left the warehouse at 8.00am. I don't believe in 8.00am. It exists, though. 8.00am is incontrovertible evidence that evil dwells in the world.

In case you hadn't noticed.

Yet evil serves its purpose. At 8.00am, Johnston Street is a clearway, its lanes clogged in and out with

127

cars and vans and buses heading to and from the city. Parking is prohibited.

That meant vehicular observation was impossible until the road rules relaxed at ten o'clock. There were pedestrians on the pavement, all head down and moving, or clustered sour at the bus stop. It was raining. Anybody hanging around couldn't help but look suspicious. The shops were still mostly shut. Most of the buildings in the immediate vicinity had frosted glass in the upper storey windows. I figured it was possible, even probable, that my watcher, or watchers, whether through instruction or prior observation unobserved, would punt on my sticking to routine, and expect me to emerge mid-morning.

I betrayed their faith, but at appalling cost, for I had no coffee within me. I had to walk up Johnston, cross Smith, trams and all, continue past the Bradford, the row of little shops, the used car lot, the garage, cross a side street, past the Rochester Castle hotel, the terrace of cottages, another side street, the offices, the massage business which may or may not be a brothel (it was open, whatever), the flash design store, then cross at Johnston and Brunswick, grid-locked and tetchy, east to west, then north to south, trying unsuccessfully not to bump into the other hurrying pedestrians, past the Provincial pub and in, finally, blessedly, to Mario's Coffee Shop, barking for a latte, double strength, before slumping into a chair, fighting addiction and nausea both.

It wasn't all bad, though. As I turned out of the alley

I trod on a syringe. I took it as a good omen for the day, a reminder that someone, somewhere, needed me.

Free to move now, I figured, I relaxed, letting the latte do its work. I grabbed the morning broadsheet from the rack, flicked through, trying to concentrate against the hazy creep of my first Dunhill. There was a photo story on page three about Shelagh Purdey's funeral. The story said nothing much, inquiries continuing, bit of colour, bit of sob. The photograph, taken from the foot of the grave, showed the Methodist at the head, mourners to the side. I recognised Graeme and Elaine Purdey, heads down; Corrigan, head up. Details were misty, the drizzle of the day combined with the golfball-grain of a long lens rendering others indistinct. I thought I recognised the Sophia woman behind Graeme Purdey, by her height at least, although it could have been a child. I thought, too, maybe Gordon and Pordelli, back a bit, cropped by the margin. No one else was clear.

The story had a kicker at the end: *Shelagh Purdey—Why She Died*, Features, page 15. A favourite technique of the paper. I turned to the article. There was precious little biographical stuff. *Parents separated early, her mother moving away*. No name. No mention of incest, just straight to the chase: on the street in her teens. There was lots of material about percentages of adolescents living away from home, the socio-economic spread thereof, the hypocrisy of state and federal governments which both bewailed the problem and then slashed youth allowances, closed community centres, denied

129

funding to help-lines and did everything they could to preserve the sanctity of the family unit, however violent. Quotes from the usual sources—social workers and psychs—bar Corrigan who, for a change, had managed to keep his mouth shut.

I had the feeling other forces, and not just the cruel caprice of capitalist circumstance, were at work in young Shelagh's case. Crucifixion is usually a helpful clue in such matters.

Two coffees down, two butts crushed, thus enlightened and grounded both, I left Mario's and headed down Brunswick, staying among groups of late workers and early shoppers for cover, past the boutiques and cafes, towards John the Baptist's place. The rain had stopped. I cut into the housing estate at the closest end, figuring the Gertrude Street side by the telephone box might be under surveillance.

The stairs nearly killed me, like they always did. I'd long given up trying the elevators. I had little patience for anything which promised to raise me up and then reneged. John answered quickly when I knocked on his door. He doesn't sleep much. He was dressed in a pale green, threadbare dressing-gown, skinny varicose legs on open and unwelcome display, his smile gappy, breath fetid.

'Come in, son,' he wheezed. 'Early for you. I'll put the kettle on.'

He crossed the floor and into the kitchen. The place hummed with the heavy odour of boiled flesh. A fresh skull, clean and white, was nailed to the far wall at knee height, a full, perfect and sufficient sacrifice, even if John's resulting messages of fathers and light were harder to interpret than the entrails of a Roman martyr spread beneath a statue of Mars. A cheap little transistor radio, propped on the windowsill, babbled about horses, races, track conditions, odds and bloodlines. I followed the old man into the next room.

'Won't be long, son,' he said, his back to me. He plonked his blackened kettle on the gas stove and faffed about with chipped mugs. 'Tea, yeah?'

'Yeah,' I replied. 'One sugar.'

The smell was rancid, worse than in the lounge room, complemented by the gnawed, coagulating contents of an ageing KFC box on the 1960s laminated kitchen table.

'I seen you down below last night,' John was gabbing. 'Thought about popping down to say hello, but you looked busy, talking to the youngsters. Course, anyone asks, I know, son, you wasn't there and I didn't see you there. No grasser, me, you know that.'

There was a sticking plaster across his hand. The KFC was starting to make me feel ill. I walked back into the lounge, to suffer not its sight, and lit a smoke. Horse number nine, Queen Berenice, looked good in race four at Randwick, apparently.

Ahh, memories. Or their absence. Whatever. She starts as a key player, unwittingly, in the growth of my cult, and ends up as a two-year-old filly running the mile on a wet track. So it goes. Pauly wouldn't have liked the irony, no doubt. Humourless bastard, like all

131

cops and salesmen. She was alive when I was around, was Berenice, just. Herod Agrippa's daughter. She married her uncle, another Herod, birthing two sons, inbred and powerful. Then she moved in with her brother, King Agrippa II, and was widely believed to have fucked him senseless for years. It was Agrippa II who let Pauly stay at Caesura, writing the brochures, setting up the gig, working the flim-flam.

Almost thou persuaded me to be a Christian, the king said. Almost. I wonder. What persuasion? Did Pauly tell him that cleaving his own sister was fine by me, given the circumstances prevailing and the fact that the king let him have a house rent-free for two years?

Did he think to check?

Not that he could have done so. I did not leave detailed instructions. I did not leave a contingency plan. Perhaps he had one of his own: In case of emergency break Commandment.

John walked in with the mugs. 'There you go, son,' he said, handing me one. 'Do you a power of good.'

I looked down at it. There were oleaginous bubbles floating on the surface. I took it, once more laying hands upon the afflicted. He bade me sit, but I declined and propped my arse against the windowsill instead. I was in silhouette with my shadow cast over him. It's important to remember the visual impact of such things. Anyway, I didn't fancy the sofa. He sat himself, demurely flicking his dressing-gown over his legs.

'I need some information, old man,' I said.

He took a dribbly slurp from his mug and looked

up just a second too early. A thin trail of tea fell from his lip onto his chest. He didn't seem to notice. 'Knowing's your department, my son.' He smiled.

'Not this time,' I said.

Worry creased his face. 'But I thought—'

'Never mind. This is before my time.'

He started to cackle. I fixed him with a glare to make him shut up, but it didn't have any effect. Then I remembered: some things don't work in silhouette. I stood up straight instead. That did the trick.

'Sorry, son,' he said, catching his breath, 'but I know jackshit about Julius Caesar.' That started him off again.

I didn't have time for this. I took one step forward, pointed towards him, and commanded, 'On your knees, sinner!'

He stopped laughing and started to apologise. One more step and he was in reach. I clipped him across the temple, once, not hard, and repeated my command. It took him a couple of minutes, what with having to put his tea down, and his legs weak and fragile from age and undernourishment, but he made it. He clasped his hands in front of him, in the manner of fervent prayer. I slapped them down.

'Before my time *here*, old man,' I said, voice quiet again. He just nodded, wobbling slightly. 'I need information on a woman, used to hang around here, maybe still. I need to find her.'

When he spoke, his voice was thin, trembling from the effort of supplication. 'Who?' he asked.

'Theresa Mary Farndale,' I said.

He was quiet for a moment, whether through thought or suffering I knew not. 'Doesn't ring a bell, son. What's she look like?'

'You tell me.' I took a sip of the tea and instantly regretted it. 'Think back maybe ten years. Youngish, then. Maybe on the streets, maybe on the game, maybe on the spike. Hung about with Corrigan, the priest, for a while. Maybe went a bit screwy at the end.'

'Can I get up?'

'No.'

'Name again?'

'Farndale. Theresa Mary.'

'Corrigan's friend?'

'Yes.'

Little droplets of sweat were gathering across his forehead, despite the cold. He was starting to sway rather noticeably. Could be the onset of charismatic ecstasy, I thought. Or rheumatism. I turned around and gazed out of the window. Down below, a man stood, almost directly under the window, near the entrance doors to the tower. He looked nervous, folded into a beige sports jacket above a dark brown pair of slacks. He also looked too well dressed to be a local. A group of kids in mismatched tracksuits sat some distance away, glancing at him, quiet and hard.

'I think, yes,' he muttered. He began to nod in his own confirmation, then changed his mind as his whole trunk took up the idea. 'Didn't recognise the name. She was known round here as Easy, if it's the one I'm thinking about. Easy. Theresa. Makes sense.'

Easy Farndale. Now there's a good name for a character witness, for or against. 'Tell me, old man.'

His voice was starting to croak, his breath coming in short, jagged spurts. 'Plump girl,' he said. 'Nice kid. Ginger hair. Would've been, oh, about nineteen, twenty, when I last saw her.' He looked up at me, suddenly. 'She was no needler, son. Clean that way. Mind you, she was no angel either. Took what she could, if you know what I mean. Had to. She lived down, let me see, down in a squat on Lester Street, old factory, red brick. Long gone now, all apartments. She was a kind kid, son. Always had a word for me if we met on the street. I told her once she should have a baby then I could baptise it for her. Remember, she laughed and said you never know, but could babies be baptised twice? Didn't know what she meant by that.'

I did. 'What happened?'

'Don't know, son.' Reflexively, he went to put a hand on the carpet to steady himself. I twitched. He withdrew it. 'Like you said, she went strange. Not long after that conversation, now I come to think about it. I saw her, from up here, once after that. She looked bloody dreadful, real gone to pot. Some of the other kids were teasing her, I imagine. They were laughing. She was shouting, crying maybe. She ran off.'

'And you've not seen her since.'

'No, son.' Mild panic in his voice now. 'I swear.'

'Stand up,' I said. 'Go fetch the kettle.'

His knees had locked. He had to take his weight on his outstretched right arm and let his body fall sideways

135

to the carpet. Slowly, he extended his legs, then rolled onto his stomach. He inched himself up, bony bum rampant, in a sort of reverse push-up. It would have been polite to assist I suppose.

'Kettle, yes, right,' he stammered, trying to get both his balance and his breath back. 'Me tea's gone cold, as it is.'

'No tea, old man. Get the kettle. Bring it to me.'

He did. I waited. The man down below was trying to stamp his feet against the cold as unobtrusively as possible. He never looked up. They've got the building, I thought, but maybe not the flat.

John the Baptist walked back in, holding the handle of the kettle in a dirty tea-towel. I took it from him, tossing the towel aside. It hurt like fuck, but can a man take fire in his bosom, and his clothes not be burned? I held on, numbed the pain, took it inside.

'Now, John,' I said. 'Easy. Theresa Mary Farndale.'

'What?' Fearful.

'I want you to find her for me. Fast.'

His fear evaporated, and his gappy grin returned. 'I'm on a mission?'

I nodded.

'Better get meself a dog then,' he beamed.

'Indeed.' I turned from him. With my spare hand I unlatched the window and pushed it out on its hinge. Open, it was almost too narrow to fit my head and shoulders through. I extended my other arm, the one holding the kettle, out first, and then squeezed my top half out. The drop was dizzying. The man below had his hands in his trouser pockets. 'Lift up your eyes on high, and behold,' I yelled.

He did. I was too far up to get a clear impression of his face. No matter. I upended the kettle. A second later, he screamed, ducked, tried to get his hands free and ran all at the same time, deaf to the jeers of the tracksuit kids. One of them looked up, hoisted his thumb at me.

That should give me five minutes to get clear, I thought.

John the Baptist said nothing. Possibly he even thought nothing. Difficult to tell sometimes. I gave him back his kettle. He grasped it, winced, and dropped it on the floor. I reached in my pocket and pulled out a ten-dollar note.

'Find that woman, old man, and quickly,' I said, handing him the money. 'And put that for yourself on Queen Berenice, race four, Randwick. If she's anything like her namesake, she'll show her arse to the lot of them.'

✝

I jogged down the stairs as fast as I could, while trying to conserve enough breath to avoid looking shagged out and gasping when I emerged, countless dogleg turns later, into the damp air of the grounds. I was only moderately successful. The most direct path out, to Brunswick Street and the probability of a tram waiting at the intersection lights, would have taken me past the group of youngsters.

Not a good idea. If they recognised me as the face from the window a few minutes before, they might cheer my triumph. They might also be susceptible to inducements offered by the scalded watcher, wherever he might be, or his associates, if he had any. They were not clients of mine. They owed me no loyalty beyond price. They might well, for monetary considerations received, point in the direction of my flight.

Davey Parker did, after all.

I turned sharp right and spared them their lives. My mercy is infinite. Up to a point.

I cut back through the gardens, the rain-soaked grass dampening my trouser legs, past another tower block, out into the back street, quiet and speed-humped, then zigzagged through the back ways to Smith, hitting it, as I planned, by one of the medical clinics, the one with the taxi rank beside it. As I took hold of the car door handle I chanced a backwards glance. Nothing.

I told the driver to take me to the Clifton Hill railway station, a couple of klicks further out of town. The rest of the day was going to take some planning. I was wearing a pair of grubby black denims, my old Rossi boots, the Smashing Pumpkins tee-shirt and the black leather jacket. Perfect for around Collingwood, Fitzroy, but lacking the requisite anonymity for where I intended to spend the afternoon. I couldn't go back to the warehouse to change, not if I wanted to move freely.

That was Problem One.

Actually, no. It was Problem Two. Problem One was that it was about 10.30am. Waking up time. Mine hour had come. Trouble was, I'd already been up and about for three. The lattes had worn off, and a certain, unpleasantly familiar, irritable doziness was descending upon me.

First things first, then.

I hung about on the station platform, making like I was waiting to catch a commuter train north, away from the city. There were three other people waiting: a teenage couple in different private school uniforms, obviously playing truant, and an enormously fat woman in a faded mauve dress, one hand tightly on the handle of her shopping trolley. None of them would hold my gaze. The rain had started again, gently but with the promise, if not of rage, at least of petulance. The trio crammed under the little brick shelter thoughtfully provided. I remained outside, near the edge. The drop to the tracks was only about three feet.

After five minutes, I saw the shape of a south-bound train heading in. I waited until I could almost see the driver's face and then jumped. Three strides across, carefully placed, another jump, and I was ready for it. The electric doors hissed open and I strolled in, selected a seat next to the aisle, a middle-aged man helpfully reading the morning broadsheet between me and the window, and slouched down as much as I could without appearing drunk or strange. The guy glanced at me, nothing more. A wise man, seeking no knowledge.

I got off the train at Flinders Street, the busiest station in the city, and joined the flow heading for the exit lanes. Uniformed flunkies were checking everybody's tickets as they went through. Of course I didn't have one. Living black, you learn to be economical. My inspector was a little man, paunchy, with skin like a dry dumpling. He demanded. I stopped in front of him, blocking the lane, staring at him, willing him to meet my eyes. He did so halfway through repeating himself, paused, let the words wither in his throat and waved me through. To look upon the face of the Lord is a fearful thing.

Especially when he's hanging for a cup of coffee.

I headed out, glad of the crowds, crossed to the milling tram safety zone in the middle of Swanston Street, jumped the first one that rolled along, jumped off again three blocks later. There was a pharmacy nearby, big and satisfyingly anonymous. I walked in, purchased a packet of cold-and-flu capsules, two crepe bandages, a steel nailfile and a small box of disposable plastic gloves, the sort counter-hands use in snack bars. As I did so, I checked my financial reserves. A smidge under two hundred dollars. It should be enough, I thought, given prudence.

Back on the pavement, I jumped another tram and headed three blocks uptown, stepping off before the conductor reached my seat. The rain was gathering strength. Most of the pedestrians were now either trying to balance umbrellas in the breeze, or jog-walking, heads down and concentrating. I entered a small but reassuringly pungent coffee bar, took a stool at the far end of the counter where I had a clear view of the front window, ordered a machiatto, double strength, and a glass of water.

There were four other people in the place, all absorbed in supping their brews, all flicking idly through newspapers and magazines. One man, in a crisp white business shirt, grey two-piece suit and, I was disturbed to see, brown shoes, looked about my height and weight. He was on his own. His briefcase, also brown, was one of those extra large numbers with a clasp at the top, the sort lawyers use.

The coffee and the water arrived. I paid for it immediately. I pulled out the cold tablets and studied the box. They were the day and night variety. Both types contained paracetamol and dextromethorphan hydrobromide. The day ones also contained pseudoephedrine hydrochloride, thirty milligrams. The night ones contained chlorpheniramine maleate, two milligrams, and came with a warning about drowsiness, alcohol and machinery.

I punched out four of the day ones and washed them down with the water. A hundred and twenty mills of pseudo wouldn't do all that much, not to me, not with my system, but hell, I needed to be alert and every little bit helped. As soon as it was cool enough, I necked the coffee in one go. Then I sat back, spinning slightly, and waited.

Ten minutes later, the man in the suit hefted his briefcase and walked out. I patted my jacket pocket to make sure I had what I needed, and followed.

He had paused to look in the window of a gift shop when I reached him. A narrow lane extended down the side of the shop, a conduit to wet and scrappy loading bays. He was looking at something towards the front of the display, head down, the back of his neck exposed.

I laid the tip of the fresh syringe against his skin, ever so gently, just beneath his hairline.

'Do not move,' I whispered. 'This is a fit. It contains my blood. I might be HIV positive. You never know.'

He said nothing. His shoulders tensed visibly. Somewhere inside his head, reptile wings scraped closed behind him, talons scratched the flagstones, demons woke.

I continued talking, calm. 'Turn to your right. Slowly. Walk down the alleyway. Be careful. My hands aren't too steady these days.'

Blessed are the meek. He did as he was told.

The second loading bay belonged to a Chinese restaurant that only opened evenings. There was no sign of life, no hint of noise. It stank of rotted food. 'Turn left here,' I said. He did. 'Now stand still.' He did.

With my spare hand I reached in the other pocket and pulled out one of the crepe bandages, already out of its wrapper. Carefully, ever so carefully, I pulled the fit away and slid the needle into the stitching of my jeans, barrel up like a pistol in a holster. Rigid with panic, he didn't notice.

He would, though, in a second, so the move with

142

the crepe had to be brutal and fast. I brought it over the top of his head and pulled back hard so it covered his eyes and nose. I stretched it as tight as I could, wrapped it around three more times and then secured the fastener at the back. He was breathing heavily now, moaning in fear.

'Stand still and you will survive this,' I said.

'My wallet,' he stammered.

I reached around and stuffed the crumpled paper bag from the pharmacy in his mouth. He started to gag. 'A fool uttereth his mind,' I whispered close, 'but a wise man keepeth it in till afterwards.' His shoulders sagged.

'Drop your briefcase.' He did so. I flicked it open. It contained a dozen or so ring-binder folders, bulging with documents. I took them out, didn't even bother to read them, and piled them on the glistening asphalt. I looked inside, and saw it was good.

'Now take off your jacket, your shoes, your trousers and your shirt. Keep your socks. Do not turn around. Do not drop them on the ground. Hand them backwards, slowly, to me.' He did so, moving like a robot, his cheeks barrelling and squeezing with his efforts to breathe. His wallet was in his inside jacket pocket. It contained two five-dollar notes and a lot of plastic. I took out just his Visa card, left the cash and put it on the pile of files. Greed is a sin, after all.

I folded his clothes into the bag. He was standing, elbows tight in, in a plain white tee-shirt and pale blue Jockettes, shivering from who knew how many catalysts. For a moment I looked at him and felt pity for the man.

143

Pale blue Jockettes.

It passed. Adam and Eve covered their nakedness with leaves. If they'd used pale blue Jockettes instead, the way of the world would have been very, very different.

'Put your hands behind your back.'

He did so, compliant, palms out. He thought he knew what was coming.

I wrapped the other crepe bandage tight around his wrists. There was a large rubbish skip to the left. I yanked him over to it, harshly, one step, and ran the remainder of the bandage, a metre or more, through its iron padlock ring.

Then I yanked his underpants down to his knees. He tried to scream, and nearly choked. Quickly now, I took the bandage between his legs, pulled it taut, tied it tight around his scrotum and rapidly shrivelling dick, and knotted it off. Movement in any direction would cause acute pain. He seemed to understand this. Passionately. Finally, I moved around to the front of him. There were six night tablets in the packet. I popped them all, removed the paper bag from his mouth, and fed them in, massaging his throat each time to make him swallow.

It was probably not enough to knock him out, but it would certainly make him dozy when they kicked in ten minutes or so. 'If thy faint in the day of adversity, thy strength is small,' I said, picking up the briefcase. 'And, oh, try not to operate any machinery for a while. That's what it says on the packet here. Best to be careful.'

And thus did I abandon him.

Like father, like son.

Fifteen minutes and a visit to a public lavatory later I was resplendent in grey, walking with renewed confidence, my own clothes crammed in the briefcase, and trying very hard not to think about the fact that I was wearing brown shoes.

The sacrifices I make.

Actually, truth be told, I'd have preferred not to have visited random violation on the man, despite his crimes of fashion. I have nothing against doing things legitimately. I covet it, in fact. For the best part of two millennia I have walked this earth anonymous, denied papers, a stranger to credit, denied identity. I have never been an approved customer. Conditions have always applied.

I would have it other. But I do not, and there seems nothing I can do about it. I have grown long used to it, to living black, to scraping, to selling, to stealing. I have no influence in the kosher world. Which is odd, when you think about it.

I have learnt to survive, though. I have learnt to curb my desires. I have learnt to want less. To ask not. To practise undesire.

There's a parable in there somewhere.

I practised it now, wanting less. Conserve resources, I thought, expend only what is necessary. I wanted two things. One of them, I realised, was a mere indulgence, a fop to habit, a needless expense. I rejected it.

No McDonald's for Joshua, then.

Which left only the speed.

I caught a tram down to King Street, the crass night-club strip. The door to the Omega was unlatched, as I figured it would be. It was close on lunchtime. The cleaners would be in by now, wiping up the detritus of last night's hedonistic sorrow. Jimmy was in there, buffing the dance floor. I know Jimmy vaguely. He lives not far from me, somewhere. We're in the same business, sort of, which meant he wasn't all that pleased to see me. No matter. He sold me the two grams of amphetamine at forty-five bucks per, a measly trade discount.

Half the money gone, all but.

I spent another six bucks in a discount book store, buying a remaindered tome on vegetarian cuisine. It was everything I needed in a book: large format, thin, and hard cover. It balanced on my knees in the toilet of the pub up the road just nicely, providing me with a firm, steady platform on which to chop up a small line of speed with the edge of the Visa. A toot. An edge. Enough. I rolled up a twenty, inhaled, and then sat back with a Dunhill, waiting for the inevitable mix of chemical and mucus to slide wetly down the back of my throat.

It did. And it was good.

✝

Toorak is a long way from Collingwood, in every

sense, but mostly financial. It is the home of money, big money, money new and old, money inherited, money earned, money extorted, money immanent, money transcendent, money the cause, money the mover.

By the time I had paid the cabbie to drop me off at the corner of Chapel Street and Toorak Road, a clogged intersection at the end of the most expensive boutique, gallery and restaurant enclave in Australia, I had just ninety-two dollars, one-point-six grams of speed and a stolen suit to call my own. I stood there for a moment, watching the passing Mercedes and BMWs, the jolly red cabriolets, shiny with youth, the wool-coated matrons, the solarium-harsh young women wrapped in the figure-fawning embrace of Lacroix and Karan and Miyake, ripe with the confident fecundity of wealth, forgiving iniquity and transgression and sin.

I needed the practise.

Then I turned and in the clearing rain headed for the back streets. Two blocks in, one block across. I quickly left the bustle behind me, and started to feel more and more uncomfortable as I walked, my sense of alienation heightened, no doubt, by Jimmy's fine produce.

Actually, it wasn't all that fine. I was alert, I knew that, but there was no buzz, no sharp sparking wire at the heart of my senses. A pretty pass this world has come to, I couldn't help observing, when even the Messiah can't get good speed.

147

The residential streets were as quiet as cancer. They meandered insolently, the houses either old and large or new and very large. Each one was walled or fenced or hedged, high and sure, the barriers broken only by the insertion of huge double wrought-iron gates, providing a glimpse of a curving driveway, the tail end of a Jag, and a neatness of lawn that bespoke solidity, conceit and hired help. No one walked the pavement, bar me. In Collingwood even the side streets find strollers, day and night, nosy, content, destitute, heading out, hanging round, hunting, keeping tabs, idly chatting, doing business, staggering drunk, whatever. One thing was the same, though: if death came sudden and violent to either place, you'd never find a witness.

Beatrice Cowper's place of residence did not have double gates, at least at the front. Corrigan had failed to mention that, but I'd identified the place readily enough, thanks to the priest's principal comment about the exterior appearance of the house of Shelagh Purdey's long-estranged mother. 'The fucking hedge, man,' he'd said. 'You should see the fucking hedge. Take more than a fucking trumpet blast to knock that little lot down.'

I could see what he meant. It was dense and disciplined, running from one boundary to the other, at least two metres high and God knows how thick. No light filtered through from the other side, but I did pick out one little detail the priest had missed during his drive-by tailing mission. Deep in its abundance I could make out the regular shine of steel posts and the whip of taut-strung cable. What came first, I wondered: the hedge or the electric fence? Which was cause, and which effect?

The gate set at the midpoint of the boundary was only a metre wide, clearly not designed for vehicular traffic. It was made of solid steel, as high as its surrounds, bolted and locked securely to strainer posts that looked like they could take an armoured personnel carrier at full pelt without so much as wobbling. On the right-hand post was an intercom box, with button and grille. I pressed the button.

I had used the walk to plan my approach. I had discounted the grief counsellor line for two reasons. First, I doubted that anyone with the will to abandon her only daughter would give two shits about the mental state of whoever found her body. Second, and marginally more important, I didn't know whether Ms—or was it Mrs?—Cowper was still in contact with her ex, and, if so, whether my little interrogation of poor Elaine, no doubt embroidered by now, had been mentioned. Frankly, I doubted it. Graeme Purdey was doing all right, but his was a neighbourhood of stout Rotarians, pompous small business people, superannuated middle managers. This was the habitat of bankers and barons and bishops. The former Mrs Purdey had done well for herself, very well, and I had a feeling that the rejection of all things past and imperfect had been a necessary prerequisite.

Still. I had settled in the end for being Kevin Wheatstone from the Public Trustees Office. Sorry to bother, but some fiddly legals remained regarding the matter of Shelagh's estate, piffling matters of disbursement, really, but as her biological parent there were some standard forms to be signed. Won't take a minute.

As far as I knew, the physical possessions of the late Ms Purdey amounted to a ghetto blaster with a busted tape deck, a black-and-white television, a mattress of more interest to forensic pathology students than even charity shops, a handful of broken-spined paperbacks and a garbage bag half full of clothes. Whether Beatrice Cowper knew that, however, was a moot point. There was also the possibility, of course, that either she or Graeme Purdey, or both, had been quietly paying her an allowance, or stocking up a trust fund for her. I might find that out. It might be handy to know.

As it turned out, Kevin Wheatstone remained forever an idea, never realised in any meaningful sense. A bit like me, really. Ten seconds after pressing the button I became aware of a whirring sound above me, to my left. I glanced up and saw a camera, its lens sliding smoothly in and out, finding its focus. It paused, unblinking. Then a voice, a female voice, crackled through the speaker.

'Mr Panther,' it said, evenly, 'I've been expecting you. When you hear the gate lock buzz, please enter and walk to the front door. The garden path is not the most direct route, but I advise you very strongly not to deviate from it.'

'Make thy way plain before my face,' I said, adapting fast. The gate buzzed. I pushed it open.

The house was enormous, newish, and hideous. The bulk of it stood two storeys high, made from variegated red brick. The front door was sheltered by a pillared porch with a triangular roof, all white and vaguely Grecian. Three windows, floor to ceiling, sat on either side, white-bordered and each divided into ten component panes. Eight more ran across the top floor. To either side of the main building, a single-storey wing extended, inherent rather than added, offering five more windows each. For all its glass, its immediate impression was one of being solid, unforgiving and sealed. The front garden was as immaculate as it was unimaginative: an organic layout of kidney-shaped flower beds bordered by manicured lawn. An alabaster fountain, complete with horribly naff naked cherub, stood to one side, pissing in a goldfish pond. The garden path was crazy-paved in the suburban English style and meandered about, drunk on its own surrounds.

This, however, was a fleeting impression. The thing I was most keenly aware of as I swung open the gate was the Rottweiler. It was as black and muscular as a tropical storm, with exactly the same promise of fury. It was waiting for me, hackles up, haunches tensed, growling with such practised ease I thought for a moment it was going to break into a Roy Orbison song. The gate swung shut of its own accord, slamming with a lock-down clang that made me jump. The growling increased by several decibels. I could see a small brass plate on its thick black leather collar. It said 'Cerberus'.

151

I hate it when someone else's mythology barges in on mine.

I walked along the path, wending this way and that, Cerberus keeping pace all the way. I had no illusion about what would happen if I strayed, so I didn't. The dog was a metaphor, but I don't think it cared.

It halted when I reached the two steps leading to the porch. I took them slowly, one at a time, in case it was a trigger for his party trick. The front door was ajar. Cautiously, I opened it. It was quite thick, the edge revealing what looked like a sheet of steel, sandwiched between two solid pieces of mahogany. I was presented with a view down a wide and shadowed passageway. Archways extended from either side of it, a winding staircase of white marble curling up to the left, halfway down. What I could see mostly, however, was a vision. At the far end of the passage, framed by diminishing perspective, was what appeared to be a rectangular panel of bright, almost blinding light. In its centre stood the black shape of a woman, a curved silhouette, legs slightly apart, strong and perfectly still, her shadow extending towards me. All was silent for a moment and then I heard the voice.

'Come here,' it said, commanding, unhurried and smooth. 'Joshua Ben Panther, come to me.'

By the grace of God I should taste death for every man. Such grace was never granted. I have read, however, of other deaths denied, of near–death and comfort. When you die, they say, you float down a tunnel towards a being of light. That is not my journey.

I am incontrovertibly alive. So this. I smiled to myself. So this. I took a step now, curious and without prayer, towards the angel of darkness.

✝

# 5

LIKE ALL ANGELIC APPARITIONS, this one, too, was a cheap illusion. The long corridor, I soon noted, led to a conservatory, the sun, even in its clouded shroud, a powerful back-light.

However, that was all that seemed cheap about the domicile of Beatrice Cowper.

As I walked with deliberate unhurriedness through the building, my heels clacking on the parquet floor, I took in what I could. There were two archways either side, each revealing a large room, opulently furnished, closed double doors at their far ends. The pair to my left each contained a couple of Chesterfield lounge suites, sturdy darkwood coffee tables, heavy cabinets and bookcases, rather in the manner of a London gentlemen's club. The ones to the right were more modernist: easychairs and two-seaters, all black leather and chrome, Art Deco lamps, fluid Art Nouveau figurines atop large but minimalist mantelpieces. Everything hummed with arrogant wealth. These were plainly designed as reception rooms or entertainment areas, sites for human warmth, yet showed no signs of having been used as such. Everything was regimentally tidy, devoid of anything scattered or dropped or ephemeral. The place could have been a display house for a real estate development aimed at the obscenely rich.

The air was as still as Golgotha at dawn.

She moved from the doorframe, out of view, while I was still a good forty feet away. By that time, her image had firmed, still black, the light's tricks nullified.

She knew that.

There was no hesitation, no accidental movements. Just performance.

The conservatory was roughly half as deep as it was long, and stretched from one end of the main body of the building to the other. It contained ten red and white vinyl armchairs from the fifties, immaculately restored. They were adrift in a semicircle, facing the rear, on the vast, bare, polished wood floor, served by low teak coffee tables, and, to the right as I entered, a black, leather-fronted bar of generous proportion and elegant line. The back garden was much as the front—contiguous, I assumed, given that Cerberus had taken up a position just outside the glass, looking in, watchful, tense.

I wondered if he could get inside of his own accord.

The rear garden fence was two metres high, comprising corrugated-iron bolted to a sturdy framework of jarrah posts. Two lines of barbed wire ran taut and expectant along the top, spaced about ten inches apart. The wrought-iron double gates were there too, covered with opaque white plastic sheeting. Immediately inside them stood a large, brick garage, big enough, I estimated, to hold three cars.

'A drink, Mr Panther.'

It was not a question.

'You prefer whisky, neat. I have no Jamesons, but Laphroaig will suffice, I imagine.'

Neither was that.

I said nothing. She stood at the bar, about ten feet away, with her back to me. She was tall, not much under six feet. Her hair was black, glinting in the refraction of the glass, unobtrusively styled and hanging to just beneath her shoulder blades. She wore a long black dress, the fabric shot with gently reflective fibres, the back cut away in a deep plunge that reached its resolution midway down her spine. It was well styled and shaped, extending to her wrists to her ankles in a teasing and prudish counterpoint, efficiently embracing and enhancing a body that was lithe, muscular, and ripe. The shoes were also black, raised an inch or so on modest heels, a glimpse of stockings or tights just visible between the top and the hem.

'Mrs Cowper—'

'Ms,' she replied, matter of fact, without turning around. She was fixing herself a drink, a vodka tonic it looked like. 'Take a seat, please.'

I did, putting the briefcase on the floor beside the chair. I thought of two things simultaneously. This was curious. This was odd. Vanity is not my curse, beyond the necessary conceits of style, but it is true to say that normally my presence prompts a stirring of the passions among strangers. There are shudders of fear, stabs of caution, a welling of unease and trepidation.

That is not a condition of my identity. It is a condition of being alive and male and unvouchsafed. It is predestined.

It is also a good start.

But not in this case. There are two types of assistance, wrote Augustine. There is the assistance without which a state of affairs does not come about, and there is the assistance by which it does come about. God knows what he meant, but Beatrice Cowper had evidently been in receipt of the latter. She knew my name. She knew my likeness. She knew my drink.

That was one thing I was thinking, as I sat, silent, and watched her as she bent forward slightly over the bar, lifting her heels, extending her right arm, picking ice cubes with a pair of tongs from a small silver bucket. The fabric of her dress lifted and tightened as she did so, gently caressing her hips.

And that was the other thing I was thinking: boy, was this woman *built*.

This could be fun, I thought, as she shifted her weight from one foot to the other. Do the voice. Do the look. Do the laying-on of hands.

'What is your business, Ms Cowper?' I asked.

'None of yours, Mr Panther,' she replied, dropping a sliver of lemon in her glass and straightening her back.

And then she turned, the light now upon her, and the world howled.

I was looking at Brigid.

And not Brigid. Brigid, my Brigid, fifteen hundred years dead and mouldering in the soil of Eire, bade cows sleep peaceful at her feet, udders distended in offering. She made butter as if butter were the greatest gift, transformed her own bath water into beer and stood naked aside and unblushing as thirsty priests drank their fill. She gave herself in spirit and flesh, her eyes brown and gentle, in willing sacrifice and hope. She knew my name and doubted not. She knew my sins and forgave in tender straddle, the chosen bride of Christ. Wrapped in coarse fabric outside the wooden walls of the double monastery at Kildare, night after night in whispers and silence and warmth, she made it all go away.

Beatrice Cowper could shrivel a slug at thirty paces. The face, the hair, the eyes, the lips, the build were all identical to Brigid's, but instead of the glow of forgiveness, she radiated the pure light of betrayal. The eyes were hard and cold, her bearing determined and calculated, her face in its perfection mocked and derided the flawed of the world, her body moved without pity and invited only sufferance and discard.

I noticed I was developing an erection.

'You're staring at me, Mr Panther. Do not. It's impolite.'

My drink was in front of my face. She had walked the distance between us without me realising. I took it, nodded, and crossed my legs.

'You remind me of someone I used to know,' I said.

'I doubt that very much.'

She walked back to the bar, where she had left her own drink. She leant against it, facing me, one hand holding her glass, the other resting lightly behind her, her hips pushed slightly forward. I took a sip from my scotch and met her eyes, waiting. I needed an edge. It was her play.

'I trust, Mr Panther,' she said, meeting my gaze, 'that you are not going to try to assault me, as you did my ex-husband. Cerberus has a nasty temper on him, for all his training. I trust, too, that you are not going to grope me, as you did to poor spineless Elaine. Even you, Mr Panther, I'm sure, can see that would be a very, very foolish thing to attempt.'

She moved the toe of her right shoe slowly up and down her left shin, hitching the dress hem as she did so. Despite myself, I looked downwards.

Point, to her.

I turned my head away and glanced out into the garden. Trees, eucalypt and elm, swayed in the wind. Cerberus looked back, patient. Must take a lot of up-keep, place this size, I thought.

Time for business. My serve.

'How do you know of me, Ms Cowper?'

'I was warned, of course,' she said. 'You visited Elaine, you visited Graeme. You have a pattern, Mr Panther, and are thus predictable. It was odds-on that I would be next.'

Interesting. 'Who told you? Which police officer?'

'I forget.'

'What else did they tell you about me, Ms Cowper?'

She kept staring at me, like she was weighing me up. In the silence, just for a moment, I thought I heard footsteps coming from somewhere behind me, inside. I turned my head. Nothing. It must have been the blood pulsing in my head.

'That you are a heroin dealer of no great value or import, a nuisance just tolerated and contained,' she said. 'That you can be violent and cunning, although, until lately, not in the habit of injuring anyone of significance. That you fancy yourself as an amateur investigator, and that the priest who found my daughter's corpse and is currently suspected of her murder has asked you to clear his name. That you employ, habitually it seems, an elevated and studied pattern of speech which reveals a fondness for the biblical and theological and also, runs the suspicion, a deep-rooted state of personal delusion.'

'Then you have been misinformed, Ms Cowper,' I replied. 'I have no delusions.'

I just think I hear things occasionally.

'Of course, Mr Panther. Whatever you say.'

Point again, to her.

I kept staring at the garden. Cerberus kept staring at me.

'Why did you let me in?'

'I get turned on by hazard.' Her tone was as sexless as coal.

'You didn't weep at your daughter's funeral.'

'How did ... ?' A pause. Brief, but there. Point, to

me. She laughed, lightly, to cover herself. 'Of course, the priest. An observant man, for all his troubles, and faithful to his servant. What else did he observe, Mr Panther, I wonder?'

'That you'll never get slapstick at a Methodist funeral.'

'Did he tell you, did he observe, Mr Panther, how mourning becomes me?'

Her voice was suddenly louder. I turned my head back towards her and she was right there, her foot in front of my folded knees, her belly tight before my eyes.

'Did he comment on how I look good in black? How the dress I wore accentuated the turn of my hips, how the breeze wrapped it close about my thighs, how the light played gently off its weave as it curved about my breasts, Mr Panther? Did all that escape his notice? The priest is a man, after all.'

I felt under attack. 'Step away, Ms Cowper,' I said softly. 'I might bite.'

'I think not, Mr Panther. Not twice.' Nevertheless, she took one pace back. Point, moot. It was all I needed. I stood up, managing not to brush against her. Standing now, but inches from her face, I thought to stare her out, but my eyes and my mind were not in harmony. My vision alternately dissolved her to a repugnant geometry or melded her into love. The first was useless; the second unbearable. I stepped to my left, careful not to touch her, turned my back and started walking towards the end of the conservatory. Cerberus kept pace. I fished out a Dunhill, lit it.

Time for a hard ball.

'Did you know your ex-husband had abused Shelagh when she was younger, Ms Cowper?'

I heard her laugh again, but not the nervous laughter of last time. This was the laughter of mockery, robust and violent. It made me turn on the spot. She was still standing near the chair, one hand on her hip, the other holding an empty glass. Her eyes could have chilled the sun.

Or the Son.

'Graeme Purdey is weak, stupid and unimaginative, Mr Panther,' she said. 'He has never had an original idea in his life.'

'Incest is hardly original,' I replied.

'I'm going to prepare myself another drink,' she said. 'Your glass is here, by the chair, almost empty. Would you like a top-up, or does too much alcohol interfere with whatever medication it is that you're supposed to be taking?'

I let it pass. 'Please.' I nodded.

She walked back to the bar, with me watching, despite myself. Have I not remembered thee in my bed: and thought upon thee when I was waking?

'Pardon, Mr Panther? Speak up.'

I hadn't realised. 'Nothing,' I said. 'Just thinking aloud.'

She was doing things with bottles once again. 'A psalm, if I remember,' she said, not looking up.

'You didn't answer my question, Ms Cowper. Did you know that Graeme Purdey had penetrated your daughter, time and again?'

She turned towards me. She was holding a piece of lemon in the tongs. With her free hand, her eyes not moving from mine, she took the lemon by the peel and held it to her mouth. Her lips curled back above her teeth. She bit down, controlled and firm, through the flesh of the fruit, chewed briefly, swallowed, and did not wince. A thin line of juice slid down her chin, unregarded.

'No, Mr Panther.' Her face was still. 'But I thought he would.'

I realised something at this point. I was afraid. That disturbed me greatly, because I couldn't remember the last time I'd felt afraid. Not in the Inquisition; not when I was caught in the bloody street fights between the followers of Lawrence and Symmachus in the fifth century, when screams rent and bones snapped as two rival Popes turned Rome's streets awash in a battle to be my vicar; not in the plague. Pain has no meaning with the certainty of healing. Dying has no downside with the fact of resurrection. But there was no death here, no shadow over Beatrice Cowper, no threat of ending over me. Only life, brutal and driven and determined. In both senses of the word.

Oh Brigid.

I took a deep draw on the Dunhill, ashing on the floor. Early start, I reminded myself. Tension. Strong coffee. Adrenaline in a puddled loading bay. Flu tablets. Speed. The unfamiliar, so familiar. The day predicated anxiety, the fear not real, a flustered bio-chemistry is all. Internal states and external worlds rarely correlate. I'm fine. Really.

She sighed, tossed her hair, changing tack.

'Walk for a moment, Mr Panther, in the garden with me, while the rain holds off.' She held out a glass to me, indicating the grounds with an unnecessary but disturbingly attractive incline of her neck. I nodded. Fresh air sounded like a good idea.

She flipped a latch and slid back a large section of the conservatory glass. I noticed the light gleam off thin silver tape running around the edges of the pane, a common enough alarm system, and felt the day's chill slap my face. I walked over to her, and together we stepped out onto the crew-cut short grass.

Cerberus let out a menacing growl and tensed up.

'Mozart!' Beatrice Cowper snapped, and the dog immediately sat. 'Now, Schubert,' she added. The brute lay down, jaw on its folded paws.

I couldn't help it: I was impressed. She must have caught the look in my eye. 'In the beginning is the Word, Mr Panther,' she said, 'but when you're training a guard dog it pays not to make that word too obvious.' She started strolling, parallel to the house, sipping at her drink. I stayed by her side.

'My father was an important man,' she said. (I could have made a comment, but refrained.) 'He was a school master at a very wealthy private boarding school. He was a pillar of the church, a JP, a man who had his suits imported from Savile Row, a conservative stylist, an astute investor, a minor philanthropist and a much sought-after dinner guest.'

'And he gave you all this,' I said, pointedly looking around. 'Nice camellias.'

Or hydrangeas, or petunias, or triffids. I live in a warehouse. I don't know from plants.

'He gave me *none* of this,' she retorted, sharp. 'All he gave me, Mr Panther, was his attentions. I was nine when he started. You don't need the story. I fled that house as soon as I could. I was sixteen.'

'I don't need the story, Ms Cowper, like you said.'

We had reached the end of the right wing. Each of its windows was covered with a thick, black blind. We turned the corner, into the narrow but well-tended shadowed strip which ran down the side of the house.

'This one you do, Mr Panther. I am not a natural victim and that mantle did not sit easily with me. The rest of it I could deal with, eventually, whether by rationalising it, blocking it or dismissing it, that's not for me to say. But the idea of being a *born* victim: that was—is—too hard to bear. So I worked my arse off, not on the street, but in bars, in restaurants, in sandwich shops, whatever: serving, waiting, pouring beers, watching and learning.'

'And what did you learn?' I asked.

'Not much, just then,' she said. 'I'd been doing some reading, some talking. I thought I understood but I didn't. I thought I needed *healing*, and that healing would only come through security, through what I took to be normality. Graeme Purdey was a weak man,

165

desperate for sexual status among his peers, earning good money as a copywriter. He took to me.'

I could believe that. 'So you took him.'

'Do not presume to judge, Mr Panther.'

'That day will come, apparently.'

'Pardon?'

'Nothing.' Near the front of the building, I noticed ten, maybe more, telephone junction boxes in a line up the wall.

'I accompanied him to work functions, dinners with clients, the whole bit, hanging off his arm. I made him look successful, Mr Panther. I was good for business. I look good in a cocktail dress.'

I had fallen half a step behind, bemused by the telecommunications. I glanced at her bum. You'd look good in a car accident, I thought.

She was still going, loitering now, just in the front garden, beside the fountain, explaining how the pair moved in together, he supporting her while she went to university. 'I dropped enough hints and he soon proposed. I said yes and fell pregnant with Shelagh soon after. She arrived before our first anniversary. Even before I'd finished suckling I knew I'd made a mistake. It wasn't the kind of security I needed. I needed *real* security: the security of power, the security of self-determination, the security of single purpose.'

'The security of egocentrism?' I get tired of histories. I have seen too much past to find them illuminating.

'If you like,' she said. 'If you like. I needed strength, Mr Panther, and I realised no one was going to grant me that but myself. I have no social life, Mr Panther, only my work. That was the lesson I should have learned during my school years, and spared everyone a lot of trouble.'

'Not to mention sparing Shelagh the burden of life.'

There: just then—a fleeting glint of sadness across her face. She seemed to have lost interest in our stroll. She stared down at her drink, swirling it pointlessly in its glass, and then downed it in a gulp. I waited. Here we go, I thought. More history: the determination of fate. Probable cause. After a moment she looked up again and fixed her terrifying eyes on mine, stilled now, the sadness stowed away.

'Many people abused as children go on to become abusers themselves, but you know that,' she began. 'Sometimes that process is indirect. Evil needs only possibility, not pathway. Graeme Purdey is a weak man, Mr Panther. He is socially inept, uneasy in company, unadventurous, and ambitious only insomuch as that ambition will further his myopic stability. I despise him, and always did. There was no love in Shelagh's conception, no hope of blessings. It was part of my healing process, that's all. Graeme was merely a facilitator, a dick-on-call, and I, I was just another of his business tools, a social and professional investment.

'I saw him look at women with lust, or something diluted which served as lust, in his eyes. He liked them small and vulnerable, and I was, am, neither.'

That, I reflected, might explain his current receptionist, in form if not in content.

'I have my pride, Mr Panther,' she was saying. 'I kept quiet about my past. I didn't want to mention it; it might have jeopardised the arrangement. Eventually I told him, though, six days after Shelagh was born. I felt I had to. I remember the day. I was sitting on the edge of the bed in my dressing-gown, the baby in my arms. Graeme was squatting on the floor in front of me, one hand on my knee. We were both a bit weepy, blown away I guess, in the glow of birth.

'I confessed. It *felt* like a confession, Mr Panther. I hated that. He listened attentively. When I had finished, my eyes were still dry. I was empty. He stared at me for a moment, and then moved his gaze down to Shelagh. That was when I learned something, Mr Panther. Right then. I looked at his face. I did not see a surge of paternal protection when he looked at his firstborn, neither did I see—what?—sympathy, shock, even rejection, when he looked at me. I saw a dark epiphany in him: the dawning of the notion of the possible. I saw him struck by the sudden sly solution of the eventual ageing of his wife—something of which he was terrified, given that my own value to him was aesthetic. And I saw him, Mr Panther, assume me to be complicit. He had found his path of least resistance.

'And I knew then what had to be done. As soon as it was possible, not long after she was off my breast, I left without a backward glance. That was my gift to my daughter, Mr Panther. Strength. Strength to the fucking *core*. The strength to endure. The strength of trusting no one. And now she has been found wanting

168

in that strength. My gift to my ex-husband was guilt, the ever-present threat of damnation, unpardonable sin. And then I went to work on my own salvation. I *own* all this—this house, these grounds, and much, much more. Outright and without regret. Do you think me evil, Mr Panther?'

I looked her in the eyes. She was not asking for absolution. Merely an opinion. It was *I* who was being judged, not she.

'Therefore all things whatsoever ye would do that men would do to you, do ye even so to them,' I said.

She looked at me strangely. 'Do you really believe that?' she asked.

I did not answer. If she wanted reaction, she was asking the wrong person. All I had to offer was theatre. So I chucked in some more. I wanted her angry. 'She that liveth in pleasure is dead while she liveth.'

It didn't work.

'Timothy something,' she said, quite calmly. 'My father used to quote it often at school assemblies. It was a boys' school. Such is the wisdom of Jesus.'

'Timothy never met Jesus,' I said. 'He was a follower of Paul's. Paul circumcised him, in fact, shortly before he realised circumcision was a turn-off for the Gentiles and dropped it as an entry requirement. Timothy was clubbed to death when he tried to break up a festival of Dionysus. No one likes a party-pooper.'

She smiled at that. I stabbed in, fast.

'Do you accept responsibility for your daughter's life and death, Ms Cowper?' I asked, voice flat.

169

'Yes,' she said, matching me.

'Did you commit her death?'

'No.'

'Have you seen your husband since?'

'Ex. Not even for the divorce. Only at the funeral.'

I paused. I wondered. Slowly now, selfish, finding a measure for myself: 'Do you repent your actions?'

Beatrice Cowper never blinked. She held my gaze, calm, strong, centred, harm in a lover's mask. 'No,' she said. 'I take responsibility. No more is necessary.'

And suddenly she is laughing again, her glass now fallen to the grass, her right hand clasped demurely across her heaving chest in a gesture to good breeding. And now she has taken a step towards me, her eyes bright, her mouth a–grin, arms loose about my neck, looking down on me. And now her lips are brushing my ear, her pelvis so close to mine I can feel the heat of her delta.

'Is that it, Mr Panther?' she is whispering. 'Is that who you think you are? Do you think yourself the Christ child reincarnated?' Her breasts are pushing against my torso. 'And am I the sinner unredeemed? Is that what this is all about, Joe Panther? The inanity of your imagination, oh Lord, the poverty of your sad existence?' She is sliding down the front of me, onto her knees. Her hands are on my trouser button. 'Would you like me to kiss your loins, master? Would you like a second coming? Would you like some meagre feeling of conquest and power? Will you go away and not come back then, and leave the dead to rest till Judgement Day?'

I place my hands on her head, gently. She takes hold of my fly with delicate pinch, looks up at me, her eyes tar-pit shafts, sheer, without end. I meet her gaze, even. 'I can help you, you know,' she says. 'I could be the answer to your prayers.'

Vertigo surges. I push back sudden from the edge, hard, sending her over, sprawling, backwards, towards the fish pond. She lands, her head at the base of the pedestal, her naked back arched in the air, hands in the water, holding her body above it, bum on the grass, knees open to the world, Cupid, unconcerned, pissing between her breasts.

That was close. I have standards, after all. In the field of human behaviour, no matter what the moral yard-stick, a line must eventually be drawn. I have abased myself in many ways, but I will not consent to oral sex in another man's suit.

Especially a man who thinks brown shoes are cool.

From the corner of my eye, I thought I saw a glint of light in one of the windows of the wing. I looked around, but saw only the glass and blind framing ghostly reflections of foliage shivering in the breeze.

'I always enjoyed Leviticus, Ms Cowper,' I said, turning back. 'And if a man lieth with a beast, he shall surely be put to death: and ye shall slay the beast.'

She did not move nor speak for a moment. Her eyes were ravens' beaks. And then, still not moving, water soaking her front: 'Stand on the path, Mr Panther.' I am no fool. I did so. She leant her head back, chin uppermost, exposing her neck. '*Beet*hoven!' she called.

171

It took Cerberus perhaps fifteen seconds to arrive, turning the corner of the building in a haste of fury and unwieldy inertia. He stopped, front paws inches from the paving stones, growling, snarling, lunging, drooling. Beatrice Cowper regained her feet as gracefully as possible.

'A final word before you leave, Mr Panther,' she said, her poise returned despite her ruined apparel. 'Get help. You need therapy. Illusions kill.'

'You are not an illusion,' I answered, with, frankly, more certainty than I felt. I walked slowly and, of necessity, circuitously, back to the front gate, Cerberus shadowing me all the way. She said nothing more. Just watched.

As the steel closed behind me, I heard her laughter once again. Game to her, she thought. I wasn't so sure. I realised I had left my briefcase in the conservatory, which was a pity. I liked those clothes. Never mind. I didn't feel much like going back in to get them.

And then I realised I was still holding my glass of whisky, still a finger-measure full. I chugged the drink in one, and then lobbed it over the hedge. A dog yelped, then growled.

And then silence. I liked the silence. The rain spat like mockery as I headed for the tramlines.

The tram back into the city was full, rush hour having

started, which meant I had to stand. The young office worker strap-hanging next to me kept averting his head, offended, I assumed, by the fog of scotch and cigarette fumes coming from my mouth and nose. That made me smile. He thought *he* had a hard time of it.

There was much thinking to be endured. I still had plans for the day, but nothing could be done about them for several hours. Rocking in rhythm with the tracks, I started to swill things around.

Item one, in big letters: GET YOUR HEAD TOGETHER. Beatrice Cowper was a lot of things, most of them not very nice, but she was *not* Brigid. The perception was irrational, I reminded myself, and therefore unhelpful. If I was going to get out of this fix in one piece, my paranoias had to be kept in check. Brigid was a woman, a cowgirl, a nun, a saint apparently, born in Uinmeras, died in Kildare. Of course, I'd long left the area by then, so I never saw her corpse, but, yah, everyone dies. (Except, of course, me, and apparently one of the sons of Zoroaster, who is alleged to be still banging about somewhere, armed with a magic pomegranate. Useful, that. I wonder if it works as a mobile phone.)

No matter that she used to say, in hushed explanation, looking at the stars, how she was Irish before she was anything, how her spirit had sprung from the soil when the Tuatha de Danaan, the ancients, had arrived, long before even the Gaels set foot from the east. No matter. She was speaking of place, spirit and ancestry, conditions constant and independent of scripture.

173

Denied an understanding of the physical world, as we all were, she sought sense in the mythological one. The new church, or the old trees? In the same century, some Roman theologians condemned the wearing of amulets bearing the names of angels. The angels were really demons, they said. The demons were really the past.

The BC. The not-me.

Reason, therefore, required the ordinary death of an Irish nun. She is not Beatrice Cowper. (*Yet she recognised me.*) We were lovers. (*Yet I left her without farewell.*) This one is cruel. (*People change.*)

Good. That one was sorted out, then. What else?

A car parked in Beatrice Cowper's street would have stood out a mile. There was no car when I arrived, nor when I left. I had been successful, therefore, in throwing off my watchers after leaving John the Baptist's flat. Also good.

And yet: somebody—the cops I assumed—warned Cowper I'd likely visit her at some point. They knew that. Why then, given that they lost me, did they not set up surveillance at all likely destinations, one of which, even by their own logic, was the house in Toorak? Three possibilities: they don't care, they don't have enough manpower to cover all positions, or it's not the police watching me.

Which led to more immediate concerns. Namely, was I going to drift aimlessly and unpredictably around the city for the next several hours, just to keep my arse tail-free, or was I going to head back into my own territory and then deal with losing the shadows again as the night wore on and purpose grew in focus?

I am not the most paranoid person I've ever met, not by a long stretch. I knew an Inquisitor in Arras in France in the fifteenth who was utterly convinced that one-third of the people of Europe were witches. The first three people he tortured and burned were a hermit, a prostitute and a poet.

Such things that are done in my name. It's no wonder I get a bit edgy.

I asked the chap next to me for the time. Five o'clock, just gone, he said, turning away quickly. I bumped into him as the tram halted to pick up passengers, apologised, and put the twenty-dollar note I'd lifted from his pocket into mine.

Whatever. It passes the time. You have to have a hobby.

We reached the city, where, if I was going to head home, I'd have to change lines. I jumped off and headed into Young and Jackson's, a large, locally famous and tourist-riddled pub opposite Flinders Street station. I grabbed a Jamesons, just to be polite, and found the public phone. DSS Gordon was still in his office.

He was gruff, but not his usual antagonistic self. It must have nearly killed him, but I was a conduit to someone he wanted and, for the moment, that made me his ally. He thought. I told him that inquiries into the whereabouts of Theresa Mary Farndale were in train, utilising methods and networks he neither knew nor would care to know about. What would make life easier, I added, was a photograph of the woman.

Gordon replied, in a long-suffering kind of way, that he'd already thought of that, way before he showed me the secret report. There was none with the paperwork, and none in the criminal records files. I'd assumed as much, I said, and then gave him her street name, and the name of the street in which she had been squatting at the time of the trouble. Double-checking the street against other records for the period, I suggested, might just throw up the names of some of her squat-mates, and they, in turn, if located, might possess an old snap. It was worth a try.

He grunted. I grinned. Maybe, he conceded, but it would take time, at least a day. What were my movements tomorrow? No idea, I said. Following leads. (Nothing annoys a cop more than appropriating his clichés.) I told him to drop the shot, should he find one, over at the warehouse. Slip it under the door if I'm not in. Then decamp. (I swear, I could hear his jaw clench.) I hung up on him.

I'd thought about asking him to explain the surveillance, but changed my mind. If he wasn't going to mention it, neither was I.

I stood for a moment, still near the phone, in the grips of indecision, then had an idea. I grabbed the A–K phone book and took it with me to the gents. The thing about speed, I find, is that you must never let it rule you, especially in its absence. This day was going to be over when *I* said it was, not before.

✝

In the end I stayed in the city, doing nothing much. I hiked a few blocks, picking up a newspaper on the way, and found a synthetic Irish pub, themed and sculpted *in extremis*, leprechauns aplenty. It seemed appropriate.

I caught the evening news on the wall-mounted television while enjoying my first pint of Guinness and a plate of steak-and-kidney pie. Second item in was a dreadful tale of how someone, 'possibly a heroin addict', had robbed, stripped and bound an insurance assessor at syringe-point in the city. Police were concerned by this 'disturbing new trend'. The victim was deeply shocked and receiving counselling, but had not seen his attacker's face or appearance.

Hey, I thought, I'm a *trend*. I nodded to myself in quiet satisfaction. It is part of my role, after all, according to some, to bring mystery to the world of men.

The story would no doubt make it to the papers the following day. The one I had featured headlines about a government plan to restrict abortions, and a report about how an entire generation of Aborigines had been ripped from their parents and placed in missions to be saved. There was a headline on the back page—BUDDHA BROKE MY NOSE—but I think it was about a footballer. I didn't feel like reading any of it. Instead, I lost myself in the cryptic crossword for the next several hours until midnight closing. I had four more pints of stout, but hardly felt the first couple. There was no need to worry unduly about the effects of the rest. I had the get-sober solution in my jacket pocket.

I couldn't finish the crossword, which irritated me. You'd think, wouldn't you? I mean, *really*. Talk about short-changed by destiny.

✝

The walk to Image Makers took about half an hour, the wind confusing a gullible drizzle with contradictory directions. The trams had finished for the night, and grabbing a cab seemed unwise.

My route took me past the casino, its lights and signage bright with the hope of false promise, like all temples. For once, I was glad of its monstrous presence. Anywhere else in Melbourne, a man walking alone and unsmiling in a good grey suit in the middle of the night might arouse suspicion. In the streets around the gambling palace, where the imperatives of earth and tide find no purchase, and daylight is anathema, such sights were commonplace.

The car park next to the advertising agency was empty. Neither its building nor its twin neighbour showed any light. I walked around to the rear, checking for other pedestrians beforehand. There was no traffic on the street, although the main road nearby still roared and moaned with cars and trucks.

Funny thing: find any car park, and somewhere within it will be half a brick. You learn to value such constancies. In this case, it lay among the weeds that grew stubbornly at the base of the back wall. I noted its position.

The back door to the building was set in a comfortingly dark alcove. It was a strictly functional item, made of steel and wire-reinforced glass and a single hefty lock. I stared at it for a moment, tension not the only factor behind my clenching jaw, and prepared to go about my mission.

At this point I discovered a minor problem. I had only one pair of plastic gloves in my trouser pocket. When kitting out my freshly acquired sartorial rig, I had realised the glove-box was a little too bulky to conceal in the jacket. I'd pulled out just a single pair, in case I needed them at Beatrice Cowper's house. The box itself I'd dropped in the briefcase.

I tried to remember what else I had left behind in Toorak, apart from my clothes. The money, my keys and the rest of my purchases I had transferred to the suit. My trouser pockets, I decided, probably contained nothing of great import, even if Ms Cowper should decide to have a look: a couple of old tram tickets and shop receipts, perhaps; a few small coins, my rosaries, fluff, a used tissue, not much more.

The gloves, then, were the only issue, and that purely because of their fragility. Disposable gloves rip quite easily. Their surface can moisten in the air, making them slightly adhesive. They can tell as many tales as they conceal. I read that somewhere. I had planned to use several pairs, changing them every couple of minutes, disposing of used ones at a time and place to be determined. I don't really understand the possibilities of forensic investigation. For most of my life, after all, criminal detection relied on omens and auguries and the steaming guts of slaughtered beasts. Either that, or red-hot irons, spikes and thumbscrews. Or dogma. Whichever, electron microscopes didn't really feature.

I have grasped the principles involved, however, and look for comfort in history. Forensic science is a body of knowledge known to some, but occult to me. Therefore it is best to treat the whole subject as powerful, effective and inherently hostile.

I am not, after all, a master criminal. I am simply a messiah, fallen on hard times. I cannot be expected to know everything.

One pair, then. They would have to do. The right-hand one gave a pleasing snap as I pulled it on.

The lock gave after about five minutes of careful manipulation with the nailfile and the tip of the syringe, the door swinging smoothly back into a dark, tiled room that smelled of disinfectant and insect spray. I eased my way in, shuffling my feet to avoid tripping over, closed the door behind me and stood still a moment, waiting for my eyes to adjust to the light. I considered alarm possibilities. There were two businesses in the building, neither of them particularly attractive to opportunist burglars. I figured the security system would be nothing special. I'd been hoping it was one of those that simply set up an almighty racket and a blue flashing light, because everyone ignores them. There was no sound or fury, however, which meant it was expressing its distress elsewhere—either in a police station or, more likely, in the control room of a private company.

Most alarm triggers are accidental, and I was relying on that. If the signal went to the security firm, a protocol would be followed. A patrol car would be diverted to check it out, I thought. That would take a while. Either that, or the company would place a call to the business, seeking an answer, a secret word, and confirmation of a false alarm. Police, too, would probably drive past or walk around the perimeter, their pulses far from racing, discovering no signs of forced entry. Of course, the business owners would also be called, possibly aroused from sleep. They might consider the matter rather more urgent, especially if they knew something no one else did, but, even so, I calculated twenty minutes would be a fairly safe margin in which to operate.

To work. In the dim ambience created by the street lights, I realised I was standing in a small storage area. I could make out a couple of mops leaning against the wall, a bucket, a stack of old newspapers, sundry tins and tubes of cleaning agents. The door opposite was open, and as I moved through it I was relieved to see that it led to a short corridor, which, in turn, opened out into the communal foyer.

The light here was good, because of the predominantly glass ground floor front wall. Too good, in fact, rendering me plainly visible should anyone pass by. In my suit, I doubted that I would pass for the cleaner. I took the stairs two at a time and reached the agency door quick-smart. Its lock was plain and simple, and clearly not designed to withstand sustained and determined assault. It yielded after less than a minute of fiddling.

Inside the reception area, I walked briskly to the window and risked half-opening the vertical blind. No cars. No patrols.

The door to Purdey's office was unlocked. It had only one window, albeit a reasonably large one, hung with a blind of its own, and facing the rear. I twisted the fabric shut, and switched on the desk lamp, its head bent low to the surface. Three minutes later I had opened every drawer and cupboard in the place, none of which had been locked, and found nothing but the clerical detritus of a small business being run by a small mind.

Mind you, nothing was exactly what I was looking for. Nothing in particular, anyway. Short of finding a signed note admitting to Shelagh Purdey's murder, I couldn't actually imagine what incriminating evidence might be left lying around—if, indeed, incrimination was either possible or necessary.

There was a very good reason for this. I didn't have a clue what I was doing.

Investigating a murder was pretty much a first for me. I'd committed a few in my time, when circumstances dictated, but that really wasn't proving to be all that much help. My personal experience from a victim's perspective was also less than illuminating. The various tracking missions I'd performed for Corrigan over the years hadn't exactly given me a wealth of knowledge either. With most of them, after all, I'd had a pretty good idea where the missing person could be found. More often than not, where I'd left them. The few who I truly didn't know also presented little difficulty, given that they always knew someone who knew someone who knew me.

But this—murder, ritual, abuse—this was an entirely different set of gospels altogether. If I was honest with myself, I'd have to admit I didn't have a clue what I was doing. Luckily, however, I am humble, and will not do for me what I will not do for others.

One must seek consistency, after all.

On my bewildered head and inexperienced shoulders, Corrigan's fate was resting. The priest assumed I could do the job, and somehow I'd neglected to disabuse him. He had hired me under false pretensions. Two lots thereof, actually.

Still, he had faith in me.

Ditto thereof, did he but know it.

But not, perhaps, trust. Was, as Gordon seemed convinced, the business with Theresa Farndale indivisible from the current mess? Did the priest have a duty to tell me? Had he denied himself, and taken up his double-cross?

The second office was also unlocked, and even more barren than the first. The desk drawers contained no notepads, no diaries, no indication, in fact, that anybody ever used it. Payroll tax was clearly not a big item in Image Makers' expenditure. The only remarkable object in the room was the computer. It looked like the standard desk-top jobs in Purdey's office and on the reception counter, except that even I could see that it was larger. It had small speakers either side of it, and an extra plug-in drive of some sort.

As fat men are to pretty women, so am I to computers. I see them everywhere, but almost never get to touch them. Their possession requires money. Their use as a communication tool requires accounts, and accounts require identity. I had used Corrigan's machine on a few occasions, just to read things, mainly when he asked me to cast a fresh eye over this or that parish announcement he was drafting on it, but that was about it. Nevertheless, I was pretty sure I could fire up the one I was now regarding and have a nose around, mainly because there was a switch at the front labelled ON/OFF. I decided against it, however, because I wasn't sure whether the time and date of my incursion would be logged somewhere deep inside it. They did that, I read somewhere.

Next to the plug-in drive stood a plastic box containing a dozen or so disks, like floppy disks but thicker. I picked one up and squinted at the label on it, which, in the gloom, appeared to be mainly orange and red. It said: KUMQUAT FACT PACK: YOUR GUIDE TO HEALTHY LIVING.

I have a thirst for knowledge. I knew nothing about

184

kumquats, except that the name sounded vaguely rude. The other disks were all identical, so I popped the one in my hand into my pocket. One little disk among many; no one would miss that.

Behold, I come as a thief.

The reception area looked extremely unpromising, the drawers revealing nothing more than that Sophia had a habit of stashing apple cores in the top one. A large appointments diary and phone log, one day to a page, lay next to the telephone. Going through the motions now, annoyed that I had put myself in danger, stayed out late, and shunted so much speed into my nostrils that sleep now seemed like an unlikely prospect for the rest of the night, all for bog-all, I started flicking through the pages. They were full of mundane notations: calls from clients, calls from salespeople, meetings and sales presentations with the businesses already represented on the office walls, a few others, nothing exciting.

I was on the wrong track, I decided, and blamed John the Baptist. Mystics: who'd have them? No wonder people used to burn them. All his twaddle about fathers and light had misled me. Elaine Purdey's tale of her husband's filmmaking fantasies, I had been convinced, was where the light bit came in. It had all fitted together, with just one little problem. It was all bullshit.

And then I saw it.

The handwriting changed.

I flicked back again through the pages, just to make sure, but there it was. One hand, presumably belonging to Sophia, had made all the entries for the past, what was it, nine days. Everything before that, right back to January, was in another.

I was still mulling over this discovery when the phone rang. The security company, more than likely. I didn't answer it.

Quickly now, I walked back into Purdey's office and pulled open the top drawer of the filing cabinet. It took a minute or so, but I finally found my quarry: the staff files. Rebecca May Goodwin had worked for Image Makers for nearly eighteen months before leaving. I found a copy of the reference the boss had done for her, which, like its author, was shortish, predictable and emptily flash. There was no letter of resignation, or of termination. There was, however, a home address.

Anxiety growing, jaw chomping, it was clearly time to vacate. I checked that nothing was out of place, and the desk lamp off. Farting about with the door at the top of the stairs so that it would lock again used up precious minutes, and I nearly impaled my finger on the syringe during the process. That would have been unfortunate. I can't bear needles.

The back door was much easier, simply locking as I closed it behind me. Outside, the drizzle had become more forthright, and the wind had found a purpose. I picked up the half-brick, and hurried around to the front of the building, checking at the corner to make sure no one was about.

The brick hit the centre of the ground floor window with a violent smash and a bell-like clattering that sounded like a riff from Satan's percussionist during the climax of a particularly indulgent King Crimson number. The police, or the security guards, when they finally turned up, would almost certainly assume the alarm had gone off in response to an act of vandalism aimed, if at anything, at the graphic arts studio. Nothing inside the building would lead them to suspect otherwise.

I hooked the collar of my jacket around my neck and started walking away, crossing the street and heading down a laneway. The main road, when I came out on it, was still brisk with traffic. It was 1.30am, and one lane was clogged with cars waiting to turn into the casino car park. Wide, I reflected, not for the first time, is the road that leads to destruction.

I jumped a cab, told the driver to head first for a 24-hour bottle shop in Carlton, and thence to Fitzroy. I was strung out and niggly and pissed off. I wanted to sleep, but knew that I couldn't.

And if I couldn't, I reasoned, why should other people? This suffering on behalf of everyone else has knobs on it. My work is never-ending, my presence always asked. I fired up a Dunhill, ignoring the driver's requests and stub-fingered points towards the No Smoking sign, and made a little plan.

The priest would or would not be pleased to see me, but never mind. I came not to send peace, at least as Matthew would have me say, but a sword.

✝

187

# 6

IT WAS A PHYSICAL SENSATION, up there on the cross, near the end: a sort of shuddering *petit mal*, a turbulent absent instant I did not recognise but knew immediately. The abandonment. The spirit, the ancient elemental hand which had been holding mine, upped and left. Just like that. I believe I commented on it at the time.

But faith is a terrible addiction. My last thoughts, as my swollen eyelids curtained over parched corneas, were these: now the message ends, now it happens, now it begins, now will love descend, now will the loving father triumph.

And then I woke up. You know the details.

I was devastated, not to mention sore. I had been wrong. I found courage, however, in my error. Great courage, spurred by some limbic, reptilian revelation of life retained, some deep unacknowledged serpentine me for whom ideology and higher purpose were no more than smudges in a slow-blinking peripheral vision. Now I knew the score: the *real* score. I had made the journey and discovered the map a forgery.

This surprised me: I found reassurance. Even in the heaving shock of profound disappointment, I received a greater knowledge. Most of what I'd spent the previous few years proclaiming was on the mark. Only the reason—the end-point—was wrong, and now I could truly set my people free, free of *all* masters, real and imagined. The path was at last clear: turn left at free will and don't look up.

If the bugger's there he doesn't care.

I didn't wait for the wounds to heal. I didn't even know if they would. I had to get out there, brimming with the truth discovered, and *tell* people. I had to repent. So I ventured into the garden—you know this bit—and told dear Mary, and Mother Mary, and Salome. I was a bit befuddled at the time. I don't think I made much sense. They thought I was a bloody gardener at first. I ask you.

Ahh, that dreadful addiction. I had been shot full of cosmic Narcan, but I alone. The women saw, not me, but the idea of me, the prediction of me, the prophesy of me. They saw themselves vindicated. And, sad to say, I had no patience with their blathering and fawning and poking. If I had stayed and explained then things might have been very, very different today. The ocean of blood that has been let loose in my name might not have been so spilled.

For that, and only that, I apologise. My energy was

low. I felt run–down. It had been a bad week. I was only human, after all.

So I walked away; in plain sight and without illusion, I walked away. This came to be widely regarded, the nature of rumours being what it is, as my ascension to heaven. The start of a life on the lam would have been more accurate, but there you go. It *had* begun. I heard the stories, and I am not without conscience. I tried again, to the Twelve, to brother James, to strangers in the village of Emmaus. I was getting a bit desperate by then. Also hungry.

To no avail. So I walked, alone and in torment, out of the district. People have been waiting for me to return ever since.

And now, for the unsuspecting Father Corrigan at least, it was about to happen.

At the bottle shop I'd purchased a bottle of Jamesons and a stubby of Tooheys Red. The stubby had died fast and cleanly, although the sight of me necking it in the front passenger seat had sent the cab driver into apoplexy. I don't know why. I didn't spill a drop. He demanded that I leave his conveyance forthwith, until he turned and met my eyes. Then he shut up and drove.

I got him to drop me off a block and half from the house, and stood fishing for keys at the gate of some stranger's home in case he took his time in leaving. I needn't have worried. The car sped off with an impudent scorch of rubber. I don't think he liked me.

The priest's house was dark and silent, a light rain,

190

constant as prayer now the wind had decided to take a break, muffling any noise I made as I edged my way carefully along the thin strip of weeds, full of empty drink cans and chip wrappers, between the wooden fence and the window of Corrigan's bedroom. My jaw felt increasingly tight. Chewing gum would have been a good idea.

So would heaven, but what the hell.

The window, in the faint-hearted style of the district, was barred on its bottom half. It took me only a few seconds to insert the nailfile through the gap between the upper and lower wooden frames, and push the catch to the side. The sash was good and gentle, the top pane sliding down behind the bottom one at my touch. It made a slight squeak, nothing much, and in the breathless silence that followed I could hear only the faint sound of snoring coming from the darkness within.

I put the Jamesons in the generous side pocket of the suit jacket—a popular feature with many of the op shop customers around—and kept hold of the empty stubby. Slowly, I hoisted myself onto the sill, and then above the bars, until my feet rested on the top of the frames, the bulk of me crouched above. I looked very scary there in silhouette, I fancied, like a fusion of one of Goya's demons and an assistant bank manager. A full moon to the rear would have been good, but you can't have everything.

I waited a moment, balanced, uncomfortable, until my eyes adjusted to the interior. I could make out the shape of a single bed, hard against the wall, a looming, crumpled swell indicating where Corrigan lay. A dressing table, warped and wonky, stood to the other side. I could see clearly a small wooden crucifix, complete with the tortured body of yours truly, on the wall above the bed-head.

Wish I had the copyright. Would have made all the difference these last few centuries.

What strange history commands the servants of goodness sleep sound beneath the sign of mutilation and be thankful? If thine eye offends thee, pluck it out. Origen cut off his balls in the service of God. They called him a father of the Church.

What rough beast . . .

I leaned forward and jumped.

In one chaotic, scarcely managed stride I was across the room. The bottom of the stubby shattered with a sociopathic crack against the dressing table, shards shooting heavenwards. Before the priest's eyes had time to reflex open I had the jagged remnants of the neck pressed into his throat, hard. I sat on the edge of the bed, my face close over his, blocking out what little light persisted.

'I am Azazel and Baal, Marduk and Belial,' I whispered harsh. 'I am Bethor and Och, Hagith and Ophiel, Samael and Anael, Astaroth and Nambroth, Butthead and Beavis. I come in darkness, a satan of Yahweh Saboath, righteous and cruel—'

I smelled urine.

He started, body suddenly stiff. 'Holy Mary, mother of God—'

192

I pressed the glass a little harder. 'Silence! I come to claim the debt that is due, deceiver of worship, fornicator, blasphemer, harbour of carnality, keeper of secrets, defiler of girls, betrayer of trust.'

No one, I think, has ever really credited my skill at adlibbing. Whisky helps.

I could feel Corrigan shaking now, his voice frail, distant: 'Miserere mei Deus, miserere mei Deus, miserere mei Deus . . .'

'There can be no mercy without repentance, Brendan Pearce Corrigan.'

'I am a man of God!' he whispered as if through blood.

'Even Satan disguises himself as an angel of light. So it is not strange if his servants disguise themselves as servants of righteousness.'

A sudden stillness came upon him. The glass ceased to tremble in my hand.

'Paul. Corinthians.' He said it to himself.

'Autobiographical, I always felt.'

'Jesus fucking Christ. Panther, you arse . . . you fu—What do you think you're bloody doing, you bastard? Breaking in . . . It's the middle of the bloody nigh—'

He tried to push my arm away. I leaned in behind the jagged edge against his throat. His arm dropped fast. He made awkward, staccato, grating sounds.

'It's time to talk, priest. Now. I need your secrets.'

'I *know* you, man.'

'No you don't.'

He was silent for a minute. My hand was steady.

Eventually, quiet as contemplation: 'What?'

'Theresa Mary Farndale.'

Another silence, an inhalation coloured, I thought, by tears. 'Miserere mei Deus.'

'Perhaps. If you're a good boy.'

'I'll not lie, Panther, but I'd've chosen a holier confessor.'

'You'd be hard-pressed, priest. Let not your heart be troubled: ye believe in God. Believe also in me.'

'Take the bottle away and turn on the light. Your breath reeks, man. Must I lie in my piss?'

I didn't answer him. He made no move when I put the weapon aside. I stood up, glass crunching beneath my boots, found the door and the light switch next to it. He looked pale and old and very scared in its brilliance.

'What do you fear, priest?'

'Not you. What comes after you.'

'You've already had the flood. After me comes nothing. You simply remain.'

'That's more than enough to fear, Panther. More than enough.'

And so it began, the tale of Farndale. He lay in his bed, on his side sometimes, propped on an elbow; on his back at others, staring at the spider-cracked ceiling, hoping not to see his Creator looming beyond. He didn't try to lift himself from his waste-soaked mattress, and I never suggested he did. Degradation helps humility, I find.

I sat on the floor, on the carpet, beige, thin and

194

dusty, leaning my back against the wall. We shared the Jamesons, swigging from the bottle. I used the still intact bottom of the empty, retrieved from by the bed, as an ashtray.

The hours passed, creeping unto dawn. The story was slow in coming, seeping from him as fluid from a wound reopened.

He had known Theresa Mary Farndale, he said, for perhaps a year before carnality phased into the equation. She was, it seemed, the same girl John the Baptist had reluctantly identified, at least inasmuch as she was a red-head, plump and went by the street name of Easy.

Ms Farndale, according to the priest, was a convent school drop-out who found herself on the streets of Collingwood and Fitzroy in her late teenage years, the result of violent disharmony in her parental home.

The priest had hope for the maiden. He knew that she sold herself when money got tight; knew, too, that she flirted with chemicals, blasting speed sometimes, taking Rohypnols and other benzodiazapenes when opportunity presented itself in the form of black-market scripts or a clinic doctor with a reputation and a mortgage to pay. She was not above swapping her sex for medicinal favours, he said, but was smitten with ingrained guilt each time she did and, eventually, lulled and reassured by the bluff and boozy cleric, made her way to St Cuthbert's to confess.

Corrigan forgave her, of course, 'in dogma and in life'. She was a victim first, he said, immoral second. Her inculcated faith had persisted, despite her troubles.

She needed confession, forgiveness, and seemed to listen when the priest veered from the script and talked, he hoped, with streetwise pragmatism.

After irregular visits to St Cuthbert's, usually for confession, occasionally to sit in on a Sunday service ('always looking like any moment she expected someone to tell her to piss off out'), she started visiting the house. At first she came, hesitant and apologetic, suspiciously close to meal times. Corrigan obliged, sharing with her his food. 'A whisky, too, if she asked for it, no matter that she was officially too young to be seen in a decent pub.'

She was often cold, he said, scant protected in clothes, op-shopped or stolen, from the biting Melbourne weather. And often miserable too: alone in the world, he said, carrying some terrible grief and burdens, never spoken aloud. She asked for a hug—'a simple hug, man'—one evening, teary-eyed and quiver-lipped. He obliged.

'She clung to me like a woman clutching life itself,' he said. 'Clung on and clung on, her head against my chest, dribbling, snotting, crying, my shirt gone sodden, apologising for her weakness, she'd be all right in a minute. I held her, man, held her up against her own failed strength and will, and felt, just then, like for the first time I was doing what God had called me to do. No liturgy, no Latin, no ultimate agenda: just giving comfort to the destitute and asking no return.'

The return came, however, by turn and in time. For Easy Theresa sexual activity was the only form of commerce completely in her control. She used it to acquire, and she used it to thank. She was a young woman generous in spirit, for all her woes. The evenings progressed and multiplied, with Theresa around at the house, cuddled often, chaste, into the shoulder of the priest as the pair watched television or talked of nothing into the night.

After several weeks, her hands started to stray, he said, and her lips to murmur things that should never be murmured to the holy. He resisted, he said, 'with a vehemence I didn't really feel'.

It was her gift, she explained, a gift not given lightly and never before given freely, out of friendship. He had taught her that, she claimed. He had taught her that it was a blessed thing to give without thought of advantage. He had, in his way, given flesh to the dried bones of belief she had gnawed on all her life. Would he take that away from her now?

'I'm a man, Panther,' he said. 'For it all, damn it, I'm a man. I'd never . . . The hardest thing for me in taking the vows was the one of celibacy. It tormented me my life. I've never really understood how denying the love of the flesh increased the knowledge of God. God always seemed, I don't know, bigger than that. I think I took to the whisky as a young man in the secret hope I'd make myself impotent and not have to worry after a while. I pretty much succeeded too, I discovered, in the flesh, but, damn me, not in the will.'

'For so strong is the appeal of pleasure,' I muttered, more to myself than anything, 'that it can bring about a prolongation of ignorance with a resulting facility for sin, or a perversion of conscience leading to self-deception.'

'Who said that?'

'Tertullian. Illusions kill.'

'And that?'

'No one you know.'

And thus did their mutual journey of discovery begin, a journey that was to end in hatred and disaster. There might have been love developing, bar that neither knew its name or nature.

'And then her nightmares began,' he said. 'She began to dream that she was, well, Mary Magdalene, sometimes, the Blessed Mother others. She had torment, Panther, such dreadful torment. She would wake screaming, so often screaming. She dreamed of Mary, whichever Mary, being Mary, Mary strapped and crucified, Mary raped, Mary humiliated, Mary stripped bare and penetrated.

'And she woke each night in terror and dread. She'd punch me away, and then grab me, hold me, like a baby. It was a circus, man, I tell you. I didn't know which way was up, had no idea what to do or help. I've no experience, man, none at all.'

I was getting bored. It was all sounding rather rehearsed. Never before spoken aloud, perhaps, not in this manner, but mulled over in its elements, nevertheless. The story had the air of something contemplated, half-refined, in the darkness of late night insecurity, some basic preparation in case, sometime down the track, the Holy Spirit should ever hit the fan.

198

An innocent, for all his years and learning, the priest did something terrible. He told Easy Theresa he thought it best if their relationship ended. He meant well, he insisted (for whom, though, I wondered), but realised shortly after that he'd merely added the weight of cruel rejection to her already considerable problems.

'And there it was, I suppose,' he said, his voice faltering. 'When we were together, even when I was inside her nakedness, I still felt, although god knows I was wrong, that I was acting as a *priest*, Panther. I was in some sort of communion, however unorthodox.'

'You were in good company,' I said. 'Augustine was a root rat. Give me celibacy, he wrote, but not yet. Martin Luther used to bang his wife to scare away the devil.'

'Don't render me banal, Panther, for pity's sake. Don't strip this of meaning. When I pushed her away, when I ended the thing, then Panther, then, for the first time, I was acting as a *man*. It was then that I sinned.'

I disagreed on the timing, but kept my mouth shut.

It was after that, he said, that the girl went over the edge, no longer able to distinguish between the reality of her dreams and the fantasy of her life. She felt as if the spirit of Mary—which Mary, apparently, depended on the day—dwelt within her and gave her both mission and aim. That mission, it turned out, was the destruction of Corrigan, a man she now saw as the prime seducer in her young life full of unwanted seduction, a man who added the betrayal of trust and the betrayal of the Lord to the standard sadism of lust against the young and vulnerable and carrot-topped.

'Next thing I know I've got that ass Scopemi—Father Dominic Scopemi from Clifton Hill, the socialite, all tea and cakes and cocktail evenings—I've got him on the phone. He's telling me Theresa's been to see him, making all sorts of wild accusations. He's warning me. He thinks he's doing me a favour.

'He's a fool. He's a man who thinks people will find the love of the Lord if he turns his church into a club and cons the parish into mistaking social chitchat for contemplation and worship. I despise the man. He's a creep. He should be an Anglican. I've spoken out about his ideas from the altar, and he about mine. Thinks I'm too political or something. Now he's on the phone being all collegiate and nudge-nudge. That made me sicker than anything, Panther, I tell you, sick to my fucking guts.'

'He called Farndale a harlot.'

'He would. He hasn't got a clue what it's all about.'

'And you do, fornicator?'

'I sin with open heart, Panther. I sin against myself more than against others.'

'Try telling that to Easy Theresa.'

'I did.'

I laughed at that. It tasted like chilli in my throat.

'I *did*, man. I tried. She wouldn't listen. Wouldn't even look me in the eye. And then I've got the heavies on my back.'

'It could have been the cops, priest. Think on that.'

'No. It was a church matter.'

'Not any more, it's not.'

Like I cared. True, it was a side to Corrigan I'd never seen, and which I didn't like, but it hadn't surprised me. He was a priest, after all, and I've seen more evil, in whichever way you define it, perpetrated by priests and the holy than there are martyrs in the lists. In 1118, thereabouts, I watched as Geoffery, Archbishop of Rouen, sent his staff to beat and mutilate his own clergy in their churches. Many died in agony. Two centuries later, I watched as a mob slaughtered all the Jews of Strasbourg, blaming them for the plague, urged on and sanctified by Bishop Berthold II. The Farndale woman was small potatoes. She wasn't the first; she won't be the last; and her virtues and faults will all come to one. Or none.

Perhaps it was a case of old habits dying hard. Or perhaps the sorrow and anger I was feeling were for myself. Now look what you've gone and done, Joshua. Now look.

Just *look* at it.

'What happened to her, priest? She heard you were cleared by the bishops?'

'I guess. Scopemi phoned to congratulate me, the bastard. Can you believe that? Said we all had to stick together in this business, or some such bullshit.'

'What happened to her, priest?'

'I don't know. I asked around for a while. She went completely screwy, I heard. Then she disappeared.'

'Into the abyss.'

He fell silent, eyes closed. His lips moved.

'That's a waste of time. Somebody has to care before forgiveness can happen, Corrigan.'

'*I* care, Panther. Christ—'

'That trick never works. Offer a prayer to St Cuthbert, at least.'

He regarded me balefully. 'Cuthbert,' he said, 'is the patron saint of otters.'

I stood up. My bum ached from the hardness of the floor and the chill of the early morning. The whisky was gone.

The priest didn't notice. He was sunk in self-pity, maudlin drunk.

'What will happen to me, Panther?' he mumbled, not expecting a reply. 'I acted in good faith and the love of the Lord with Theresa, and I ballsed it up completely. I never laid a hand on Shelagh, Panther, not ever, not even in my dreams. Yet she died, Panther, died horribly, displayed in the house of God. *My* house of God. You know of Theresa. I take it the cops know, and I know what they must be thinking.'

'Do you blame them, priest?'

'No, I do not. I'd think the same, if I didn't know in my heart things were different. If I am trapped by the law and made to pay the price, then I'll set my face to that wall, Panther. I'll accept that fate, not as their punishment, man, but as *mine*.'

'Martyrdom is masturbation, priest.'

'Maybe it all is, Panther, in the end. Maybe we've all got it wrong. I'll find out in the end. What will be the judgement of the Lord upon his servant, a man who loves Him beyond life, a weak man who acted in weakness, mistaking it for the acts of a healer?'

'Nothing will happen, priest. If there is a god, he will not raise his hand to you in heaven.'

He stared at me, this desperate fool, ready to receive hope from any quarter, however hopeless. 'You think so?'

'I do. For he that spareth his rod hateth his son.'

And the priest wept, full of whisky, soaking in piss.

'I need that information on Shelagh Purdey, Corrigan, anything you can from the sex abuse support groups,' I said as I opened his door, the dawn chorus of myna birds and sparrows mocking in its joy. 'I need it tomorrow. Before the memorial service. Don't fail me, priest. Don't fail me as well.'

Outside, the morning had broken, like the first morning. A weak sun struggled, promising warmth in the day for the first time in months. That promise would be broken, and no one would be surprised.

My progress home was monitored, of course, by agents and agency unknown. There was a man in a suitably anonymous white car, a Daewoo, it looked like, parked on the opposite side of the road to the priest's house—not the commonest of sights at six in the morning. It stayed where it was, at least until I'd turned the corner.

The guy probably just radioed my movements to his colleague, a younger man, parked in the brown Falcon in the side street off Johnston, near the alleyway.

I waved to him as I walked past, carrying the cigarettes, milk and morning newspaper I'd picked up at the BP on the way. He turned his head away quickly, slid down into his seat.

Dipstick.

Some good news had awaited me at the BP. Taped to the window, near the door, was a handwritten notice, poignant with despair and loss. HAVE YOU SEEN OUR MUFFY? it said. WHITE SHIH TZU CROSS, BLACK COLLAR, REG TAG, VERY FRIENDLY, PART OF OUR FAMILY. LOST NEAR BRUNSWICK AND KING WILLIAM STS. REWARD. NO QUESTIONS ASKED.

One thing you could say about John the Baptist: when you put him on a case, he doesn't slouch about.

Once inside, I put on some music, gulped a pint of water, and sat on my uncomfortable sofa, left behind by the previous tenants. I rolled a joint to nullify the last nagging twitches of the speed, preparing for the sleep I knew I needed, and picked up the paper.

There was a Purdey update down low on page five. It noted that Corrigan's memorial service was scheduled for tomorrow afternoon, and was expected to draw a large attendance. Her death, the article noted, had sent 'a shiver of fear' through the community, and the service could be regarded as a symbolic act. Her murder served to remind everyone that the young and underprivileged were the most vulnerable members of society, and that her killer, or killers, had done to her in physical terms what the rest of us had already been doing to her in economic ones.

Four paragraphs from the bottom of the article was a quote from Gordon, indicating that he felt 'confident of a breakthrough very soon'. The last two pars, with a bullet indicator, noted that the body of a young man had been found in a house in Fitzroy, heroin overdose the suspected cause of death, confirmation pending, name not released.

Davey Parker.

Oh well.

It had been a few days. Decomposition would have been well under way. Even though the amount of smack in his system would still yield high—perhaps, indeed, record—results, the police would have a devil of a job constructing any sort of case. I doubted that young Parker had the sort of family or connections that would make a lot of fuss.

Gordon and Pordelli would have their suspicions, of course, but I was pretty certain that everyone else, from the coroner down, would work from the assumption of death by misadventure. Just another dead junkie in another malodorous room. There would be no come-back.

Anyway, I was apparently important to someone. If it was the cops, then that represented an extra level of protection. For now. If it wasn't, then, well, perhaps I had more pressing things to worry about. And perhaps I was so full of booze and amphetamines and marijuana and tiredness and confessions and violence that I couldn't give a shit.

And perhaps I had lost all grasp of reason and reality, endangered, as Beatrice Cowper had charged, in my delusion. I have thought about that, many times: that I am mad: commonplace, mortal, middle aged, and mad, no more Messiah than Yannis, the wide-eyed Greek man who wanders Smith Street in billowing silks, proclaiming himself to be Zeus on good days, Demis Roussos on bad. Of course I have. It gets to me sometimes, on dawns of cold and thanklessness and mire. How could it not?

But I am not mad. I know that. I know that because I choose to believe it. And when you take away the absolute, all that's left is choice. Because you never forget abandonment. Because I have suffered in your name, mocked and unregarded, for nigh on two millennia.

And I don't have the injuries to prove it.

I flicked through the rest of the paper, head resting on the sofa arm, my eyes skimming, brain doing whatever it would. MAN KILLED MOTHER 'FOR GOD' said one headline, SUICIDE FEAR IN PERTH CULT, another. Nothing really grabbed me. The joint was down to its filter. I'd have another, I thought. In a minute. Do the job properly.

The traffic on Smith and Johnston was building up for its daily rush-hour blockage, an ambulance trapped and screaming somewhere in its midst.

Shelagh Purdey a martyr.

Thus do saints begin. Thus do things reduce.

There was room for a Saint Shelagh, the name as yet untaken. In time, perhaps, it might come to pass. First the beatification, like Mary McKillop, and then the full megillah.

Of what would she be the saint, I wondered? The headless? Incest victims, perhaps. That one was still going spare.

There are many ways to glory in the heart of the Lord.

My favourite is Saint Juthwara. I never met her. No one, now at least, even knows whether she really existed, which is fine: non-existence has never been a barrier to advancement in this business. If she did, it was sometime before the turn of the first millennium. Her hagiography suggests she lived in Cornwall.

She had a pain in her chest one day. Her stepmother told her to put cream cheese on her tits.

And that was it. They made her a saint. If you can find an image of her, look: there she is: pious, virginal, with cream cheese all over her tits.

Her cult never really took off, which I regard as perhaps the single greatest failing within the history of the religion. The spin-doctors preferred more ballsy fare: St Joan, burnt at the stake; Crispina of Tagora, shaved and beheaded; Catherine of Alexandria, broken on the wheel, remembered now as a firework; St Dympna, raped and murdered by her royal father; more, more, endlessly more.

Imagine it, now, though. Thousand of nuns, all over

the world, pert and poised, walking around with naked breasts smeared in camembert, in brie, in warm mozzarella . . .

I noticed my hand was in my trousers, the newspaper splayed and spreading across the floor. I closed my eyes. I was turning and spinning and smelling cheese and skin, musty from enclosure, released into the morning chill. I tried to find a face, a face I knew, to place above the breasts. Not Brigid's. This was no act of love.

Beatrice Cowper.

Have I not remembered thee in my bed: and thought upon thee when I was wanking?

I felt the *petit mal*. Her face, for a moment, morphed with the tight-lipped image of Augustine: Late have I loved you, he was saying, beauty so old and so new; late have I loved you.

And then back, a lascivious curl to her lip: I trust you're not going to grope me. Surely, even you could see that would be a very foolish thing to do.

A slender dribble of cheese ran over her hard-topped nipple, curling, curving, extending into a smooth and viscous droplet, teasing towards my open mouth.

And then Brigid, wind-kissed, shadowed by concern: Not that which goeth into the mouth . . .

It was mid-afternoon when I awoke, cramped and uncomfortable, my arm numb from the pressure of my waistband, it's mission uncompleted, its aim now unachievable. The CD had been stuck for hours. *Amen-amen-amen-amen-amen*, it went.

✝

Many things are said, the truth of which is duff. I founded Christianity, for instance. That's one. Mariah Carey sings good songs. That's another.

And the day after a speed hike is suffused with nameless depression. That, too.

With me, at least, it usually takes twenty-four hours. My daylight nap, therefore, left me feeling surprisingly perky. I knew it wouldn't last, though: a couple of hours, not much more, and a leaden tiredness would descend, a gentle precursor to another long bout of sleep, and morning dawning dark and dismal, demons padding barefoot and surly.

After a shower and a shave, I pulled on some clothes—black jeans, Wallace and Gromit tee-shirt, frayed black denim jacket, spare boots—and boiled some water for the plunger. The light was already fading into winter dusk, the sky, for once, dry and only lightly salted with clouds.

There were just two matters on the agenda, before a restful evening in preparation for the morrow. The first concerned a suit. The second concerned a Shih tzu. Both, I decided, required a single strategy. I emptied the pockets, stuffed the trousers, shoes and jacket into a green plastic garbage bag, placed that inside a stiff brown paper carrier bag left over from an old clothes shopping expedition, and headed out.

The Falcon had been replaced by a Honda Civic. It

didn't move as I walked past it. Its driver, a plump middle-aged woman with a severe haircut and a bulky hiking jacket, didn't acknowledge me. I presumed someone would be assigned to follow me on foot, given that the traffic was harsh and they had no idea where I was heading. Which made two of us. I didn't try to identify which of the dozens of pedestrians around, local and stray, all quietly celebrating the rare period of clemency, was my tail. I had no need to move unobserved.

John, when I found him twenty minutes later, was several sheets to the wind and in fine form. He was sitting on a slatted bench in a tiny playground in one of the side streets, glass of pub water in one hand, skinny cigarette in the other. In front of him stood three small and solemn children, Caucasian, African and Asian, glancing at each other, and then at their mothers, two of whom were smiling, reassuring the third as they sat watching on another bench nearby.

As I walked up him, two of the youngsters had already been admitted to the old man's mystery, standing with glistening foreheads, watching an arthritic finger inscribe a sodden cross on the third, listening again to his meaningless gift.

'Mercifully hear our prayers, O Lord,' he mumbled, 'and graciously accept this oblation which we thy servants make to Thee. You are the Source and the Silence, the Mind and the Truth, the Logos and the Life. Your cruelty is our glory, for ever and ever. Amen.'

'What's it mean, mister?' the convert asked.

'Wouldn't have a clue, son.' John smiled. 'I just follow orders.'

I sat down next to him. Two of the children took a few paces back. The third ran to mother. The adults stood, suspicion in their eyes, called the pair and walked away, one staring back hard at me as if I'd just defiled her day. 'I am what I am, ladies,' I called out. 'I can't help it.'

John watched them go and then turned to me, a frown across his face. 'It must get to you, son,' he said.

'I'm used to it,' I replied. The pedestrians were fewer here, away from the shops. I thought I saw a man, perhaps the Falcon driver, familiar anyway, pause for a moment across the road, and then walk off. That made sense. They were watching my movements, but trying to be hip to discretion. A watcher here would stand out like a dick joke in the Mass. There were only two directions I could go, and no doubt someone would be waiting a block further up, or down, when I did. No problem. I would not disappoint.

I pulled the garbage bag from the carrier and put it down at John's feet. He looked at me quizzically. 'Ask not,' I said. 'Find an incinerator, and cast it into the flames.'

He nodded. 'Whatever you say, son.'

'How did the horse go?'

'You blew your cash, son.' He shook his head. 'Fell at the first corner, broke its neck, dead on the spot. Never seen anything like it.'

I grinned. There *is* justice, after all. 'Tell me about Muffy,' I said.

He just stared at me. 'The *dog*,' I prompted.

'How did you know I'd . . . ?' he started, and then smiled. 'Of course, you being you. Sorry, boss.'

'Is it done?'

He nodded. 'Poor little thing. I've got the nail in the wall, but there's still the boiling waiting.'

I made a mental note not to visit him for twenty-four hours. 'And?'

'She's alive, boy,' he said, suddenly animated. 'I got that much. For sure, alive. That's the good news.'

'And the bad?'

'She's alive in a cell somewhere. I got walls. I got a bare floor, a small room. A cell. There's a small table in one corner. Objects on the table: something, stuff, son. She's been there for years, doesn't expect to leave.'

I disagreed with his interpretation. This was good news indeed. A stationary target. 'Where?' I asked. 'What cell?'

The old man shook his head. 'It don't work like that.'

Typical. 'Anything else?'

He looked at me, a sudden squall of unease distorting his features. Then he turned away and stared at the glass in his hand.

'What?' I asked.

He closed his eyes for a moment, took a deep breath into his reluctant chest, let it out, and swallowed his holy water in a single gulp.

'She knows you, son,' he said, fear in his voice. 'She knows you.'

✝

# 7

I AM THOROUGHLY DISLIKEABLE. I know that. I am
perfectly aware of that. I am obnoxious, obscene,
violent, lustful in my thoughts and bitter in my memories. I am untrustworthy, deceitful, opportunist, sly,
brutal, usurious, unstable, uncharitable and vengeance,
always, is mine. I am a drunkard and a drug abuser. I
am capricious and heretic, appalling and cruel.

I am the son of Man.

I am all these things and victim. I went to die for
your sins, and ended up their living validation. I abhor
myself, but repent not in sack and ashes. I have nothing
to repent. I did not ask for this. You gave it me.

I wish only its return.

Come: take it back. Carry your own burdens.

Fat chance.

Refer, now, to my recent assertion that a twenty-
four-hour window of comparative buoyancy exists
between the anxiety of speed and the depression of its

passing. Such matters are imprecise, and biochemical mysteries complex. That which pertained in the past does not necessarily predicate the future. Fate can be tempted. Life is a bastard. The universe is hostile.

Whatever, by nine o'clock that evening I was feeling like shit, pinned to the sofa by a creeping poverty of spirit which rendered everything irritating and inane. The previous day, I realised, must have been just too demanding and disturbing. I'm not as young as I used to be, after all. It takes it out of you, eternal early middle-age.

I was getting somewhere, I knew, unravelling the mechanics of death. Where, though, I didn't have a clue. I decided my best strategy lay in ignoring the iniquities of the world for the evening, letting the downer run its course, and waiting to see if fresh ideas occurred in the coming of the morning.

I'd had a couple of snorts at the Bradford after leaving John the Baptist to his rounds. It was then that the depression started to descend. Two joints back at the warehouse had levelled things off a bit, and all I needed, I knew, was something to occupy my mind for a while. Trouble is, I have a lot of mind.

The television offered only banalities. The adverts warned me not to drink and drive, not to smoke, not to lie out in the sun and not to neglect my milk. Another assured me my life would be better if only I sang a twee little song with my name in it. I switched it off, apostate. Patti Smith had seemed too uncomfortable, too close; the Smashing Pumpkins too prone to bursts of guitar-led fury which I didn't need. I tried Tori Amos, but she sang about crucifying herself.

I had tried reading, but there was little in the house of a contemporary nature. There are times, sad to say, when glancing through Tertullian's *To the Martyrs*, or Bede's *A History of the English Church and People*, simply doesn't push my buttons. I glanced across again at the pile of books, trying to remember if there was any-thing—anything at all—in it which might distract. The fat floppy disk I'd removed from Image Makers was over there, leaning up against my translation copy of the gnostic gospels of Nag Hammadi.

The image amused me, for a moment, as much as anything could. The gnostic gospels were written by a bunch of mystics, maybe a hundred years after I failed to die. They were Christians, in a sense, although the term probably would have meant as little to them as it does to me. Peaceful types, by and large, they thought believers who yearned for martyrdom were stupid. They held men and women to be equal. They thought I was okay—pretty special, in fact—but it didn't do much good to get hung up on me. They thought God, Yahweh, maybe any god, was a *demiurge*, a false god, a shallow destructive thing obscuring a bigger, better, more distant spirit beyond. If they were around today, they'd all be in Greenpeace.

They were ruthlessly vilified and exterminated, of course, by just about everybody, these harmless lovers, including Paul's mob. Bishop Ireneaus hated them. Tertullian thought they were evil. They were ended in blood, and their writings, scratched on papyrus and excluded from the Testament, were found buried in an urn in 1945 in a village in Egypt. The man who found them had been on his way to murder a chap who had killed the first man's father. His mother used many of the texts as fuel for her cooking.

With papyrus and pigment the Gnostics pondered peaceful philosophies. Two thousand years later we use floppy disks to flog kumquats. Thus do we progress.

And thus do we become depressed again.

I needed to pacify myself, so decided, for a change, to haul out the sonic big guns. I grabbed a recording of Allegri's *Miserere*, done by the Tallis Scholars. The mood I was in, I reckoned it was the only thing which could shift it.

I first heard the piece sometime in the early seventeenth century, when I was passing through Rome looking for work. Gregorio Allegri wrote it specifically for the papal choir, and it was so beautiful, so gorgeous and lush, that even the most cloth-eared cardinal recognised it as something very special indeed. That was why, in the spirit of giving, the powers that be kept it a secret, promising severe and physical punishment for anyone who attempted to smuggle the score out of the Sistine Chapel. I know, because I tried.

Mozart did it, in the end, lifetimes later. He heard it and remembered it, note for note, carrying it away in his head.

Mo*zart*!

Sit, boy.

I did, firing up another joint and closing my eyes as the voices of the scholars began their slow ascent to glory. The text is Psalm 51, thankfully in Latin.

*Ecce enim in inquitatibus conceptus sum et in peccatis concepit me mater mea.*

Behold, in guilt I was conceived and in sin did my mother conceive me.

Not me, baby, not me.

I felt the muscles in my shoulders relax as the voices washed over me, the rolling, meditative incantations below, and the flying, swooping falsetto above, far too strong and blood-rich to be shackled by the penitence of the words. It was not a cry of triumph in a new church, but the keening of the wind through the mutilated branches of the old trees, subversive and seditious. Did old Gregorio realise? Did he wonder from where his sudden passions came? Did he just ascribe them to yours truly?

Well off the mark. I was just a punter and, man, he blew me away. He was one of the greats, up there with Palestrina, Puccini, and Iggy Pop.

By the second half of the final verse, when the aching yearnings of the soloists and choir at last find common ground and greater strength, I was flat on my back, slack jawed, watching lava lamp impressions on the inside of my eyelids. I had reached, at last, a place of peace, and didn't want the sound to stop. I never do.

It always does, though.

William Mundy's *Vox Patris Caelestis* was coming up

next, a shallow and mediocre piece, by the end of which, I drowsily reflected, I should be well asleep.

My ears, however, were not the only ones tasting love. The *Miserere* ended, and in the silence that followed there came a knock on the door: three taps, sharp, solid, polite, origin unknown.

I sat up, snap-awake again, more annoyed than unnerved by the interruption, my head spinning from rising so suddenly. There was a couple of possibilities, I figured. The police were clearly at the top of the list, but the impact of the knock didn't sound like it had the weight of a short-tempered detective behind it. It was unlikely they'd be so restrained.

Anyway, if the cops had anything for me, they could just shove it under the door, as per instructions.

Maybe it was one of my clients. Davey Parker had known my address, after all, and I hadn't been at my usual spot for a couple of evenings. Rashid, Spring-Head, shaking and sick, seeking salvation? Caroline, perhaps, with information?

I doubted it, though. There is no romance of the street, no chivalrous code innate among the scorned and disturbed. There was no legion of the wretched out there anxious to help good old uncle Joe in his quest for justice. Heroin addiction precludes altruism and, anyway, good old uncle Joe was a bastard.

At a stretch, it could be someone lost, someone looking for one of the businesses in the area, or one of the other inhabited commercial spaces. It had happened before. (Hello, is your name Jim and are you a sculptor?

No, my name is Joe and I am the ineffable love of God made flesh. Jim lives two doors down.)

At that point, whoever it was made it plain they weren't going to go away. A second tattoo sounded, a little harder to compete with the first notes of the British composer. (Tell me why, I thought, I don't like Mundy.) I stood up and started walking softly to the door. I wondered for a moment whether it might not be Beatrice Cowper standing on the other side. I didn't like that thought.

It required both hands to open my door, which swung inward; one for each lock. There was no light on the landing. Slowly, I clicked the latches, top and bottom, took a half-step back and pulled the door with me, half a cubit, peering around from its protection.

There was a split second to react before the boot hit my face. I managed just to turn cheek, and copped the toe full-bore on my jawline. The impact and the surprise knocked me off balance, making me let go of the door and stagger backwards two steps in a reflexive attempt to remain upright.

This, in retrospect, was not the wisest move I could have made. Some deep part of me was still coming to that conclusion as, head down, I checked my momentum and started to turn back to face my attacker. A forearm slammed into my other cheek, knocking me off-kilter in the opposite direction. It was, I sensed, the first instalment of a two part combination, so I rolled with its impetus, spun and dropped to one knee, feeling the slipstream of the follow-up whisper past me like slander in the market place.

I landed, back to my attacker, within reach of one of the folding director's chairs by the table. Continuing the arc I'd begun in defence, I turned to attack, grabbing the back of the chair with both hands, swinging it and rising to my feet in a single fluid sweep.

Until that moment I had not identified my assailant. There had been no time. I knew only that the assault was serious and professional, requiring my full attention. I swung the chair at head height, putting all my weight behind it. At the limit of the swing, at the moment I expected to feel a jarring resistance along my arms and hear the sound of tubular steel bludgeoning into flesh and bone and cartilage, I felt just the resistance of empty air, and realised my mistake. Sophia Ognenis stood only five feet tall, and with the merest nod of her head ducked below my weapon's trajectory and stepped inside my guard.

I caught a fleeting glimpse of her face: set, straight-lipped, calm. The heel of her left hand shot round and set off a thunderclap in my right ear, her right knee thumped home into my crotch, flashed back, hit the ground and lent tactical support to her left leg as it stretched out parallel to the floor and short-kicked, once, twice, into my side between ribcage and hip. The chair clattered to the ground behind her.

Bent over, moving backwards and trying, with little success, to think, all at the same time, I lashed out a blind defensive backhand and felt my knuckles glance home, somewhere near her temple but missing her eye. I heard a sharp intake of breath and a swearword. Then lights flashed inside my brain as her boot came through in a savage round-house kick to my head. The force knocked me to the floor again, onto my back. I could see her, still upright, close and to my side, weight on her left leg, the right one moving back, ready to strike.

For a moment I considered surrender. I considered begging for mercy, for release, for compassion. I was ready to commence dialogue.

Then I saw into the mind of god. There, lying on the floor. There, battered. There, in a moment of min-uscule length and immeasurable depth, silencing the roar inside my head, bringing balming comfort to the gritted contractions of my face and belly and balls. There, in degradation and defeat. There, a glimmer of infinitude.

No Yahweh was this, no El Shaddai, no sharp and jealous demiurge, no sectarian warlord. This was a glimpse inside unspeakable perfection, the resonant not-there where everything is and nothing becomes. This was where all exists, and doesn't form, a place that is not a place, yet is, and is full of nothing but possi-bilities, unending possibilities chanced upon among an eternity of possibilities, found and unfound, possibilities nevertheless, waiting only to be given form, defined, limited, rendered, made whole, fragile, cut-price, and diminished.

Knowledge descended upon me and, with it, entered hope.

I knew at that moment, as I had never known before, of contemplations discovered five hundred years before my birth in a land as far away as travel and imagination could permit. I knew, suddenly, of K'ung-Fu-tzu—Confucius—and his followers Lao-tzi and Xung-tzi. I received their names. I knew of their contemplation of *dao*, their ponderings and passive discoveries. I knew, mostly, of their thoughts of conflict, their strategies for survival, their quiet understanding of the paradox of blood. I knew of Xung-tzi's book, a holy book called *The Art of War*.

Had I known of it before? Is there a difference between revelation and remembering? Is one a greater gift than the other? What happens when the mind is jogged by an eight-hole boot with genuine leather upper and acid-resistant sole?

I knew, immediately and passionately, that somewhere in that body of understanding lay the thought that would help me defeat my enemy. All of a sudden, the spirit moved, and entered me.

Unfortunately, I knew something else, too.

I had never read *The Art of War*.

Sophia Ognenis's right boot slammed into midriff.

I must do that, I thought to myself.

The boot slammed again, into the top of my head.

Soon, I concluded, as my mind became one with the *dao*.

✠

I did not try to move when I woke up, not even my eyes. I remained still and tried to understand. My position was horizontal, and hunched. I could feel the cold hardness of the floor beneath me, the fluttering of dust particles at the front of my nostrils. Must sweep up tomorrow, I thought, and then realised that it was not perhaps the most useful thought to be having right at that moment.

There was no music, which meant—what? After Mundy on the album was Palestrina's *Missa Papae Marcelli*, comprising the Kyrie, Gloria, Credo, Sanctus et Benedictus and two Agnus Deis, so I'd been maybe forty minutes out in all. Now there was silence, or what passes for silence in a warehouse in a crowded inner-suburb.

Or not quite. I kept still for another couple of minutes, to confirm. There. A slither of sound: a susurrus of paper, somewhere else in the room. I forced my eyes open. They were not swollen, but with the admittance of light came the awakening of my body and a dull rush of pain. I held it in, and concentrated, willing focus.

Sophia Ognenis was sitting cross-legged on the sofa. She was wearing a black, red and white Moschino tracksuit jacket, over a red crew-necked top. Her trousers were black and baggy, her boots by Blundstone. Her face, I could see, was a mask of contentment, unmarked by my one practical thump. She was reading a book. I couldn't make out which one.

I groaned. It was not a conscious decision. The

224

receptionist looked up, and smiled, bright and sharp.

'Hallo again,' she said, all jolly. 'Like you said, I'm laying my calves on your altar. Listen to this—' She jabbed quickly at the open page of her book. 'Listen, I mean, sorry, what crap: "Our fathers were religious men and feared God. Now in their places a wicked generation has grown up, sinful sons, falsifiers of the Christian faith, who run the course of all unlawful things without discrimination." Don't these people *know* it's the twentieth century, nearly the twenty-first?'

She giggled, shaking her head like a schoolgirl delighted by a pop star's scandal.

I groaned again, searching to find the reference. My jaw worked only with great reluctance. 'No,' I said, the word sounding muffled and swollen. 'It was written in the twelfth, by William of Tyre. He reckoned the crusaders weren't tough enough.'

She flicked back a couple of pages, grinned. 'Ten points!' she exclaimed. 'Well done. Then again, it's your book, isn't it, so you should know it.' She closed the paperback, and tossed it on the floor. I felt its impact through my cheek. 'Why do you read this stuff? You've got an awful lot of it. Shit-loads. Who are all these people? Are you a fundamentalist or something?'

'No,' I replied. 'Merely fundamental.'

Very slowly, I pushed myself up into a sitting position. My head spun and my focus swam, momentarily distracting my attention from the pulsing traumas of my body. Gingerly, I ran my hand over my stomach, my ribs, my balls, my jaw and my head. Sophia watched

225

me, head tilted to one side, curious and amused.

'Don't worry,' she chirped. 'Nothing broken, no lasting damage, I'm better than that.' She picked up my Dunhills from the floor by the sofa, shoved my lighter in the packet, and tossed it toward me. It scudded to a halt in reach. I grabbed it, but decided my hand was shaking too much to chance a burn just then.

'Why did you come here?' I asked, doing a slow, experimental turn of my neck.

She raised her hand and waved it. In it was the floppy disk. Her answer raised lots more questions—so many, in fact, and so fast, that they cannoned into and tripped over each other in the rush to get to the front of my brain. Luckily, I had another to hand, one I'd prepared earlier.

'How did you find me?'

She dismissed it with an airy wave of her small hand. 'Oh, I just asked around, Mr Myra.'

That stopped me. In the beginning was the Word. And the Word, in this case, thus revealed, elliptical and gleaming, was *bullshit*. I decided not to employ it. Just yet.

'How did you know I had it?'

'Because it was missing, of course,' she said in a tone which indicated, clearly, that I was being a bit of a silly-billy. 'There are only a certain number of them, and one was missing. Someone chucked a brick through the window downstairs but didn't take anything. Mindless vandalism, said the cops, and that's what the boss said to me, too, when I went into work. Mindless vandalism—well, it's okay, but I don't believe too much in mindlessness. I don't think it's possible, not without surgery. So I did a quick inventory upstairs and, hey, it took me a while, but I found one of the zip disks was missing. Now, that's a no-no, because the boss is very careful about these things. He's very insistent. Only *he* can handle them, and only he can send them out. He was very definite about that: authorised customers only, the client's express wish, deal-breaker otherwise.

'Now, I figured, Mr Myra. Who'd want one of *them*? Well, strikes me I didn't know, because, hey, you know, kumquats, big deal, but, there it is, one missing, and it sure wasn't a poltergeist. Nothing just *happens*, you know? So, I thought, maybe whoever took it just, you know, took it, like a souvenir? Yeah, maybe. So who would do that, I think, who would go to all the trouble to break in, cover it up, and nick off with something worthless to them? Well, from there it was easy. From there, it was just a matter of thinking: have there been any vengeful and violent loonies in recently? Well, isn't it, it wasn't a tough answer.'

I'd managed to get a cigarette into my mouth, lit. I puffed on it, but decided not to risk taking it out again. I nodded at her, paying tribute to her wisdom.

'So you looked up Nicean Films in the phone book, and here you are.'

She covered it well, nodding back. 'Pretty much.'

'Why are the disks—what did you call them?'

'Zip disks.'

227

'Why are the zip disks so important to Graeme Purdey, Ms Ognenis?'

'Sophia, please, and I don't know. They just are. Why are they important to you?'

'They're not. It was, as you surmised, just a souvenir. Why did you attack me? Why didn't you just come around in the morning and ask me for it?'

'Two reasons, Mr Myra. First, the boss doesn't know it's missing yet, and I'm all for a quiet life. I believe in stopping problems before they start. Second, you've shown yourself to be nasty, and I wasn't going to take any chances. I'm only a slip of a thing, after all.'

I chuckled. I couldn't help it. It made her eyes narrow.

'Also, I think you should know,' she said, an edge having crept into her voice, 'I don't believe it, but I've been told it, up to you, whatever you make of it, I've been told I have a borderline personality disorder, I think they called it, a propensity to violent overreaction. I am a stranger to remorse, apparently, which, coupled with the fact that I've trained in various martial arts and kick-boxing since I was nine years old, makes me a bit lethal. I don't believe it, of course, never have. I've got a much better explanation: I just like beating people up.'

'When they deserve it.'

She smiled again, testing the idea. 'Sometimes,' she said, shrugging. 'You know. Whatever.'

My jaw was clenched so tightly as I levered to my feet I nearly bit the cigarette filter in half. Sophia watched me, intent but with professional dispassion. She knew the damage she had done, and saw in me, correctly, no immediate threat. I did a reasonably good job of projecting a certain battered dignity as I walked slowly across the room, past the sofa, to the whisky bottle. She shook her head when I waved it in her direction.

'Why *did* you break in, Mr Myra?' she asked.

It was my turn to shrug. It hurt. 'Nick. No reason. I don't like being humiliated. Why are you still here?'

'Not very polite, Nick. Come here and sit down. The business is done, and I don't, you know, like being all business. I like a bit of a chinwag at the end of a long day. Know what I mean?' She patted the sofa. Glass in one hand, smoke in the other, I perched on its edge. It took me a while. She smiled. I'm not very good at small talk, especially when my teeth are rattling and my tongue is swollen. I did my best.

'I thought you were wearing Doc Martens last time you assaulted me,' I managed.

She looked at her boots, shucked her shoulders, giggled. 'You have to be versatile. It makes life easier. There, isn't this cosy? Now then, Nick, tell me, something I wanted to ask you, tell me, given your beliefs, all this book stuff here, tell me: How would what's-his-name, William of Tyre, yeah, rate you as a crusader? See, I remember it. How harsh would his judgement be on you?'

A series of horrible possibilities went through my mind. What on earth was this woman, this avowedly *dangerous* woman, on about? I said the only thing I could. 'What on earth are you on about?'

'Your Russian merchandise, Nick, you know, daddy, daughter, with hair, without.'

So this is the gig, I thought. The outraged refusal, the maintenance of respectability, the violent penetration, the sly offer via an underling. Fine. Graeme Purdey was coming to the party, after all. The view from the mountain can be breathtaking. He was of his nature, denials to the contrary; as in the first person, so in the third, substance indivisible. Shelagh's father edged back to the top of the suspects list.

The problem with a cover story invented on the spur of the moment is remembering it in the fullness of time. I thought fast. Sin, falsification, judgement. Address the question. Keep it going. Ignore the pain.

'Royalties,' I said. 'Like I told your boss, they're all on royalties.'

'Transnational royalties, Nick.' She shook her head in mock disbelief. 'I'm impressed. Big job, that, I'd expect. You'd probably need bookkeeping, money transfers—trust funds, maybe?—destination accounts, probably, I'd think. What about contracts, Nick? I'd doubt that, but, you know, royalties in Russia on sales in Australia. Currency exchange. Disbursements. Accounting. Phantoms. That'd take a fair bit of organisation, eh? Big job for just you.'

My head was pounding. I was in the wilderness. I nodded. I shook. I tried to see where this was going. 'I've had bigger jobs,' I managed. 'I've been at the top of some pretty big organisations in my time.'

'I had a look around, Nick, while you were out.'

I was supposed to laugh at the pun. I didn't. I met her eyes, stared, still, held them, did the look.

'I thought, well,' she continued, not worried in the slightest. 'I thought, you looked around in South Melbourne, I'll look around here. Equal and opposite reactions, yeah? Fair for you, fair for me, right, that's how it works. You've no computer, funny that, and, see, Nick, I can't see how you could work the business without one. You need records, information, data transfers—I mean, you're here, not Moscow—'

'The details take care of themselves. My father set up the company.'

Straight away: 'Is he still in the business? How do I get in touch with him?'

'I don't know.'

She didn't believe me.

'Whatever. You're not there, you're here, and, like, you can't be everywhere at once, can you?'

'You'd be surprised.'

'I doubt it.'

'You think I work from home? I'm not that stupid.'

'Where do you work from, then?'

'I'm not that stupid, either. Your point, Sophia? My hospitality is running thin.'

Her eyes sparked. Her head tilted left, a perky smile flicked on, one shoulder shifted back, half an inch, enough. 'You want to try to throw me out, mister?'

she said in a little girl voice. I said nothing. It was all I could think of at the time.

'The point, Nick, is this. I think there's less to you than meets the eye. I think you're a try-hard—no offence, but I do. I think you've maybe got hold of a good deal, but one that's a good deal bigger than you. I think you're in way deep and doing your best to get control. Nothing wrong with that, Nick, good on you, but, you know, I think maybe you could do this thing a whole lot better, you know, in a partnership situation.'

Aha.

'With your boss?'

'He might be interested, yeah, you never know, letting bygones be bygones and all that. Really, he's a nice guy. You caught him on a bad day—troubles at home, I think. His daughter was murdered, did you read about it? Then his wife had a prowler, or something, I don't know, and now, you know, there's a pride thing for him, but, whatever, he'll get over it. He's got the office. He's got the potential cover. He might like a slice. All you need to do is show him the figures.'

'What figures?'

'Naked and numeric, both lots.'

And I'm thinking: Shelagh Purdey's post-mortem crucifixion was theatrical. More. It was cinematic. I could almost see the final shot, pulling back down the aisle, her greying, purpling body growing smaller, slipping into blackness, violin music on the soundtrack and no credits rolling. Fathers and light. The light of the father. The dog had not died in vain, after all.

So: will he show me his, if I show him mine? Of course, he'd have to show me his *first*. That's the way these things work. He's making the offer. He has to establish his cred.

And, anyway, I didn't have any. Of either.

'Maybe,' I said, crawling crabwise to conclusions. 'This is a specialised market. What experience does he have in—'

There was a knock at the door.

The moment froze.

I looked at Sophia. She shook her head, tight, short. She looked at me.

I kept looking at Sophia.

'Honestly,' she said.

She uncrossed her legs.

This was too coincidental for my liking. *His wife had a prowler, or something, I don't know, and now, you know, there's a pride thing for him* ... Twice slighted, Graeme Purdey, twice violated. A proud man. Was this to be his reply, the reclaiming of his manhood? Had he sent forth his assistant, his *accomplice* (his *amour*? He likes them small, his ex-wife had said), to soften me up, damage me, render me incapable of retaliation? Had he now arrived, as planned, to finish the job (it's *man's* work, brutality) with a baseball bat, a knife, a gun, aided and abetted by the creature to my side? It wouldn't surprise me. It's the sort of thing I'd do.

233

And I am full of the likenesses of you. Open up, and let me in.

Again, the knock, controlled but impatient. Sophia shook her head again. Her eyes gave vent to the presence of secrets, to knowledge unrevealed.

'Did you lock the door?' I asked.

'Nope.' There was no triumph in her voice.

I leaned into her, fast, and put my left arm hard around her small shoulders, ignoring the pain in my own, pressing her into my side. I slipped the other up to her neck, loose, like a precursor to leaning into a kiss, except that my thumb and forefinger pressed in each side of her windpipe, lightly but with undeniable threat. 'Come in!' I yelled.

She tried to move, to position herself, but I hung on tight and buried my lips in her ear. Her neck smelled like sanctuary, pale downy hairs now visible on the back of it. 'Listen, bitch,' I whispered. 'If this is anyone you know, you shall be the shield of faith, wherewith ye shall be able to quench all the fiery darts of the wicked. You will be the helmet of salvation and the sword of the spirit. Anything comes flying my way, you'll cop it first.'

She was out-manoeuvred and knew it, pro that she was. She twitch-nodded, and looked to the door. Her eyes went wide.

Two uniformed police constables walked in, hats off. One of them was carrying a large beige envelope. The other held a clipboard.

We held the pose. What else could we do? 'Mr

Panther?' said the one with the envelope, diffident. 'Mr Joshua Ben Panther?'

I nodded. They seemed a little embarrassed at the scene, and I could see they meant no harm. In their mouth was found no guile; for they were without fault before the battered sofa of God. It would have been polite to stand and greet them, especially since I'd already figured out what was in the package they had brought. To do so, however, would have been unwise. My hand felt Sophia's skin go hot and taut, thrumming with the anger of deception, her blood fired by sudden war and rumours of war. To the casual observer, she probably looked calm and comfy—she was good, no doubting that—but there are no secrets from me.

She was as still as the dead, awaiting salvation, prepared for fire.

The cop waggled his hand about a bit, unsure whether to offer it or not. I didn't reciprocate. I could hear Sophia breathing, slow and even, slow and even. Warrior breath. Psycho simmers. Building.

The envelope was proffered. 'Detective Sergeant Gordon said you were needing this, sir,' the constable said, oblivious to the terrible power of his phrasing. 'It's a photograph of—' he quickly pulled his notebook from his top pocket—'one Theresa Mary Barndale.'

'*Farn*dale,' I corrected, stupid, fallible and anal, as I am.

'Sorry, sir. The ink's run in the rain. He said we were to drop it off whenever we were in the area tonight and not tactically engaged. He said you

235

wouldn't mind the hour because you wanted to get on with it. Farndale, as you said, wanted for questioning in connection with a murder inquiry you're helping with, is that right?'

Ever held a hand grenade, status of pin unknown?

I thanked the officer, and turned to Sophia. 'Isn't that nice of them, dear?' I said, my finger and thumb flexing gently into her throat, my meaning violently clear. She nodded, said nothing.

'Well,' I said, attempting bluff, 'thanks a lot. Perhaps you could just leave it on the table on your way out?'

The second cop shook his head. 'Sorry, sir, but you've got to sign for it.' He wiggled his clipboard. 'If that photograph ends up needed as evidence, we'll need to know who's got it, won't we?'

He smiled. The dickhead smiled. Then he held out the board, but did not step closer.

I was left, thus, with little option. I grinned at the cops, raised my eyebrows, trying to be both knowing and apologetic. 'Don't move, darling,' I said to Sophia, brushing my lips against her ear, 'this won't take a moment.'

I was right. It didn't. The nanosecond I lifted my hand from her skin, she struck. Her right arm, which I had hoped was pinned tightly between our torsos, sprung free and up, sharp at the elbow, delivering the back of her fisted hand right into my nose. I leant away on reflex, which gave her just enough room to follow through with her elbow into my cheek.

I'm not quite sure what happened next, except that

it involved somehow another close encounter between her Blundstones and my head. She was standing in front of me, me still seated, shouting a lot, shouting questions, and not giving me time to reply.

'*Panther!*' she was yelling. 'Panther? Myra? Panther? Who the fuck *are* you? You're a *cop*, you bastard, you're a fucking *cop!*'

Then she slapped me across the face, which demonstrated just how good she was, given that it was swaying back and forth on an unpredictable trajectory at the time. At this point, the two shocked young constables decided they had better intervene, domestic or not. They grabbed her under the shoulders, and forced her hands behind her back. She struggled and swore, spitting at me.

'Jesus,' I managed, playing the role, 'you're a mad woman. Get the fuck out of here.'

'Fucking *cop*,' she spat again. 'Pig. Bastard.'

'Come on, Miss,' said the one with the clipboard, 'I think you'd better come with us.'

Sophia Ognenis raged and strained against the arms of her captors, fury in her face. There was more yelling and scuffling as the threesome made it to the door, and more still, I heard, as they crashed awkwardly down the stairs.

I had stopped paying attention by then, however. There were other things to think about. Three of them, in fact.

There was the fact that I had not signed the clipboard. That was good.

There was the fact that my nose was bleeding rather profusely. That was bad.

And there was the fact that next to me, on the sofa, in the fragile, warm indentation made by Sophia's buttocks, was the zip disk. She hadn't stashed it. She hadn't thrown it. She hadn't dropped it. She had *left* it there.

That was strange. Very strange indeed.

✝

Morning came in a mess of contradictions, as usual.

I was sore as hell, with more swellings in unusual places than a beauty-pageant in a cancer clinic. My nose ached, but wasn't broken. Despite appearances to the contrary, Sophia had pulled her blows during the previous night's denouement.

Did that mean she liked me? Probably not. Probably it meant she had a use for me. Or her boss did.

Whoever I was.

Which meant she *didn't* think I was a cop, appearances, once more, to the contrary. Also, of course, she didn't think I was Nick Myra of Nicean Films, see previous clause. She never did. I knew that, from the moment I woke up on the floor and asked the right question for a change. She didn't ask around for my address and she didn't look me up in the phone book.

Which left several blindingly obvious questions and not a few disturbing possibilities. If she had known of the fiction of Myra, had she known also of the fact of

238

Panther? If so, who had told her? For once, I was prepared to bet against Gordon. I was pretty sure the pair had never met. His knowledge of her would have come purely from a written report circulated from the South Melbourne cops. If it *had* been him, then she would surely have had some inkling of my reputation with the man, and perhaps even the uneasy alliance which currently persisted. No one sane—or even borderline sane, as she seemed to be—in possession of that type of information would have then gone off the deep end as she did when the uniforms walked in.

Unless the performance was *all* for my benefit, instead of just partially.

Probably not the cops, then.

Then who? What sort of information network did Graeme Purdey have? Did he genuinely not know of his receptionist's violent visit? And his interest, suddenly, in the incest films ... Surely, surely, the man must have had an inkling at least that the bearded monster who groped his wife and the bearded maniac who cracked his nose were one and the same. I had violated him, his home and his spouse, once in the name of his murdered daughter, and once in the name of the horror he brought to her life.

Not a good basis upon which to establish a clandestine and thoroughly illegal business relationship, I would have thought. A very good basis on which to set me up, turn me in, achieve his revenge and leave the world safe for ordinary decent folk who prefer to destroy their children in private, though.

239

I pushed the plunger down through water silted by Lavazza, hungry for understanding. None of my questions would be answered while Sophia remained, as I was pretty sure she would, in police custody. Whoever she was, and whatever agenda she was pursuing on behalf of her employer, she was of no value to me behind bars. And, anyway, there was the matter of the zip disk, which she had deliberately left behind, a strange move considering that she had earlier tracked it down and beaten the crap out of me to retrieve it. Graeme Purdey obviously hated the idea of unauthorised persons grabbing his kumquats, but even that, apparently, was preferable to having them fall into the hands of the constabulary.

I remembered my own night in the cells, the harshness, the stench, the schizo, the fear soaked into the paint, the danger and despair, the terrible vulnerability of being a prisoner. Truth be told, I have experienced that many times, and many times worse. But did I really want to feel responsible for putting someone else through that, someone whose last act, in an evening of mystery, had been one perhaps of contrition, an ambivalent reaching out, an attempt at allegiance, a small secret signal to suggest the common ground of the bereft?

Of course I did. She left the damn disk with me because she considered me easier to bash up than the police.

That was an unworthy thought. I reminded myself forcefully of who I was. I had, did I not, an elementary responsibility to find forgiveness in my heart.

When it suited me, anyway.

Actually, I thought again, it was her *second* last act, dropping the zip. Her proper last act had been to kick me in the face.

I took rather longer than usual over coffee that morning.

It was raining, of course, a thin chant of nurture on the corrugated iron of the roof, constant, without need of converts. Through the spackling grit of the window the sky seemed uniform, heavy and white, more self-assured than threatening, promising a bitter-silent backdrop for Shelagh Purdey's commemoration that afternoon.

The envelope was on the table, where I had tossed it the night before in the hour of locking up and calming down which followed the departure of my visitors and preceded the descent of anaesthetic sleep. I slit its edge and withdrew a ten-by-eight photograph, a degraded reprint of an opportunist colour snapshot.

Theresa Mary Farndale, at the time, had been smiling, saying something perhaps, nothing important, turning to the lens, hailed, instantly amused and disconcerted by the flash. The shot had caught her from the chest up, fairly tight, capturing her whole head and a little air above. The background was indistinct, the light insufficient to reveal more than that she was inside a building, a large room, like a warehouse squat. I could make out a plane of bare, ruddy brick, diminishing along a sharp perspective, broken by what appeared to

241

be, I was pretty sure, a dog-eared poster for the Madonna film *Who's That Girl?*

That established two matters in my mind, both obvious. First, the date must have been around the time Farndale was starting to visit St Cuthbert's. Second, the poor girl had clearly needed help.

Her hair was certainly gingerish, although the precise shade was impossible to determine, a babble of robust and idiosyncratic curls which writhed about to just above her shoulders. The face was plump, but gently so, blemished around the chin and pallid. The lips were precise, wide and firm, frozen between passing smile and emerging pout. The nose was aquiline and proud. The flash had caught her eyes, painting her pupils, wide in the dimness of the room, blank and red, cold suns full of the silent knowledge of violence and betrayal.

The image and the instant rendered her a paradox: concrete but ephemeral, a teenager Gothic-eyed and ancient, a woman-child forever present in a moment constant gone, an innocent succubus, a wretched perfection, affirmed by her flaws.

I could see why the priest had had trouble. There had been deep secrets inside Theresa Mary Farndale. And nothing is more seductive than the promise of mysteries revealed.

I stared at the photograph for the duration of a Dunhill, searching for explanations, clues, hope. I recognised her. I had never seen her before. Many times. The gnostic gospels came to memory, again. There was a poem found in that urn, author unknown, called "Thunder: Perfect Mind". Part of it rose now from her blood–sun eyes:

> For I am the first and the last.
> I am the honoured one and the scorned one.
> I am the whore and the holy one.
> I am the wife and the virgin.
> I am the daughter.
> I am the members of my mother.
> I am the barren one
>     and many are her sons.

She is in a cell. She knows me, this stranger, John had said, swallowing his sacrament in haste.

And now I knew her. Wherever she was, no matter that a decade may have etched and stretched her with a cruelty denied to me, I would recognise her. I would not forget the face. Why had the verse come to me, I wondered. Was it because of the couplet with which the poet had prefaced it?

> *Do not be ignorant of me anywhere or any time. Be on your guard! Do not be ignorant of me.*

I slipped the shot back in the envelope and threw on my denim jacket, wishing I still had my leather one. The zip disk went in the breast pocket. Before leaving, I telephoned the Collingwood police station and spoke to the desk sergeant. It was all a misunderstanding, I said, a tiff, no real harm meant or done. I didn't wish to press charges. Please, set my person free.

The Falcon was on duty in the side street, beaded by rain. The bloke in the driver seat was hunched into a fat padded hiking jacket. His side window was a

243

quarter open, no doubt to prevent the cabin fogging up. I knocked on it with one bent knuckle. He looked at me, saying nothing, very still. I could see both his hands, which were holding a glossy gossip magazine. The morning tabloid, I noticed, was on the seat next to him. The main headline said FORMER PUPILS ACCUSE NUNS: HUNT FOR BODIES AT EX-CONVENT SCHOOL. I could also make out LOYALISTS, IRA, CLASH AT 'MARTYR' FUNERAL, and, near the bottom of the page, HUNDREDS EXPECTED TO GATHER FOR MUR-DERED GIRL.

For whosoever shall call upon the name of the Lord shall be saved. At least according to Pauly. Me, I don't have an answering machine.

'Do you know Graeme Purdey?' I asked.

Nothing moved, not even twitched. He looked familiar, this close. Not the man in the Honda Civic. Not the man beneath the kettle cascade. Somewhere else, somewhere else.

'How about Sophia Ognenis? Detective Senior Sergeant Gordon? Pordelli?'

Still nothing.

'The Bee Gees, then?'

'Fuck off,' he said. He didn't smile, though. Maybe he liked the Bee Gees, in which case I was in more trouble then I thought.

'As you wish,' I said. 'Look, I'm just going to pop down Smith Street to the chemist. The second chemist, not the first one. The one near the video store—that's the video store on this side of the street, not the one across the road. I'll be in there about ten minutes. Then I'll be going round to St Cuthbert's, then lunch, then back to the church again, okay?'

'Fuck off,' he repeated, and then added, unconvincingly, 'whoever you are.'

'Who, indeed.' I nodded. 'Who indeed. You couldn't give me a lift, could you, given that you'll probably have to head that way now?'

He wound his window up and pretended to study the magazine, which was silly, given what it was.

✝

The walk along the street was uneventful. Most of the shops were open, but it was still too early in the day for the dealers or most of the flock to be abroad. A group of men sat at a table, a concrete-stumped public amenity on the corner by one of the Vietnamese food stores, barking with brutish bonhomie, passing around a flagon of sherry, oblivious to the drizzle. The Asian traders were busy as usual, dodging shoppers and prams, trundling trolleys laden with sweet bananas, jackfruit and yams. Young ravers promenaded, all pinks, reds and electric blues. A dirt-brown feral stood outside the Safeway, scratched acoustic round his neck, murdering REM's "Losing My Religion", the stud in his pierced lip wobbling like a metronome. A forty-something woman in a grubby floral dress and a preposterous blonde wig stood near him, sucking on a cigarette, staring, swaying out of time. Trams chimed, cars revved and fretted in the clog.

No one saw a thing.

The chemist I wanted contained a photo lab. Between it and the video store was a briskly busy medical clinic, a large sign on the door proclaiming that no cash or drugs of addiction were kept on the premises. Caroline was sitting on the tram-stop bench outside it, clad in a mismatched, cheap and shiny tracksuit, cadging money from dry-eyed passers-by. She smiled thinly when she saw me, and asked for a cigarette.

I fished out a Dunhill and handed it to her. She took it. I pulled out the shot of Theresa Farndale and put it in front of her face.

'This is her,' I said. 'Recognise her?'

She shook her head. 'She's like you, Joe. Could be anybody.'

'I'll get you a copy. My offer stands.'

'Offers don't stand, dealer-man,' she replied. 'Offers lie in wait.'

She fingered the cigarette, looking down at it, turning it over and over, around and around. She kept glancing at the pedestrians, quietly annoyed because I was in her way. Her skin looked awful.

'Are you going this afternoon?' I asked. 'To the service?'

She shook her head, no expression on her face. 'Shelagh's gone,' she said. 'Shelagh's in the past. I can't be doing with the past.' Her fingers snapped the cigarette in two. She slipped the filter in her pocket, threw the rest into the wet. 'I've got my whole life to look forward to.' She stood up. 'Might see you this evening, though.'

I nodded. Then she was past me, walking backwards, feigned sadness on her face, explaining to a trio of black-shrouded Goths, ghostly and glum, how her sister was in Bendigo, having a baby, and her wallet had been stolen, really bad, and how she needed money to catch the bus . . .

I blessed her beneath my breath.

In the chemist, I ordered two dozen reprints of the Farndale shot. They could do that sort of thing, even without the neg. Judy, behind the counter, nodded, then apologised and asked for my surname. When she'd first arrived in the area, about two years ago, she had worked for a short time behind the jump at the Bradford. She knew me by sight, remembered my first name.

She also remembered that I knew Corrigan, apologised again, said, tut, wasn't it *terrible* about Shelagh Purdey, such a nice girl, not that she knew her herself, you understand, but she had *heard*, it's what everybody was saying, even the papers, and would I by any chance be seeing the priest in the next couple of hours.

I told her yes, straight away in fact, so she apologised once more. Then she disappeared into the lab, and re-emerged almost immediately carrying a large, flat, rectangular object, perhaps a metre high, two-thirds as wide, wrapped in brown paper. She handed it to me. It was Corrigan's order, she said, finished and framed.

Would I mind dropping it up to him, which would save him having to walk down to get it, he being busy today, after all, and what with the rain and everything.

I nodded. I like to do my bit. She was so grateful she asked forgiveness.

I found him in the church itself. The doors were ajar. He was pacing the aisle, wearing a pair of well-worn baggy brown corduroys and a musty green jumper, rubbing his chin with his right hand, clearly deep in thought. In the shadows, two of his older and lonelier parishioners bustled and limped, one trying to buff the floor, the other brandishing a feather duster.

He noticed me when I was halfway towards him. I smiled, curious to note his reaction. Even from that distance, I could see his scowl.

'Have you no fucking manners, man?' he hissed, tossing a glance over his shoulder to the crucified Christ at the front. 'Will you not acknowledge the presence of the Lord?'

'Talking to yourself is the first sign of insanity,' I rejoined, continuing my passage and holding out the package.

'Not *me*, you fool, Panther, you. What's this?'

'From the chemist.'

He took it in both hands, hungrily, clasped it to his breast and stared at the ceiling. 'Ahh, thank you,' he said. 'The good Lord does it when it needs to be done. Four o'clock yesterday I got this to the place, a tiny negative, and asked for it by lunchtime. They said

248

they'd do their best, but no guarantees. I was worried it'd not arrive, I'll tell you that.'

'What is it?' I asked.

Corrigan looked at me, his eyes bright. 'A photo, boy, what else? A photo of Shelagh.'

This concerned me. Who had been talking to whom? 'Where from? The father?'

'Indirectly, yes. I got it from the paper, the broadsheet. Their people got it from the dad. No one's ever seen it. The paper didn't use it in their stories on account of the fact the poor girl's smiling.'

'Must've cost you a bit to get it enlarged and framed.'

He shrugged.

'Couldn't the paper have done it for you?'

'Now, I asked them that and the bloke on the phone said no—said they report news, not create it. They'll be here this afternoon, though, although they were a bit pissed when I said they'd not be on their own.' He turned away and called for Mrs Collosi. The sturdy old black-clad biddy wielding a duster in a threatening manner put down her weapon and made her way across, nodding in the servile mime of the emptily devoted. 'It's here, Mrs Collosi,' he said, beaming at her. 'Careful with it, now. Why don't you unwrap it and give it a dust down? Put it up the front where everyone can see. Thank you. I have to have a word with Mr Panther here a minute.'

The old woman, grinning with fulfilment, lifted her gaze from the ground and looked towards me, joy in

249

her eyes. Her face snapped shut the moment she focused. Admittedly, I was a little more misshapen and brightly hued than normal, but, even so, I thought there was no need for her to surreptitiously cross herself as she walked away.

Corrigan noticed, too. He shook his head gently. 'Don't mind her,' he said. 'Mrs Collosi is on her own these days. She doesn't get out much. She lives in the flats, down by Gertrude. She'll not have seen you before. You probably frightened her.'

I'll bet she *has*, I thought. And I'll bet I do. She had sat herself in the front pew and was busily unwrapping the photograph, looking back at me often, a storm in her brow, shifting sand beneath her feet. First moment she gets, I thought, she'll tell the priest I'm a dealer, killing his lost sheep.

Poor Mrs Collosi.

'Don't take too long with it, now,' the priest called out to her. 'There's still a lot to do before kick-off.' He turned back to me. 'So much to do, Panther. I'd let it ride. There was chalk on the path, more in here, old bits of crime scene tape, and that powder, man, the powder they use for fingerprints, bloody everywhere, even in the armpits of the Lord himself.' He shook his head. 'Come, boy, let's go to the house, have a brew.'

We left by the front doors, and headed up the street, my head hunched against the rain, his erect. I was, I admit, a little discomfited by his manner.

'I'm surprised, priest,' I began.

'You must be, man,' he laughed. 'You've been here

five minutes and you haven't quoted that bastard Tertullian at me yet.'

'I'm surprised you're even talking to me.'

He clapped me on the back, hard. I almost punched him in the face, reflex, but just held it in.

'Ahh, Joe Panther,' he said. 'The world's a fucking circus, but at least I work for the ringleader. I'm not angry at you, man. In fact, I should thank you, not that you'd be looking for thanks, and the act of thanking itself would piss you off, so it's all the more reason to do it. Thank you, thank you, thank you, you bastard.'

He unlocked his front door, stood back to allow me entry, then continued. 'You're a mad, bad hard-man, Panther, with the manners of a pig, the temper of a pitbull, the timing of the Gestapo and the methods of the Inquisition, but sometimes I think that God himself was the one did send you.'

I could have said something. I didn't.

'Attacking me like that the other night, man. Unforgivable. I've not pissed my pants since I was five. But you know what you did?'

'Ruin your mattress?'

'Ach, that too, but you got my head straight, man, pushed it where it didn't want to go, pulled it out the other side. I'm telling you, man, this is terror, this is the greatest of burdens—'

'Pride is a sin, father.'

'So is assault with a fucking broken stubby, so shut up. The greatest burden I've yet been asked to shoulder, Panther, and I couldn't do it. I was lost. I was lost because of the demons in the darkness, and you freed those demons, man. Right there: free. Be gone. Bebloodygorrah, be gone, ye serpents. You made them stand up and identify themselves. I'd not realised before, but somewhere inside me I'd started seeing poor Shelagh and poor Theresa as one and the same. The pressure, boy, the pain of it. No edges. My guilt over Theresa was obscuring my clear conscience over Shelagh.'

We were in the kitchen. He had the jug from the percolator in his hand. He stopped suddenly and turned to face me.

'You forced me to talk through it, Panther. You forced me to set the past to one side, set it in stone. You were on a mission, boy. Whether you know it or not, the Lord was guiding your hand that night—'

Up, under your chin, I thought, jagged–gleaming, sharp, and a breath, a shove, away from murder . . .

'—and making you perform his work. You were the vessel, boy, into which he poured his love. I put my hand up for Theresa Farndale, man. That was me. I fouled up. But Shelagh Purdey is *not* the same. Shelagh Purdey is my chance to make good. She's my chance to *atone*.'

'So,' I said, looking at him there, satisfied with his own justification, 'Shelagh Purdey died to give you a second chance. God favours the opportune over the just. Sin is statistical in nature. The good go to Heaven, on balance.'

He just shook his head, tutting to himself, his spirit

resilient. Of course it was: he had a show to do, and he was a pro. 'You'll not rile me, man, with your smart ways of thinking. Not today.' He hit the switch on the perc. 'Five minutes, no more.'

'Did you get anything from the sex abuse groups, like I asked you?'

A shadow crossed his face. 'No, man. I asked all the ones I knew, of course, like you asked. Leave me shit-scared and sobbing in my bed, ask me that, and you think I wouldn't? Of course I did.'

'So?'

'So, the couple that include cleric abuse in their ambit wouldn't talk to me, and I'd not have expected them to. I know different, of course, but to them I'm a priest under suspicion of a sex crime—'

'It was about power. It's all about power. Go on.'

'The others, well, some of them I've got contacts with. I've made a few referrals here and there, over the years. No one had any records of complaints made by Shelagh Purdey. Not a one.'

'Are they *sure?*'

'Well, one mob, the woman I talked to thought their database was behaving a bit screwy, so she couldn't be a hundred per cent sure, but she tried a few different searches, and still came up empty. The others, nothing. It didn't surprise me, Panther, and nor should it you. Most cases of abuse—any abuse—go unreported.'

And Theresa Farndale found out why, I reflected, but kept my mouth shut.

'It doesn't matter,' the priest was saying. 'I'd be damn sure it happened.'

'You have no evidence,' I reminded him. 'Only faith. Without evidence, we can't deflect suspicion to the father.'

'You still think the father?'

'Oh, yes, but with nothing to give the cops, it doesn't matter what I think.'

'Faith,' he said. 'Like you say, we have faith. And faith wins wars, man. Would you like a drop of Irish in your coffee?'

'*You* have faith, Corrigan, not me. And faith *starts* wars. Yes, I will.'

'The bottle's in the study. Let me pour the cups and we'll go through.' He winked at me, like a mischievous schoolboy, or an inn-keeper offering a bribe to a simpleton. I decided to change the subject.

'Your computer, priest. Does it have a zip drive?'

He looked surprised. 'What? Since when were you interested in computers?'

'Does it?'

'Sure it does. The hard drive's too small. I bought one to attach to it. Those zip disks, man, they'll hold the same as a hundred floppy disks, each one.'

I pulled the disk from my jacket pocket, waved it at him. 'If you need to thank me, then do me a favour.'

He caught my meaning, and held his hands out in supplication. 'I'd love to, Joe, but, you know, the service coming up, there's so much to do . . .'

'Just show me how to operate it, priest, and leave me be. I'll pick it up as I go along.'

He nodded. 'Okay. Is this more of the Lord's work?'

I confirmed.

'What's it about?'

'Kumquats.'

✝

# 8

I FIRST LEARNED OF MY ABILITIES during childhood. I was a problem child, a worry to family and neighbours even then, an uncontrollable brat, a wilful repository of spite, font of hyperactive misery.

I withered a fig tree with just a glance, piqued by its barrenness. Many of my peers, second sons and third, survivors of Herod's massacre, died because of my pranks. I caused streams to run to a pool. Mocked by a playmate, I withered him, too. I rode on a sunbeam, bade others follow, watched them fall. More ran to a cave. I turned them into goats, turned them back at the weeping pleas of their terror-struck mothers, became the leader of the gang.

Oh yes, I was quite a handful. I blame the parents, myself. I remember Mary's quiet, knowing observation; Joseph's obedient complicity. Nothing said; nothing explained. I remember, too, the first inkling of the secret, the reason why little boys and girls followed me in fear, and why, later, grown men and women fell in behind me, awed in love, ready to defy themselves, willing to die most horribly. They wanted to believe. And I wanted to help.

I help where I can.

Most of the time, I don't need to. The Gentiles took Simon Magus for a god; also Paul; also Barnabas. I was nowhere to be seen, so I was especially holy.

And so it began. Divinity *in absentia*. Power by proxy. Or so it appeared. The mortal man is not the lord. The glory is not the god. The filter is not the cigarette.

There have always been people wanting to believe. Whenever I could, I have helped. I remember a young, brash man called Jorg Sabellicus, for instance, a self-confident sleazebag I met one evening in the fug-filled air of a tavern in Kreuznach in Germany, somewhere around 1507. He was pissed, angry and bitter, having just lost his job as postmaster in the town, shadowed by a scandal involving young boys.

He wanted to believe. I led him to believe. No matter that the things I whispered to his ear were without foundation, and that I, of all people, was the least qualified to speculate on matters of the hereafter. I called myself Joachim von Pantagruel at the time.

Jorg believed. And how. He left Kreuznach after a while, and the next time I heard of him he'd settled down in Heidelberg. He'd changed his name, too. He had some very strange ideas, that Johannes Faust. No idea where he got them.

Mrs Collosi also wanted to believe.

I found her in an anteroom at the side of the church, seated alone, knees together, munching a sandwich for lunch, breaking from her labours. She froze in terror when I entered, that look in my eyes.

I borrowed a line from Pauly. Its source might even have been genuine. I can't recall, but it sounded like me.

'Wherefore, my beloved,' I intoned, filling the room with my undeniable spirit, 'as ye have always obeyed, not as in my presence, but now much more in my absence, work out your own salvation with fear and trembling.'

No more was needed.

She crossed herself again, too terrified to stand. 'You are the devil himself,' she hissed.

'For it is written in the work of the prophet Tom Waits,' I said, turning away, eyes leaving last, '"there ain't no devil, it's just God when he's drunk." Get thee back to Gertrude Street, never more to speak.'

I left her in resonant silence, chewing bread in a mouth suddenly dry in the house of the Lord. The memorial service was still an hour and a half away, and a stroll to Brunswick Street for a quick foccacia seemed like a good idea.

I had spent the previous hour clicking the mouse on Corrigan's computer, and had learnt something. I had learnt that it is possible to know more than is absolutely necessary about kumquats. The zip disk had unveiled itself at the command of the priest, revealing page after colourful page of breathless praise and obsessive evocation in the name of fruit. I knew now of the kumquat's history, its uses, its nutritional components, its economies of scale, its rising popularity among certain demographics, its excellent returns, its tantalising taste in tarts and tea-cakes alike. The disk was designed for merchants and shop-owners taken already to the top of kumquat mountain, ready to be tempted by the view.

What I didn't know was why Graeme Purdey was, as Sophia reported, so anal about his stock. I also didn't know what in blind hell any of it had to do with the tasks to hand. Probably nothing. I'd shot the disk from the slot, shoved it back in my pocket, and chided myself for wasting time.

I found myself a table at Mario's and ordered lunch. Replete, I whacked forty cents in the public phone at the rear of the cafe and, using the number gained easily from Directory Inquiries, rang Rebecca May Goodwin, the predecessor of Sophia Ognenis at Image Makers. I introduced myself as a researcher from the Department of Labour—nothing to do with the Department of Social Security, don't panic—charged with accumulating data on why people leave their jobs.

Rebecca was happy to help. It had been weird, she said, and unexpected, but not at all unwelcome for all that. She'd been the receptionist at Image Makers for eighteen months, content and confident in her work. Then, one day, a fortnight back this must have been, two men in suits came to see her. Her, not Graeme

Purdey. They had waited, in fact, until the boss was out at lunch.

The men, she said, were from an employment consultancy—Corporate Somethings, she had it written down somewhere. They said they were head-hunting her. She was just the person they were after to fill a key logistic role with a major, major corporation, the identity of which, they regretted, had to remain confidential for a few days more.

She was flattered by the attention, but what won her over was the cheque for five thousand dollars they presented to her. A signing bonus, they called it, no matter that she'd not laid pen to paper. They told her to finish up at the end of the day, go home and wait for their call. There was no need to explain to the boss, they added. They would square it—they had someone, a replacement, who could start the following day.

Ms Goodwin had not heard from Corporate Somethings since. She was not unduly worried, however. She could wait a while longer; five grand could stretch a fair way.

✝

I timed it well. The memorial service had been underway about half an hour by the time I got back to St Cuthbert's.

Strangers crammed the grounds, a shuffling, shaking antiphony of mutters and sniffs, the garish circles of

260

umbrellas, the colours of migraine, weeping in the rain. The crowd spilled out of the front gate, milling on the pavement, loafers and trainers and court shoes and boots, trampling the flagstones and gutter, unknowingly defiling the path of Shelagh's final cerebral journey. A pair of cheap hire speakers rested on the porch, doing a less than adequate job of enjoining outsiders in memory.

I noticed John the Baptist hovering around near the gate. He was wearing a crumpled and frayed black suit that didn't fit him properly. He looked anxious, staring around, looking for something. He didn't see me.

I pushed my way through the pack, heading for the doors. Some people moved out of my way as best they could, humble in the presence of mourning; others stood firm, until they saw my eyes.

Squeezing inside, I positioned myself by the back wall. There were two reasons for my late arrival. The first, obviously, was so that I could observe the less tardy attendees with a minimal risk of being noticed or confronted myself. The second was so I missed the opening hymns and prayers. It doesn't matter how horrified I feel about the way my cult developed into a global fury of hate, mass murder, abuse, betrayal and arrogant wealth, I still sometimes can't resist a quiet, self-effacing 'Thank you, you shouldn't have' at the end of a good singsong.

My timing was pretty much perfect. The echoes of the last amen were fading in the rafters, the air stilling.

Sundry coughs and rustles rose from the crowd, every pew full, as Corrigan, in full battle dress, climbed to the pulpit and gathered himself, keenly aware, I fancied, of the tension he was building.

All is theatre. All, all, all.

Beneath his platform stood the photograph of Shelagh Purdey. It was a black-and-white shot, perhaps a still from a film. It showed Shelagh pubescent, perhaps fourteen years old, and was taken from a point of view slightly above her, almost directly overhead. The little, little movie star was clad in a frilly dress of some sort, something evocative of a decade long past and fragile in its opinions. She was twirling clumsily on one foot, her arms out, angled down, palms up, presenting. Her mouth was smiling. Her eyes were tundra, the pupils wide, flat and wary.

The shot, I couldn't help noticing, was well lit.

'Ladies and gentlemen, please be seated,' began Corrigan, pausing then a second to allow the momentum of murmuring to dissipate.

'Today, according to certain traditions, is the feast day of St Sidwell, a saint, I'm sure, unfamiliar to most, yet a thousand years ago was the focus for much devotion and hope. It is perhaps appropriate to remember her on this sad occasion, because she provides us with a model through which to find consolation and evidence of God's love in the tragedy that has befallen the Purdey family in particular, and this community in general—'

There were quite a few people stuck up the back,

262

in the standing area, behind the cheap seats. Most stood erect, hands clasped piously in front of their crotches, swaying slightly from the effort. I leant against the wall, ankles crossed, arms folded over my chest.

'St Sidwell was beheaded in violence and anger. Buried outside the English city of Exeter, her grave became a centre for pilgrims from far and wide. Devotions at her site, it was said, could bring about miraculous cures. Many were healed by the love of the Lord, accessed—to use a word from the computer age—via the contemplation of her uncorrupted, virgin remains—'

Graeme and Elaine Purdey were seated right at the front, together, but not touching. His suit was black, although I could just make out a scimitar of bright green, the back of his shirt collar, struggling to girdle his neck. She wore a navy blue twin-set, not cheap, but common. She had a new hairdo, too. A new hairdresser would have been a better investment.

'Ladies and gentlemen, the horrific murder of Shelagh Purdey, her body left, here in this house of God, would be unbearable were it not for the example of His compassion through the martyrdom of Christ, in who, we are reminded in Ephesians, "we have redemption through his blood, the forgiveness of sins, according to the riches of his grace."'

In the pew behind the Purdeys, directly behind the father, was a short woman, young, cropped dark hair, plain but neat black dress, woollen, perhaps, sleeves extending halfway down her sharply defined upper arms. Her hands disappeared around the front, probably cradling a folded jacket. I couldn't be sure because of the distance and the angle, but I felt pretty certain it was Sophia Ognenis, well out, groomed and changed.

'Shelagh's death speaks of all the sicknesses rampant in our society: of the abandonment of the young, of the harsh cruelty of a nation governed by market forces instead of understanding and love. And yet, your presence here today speaks also of the desire to change that—the desire to *heal* the cancer of disregard that is allowed to choose its victims from the weak and disenfranchised—'

Sophia Ognenis had never known Shelagh Purdey. She had not struck me as a church-goer. In fact, I had the distinct impression she had struck me as an atheist. She had only known Graeme Purdey a fortnight. I knew that now. She was neither friend nor family.

'Shelagh is with the Lord now, and, through her, God has chosen to pour his love into us, for by contemplating her terrible end may we see the cause of misery and find the strength to act according to that love and begin the long healing process which God, in his mercy, demands of us—'

Every minute or so, she flicked her head, an almost inconspicuous twitch, to the left and right. I recognised the movement. I have seen it countless times over the centuries, beginning with the spies the Romans used to put in the market, and the guards they positioned on top of the Temple during Passover. The stranger who gave me the donkey outside Jerusalem did it, too. It was a public relations coup, that donkey. It also sealed my fate, such arrogance. Never did find out who that man was.

'Ladies and gentlemen, we are here to mourn. But we are also here, in our legions, to proclaim: never again. Pilgrims from far and wide made their way in hope to the resting place of St Sidwell. We, now, must also become pilgrims, but of another type—pilgrims on a journey of understanding and courage, pilgrims who see at journey's end a community marked, not by its admiration for the rich and ruthless, but its true compassion for the poor and troubled. People, let us today, *now*, take the first step on that pilgrimage—'

There was the young man in a shroud in the Garden of Gethsemene, too. Don't know who he was, either. He did it a lot, there, in the hostile shadows, there, waiting, there, playing his part. Then the sound of steel and leather came between the trees and I played mine again.

'As the pilgrims were healed by the contemplation of St Sidwell, so we pilgrims can be healed—can begin the healing of our community—by reflecting on this great loss, and setting our hearts to the momentous task of making our society one which truly *values all* its members, a society which places the Christian tenets of fairness and justice—for all, no matter how disadvantaged—at the very forefront of its mission—'

Sophia, if it was her, was working. She was watching Graeme Purdey's back. But on whose orders, and to what end? Purdey was undoubtedly paying her wages, but to whom was she loyal? What hand had writ the script of Corporate Somethings? Purdey himself, just to get rid of his previous receptionist? Unlikely. Was he, too, a player in a larger game, dimly aware of the rules, unappraised of the object?

'And let Shelagh Purdey, blessed now in the bosom of the Lord, be the symbol of that trek—'

I almost felt sorrow for him. Empathy, even. Then I glanced at the photograph again.

'I believe God wishes us to see poor Shelagh as a reminder, not of the cruelty of our times, but of the promise of his love. She is gone now, yet she is also here, the thread which draws all together today—'

The other heads at the front were all neatly coifed and solemn. I recognised some; didn't need to know the rest. They were merchants, councillors, the local member of Parliament. Respectable types. Occupying forces.

'We must ask ourselves now this question: in her memory, can we find the cure we so desperately need? In the name of her agony, can we find the strength within us to make change for good? And we must ask ourselves, also, the most important question—'

There was no sign of Mrs Collosi. Or Beatrice Cowper.

'If she's so fucking blessed, how come she's so fucking dead?'

That wasn't Corrigan. That was DSS Gordon, standing next to me, stage whispering, chin a-jut, lips thin at my ear, eyes cold and raindrops beading on his hair oil. The people in earshot shuffled a distance, as quietly and as best they could.

'Outside scumbag, *now,* or I'll arrest you here, right now and very loudly,' he hissed, and started sidling away towards the door.

I followed. The service was starting to bore me anyway.

I found him around the corner of the building, leaning against the side wall, sheltered from the angle of the worsening rain. Pordelli was with him, naturally, not quite able to get his girth wholly in the dry.

'They let drug dealers in churches now, mystery man?' leered the detective constable, attempting a rhetorical question.

'My sins, which are many, are forgiven,' I said, not smiling.

Gordon snorted obscenely. 'Who by, Panther? That degenerate priest?'

'Probably, the ones he knows about, but mainly by me.'

Pordelli shook his head, mocking. 'Don't think it works like that, mate. Not if what they taught me in Sunday school was right.'

'It wasn't,' I replied. 'Trust me on that one.'

Gordon snorted again. 'I'd rather trust a dingo with a firecracker up its arse. Where's Theresa Mary Farndale, Panther? Found her yet?'

'She's in jail. She's in a cell.'

'Not in Victoria, she's not. We checked that long before we talked to you.'

'Then somewhere else. Check interstate.'

'Who told you?'

'Muffy.'

'Who's Muffy?'

'A snout.'

Gordon sighed. Pordelli leaned in, face up against mine, another set routine. 'Why was Graeme Purdey's receptionist at your place last night, filthy boy?'

I didn't get a chance to reply. 'Let me tell you,' said Gordon. 'She wanted to talk to you about a break-in at Image Makers.'

This was a bit worrying. When they came at Gethsemane, they arrested the boy in the shroud. Then they let him go, naked, into the twisted blackness of the grove. They seemed pleased with him. He seemed pleased with himself. 'Did she tell you that?'

Gordon smirked. 'No. You did, just then. Haven't spoken to her. The uniforms left a note in my pigeonhole, like I asked them to.'

'What break-in?'

He turned on one foot, grabbed my lapels and shoved me back against the wall. He had eaten KFC for lunch, I could tell. A couple of teenagers, awkward in formal black, had been watching us idly from near the front of the building, glad of the distraction. At the first hint of violence, they melted away.

'You know damn well what break-in, Panther,' growled Gordon. 'I can't prove it was you and I don't know what you thought you were after, but it *was* you, Panther, I know that. Oh yes.'

I tried coy. 'Oh yes?'

Coy didn't work. He stiff-armed me against the bluestone. 'Oh fucking yes, Panther. I know lots of things. Want to know what I know? I know you broke into Image Makers. I know I told you to stay away from the Purdeys. I know you haven't. I know I told you to find Theresa Farndale. I know you haven't. I know a man was robbed and stripped at needle-point in the city. I know you killed Davey Parker with a massive overdose of heroin because he assisted us with our inquiries.'

Pordelli chimed in. 'That was your fit in the clothing bin, mystery man. No prints, smart man, but *we* know, don't we? It's down to you. It's on your conscience.'

It wasn't, actually.

Gordon resumed his theme. 'I know you're a piss-poor dealer, Panther. I know you're a murderer and a thief and a molester of women. I know I've got you on a slab. You want to get off the slab?'

'I've done it before.'

'The deal, Panther. Listen. I can't use the church report. I'm not supposed to have it. You find me the Farndale woman in forty-eight hours. I get a statement off her, sufficient to establish priors for the priest, sufficient to pull him in again and grill him, then maybe, just maybe, I let you leave this town. You fail, and I bust you big time. Your charge gets upgraded, you get caged, your warehouse gets raided and searched, your smack gets proffered, the charges mount, and you go so far down you could suck the cock of an earthworm.'

He stiff-armed me again. 'Got it?' he snarled, dropped me, turned and walked away, Pordelli rumbling and rolling in his wake.

'Are you having me followed?' I called out after them.

The reply, if there was one, was lost. At that moment the clouds blackened and strained, the light thinning as if a witch had stolen the sun, and the rain trebled in strength, sheeting down with a singleness of purpose and a roar on the shingled roof. The cops hunched and ran, heading for their car.

I walked to the front of the building, deep in thought. The mourners were unsettled by the cloudburst. Some, beneath brollies, stood stoic, determined to finish the ritual. Others found their compassion dampened. With nods and shakes and stamps and much belting of coats, they turned, apologetic, and started to file from the grounds. I noticed John the Baptist dart, with surprising agility for his age and disabilities, into where the crowd milled thickest.

The cops knew of my deeds, yet could prove them not. Nothing new there. No comfort there, either. I never did find out the first lot of charges against me, no matter that I asked the guards, their Sanhedrin escorts, the high priest, Pilate himself, and my interrogator, the Pharisee, the man Malchus, as the salesman called himself that night.

I never knew them with Brother Francesco, either. Not in detail. Something about goats and toads. Something about a heretical belief in the poverty of the Saviour.

Well, I mean. Look at me. Could you blame me?

Nor in Los Angeles. Something about doing the bidding of the Beast. It didn't bother me until he pulled out the hand gun.

In all, I think, I have little faith in the evidentiary standards demanded by my persecutors. They're almost as bad as those applied by my fans.

Gordon, however, had told me something very useful, in his own, funny, inadvertent kind of way. He had not chided me for visiting Beatrice Cowper. The mood he was in, he would have done, had he known about it. Which meant he didn't.

Which meant she hadn't told him, despite the warning she had received, despite my rebuff, despite the angel pissing on her breast.

The rain was a truck engine on the roof, a snare drum tattoo on the ground, ball bearings down the drainpipe. Above the noise, however, I still heard the high-pitched shriek from within the crowd, felt the start of chaos.

I looked up to see John the Baptist now walking out through the gate, wide-eyed, hunched, hurriedly enfolding something struggling in his suit jacket.

'Jeremy!' came a matron's shrill cry from the crowd. 'Jeremy! Where's Jeremy?'

I knew what I had to do.

✝

The rain was still pelting hard when I started to walk along the wide alley that bordered the back of Beatrice Cowper's house, about three-quarters of an hour later. Dusk was not due for another hour, but the cloud cover had rendered the light so miserly most of the cars on the road during the journey had long since switched on their headlamps.

The Daewoo hadn't when it fell in behind my taxi, which had been fortunate. No doubt its driver—the plump woman, I thought, although it was difficult to tell through the rivulets swirling across the wind-screen—had been sitting in the damn thing for hours, her eyes gradually adjusting, probably not even noticing the fading light. I'd hailed the cab a block from the church, as it pulled out from gassing up at the BP. The watcher car had slotted in not long after, and stayed behind—sometimes directly, sometimes letting another, innocent, vehicle slip between us—during the short slow drive into the city. It had not come as a surprise.

Many of the main intersections in the Melbourne CBD have idiosyncratic turning rules. It's a tram thing. You have to turn right from the left lane. When the lights go red, the turning cars head off at speed, just ahead of the on-coming traffic.

This road rule comes as a dreadful surprise to tourists on self-drive holidays. It does, however, have its uses. It is particularly handy for people who want to escape being tailed and avoid paying cab fares simultaneously. It works like this: you tell your driver to turn right.

Then you sit tight while he's getting the cab into position. Wait for the chase car to pull up behind, exposed, declared, ready to do the same. Then open the passenger door and run like buggery.

Okay, not exactly sophisticated, but it works every time.

I found a second cab—from a different company, of course—in a side street, and told the driver to head for the corner of Chapel and Toorak. It took a while, the roads clogged with early office-worker escapees, but no one followed us. From the drop-off point I walked. I was soaking wet, the Old Man being notoriously lax when it comes to discerning between the just and the unjust in matters of precipitation.

Which is a pity. An independent assessment would be handy sometimes.

I had no wish to see Beatrice Cowper.

I told myself that, anyway.

I didn't actually know *what* it was I wanted to do, not specifically. Beatrice Cowper had not informed the police of my visit, which meant, I decided, one of two things. First, perhaps she was embarrassed by our little scene, more so because she'd been warned beforehand about what a bastard I can be, and didn't wish to bring further discomfort upon her head. I didn't believe that. The woman had abandoned her daughter to the incestuous attentions of an advertising agent. She had played me on a line, like a fisher of men. She was not the bashful type. She did nothing without premeditation.

The second possibility, then. She didn't want cops

273

in her world, not one bit, not even when a madman manhandles her, threatens her life and lobs a whisky glass at her dog.

That meant she had something to hide from the wise and prudent. Or from the police, at least. It didn't really matter what it was. What mattered was the possibility of a side deal. If I could discover her secret, then there was only one thing that would prevent me from doing my civic duty by exposing her to the authorities.

And a very large wad of it, at that.

As a potential solution it possessed a certain elegance. Gordon had no idea I was in contact with Shelagh's mother. If I could work a deal with her—no, let's be precise here, if I could extort a case full of cash from her, fifties and below, used, non-sequential—then I could afford to steal silently into the night, leaving ruin and despair behind me. As usual.

Without me, the cops would never find Farndale, and the priest would remain untroubled. Without me, also, Graeme Purdey would have to answer only to his conscience, if and when it bothered him. John the Baptist would live in peace. Sophia Ognenis would find someone else to beat up. Caroline and Spring-Head and Rashid and Feeney and Macca and Shazz and the rest of the flock would find someone else to score from. Mrs Collosi would tremble in silence. And Shelagh Purdey would rot.

All would have their reward.

Things are so much less complicated when I'm not around.

The foxes have holes, and the birds of the air have nests; but the Son of Man hath not where to lay his head.

Something always crops up, however. Didn't have a place when I arrived in Jerusalem, either, not for me or the boys. It was a man with a pitcher of water who led us to the upstairs room with the table set for supper. I'd never seen him before. I've often wondered since then, in the damp cold places of my endless walk, who it was he was working for. I never saw him again.

Probably the same as the man who gave me the donkey, or the naked child in the shroud, watching through the branches.

The director holds the script; the actors just say the lines. I am the ham of god.

It all came down, I decided, as I turned into the lane, confident I wasn't being followed, to the furniture in her house. There was simply too much of it for a woman on her own. I was sure she could throw a lovely party, be the perfect host, but she hadn't come across as the social type.

Anomalies remind me of me. And anything that shares its nature with me must be trouble.

The fence was sheer and solid, the barbed wire above it taut and glistening, suggesting a fragility that was not of its kind. There was no one else in the lane. The rain was perfect cover, confining everybody indoors. I was not stupid enough to contemplate attempting entry to the house. Even if Cowper was out, I had no doubt

275

Cerberus would be hanging around, musing on composers. The garage, though, was a different matter. It was only a few feet from the boundary line, as far as I could remember, which meant that I might just be able to jump from gate-top to rooftop without entering dog range. Then, if it had a skylight . . . Clearly she owned more than one car, and who knows what their contents might reveal.

I patted my pockets, checking for my rosary beads. They weren't there. Then I remembered: I'd left them in my leather jacket. No matter. There'd be something nearby, a piece of wire, a screwdriver, a claw hammer. Whatever.

First, though, I needed to refresh myself regarding the geography of the garden, see if my memories were correct.

I gathered myself and jumped, catching the sharp top of the corrugated iron in my hands and hauling myself up, boots slipping against the curves, jagging off wet rivets, until I could heave my elbows over the rim. I had to be careful not to catch my head on the lower of the two wire strands. Finally, after a bit of huffing and puffing, I found my balance, arms outstretched along the top, taking my weight with shoulders and elbows, hands grasping for security, my forehead resting like a kiss against the barbs.

'Good afternoon, Mr Panther. Are you having an episode?'

The concentration and threat of laceration involved in clambering up the fence had been acute, and so confident had I been that no one sensible would be out in such turbulent weather I hadn't even bothered to scan the grounds beforehand.

I did so now.

Beatrice Cowper was standing in her garden about three metres in from the fence. Cerberus lay at her feet, tense and uncomfortable, clearly under the influence of Schubert. The woman was clad in the brown and white raiment of a nun, the heavy, coarse cloth sodden with rain, ridged and clumping. Her feet were bare. The sight shocked me, made me inhale deeply and sharply as I tried to make sense of the moment, and in that inhalation I thought I smelt the rich, damp earth of Kildare, the salted flesh devotions of dear Brigid, the distant hover of burning wicks, and the promise of rest without resurrection.

So I fell off the fence. I heard her laughter peal above the downpour.

I got to my feet, mud-covered now, and wondered what to do next. If I stayed here, would she come out? Would she open the gate? Would she ask me to go round the front?

Would she bollocks. After five minutes, I realised nothing was going to happen. The next move was mine.

So I clambered up the fence again.

She had not moved.

And neither had my brain. I fought for something to say and eventually came up with a beauty. 'You're dressed as a nun,' I said.

'Do you like me better this way, Mr Panther,' she

smiled, eyes hard, 'full of virginal and sacrilegious promise?'

I ignored her and looked around. I could see the garage much more clearly from my vantage point. It looked close. I could see, too, the wing of the house behind it, the blinds on each window raised, some completely, some barely halfway. No lights shone from within.

'Your attention is wandering, Mr Panther. Perhaps you should take something to sharpen your focus.'

My focus, as it happened, was sharp as a razor, slashing about like hope in a dockside gang fight. The garage was jumping distance from the gate. And there—there, again—blinds moving slightly in the wind. Except that the windows were all closed.

There was a more pressing observation, however: Beatrice Cowper was dressed as a nun.

Was she dressed, consciously, as Brigid? How did she know of Brigid? *Was* she Brigid, vengeful and returned in defiance of every known law of existence? Am I not the living, awful, desolate proof that the universe is not constrained by our own understanding? Is it not true that despite the considerable and, many would maintain, unique advantages given me in the realm of spiritual understanding I have still, two millennia after coughing into frightened, painful, wakefulness, to discover a single proposition more subtle than *what is*, *is*, that I can regard without suspicion? Must any journey yield only the suggestion that life is fundamentally bizarre, and the more you live it, the more bizarre it gets? If my father was a soldier, is the essence of life unknown? If my father was Yahweh, is the essence of life unknowable? If my father was the Uncaused Cause, is the essence of life unimportant? In a world containing the Smashing Pumpkins, is the popularity of Mariah Carey proof that evil is banal?

Alas, we cannot seek answers until we know how to frame the questions. I returned my gaze to Beatrice Cowper, her hands clasped in mocking supplication, and framed one.

'*Why* are you dressed as a nun?'

'To please you.'

'Why are you dressed as a nun, standing in your back garden, in the pissing rain?'

'To please you.'

My arms were starting to ache.

'Does it please you, Mr Panther? Does the Lord see me, and see that I am good?' She smiled coquettishly, flipped a hip.

'Do you often dress as a nun? Have you ever dressed as a nun before?'

'Only to please you, Mr Panther.'

That was the sort of ambiguity that would give me nightmares, were it not that my unconscious long accepted that the real world could easily eclipse any horrors it could come up with on its own.

'How did you know I'd be here? Not just *here*, your house, but here, here, at the back fence?'

She started laughing. 'Mr Panther, you are so naive. Whatever happened to omniscience?'

'I don't know.'

'If you are the Lord, Mr Panther, then surely you cannot object to my trying to satisfy your every need?'

The muscles in my shoulders were on fire from supporting my weight, undoused by the rain. The fence top was sharp and slippery, the barbed wire grazing my forehead. 'And you just happened to have a nun's habit to hand?'

'Sometimes I like to be pure, Mr Panther. And sometimes I like to stand in the rain, and feel the earth rise up through my feet. It cleanses. It gives strength. I like to get a hug from mother. I have a very large wardrobe, Mr Panther. I can be whoever I want to be. That is a right I reserve. You, however, I fear do not have that right. You are condemned to be exactly who you are.'

'And who am I?'

'At a rough guess, Mr Panther? A man with multiple personality dysfunctions, probable substance abuse problems, possible schizophrenia, a desperate man forced to live in a cash economy, leading an existence brutal, sordid and, I suspect, mercifully short—a man who shouldn't feel so hostile towards the idea of seeing a shrink and going on a Haloperidol holiday. You are, Mr Panther, exactly who you seem.'

I ignored it, of course. When people start to suspect, they naturally seek explanation among the scattered and whitened bones of their own conquered demons. I'm used to it. I have been rebel and lord, messiah and mad, witch and witless, innocent of sin and to blame for the lot for as long as I can remember. 'And you, Ms Cowper, are you exactly who you seem?'

Even as I asked that question, I willed her not to answer. She tossed her head, contemptuous and dismissive.

'Oh, Mr Panther, I am many things. I am the whore and the holy one. I am the wife and the virgin. I am the daughter. I am the members of my mother.'

Of course I recognised the quotation. The question was, was I *meant* to? I never got the chance to find out. Ms Cowper stamped a foot, petulant, silent and splashy, on the grass.

'Game's over, Mr Panther. I'm cold and I'm wet and I feel ridiculous. I trust you see now that whatever it was you were planning, however you intended to defile my life, the attempt will always be futile. I see all. I know all. I'm glad you came, however. I have something I wish to give to you.'

At that, she turned her back on me. She glanced down at Cerberus. '*Mah*ler!' she snapped. Immediately, the dog sprung to its feet and bounded to the fence. It started to pace up and down along the boundary, a few feet each side of me, looking up, growling, its drool mixing with the run-off from its snout. I watched the beast carefully, craning my neck, looking down, feeling the barbs from the wire pierce my flesh, wondering if it could jump.

'And by the way, Mr Panther . . .'

I looked up again. She still had her back to me. She bent low at the knees, spine straight, took hold of the hem of the habit and in one fluid movement, lifted the sodden garment above her head and dropped it on the grass. She was naked. 'I, too, am exactly who I seem to be.'

And then she walked, without looking back, across the lawn, into the conservatory, and crossed into the darkness beyond, leaving me hanging, arms in agony, blood trickling into my eyes. Now. Excuse me, but one of the pivotal moments of my life involved being left hanging, arms in agony, blood trickling into my eyes. I did not like it one bit, and it only led to tears. Understandably, I think, anything which reminds me of it makes me feel upset. Used, even.

And yet I hung there. Alone. Looking at a well-tended suburban back garden and listening to the rumbles of a Rottweiler in the rain.

Thus do things reduce.

I was thinking. Brigid. Beatrice Cowper. BC. Someone else's past was coming back to haunt me. Was this planned, or was this just weird shit happening? The wind gusted, making the manicured trees fuss and stretch, sheeting me with water, washing the blood from my face.

Then more blood ran, taking its place, making me blink, making me think, for a moment, that I saw a white shape pass one of the upstairs windows.

Beatrice Cowper re-emerged, walking purposefully, carrying the briefcase I'd left behind the last time. She was no longer naked. She was dressed in a black latex catsuit, skin tight and total, its surface catching blades of light, flirting them to destruction as she moved. A silver-steel zip extended prominently from crotch to neck, dividing at her breasts. Her feet were still bare; her hair still sodden and flat, strands clinging to her face and shoulders.

'My apologies for keeping you waiting, Mr Panther,' she said, full of mock sincerity. 'This outfit, not that you would like it, is very tight. To get it on, I have to coat myself in petroleum jelly.'

'Have you ever met Nicholas, Bishop of Myra?' I asked. 'He would have understood your problem.'

She didn't reply, just walked to the fence, Cerberus making way, and handed up the case, just out of my reach.

I couldn't help but notice her cleavage. 'I feel like we've known each other a long time, Mr Panther,' she said.

'Perhaps we have.'

'No.' Her countenance was not merry. 'We have not. This is the end of our acquaintance, Mr Panther. It could have been other. You could have asked for my help. I have some understanding of your condition, but you made your choice. Whatever it was you wanted from me, I will not give it. I'm sure, by tomorrow, you'll have forgotten all about me. You're a busy little messiah, I'd imagine, and there are a lot more vulnerable, gullible, and available people around than me. Seek help. Take your bag. Go away.'

I reached out my right arm, palm up. At full stretch, I took hold of the handle of the bag.

Then I fell off the fence again.
Like she knew I would.

✝

It was well dark by the time I got back to Collingwood.
The chemist was just closing up when I reached it. Judy
smiled, apologised, and handed me the reprints. I told
her to bill the Victoria Police. I was damp and
depressed and desperate for a drink. The Bradford
obliged.

I'd been half hoping to find Corrigan in the bar, so
that we could have a chat, a time-out, like the old days,
before it all went strange. The past can be comforting
sometimes, if only because it's over. He wasn't there,
and I didn't feel like visiting his home. It would have
been too much like work.

Then I remembered. Tomorrow was Sunday. A day
of rest. My day. He'd be working on his sermon.

After a couple of snorts I headed back to the warehouse, bag in hand, intent on relaxing for a couple of
hours before heading out on a well-overdue delivery
run. There were hungers to feed. Needs to fulfil. Caroline should have scabbed enough for a deal by now.

The Falcon was in the side street. I waved to the
guy, the one who looked vaguely familiar. He didn't
wave back.

There was an envelope on the floor, just inside the
front door. It was blank.

Inside it was a plain white card. On it was written: *14 Roseberry St, Carlton. 2pm, Sunday. Bring the zip disk or die. Wine and hors d'oevres will be served.*

It was signed: *Sophia.*

✝

# 9

I HAD THE BRIGID DREAM again that night, which
didn't really surprise me. Brigid, in her habit, gently
and lovingly astride me, morphed back and forth, back
and forth, with Beatrice Cowper, face never changing,
identity determined by body heat and the light's
refraction in the eyes—fixed on mine, now giving,
now dryly actuarial—lust wearing love's gown, forgiveness budding in the bed of vengeance, blooming,
blood-red robust petals, luxurious, arching, bridging,
thrusting in communion, the very promulgation
pushing forth a cold seed of nascent threat, demanding
sacrifice, urgent, mechanical and bruising. Brigid's
voice to Beatrice, Beatrice to Paul, Shelagh's head and
rottenness, Paul again, a need for Brigid, Beatrice
offered, Brigid's voice, quoting Augustine, O Lord, all
that I am is laid bare before you, hardening into Beatrice, And by the way, Mr Panther, I, too, am exactly
who I seem to be, then Paul again, hail Pauly, full of

spin, For now we see in a mirror, darkly, but then face to face . . .

I made love to someone in my sleep. I don't know who. Maybe the world.

I awoke fresh and relatively relaxed for all that. I had gone to bed early, not long after midnight, my body exhausted, my brain too burdened by causes and contradictions to do more than test their weight, put them on a shelf and vow to tackle them in the morning.

The evening deliveries had gone smoothly. I'd stood in my usual place, not in the least concerned that the chap in the Falcon had evidently alerted the chap in the Honda Civic of my movements. The car was parked twenty yards up the road, its driver slumped in the shadows of his seat, watching me in his rear-view mirror.

Clearly, whoever was controlling the watchers, cops or no, had no intention of using them to bust me. They knew what I did to generate the unreliable surge and trickle of cash I laughingly call income, and seemed, for whatever reason, to accept that. Intervention, clearly, was not on their agenda.

Like someone else I could mention.

The watcher didn't arouse the suspicion of my flock. Lots of people wait in unremarkable cars in the night at the kerbsides of Collingwood, thirsting, fifty bucks in hand. This one fitted right in. One of the young Vietnamese dealers, I noticed, not without amusement, walked past and stuck his head through the open window, raising his chin, lifting his eyebrows, making

an offer. He swore as he walked away. I don't think
he made the sale.

I handed out the reprints of the Farndale photograph, repeated my offer. She's banged up somewhere,
I told each, holding back the merchandise until I'd finished—jail, probably, but maybe detox, maybe some
sort of residential facility. Check your contacts;
someone may have come across her. The flock nodded
and twitched, too sunk in devotions and need, too
anxious for salvation and forgiveness, to care. Feeney's
hand bore splint and grubby bandage; I took away his
pain. Caroline managed a smile, in between the shakes.
'You never give up, do you?' she said.

'I wish I could,' I replied.

In the shower, kettle on the boil, Iggy on the stereo,
my mind wandered again to Gethsemene, to the man
Malchus standing furious among the soldiers, bleeding
after Simon Peter clipped his ear with a sword, wiping
his wound, Judas silent in horror. He patted the
shroud-boy on the head, bade him leave, bade the
others stay. Take only the Nazarene, he said.

And so the final act became the first, and the least
in the kingdom became the most.

In that room of the High Priest, the shuttered room,
Malchus demanded answers. His minions called him
Saul to his face; the sophist from Cilicia, the hardline

Pharisee, raised among the Gentiles, to his back. His need for information was urgent; his questions tangential, irrelevant, I thought, obsessed with petty detail. Tell me about the meeting, the gathering in the guest-chamber. Not who was there. We know who was there. Tell me about the bread. What did you do with it? Then what? And said? Now the wine, the wine. Think carefully: what were your words?

The air was thick with the smell of young blood, the cries of slaughtered lambs, ready for the roast.

The past receded under the sharp retort of a cup of Lavazza and the grunt of a well-played riff, leaving only its lesson for the day. It was the Lord's Day. Not the best day to go to church, but it would have to do.

The Smith Street tramlines, heading away from the city, extended through Clifton Hill. It was a short journey. The church of St Peter's, I noted, with due reference to the telephone directory and a street map, required only a quick walk into the leafy back streets to reach. For once it wasn't raining.

On the tram, I glanced through the morning tabloid. The front page headlines said, PM NO TO BLACK GENOCIDE APOLOGY, POPE SENDS MESSAGE OF PEACE, and U.S. BAPTISTS BOYCOTT DISNEY. The memorial service made page three, nice picture, mourners downcast in the rain, a soft, tear-jerker write-up. Feel-good, with a side order of guilt.

Architecturally, Clifton Hill looked like Fitzroy with a better job. The houses were well maintained, gutted and rewired on the inside, quaintly, anally, preserved on the out. Authentic fakes, each a mortgaged statement of ostentious modesty. Pauly would have felt at home. There were Volvos around, occasional restored Lancias and Fiats, a lot of hatchback runabouts, brightly coloured and sensible. The Daewoo looked a bit dowdy. I saw it every couple of minutes, its driver slowly doing the blocks in a grid pattern, circling, monitoring, now behind me, now in front.

St Peter's appeared to be much the same vintage as St Cuthbert's, but was scrubbed and clean on the outside, set in small but neatly mowed grounds. A sign outside, donated by a local real estate concern, advertised a fete—chocolate wheel and bric-a-brac—held the week before. Another, smaller, slightly faded sign beside it advised of yoga classes, creative dance and a forthcoming exhibition, featuring that most mouth-watering of attractions, 'an array of china painting', in the hall next door. The overall impression of the parish was one of confidence, comfort and sound financial planning.

A service was not long over when I entered the gate and started the short walk to the front doors. The last few parishioners, mostly elderly and well dressed, pottered past, eyes glancing off me with practised ease, bidding each other farewell, a couple organising tea and cakes for later in the day.

As I reached the entrance, a man stepped out of the shadows and wordlessly blocked my way. He was in his late thirties, I guessed, but looked older, clad in a level-tempered black suit and tinted glasses. He stood upright, facing me, chest puffed, his feet, in plain black shoes, firmly planted, slightly apart, for maximum balance. He held his silence, chin up.

I let him.

'Can I help you, mate?' he asked in the end, lowering his head to take in my denim jacket (complete with almost inconspicuous coffee stain), Monster Magnet windcheater, fraying jeans and boots. His nose wrinkled in unexcited disgust.

'I want to see Father Scopemi,' I said, not smiling, voice neutral. 'Are you him?'

The man did not smile. 'I am the Father's assistant,' he replied. 'Who are you?'

'Curious. Are you a member of the clergy? You're not dressed for it.'

'My role and duties are secular.'

'Like what?'

'The Father is a busy man, and his life is none of your business, mate.' The hint of warning was unmistakable.

'I'm sure he has time to see me.' I lowered my voice and brows both, matching him.

'And you are?'

'No one you've met before.'

He stiffened, unconsciously repositioned his feet. I contemplated decking him, there and then. It would have been easy enough, if somewhat more painful than usual, my bruises having not yet quite faded. I heard a car pull up outside the gate and guessed, without turning around, it was the Daewoo. I decided to try the path of peace for a little while longer.

'I wish to see him,' I repeated, flat.

'He's not here,' said the assistant.

'It's Sunday,' I said. 'He is a priest. This is his church. Where the fuck else would he be?'

'Away. We got a locum.'

'Away where? Why aren't you with him?'

Actually, he didn't need to answer the second one. I already knew: he was here to deal with people like me. I took a step towards him.

'I have a deep interest in the Church,' I said.

He didn't move. 'Professional?'

'I've never been paid for it.'

Aye, there's the rub. I sometimes wonder what would happen should God come to me, a burning bush, a strobing hydrant, a talking disco ball, whatever, and say, Son, it is time for your reward, in earth as it is in heaven, what do you wish? And I would say: Are you strong enough, Father, to make a pile of cash so tall you couldn't jump over it?

My shoulder touched his chest as I took another step forward. 'I'll not be more than a minute or so,' I said.

His hand went up, pushed me back, a leer on his lips. 'I don't think so,' he warned. 'Look at you: filthy, untidy, and not from round here. This is a community church. A decent place.'

'What are you saying?'

He sighed with the exaggerated patience of a night-club bouncer justifying a punch yet to be thrown. 'I am saying, mate, this is not a church for people like you,' he said slowly. 'How can I put this? Fuck off.'

I thought of Tertullian. 'If, with slight forbearance, I hear some bitter or evil remark directed against me,' he wrote in one of the sales brochures, 'I may return it, and then I shall inevitably be bitter myself. Either that, or I shall be tormented by unexpressed resentment.'

I had no wish to be tormented by unexpressed resentment, nor to be bitter. I sought release. I'm good with a head-butt. His glasses fell to the floor. I ground my heel into them as I turned and walked back down the path.

He didn't follow. I don't think he could see too well.

I shouted to the woman in the Daewoo to give me a lift, but she was already moving.

✝

Walking back to the warehouse I made a detour to Corrigan's house, left him a message, shoved under the door. I didn't interrupt his chores. The note read: *Find Scopemi. He's gone. Where? Who is his assistant? How many of the leisure class are urged by an excessive love of arms to become gladiators? Surely it is from vanity that they descend to the wild beasts in the very arena, and think themselves more handsome because of the bites and scars. (Yep. Tert.) ASAP. Regards, J.*

I grabbed a felafel along Smith Street and headed home. It was half past noon, ninety minutes before my meeting with Sophia.

I cranked up the stereo, giving Spiderbait a run, put my feet up and munched while contemplating maybe a small joint for pudding to take the edge off the morning. Food finished, I decided it was about time to reacquaint myself with my leather jacket. Grabbing the briefcase from where I'd dropped it on the floor the night before, I flipped its clip and opened it. On the top of my clothes, neatly folded, lay a package, wrapped in plain brown paper, clearly a paperback book from its size and shape. I lifted it out.

On the front of it was a Post-it note. In elegant, cursive hand was written: *Open your eyes and seek help, Mr Panther. You are less than you believe. Follow the signs. BC.*

I sensed malice. I sensed temptation. I was not pleased. Her cold zeal had entered my house. I ripped the paper off in one go.

The book was battered, well thumbed, and old. It was called *Beyond the Chains of Illusion*, by Erich Fromm, who, at the time of its writing, I noticed on the back, was Professor of Psychoanalysis at the National University of Mexico.

Two neatly cut strips of thin white cardboard protruded from among the pages. I opened the book at the first one, saw one line in a page full of lines, baptised by highlighter pen. It said: *The more of himself man attributes to God the less he has left in himself.* It could have been Augustine, but it wasn't.

The second marker revealed a much larger highlighted passage. I read it with a clutch in my belly, reptile-eyed.

*In the widest sense, every neurosis can be considered an outcome of alienation; this is so because neurosis is characterised by the fact that one passion (for instance, for money, power, women, etc) becomes dominant and separated from the total personality, thus becoming the ruler of the person. This passion is his idol to which he submits even though he may rationalise the nature of his idol and give it many different and often well-sounding names. He is ruled by a partial desire, he transfers all he has left to this desire, and he is weaker the stronger 'it' becomes. He has become alienated precisely because 'he' has become the slave of a part of himself.*

He. Me. Not me.

Beatrice Cowper, I thought. Beatrice Cowper, human being, lost, slithering and lowly, daughter of sinners, immersed in fault, weak and frail, the fruit of humanity's corrupted womb, blighted save redemption by the sacrifice of Christ upon the cross.

Beatrice, after all I've done for you.

I threw the book across the room, willed it burst into flame.

It didn't.

I twisted the volume of the stereo, hard. Thunderous drumming, roiling bass and screams filled the air.

I walked over to the book, put a lighter to its pages.

Behold, I said to myself. A miracle.

✝

There were two extremely interesting things said to me later that day, both uttered by Sophia Ognenis. One was the phrase, 'I'm afraid I've been less than fully frank with you'. The other was 'memes'.

Both were to come in the fullness of time, however.

Carlton, an inner suburb defined in equal parts by the presence of a university, a couple of major hospitals and the biggest concentration of Italian restaurants in Australia, lay just the other side of Fitzroy, a twenty-minute walk from the warehouse. Fourteen Roseberry Street turned out to be a recent addition to the streetscape, a small, neat, two-storey, pale-brick townhouse in a line of four, tucked away behind the food strip. The Daewoo kept driving past when I turned the corner. A six foot wooden fence of horizontal planks bordered a narrow front garden containing concrete slabs and hardy-looking plants in pots. The curtains in the windows were plain ochre, top and bottom. Neither the yard, nor the tiny balcony upstairs featured any of the usual bits of domestic detritus: discarded sneakers, clothes-horses, gardening stuff. It all looked, in fact, unremarkably anodyne.

I got my first inkling why within seconds of knocking on the door. Sophia opened it without delay and bade me enter, with a smile and a vague wave of her arm. She was dressed simply in a pair of loose black trousers, elastic waisted, kung fu slippers, and an oversize white tee-shirt which featured the front cover graphic from a Red Hot Chilli Peppers album. I was impressed.

The entrance opened straight into a combined lounge and dining area. A door at the far end of the irregularly shaped room led, I presumed, to the kitchen. A flight of stairs hugged a side wall. It was considerably warmer inside than out.

The space had the air of an efficiently and comfortably furnished motel suite. The sofa and armchair were grey, flecked with quiet but twee pink curlicues. The coffee table was brass-edged. The small dining table and four chairs all matched, blackened by laminate veneer. There was a three-shelf wooden bookcase, sparsely populated, a television, mini-stereo, and not much else.

I could see three artworks on the wall. Two were routine department store prints, Australian landscapes in the style of Albert Namatjira. The other was a movie poster, taped up, with visible fold lines which betrayed its provenance as a magazine giveaway, the one anomaly in the place. It was for a film called *The People vs Larry Flynt*, which I'd read about, a movie about a man who made a fortune through publishing porn mags. The poster depicted one of its stars, Woody Harrelson (I'd enjoyed him in *Natural Born Killers*), naked save for an American flag around his loins, stretched, camera-aware and crucified, across the giant, barely covered pubis of a woman.

Thus, I reflected, not for the first time, do things reduce.

It was obvious that the place was a safe house of some sort, Sophia Ognenis its temporary resident. I decided not to share my observation. Not yet.

She spoke quickly, all ritual fuss and politeness, shepherding me to the sofa.

'You like the poster? It's good, isn't it, very striking. I like it. The film was all right, but the poster is a triumph of iconoclasm, don't you think? It must be, it was banned in America, some stupid thing about blasphemy. Anyway, sit down, please, Joshua—may I call you Joshua?'

'Joe.'

'Joe, right, sit down. Glad you could make it, thanks for coming, nice jacket, by the way. Monster Magnet, good band—your top, I mean. Make yourself comfortable, I'll just get the wine. You want wine?'

I nodded, fished out my cigarettes. She bustled through the far door and returned seconds later carrying a bottle of red, a corkscrew, two long-stemmed glasses of no particular value, and an ashtray that might have been stolen from a pub. She put the last on the coffee table in front of me, remarking that she didn't herself, smoke that is, but, please, I should feel free, it wouldn't bother her, she used to. She put the glasses down, too, and busied herself with the cork.

'Did you bring the disk with you?' she asked lightly.

'Answer me a question, Ms Ognenis—'

'Sophia.'

'Answer me a question.'

'Shoot.' She was drilling into the cork, I noticed, with a practised and beguiling ease.

'Do you intend to wallop me again? Because, I should warn you, I think, if you do I would just as soon leave beforehand, and, if that's not an option, I will not hesitate to do my best to hurt you very much.'

'I thought you'd already tried that.' She smiled. 'It wouldn't be wise. Best to learn from mistakes, I think. Anyway, no, violence is not on the agenda. Not at the moment, anyway. Did you bring the disk?'

I nodded.

'Let me see it.'

I withdrew it from my jacket, put it on the table. She sat on the sofa, the bottle uncorked, poured two glasses, handed one to me, raised hers, smiled. 'Up yours, then,' she said. I said nothing. The wine was a muscular cabernet merlot, local, not bad.

'Have you looked at it?' she asked.

'Does Graeme Purdey know about this little meeting?'

She shook her head, took another healthy sip from her glass, looked me squarely in the eye.

'No, Joe, good question, though, and I'm not surprised you asked it, given the little misunderstandings and false impressions flying around, not surprised at all. But no, Graeme Purdey doesn't know about this.'

I believed her, although was careful not to indicate so. Whatever sort of business Graeme Purdey was conducting, I thought it highly unlikely that his assets ran to a fully furnished safe house. 'Do you know where he is right now?'

She shrugged her shoulders. 'At home, I guess, with his wife. It's the weekend, after all. They've had a big week and they're in mourning.'

'Are you his lover?'

I asked that question at the instant Sophia was taking a quaff. She snorted, coughed and laughed simultaneously, forcing twin spurts of crimson from her nostrils. It was an eloquent enough reply.

Still cackling, wiping her face with her hand, she stood up and walked to the stereo, hitting the play button. Immediately, on low volume, the undulating narcosis of Portishead filled the room. I had to admit it, the woman had style.

She sat again, nodded towards the disk. 'Well,' she asked, '*have* you looked at it?'

I nodded. 'Briefly.'

'I haven't. What's on it?'

'Kumquats.'

'Don't be obtuse, Joe. I don't like it and it can, you know, make me a bit edgy, and that's not good for stress levels or, like, how can I put it, the integrity of your body tissue. What else?'

Full of grace and truth, I replied. Anything for a quiet life. 'It's a glitzy sales pitch about kumquats, all very colourful and excited. There are sections on the history of the stuff, where it came from and all that. Then there are other bits on its nutritional value, some market research, some cooking suggestions, lots of pretty pictures, polished voice-over. It's a document produced by a marketing body, intended to convince shop-owners, caterers, food manufacturers, restaurateurs and so on to buy in wholesale quantities.'

She looked at me in silence for a moment, then nodded. 'And what else?'

'What do you mean, what else? What else do you want? A free sachet of shampoo and a chance to win a holiday on the Gold Coast?'

'You're doing it again, Joe. *Joshua*. Don't. What more, lots more, what, maybe, if I wanted to get more information, if I wasn't satisfied with the sales pitch? What if I wanted to order?'

I saw what she meant. I hadn't asked those questions myself, being more than sufficiently burdened with kumquat facts and not having the slightest intention of ordering a crate-load. 'Each section had like a code at the end of it. I guess they were computer codes, but I don't know. I've never owned a computer.'

'What did they look like?'

'I don't know. Lots of disjointed letters and strokes, like some sort of modern equivalent of nineteenth century magic spells or charms. You know: say the magic words and up pops a demon called Amator or Theodoniel, stinking of brimstone and quoting from Yeats.'

Curious. A slow smile spread across her face, then disappeared. Then she babbled at me, as if possessed: 'Aitch-tee-tee-pee-colon-stroke-stroke-dubbulyood-ubbulyoodubbulyoo-dot-blah-blah-blah-dot-net-dot-com?'

Christ, I thought, the woman's a bloody Pentecostal. I replied as best as I could: 'Tetragrammaton,

Tetragrammaton, Tetragrammaton, Ismael, Adonay, three bags full. Amen.'

She looked me, glass stalled halfway twixt table and gob, as if I was stark raving mad.

I didn't like that.

I tried a different tack. 'What are you on about?'

'Internet,' she said. 'Web site addresses, you know? Most of them start with the letters H-T-T-P, followed by slashes, and have W-W-W in them, stands for world wide web, I thought everybody knew that.'

'I see. I've never seen the Internet.'

'Luddite. Makes sense, having more information on the Net, but, odd, don't you think, that ordering—you said, ordering?'

'I got that impression.'

'That ordering's done on the Net, too. It's all very modern, if it is, not to mention raising questions about encryption and security of credit card numbers during transactions and, I guess, confidentiality of order sizes if order sizes are important—do you think size would be important in the kumquat trade, Joe?—don't know, but odd. I mean, what's wrong with sending a cheque through the mail, you know? You don't know much about the Internet, then, Joe?'

My glass was empty. I helped myself to another, topped hers up. She nodded approvingly. 'No,' I replied. 'I told you. I've not spent much time with computers.'

'Oh, you should, Joe,' she said, sounding very serious. 'You should. How to put it? The Internet is a human invention grown master of its inventors. It is the sum total, not just of millions of computers throughout the world, but the millions and millions of links between those computers—a huge network, unplanned and unmapped, if you like, infinite possibilities within ceaseless change and motion, expanding and independent. The Net is fundamentally amoral—it began as a military tool—and effectively unregulated. It can't be killed; it can't be stopped. No one can turn it off now. It serves any purpose: commerce, politics, fun, freedom, dictatorship, secret, open, free, expensive, religious, secular, love, drive, profit, torture, murder, salvation and silence. It has no constraint, it's open to all, will serve any master, will bide any will, will be bigger than anybody. It can do more than anyone can ever imagine.'

It sounded like someone I knew.

Or wished I knew.

I considered my reply. I did my best. I said, 'Hmmm.'

Sophia chuckled. 'Too much for you, old man?' Then she snapped serious. 'Give me the disk. I want to check out those web sites.'

'You want to buy kumquats?'

'I want to save lives.'

The pause was pregnant with incomprehension. She looked at me, calm, assured. I lit another cigarette. 'Wandering stars,' meandered Portishead, quoting the Book of Jude, 'for whom it is reserved, the blackness, of darkness, for ever . . .'

Finally, I spoke. I knew I sounded ludicrous. 'With kumquats you want to save lives?'

Sophia sighed, shrugged, shook her head and sat back, folding her legs beneath her. She stared at me, leaning in slightly, assessing me, weighing something up. After a moment or two, she seemed to make up her mind and sighed again, preparing herself.

'Joe,' she said. 'Joshua Ben Panther, I'm afraid I've been less than fully frank with you.'

I felt my eyes narrow. Tension crept across me, tightening my muscles in preparation for fight or flight. My question came as a whisper: 'What?'

'I am a federal officer,' she said, standing up. 'Hold on while I go get the cheesy biscuits and another bottle of plonk.'

✝

Portishead gave way to Tricky, cabernet merlot gave way to claret, and afternoon gave way to dusk. I was initiated into gnosticism, availed of the occult.

Sophia would not reveal her agency. That, she said, was both unnecessary and unwise. I gave her some options: ASIO, ASIS, federal police, the Office of National Assessment, customs, military intelligence. 'Something like that,' she replied airily. 'Officially, it doesn't have a name.'

She was, she said, part of a complex international investigation, a labyrinthine and laborious exercise in inter-agency covert cooperation. The target was a type of pornography—nasty pornography, well organised, pornography involving abduction, mutilation, and death. No one had ever seen much of it, she explained, only occasional glimpses, signs and oblique references. In fact, she continued, no one in the various inter-linked agencies was even sure that it existed on the scale that was assumed, or whether they were dealing with nothing more than a few unconnected pieces of obscenity. Both theories fitted, apparently, and neither could in good conscience be ignored.

There were two strands to the mystery. The first was the nature of the signs revealed; the other was the places they were found. I leant back on the sofa, crossed my legs, pulled from the claret, crunched a cracker, and listened.

'All up,' she said, eyes bright, 'we've got about a dozen stills, you know, like photographs, but the think-ing is that they're not meant to be still, I mean, not all of them, not originally. Originally some were from films, video, something moving, different things. What and how much, we don't know. We've come across some of them as images on the Net, and others as hard copies—you know hard copy, like on paper?—at, well, I'll get to that, places in Europe and North America.'

There were four stills found on the Net, she said. They had been found at apparently unconnected times on almost certainly unconnected sites—sites run by stu-dents, hackers—net nerds, she called them—dedicated to collecting bits of weird, strange and, usually, sexually suggestive and fetishistic bits and bobs, ripped off or hacked from places unknown. The site operators, in Philadelphia, Malmo, Vancouver and Lisbon, had all been tracked down and questioned closely. 'They were all sick bunnies,' she said, 'but they knew nothing, you know, like they were opportunist feeders, bottom of the chain, carrion eaters.'

And carrion it was, their diets. Most of the people featured in the stills appeared dead or almost dead. All of them were naked; most, but not all, were women. Their deaths and suffering were profound. Sophia described some of them, her perky manner never once faltering as she spoke of one, a man, tied down and tortured with railway spikes; another, a woman, who appeared to have been stripped to the waist, whipped, and then placed alive on a bonfire; a third, also female, savaged by a dog; the last, still female, pierced and suspended, wrists manacled, the blood on her face leading observers to deduce she'd bitten off her own tongue.

Many are the ways to martyrdom. The horror passed over me, or through me, not touching the sides. Countless millions have died in defiant or grovelling agony during my life, my honour hanging above the slaughter, voiced by the victim, the killer, or both. Whenever two or more of you are gathered in my name there is death. And PR.

The wine was good. I had a thirst up. I hoped she had a third bottle.

The hard copies, actual prints, she continued, had been discovered unexpectedly, as by-products of other

306

investigations. It was only in the past several months that correspondence between agencies around the world had discovered what appeared to be—what might have been—a pattern.

'Remember Waco?' she asked. 'Remember David Koresh, his mob, called themselves Branch Davidians, up in smoke? One was found there.'

I shook my head. 'Their compound was completely razed.'

'Well not there, exactly. It was found in a house rented by an ex-member, a drop-out, a guy who quit two weeks before the siege began, lucky, eh? The Americans figure maybe there were more inside the ranch, you know, but, shit, no idea, they had trouble finding even teeth when they finally combed the ashes. Then another one was found in California a couple of years later.'

'Let me guess,' I interrupted, 'Heaven's Gate, that mob of screwed-up fundamentalists who figured the Lord was coming to rescue them in a spaceship concealed in the tail of the Hale-Bopp comet. They all committed suicide, very neatly.'

'Spot on, Joe.' She smirked. 'Good to see you follow current events. It was found in a desk drawer. Can you believe it, these guys, I mean, you know, some of them even chopped their balls off because they thought Jesus'd be pleased.'

'There be eunuchs which have made themselves eunuchs for the kingdom of Heaven's sake,' I mused. 'He that is able to receive it, let him receive it. It was quite a popular gesture once. Bloke called Origen did it around 202 AD. He became rather famous.'

She shook her head, drained her glass. 'Fucking loonies, I don't know. Anyway, you're getting, I think, the gist now. More were found at another cult mass suicide, a group called the Solar Temple, in Europe and Canada, another on an encampment used by a group of US rightwing survivalists, all big guns, God, and beware the New World Order. There were rumours about an associate of Timothy McVeigh, the guy who bombed Oklahoma in revenge for Waco, he might have had some of this shit, and a definite find in the house of an Italian man, a psychopath, who murdered four prostitutes in Naples and told the police God told him to do it.'

'Lot of them about.'

'He's a demented bastard, your God, isn't he?'

'I don't know.'

'And, yeah, anyway, a few others, here and there, in the possession of violent men convinced of the holy justice of their missions, preparing for the apocalypse. It doesn't take much, does it Joe, to figure there's a link.'

'Any more wine?'

'In a minute.'

I spoke carefully. One always should when in the presence of mystery. Or cops. 'So, you think—what?— these images are messages? Catalysts? Instructions to kill?'

She looked at the ceiling for a moment, choosing her words.

'Not that causal, no. We're leaning away from grand conspiracy, because, look at it, it doesn't make sense. If you assume that, then, well, it follows that whoever is producing this stuff knows in advance of where these cults are forming, what they're thinking, what kind of paranoias they possess, and seeks them out. And then there are the loner loonies, like the guy in Naples—it would mean that someone, somewhere, knows how to get to individual sick-pups, anyone, anywhere, out of anonymity, right around the world. I mean, Joe, follow that path and where do you end up at?'

I didn't need to name names.

'Precisely.' She tapped her knee in triumph. 'And there ain't no god, Joe, it's just the devil when he's drunk. So, no, no conspiracy, not active, anyway. It's more like, well, business. Weird attracts weird. People find these things, hunt them down, key into them. Pay for them. Violent pornography—*real*, violent pornography—helps sick bastards normalise their feelings of, what, terror, revenge, blood lust, whatever. See enough of it second-hand, it helps you overcome your fears of doing it for real. It must be okay, because other people are doing it. More: it shows it's *needed*, it authenticates the mission. Kill a person, torture them, strip them? No. Kill an image, create a tortured icon, make a mythic sacrifice? Much easier: it can be justified, the demands of a higher power.'

I thought of earlier in the day, of anger and of flames.

309

The more of himself man attributes to God the less he has left in himself.

'Who said that? One of your ancient preachers?'

I realised I had spoken aloud. 'No,' I said. 'No one important. But your theory posits intent, if not direction. Someone's putting this stuff out to help create an atmosphere of possibility. Someone wants to encourage death and mayhem?'

She grinned. 'Or meet the demand for it already there. That's the thinking. Decadence and horror precede the Second Coming—that's the theory, isn't it?'

'That's the Revelation line. It was written late in the first century by a bloke called John on the island of Patmos. Christ knows what he'd been smoking.'

He doesn't actually. But he'd dearly love to try some.

'So look where we are,' she continued. 'Doesn't matter how you measure it: *Anno Domini*, six thousand years since creation, Age of Pisces into Aquarius. The orthodox, the fundies, the bloody crystal-clutchers— everyone's expecting major cosmic changes in the next few years. Two thousand is just a number, Joe, just arbitrary, but the expectations are real enough.'

I nodded agreement. None of it had been my idea, after all. 'Prepare ye the way of the Lord.'

'Well, that's it, yes.' She smiled. 'Or the Earth Goddess or the new age of reason or the jolly green gopher-men from Mars. Do you know there are thousands of outwardly sane-looking people who think global warming should be encouraged because it'll hasten the age of the saints? Everywhere you look, Joe, the message is the same: *bring it on*. Lots of people can't wait and we're thinking, too, there's a lot more of this porn stuff somewhere, bigger, better, worse. It's not just nasty, it's food for the hungry. A lot of people out there want to see the earth as Sodom awaiting God's wrath. We want to stop it. Fast.'

I sensed that we'd reached a moment, a point in a journey I'd had no idea I was on. It was a familiar feeling. She was about to give me a donkey. 'And?'

'Wait, Joe. A lot of intelligence has gone into figuring this out, you know, this is a high priority on a lot of international agendas. The consensus is that we're pretty sure where it's *not* coming from—people have been questioned, unpleasant perverts have been grilled, phones have been tapped, mail's been intercepted. Our leads are few, but there's a thin one in Australia. This stuff has never been found in Australia. That might be significant in itself, you know?'

'What?'

'The madman in Naples. The Italian investigators cleaned his place out but good, really took his house apart, and you know, Joe, guess what they found?'

I shrugged my shoulders. She picked up the zip disk from the table, waggled it between her fingers.

'One of these,' she said. 'Not *this* one, exactly, another one, an older one, different serial number, same logo.'

'What was on it?'

'Shit about kumquats.'

'So?'

'Two things: the man had nothing to do with the fruit trade, and it was found in a box beneath his floor-boards, together with some hardcore porno magazines, a Bible, a crucifix and a branding iron.'

Needless to say, she said, the kumquat marketing body didn't exist, and the trail, eventually, exhaustively, led back to Image Makers and Graeme Purdey. The agency moved in, paying off the existing receptionist, sweetening the deal with Purdey by means of conven-ient fiction rendered plausible by the donation of money to his personal account, and Sophia Ognenis took up position, eyes well open, cover in place.

'Nothing,' she said. 'I found the zips okay, and noted, like, his paranoias, but I never got the chance to play with one. Insists on handling them himself. It's weird. I've talked to him a lot, even gone out for drinks with him—he fancies me, the sleazebag—and he's never mentioned anything, nothing, not a hint that his business is anything but above board. We've checked his finances, his accounting, his tax, the lot, and, hey, guess what, he's squeaky clean. Except . . .'

'Except?'

'Except the kumquat account is ridiculously profit-able. He gets, we reckon, fifty grand a year just to send out the disks to approved clients. Trouble is, we don't know who those clients are, nor who approves them first. We tried to trail back the money, but it gets lost in a maze of trust funds, shelf companies, offshore investments, even a church in Florida. There's no advertising, beyond one or two display ads placed in glossy skin mags, and those plug nothing but kumquats. We were beginning to think we were on the wrong track, except for two things. One of them was you walking in, offering incest flicks.'

Yep, I thought. I can pick my moments. 'But you know now that was all bullshit. What was the other thing?'

She chuckled. 'You're going to like this, Joe boy. We checked his family, past and present, his associates, even the whores in the brothels he frequents. Guess what we found?'

'Nothing?'

'Spot on, but, and here it is, guess where we found the most nothing? His ex, his ex-wife, Beatrice Cowper. She's suss to buggery, Joe. Did you know she's got a PhD? She did her thesis in mythological psychiatry.'

'What's that?'

'Analysing behavioural disorders in people who don't exist, I guess. She doesn't practise, though. Seems she applied for a research post at her university years back and was turned down, something about exercising a harmful influence on study volunteers.'

'Like lobotomising their imaginary friends?'

'Convincing students to run away from home, I heard. All very murky, anyway. She owns half a dozen rental properties, mostly small retail jobs, run at arm's length and meticulously documented. Her taxes are clean, but her income is clearly vastly more than she declares, and we can't find it. Her house is a fortress, like serious, the phone lines can't be tapped, and she's got a lot of them—'

'I know. I saw the junction boxes.'

'Coaxials at that. Industrial quality, really fast. Digital ISDN. We can't hack into her computers, remote listening device shields are up, we've tried, surveillance everywhere, but she's bomb-proof and bullet-proof, security up the arse, I reckon she'd even have a boom gate across her fanny, no bills, no accounts, no wants, no warrants, nothing. In real terms, she's invisible and invulnerable, and that's really fucking smelly.'

It sounded familiar, though. I decided to ask a dumb question. It helps, I find, asking the occasional dumb question. It makes people think you're dumb. 'So what are you going to do?'

She stared at me a moment, her eyes flashing a gamut of possibilities, mostly, I noted, sorrowful ones. Then she drained her glass. 'That's where you come in, Joshua Ben Panther. You've met her, you've been inside, you know her.'

'How do you know?'

'We've got a small automatic camera mounted on a telegraph pole outside her house. It looked like routine line maintenance. It triggers every time someone enters its field of view, which is, you know, focused on the gate. This past week there's only been you and a couple of Mormons, who went away, you know, empty-handed. You went in.'

I nodded slowly, thinking quickly. 'Just the front?'

She confirmed. 'Your mission, Joe, should you decide to accept it, is to go back in there again, find a way, win the lady's heart, let us in.'

Not again. 'The cops, the other cops I mean, Gordon and Pordelli, they know about this?'

'No, no, no, no way, none of that amateur shit. Hence the theatrics the other night, of course. They haven't got a clue what's going on.'

'Something we agree on, at least. And if I don't accept?'

She bowed her head, picked up the wine bottle, made a show of checking to see if it was empty. The Tricky album came to an end. The silence hung for a minute. When she spoke, her voice was hushed, tinged with regret.

'The confidentiality of our assignment is pretty much absolute. The very act of telling someone about it puts that person in danger—not from the baddies, Joe, but from us. You know now, and we, well, we know a lot of things about you. We know, like, there are serious charges pending against you, so, really, all we have to do if you won't play ball is let events take their course.'

'I've got that covered,' I lied.

'Maybe, maybe not,' she chirped, and then went all solemn again. 'We can cover it better. Help us, and we'll see what we can do about getting you money, getting you documentation, getting you out of the country. We are not above making deals with violent men. Some of our best friends are violent men. But, you know, if you reckon you've got the state cops under control, there's always the other option, and that's this, Joe Panther: you will die in this house, now if necessary, and, like, I think I should point out two things, here. First, have no doubt that I can and will do it and still sleep sound come bedtime.'

I hadn't.

'And, second, be aware your body will lie here, undiscovered and going all yucky, for far longer than Davey Parker's did at his place.'

The first part of that point was untrue, although she could not, of course, have realised it. The second part, though, sent a clamour through my brain and sweat to my palms. How could she have known about *that*?

I felt her hand lightly patting my knee. 'You've gone rather pale, Joe, and that won't help at all. You have a little think about things. I'll grab another bottle, while you, why don't you, put on some more music?'

✝

'So, yeah, memes,' she said. 'Great idea, don't you think, and really, what's the word, axiomatic. And reductive: the idea of the meme, which is, of course, itself a meme—the idea, I mean. I *love* that.'

We were drunk. It was dark outside. The fourth bottle was well on its way to destiny. The compact disc selection had yielded a Bjork album. The cheesy biscuits had long gone, and the subject of a home-delivered pizza placed on the agenda, but deferred. The ashtray was overflowing.

We were just jazzing, facing each other on the sofa. Paradoxically, given that I was technically under threat of death, and in the place of my threatened death, I was quite comfortable. At least no one, bar the obvious, knew where I was. Invisibility has its attractions.

Predictably, Sophia had questioned me about my collection of books. I had told her that religion was a hobby of mine. I was trying to understand it, trying to understand what went wrong. She would have got the wrong end of the stick if I told her I was working on an alibi.

'Nothing went wrong,' she said. 'It all went perfectly, well, not to plan—there was no plan—but to pattern, like, you know, the fundamental imperative was, is, survival.'

'Of humanity?' I asked. 'Surely not. Eleven crusades, countless holy wars, the Inquisition, the witch craze, bubonic plague spread by wandering penitents, reinforced poverty through dogmatic opposition to contraception, centuries of violent inequality through telling people that the *next* life is important, not this one ...'

'Yeah, yeah, yeah, all that, but that's not what I mean.' She was quite excited, bouncing up and down, suffused by her own epiphany. 'The survival applies to the *idea*, not to its believers. That's the theory of the

317

meme. Every idea is a meme. A meme is a self-replicating system, like a virus or a genetic code, something not technically alive in isolation, but capable of aggressive colonisation within a host, and aggressive replication *between* hosts.'

'Cute metaphor, but ideas change, ideas die out. The world isn't flat.'

'No, ideas are *selected out*, they are aggressively outcompeted by, by—'

'Better ideas?'

'More ruthless ideas. Better is a value judgement. Look at a virus, a really successful virus, I mean, like flu. What happens? The virus colonises, it adapts, it changes to best exploit its host, its chances of reproducing itself. A good virus can change itself almost totally—change its symptoms, change its effects, become drug resistant, become more dangerous, become, you know, more infectious. A virus has no morals, right, a virus doesn't question itself, nor does it consider the needs and wants of its host. It just does what it has to do in order to reproduce itself: it will kill, it will cripple, it will turn the brain to mush, anything.'

'So you think ideas do the same?' I asked. 'A meme adapts to each new cultural environment?'

'If it's strong enough, yes,' she said. 'So you'll never find it, Joe, your explanation, never, in any of your books. The books are products of the meme and you can't see a meme as good as that one from the inside. Like, the books assume the agent of increase to be God, and that's bullshit. The agent of increase is the *idea* of God, the God meme. Shit, look at it, take Christianity as an example: it preaches love and forbearance, but doesn't hesitate to commit acts of extraordinary savagery. That's not hypocrisy; it's the adaptation of the meme.'

'So humanity invented God, is that it?'

'Did humanity invent the flu virus? No. Humanity gave the flu virus an environment in which to flourish. What if the meme—all memes—already exist, and we just provide the breeding conditions?'

'Memes foresee?'

'Memes act, blindly and ruthlessly, I reckon. There's no foresight at the heart of the universe, Joe, only hard-wired self-referential imperatives. Look, the God meme is the most ruthless of all, never mind its choice of god. Look, look, there.'

She waved her arm at the *Larry Flynt* poster. 'There it is, in action again, perfectly willing to subvert its characteristics of respect and awe, perfectly willing to grovel in the mud as an image of sado-masochistic eroticism, just as long as it lives one more day, passes on its code one more time. That image isn't, like, a secular appropriation of religious imagery—it's a blind appropriation of the secular by the meme itself. The meme doesn't give a fuck about the Ten Commandments. The Ten Commandments were manifestations of the meme's drive to succeed. They were what was required at the time. Human beings needed an appendix once, too, you know, it was crucial, but then it wasn't, so

319

we withered it. The God meme needed religion to survive and reproduce. When it doesn't need it any more, it will simply discard it.'

Despite myself, I drifted into the discussion. 'And mutate again, maybe. The heart of god is universal power. Does god now move into a better mechanism for universal power, maybe, an empirical mechanism, like your Internet?'

She looked sad for a moment. 'If we're not careful, yes, unless we cultivate a better meme, still more powerful.' Suddenly she perked up again. 'There's always hope, Joe, always hope. There's another theory, I like this one, that says culture and genes—say, memes and genes—are linked, and, like, influence each other. They call it the thousand year rule—certain characteristics are favoured by cultural change, but the genes take a thousand years to catch up. A thousand years ago, the Christian god meme was rampant, undefeatable, but, in the past thousand years, you know, intellectually, philosophically, scientifically, we've destroyed that god. Maybe, you know, genetically, we're becoming resistant to god. The Internet's happened at millennium time, and, right, I don't think that's coincidental, I think it's predictable and mechanistic. Who knows, in another thousand years the meme may be selected out totally. I mean, you'd know this, there are many more dead gods than living ones.'

I drained the last of the pinot noir. Bjork's dispassionate cycles were hypnotic, and becoming more so. My head sank against the back of the sofa, my arse moved forward on the cushion. A thousand years. A thousand years.

'What are you doing, Joe?' I heard Sophia ask, through a fog.

'Looking forward to some rest,' I replied, and welcomed the darkness, poor simulation though it was.

✝

# 10

ZOROASTER'S SON CAME TO ME in the hypnogogic dawn.

He was old, fragile and weary, not a day over twenty-nine. He was shuddering with the effort of standing, his right hand bloodied from the sacrifice of bulls, his left grasping the wrinkled remains of a pomegranate, eyes bulging from the holy hallucinogens that fuelled his father's cult.

For three millennia now, he croaked, he had wandered the earth, seeking the certainty his old man had possessed, to no avail, to no reward. His time at last, he said, was near. To most now he was less than memory. His father's laws shaped the world for centuries, but now they persisted in the minds of mere thousands of devotees. Three generations more, he said, and peace would come for him, the momentary sleep of the immortally dead. Soon, oblivion would be his reward.

You could have that now, I said, and offered him some smack, trade discount. He shook his head and faded.

In wearied silence and red wine hangover, I lay and wondered. How long? How much longer for me?

I opened my eyes, slowly at first, and then with a start. For a moment I had no idea where I was, and all sorts of nameless fears, a swarm of shapeless memories, swept through my head. Then I remembered: I was on the sofa of Sophia's safe-house. The ochre curtains were drawn, but their warm orange glow combined with the drifting sounds of distant cars, a chiming tram, the excited shrieks of small children, told me it was well morning.

I felt creased and sore as I levered myself up, but strangely rested for all that. I needed a pee, badly. The loo, I remembered, was upstairs. Sophia was nowhere to be seen. I figured that stomping around in a house which might also contain a sleeping sociopath skilled in martial arts, operating covertly in an atmosphere of death and revenge, might not be the most sensible thing to do, not without announcing myself.

I called her name from the base of the stairs, softly at first, then louder. I called again from halfway up, and again outside what must have been her bedroom door. No answer. Gently, I turned the handle, pushed it open. The room was empty, decorated in the best Best Western style, the covers flung over the bed. The clock radio on her bedside table said it was 9.15am. She must have gone to work.

323

And I wondered, this woman, does she ever *stop* working?

I was all alone in a stranger's house. I figured there was no point in searching it, her mob was too professional for that, so I went back downstairs and found the coffee.

Before leaving I telephoned Corrigan. He'd got my message about Scopemi, he said, and gave his word he'd look into it straight away. Then I asked him about the other thing that was bothering me.

After that, I called Image Makers. Complicity, I decided, was a two-way street. Sophia answered.

'It's me.'

'Sleep well?'

'Yet a little, a little slumber, a little folding of the hands to sleep. Can you talk?'

'Sure, because, you know, the boss isn't in yet and hasn't phoned, don't know what's going on.'

'What are you doing tonight?'

She giggled a bit. 'You disappoint me, Joe. I thought you were better than that, though why, God only knows. Last night was strictly business, and serious business at that.'

'So is this.'

'What?'

'Not on the phone. When can you meet me?'

'Have to be late, because there are some things, you know, I want to do here that I shouldn't do until Purdey's left for the day, so I'm faking up some filing shit, some computer shit, reallocation of disk space to make life more efficient, that sort of thing. I'm going to, you know, offer to stay behind to finish it. He likes that sort of thing. He'll probably volunteer to keep me company, but I'll piss him off quick.'

I glanced around the room. The zip disk was nowhere in sight.

'Late is good. What's the nearest pub to your place? We need to be in that—this—area.'

'The Cardigan. It's—'

'I'll find it. Eleven o'clock. Wear black.'

'Joe, we've—'

I talked over her, asked her to do one more thing. She said she didn't know if it was possible, but she'd try. I hung up while she was explaining the difficulties, and let myself out. The Falcon drove off as I hit the pavement. There was money in my pocket sufficient for a taxi, but the day was fine, at least temporarily, the sun casting a glamour of warmth in the finger-numbing air, so I decided to walk.

When I reached the turn-off into the alley that led to the warehouse, I noted something very interesting. None of the watcher cars was around. A few metres further up, turning into the darkened car park, I found out why.

Parked in it were two police patrol cars and a divvy van.

Life went to shit.

✝

'So again, Panther, once again, slowly, just so you understand: Where. The fuck. Is Mrs Elaine *Purdey*?'

The softness of Gordon's tone did little to disguise his fury. Nothing, in fact. His face was very close to mine, looming from above. He'd had bacon for breakfast.

We were back once more in the interview room. He, Pordelli and I had been there for well over an hour, as far as I could judge, police rooms, like casinos, being clock-free zones.

My hands were in my lap, cuffed. I looked down at them and said again, 'I've no idea.'

Pordelli hit me across the cheek with the White Pages A–Z, nearly knocking me off my chair. I struggled to regain my balance, never taking my eyes from him, and then slowly, insolently, turned my head, presenting its other profile. The fat man raised the book.

'No,' snapped Gordon, halting him with an outstretched hand. 'One more bruise on this bastard and he'd hardly feel it.'

He would, actually, but it was not the time to be pedantic.

'It might help,' I ventured, 'if you stopped asking questions and started making statements—'

'*You're* the one supposed to be making a bloody statement, mystery man,' shouted Pordelli. Gordon gave him a look, and indicated to him that he should sit. He did so, reluctantly.

His boss did the same. 'Okay, then, Panther, for the record, let me tell you what you already know. Sometime last night, between 7.00pm, when Graeme Purdey

326

finished his home-cooked dinner and went out, and 2.00am, when he went back home again, his wife, Elaine Purdey, disappeared. There were signs of a struggle inside the house, but no indication of forced entry into it. There's been no contact, no messages, no demands since. That means we can probably—although not definitely at this stage—rule out a kidnapping. That means, in turn, we're dealing with a violent arsehole with an agenda of his own. Now, Panther, how many violent arseholes has Mrs Purdey come into contact with recently? One, and only one.'

'How do you know that?' I asked.

Pordelli growled. 'We know that, mystery man, filthy man. We know that.'

'It couldn't have been me,' I stated. 'There was no forced entry. Elaine Purdey wouldn't let me in of her own free will.'

Gordon stared at me as if I was a smear on a microscope slide. 'Sometimes I wonder about you and free will, Panther. Sometimes I think you could talk anybody into anything.'

He was too kind. He really was. I didn't mention it.

Pordelli leaned forwards in his chair. '*Speak*, you bastard.'

I adopted my most irritatingly holy countenance. 'There is a time to keep silence, and a time to speak; a time to love, and a time to—'

'Shut it, Panther,' said Gordon.

'He just told me to speak,' I countered, pointing, trying to point, at his offsider.

327

'Then fucking speak to *me*. You say you don't know where she is.'

I nodded.

'So prove it. You know the routine. Account for your movements last night and we'll pat you on the head, say sorry to have troubled you, and let you get on with the work you're *supposed* to be doing for us.'

Call me cynical, call me wise, but I decided that telling Gordon I'd spent the night in the company of Graeme Purdey's receptionist, who happened to be an undercover federal agent temporarily domiciled in a nondescript safe-house while trying to track down a transglobal trade in sadistic sexual snuff films, all the time not telling the local cops about it, would not have been the most intelligent thing I could have done.

'Could Graeme Purdey have set it—'

'Don't be idiotic.'

I was presented with something of an obvious problem, that of coming up with a lie which functioned as well as the truth. It wasn't so much an ethical question as a theatrical one. Truth, at least if the past two thousand years are anything to go by, is not that which is truthful. It is that which is believed. The difference between falsehood and honesty is performance.

'Well?' growled Gordon, impatient.

I performed.

'*Listen*, Gordon,' I hissed. 'I'm sick of this. You've got a murder, you've got an abduction, and you don't have jackshit else, do you? No. What you've got is an overwhelming desire to make it stop, to get it *sorted*, to

328

get back a cosy life of filling out the paperwork on overdosing junkies, domestic violence, drunks in knife fights and mad people released into the community, cluttering the streets, howling at the tourists. What a pity you've got some real work to do for a change. In the absence of the culprit or culprits confessing, all you can think to do is fit up the local outcast.'

Because that's what I am. It's what I always have been. No one has ever asked me to sit on a jury and offer judgement on my peers. Which is short-sighted, really, given my qualifications.

'Self-pitying bastard,' muttered Pordelli.

'Self-*supporting* bastard. I am a paragon of the capitalist system, an inevitable product of a free market economy. *And,*' I hammered, before Gordon could open his gob any wider, 'may I remind you that I have never been charged with anything in this town—not before this week, anyway—much less convicted, and you are therefore persecuting an innocent man, no priors, no probabilities, nothing.'

'Is that it?' sneered Gordon. 'Does the defence rest?'

'The defence *never* rests,' I replied, flying now. 'The defence, if you must know, was out all last bloody night doing your work for you. You want the benefit of my network in tracking down some bloody woman you can use to frame a priest, then you've got to let me work that game. My people (I nearly said my flock) don't live clockwork lives, don't go to work at nine and watch 'Melrose Place' come evening. They have their own routines, their own concerns, and if I want them to sing to me I've got to get in their rhythms.'

'So tell me where—'

'And part of those rhythms are silence,' I said, then swung in. 'Look, you've got nothing to link me to Elaine Purdey's disappearance. It surprises me as much as it does you, believe me. I can't tell you where she is, or whether her little sunken chest still heaves and flutters, but I *can* tell you this—you've got no fingerprints of mine, no—'

'Which reminds me,' started Pordelli.

I cut him off fast. 'No fibres, no footprints, no witnesses, no clues, nothing that points to me except your own self-affirming suspicions. I'll tell you that. And why? Why? Because I wasn't there, I wasn't anywhere near the place. Anyway, in case it's slipped your mind, I have neither car nor a licence to drive one, so, think about it, how am I supposed to abduct anyone on foot? On the bus? Roll the bitch up in the floor coverings and whack her in a taxi boot, tell the guy I'm a rug salesman on the night shift?'

'Do they do that, work nights?' asked Pordelli.

Gordon had not been so diverted. 'Where did you spend the night?' he demanded.

'We need trust, Gordon.'

'We need a killer and a kidnapper, Panther, not necessarily in that order.'

'So I need to be out *there*, not in here. Listen, deal time, try this. I've got things to do, things to our mutual benefit, for my sins. If I tell you where I slept and give you a name to confirm it—there's no

330

phone—will you let me go before you check it?'

'And if I don't?'

'Time's ticking, for you and, maybe, for Elaine Purdey, if time still has any meaning for her. You can whack me in a cell for hours if you like. I don't mind. I'll meditate or something, contemplate the way.'

He stared at me hard for a minute, then picked up his pen.

'Give.'

I held up my arms.

'Unlock him, Pordelli.'

I gave him Caroline's name and address.

'We know her,' he said. 'Junkie girl.'

There were no familiar cars outside the cop shop. I didn't know why.

Which was a fat lot of help.

In any case, though, it meant that for the moment I was free to move untailed, and that was good, because I needed to move very fucking fast.

Five minutes later I was standing on Brunswick, flagging cabs. The second one stopped, only took a few minutes, but the driver scowled when I told him I wanted to go just a couple of blocks. I scowled back. We went.

I had gambled that Caroline was still living in the flat she had shared with Shelagh Purdey, a poky white-brick first-floor walk-up hard by Alexandra Parade, multi-laned, arterial, and clogged morning and eve. I figured it wasn't much of a risk. Little enough time had passed, so it was unlikely she had yet come to terms with the looming problem of having to scrape up all the rent, given that scraping half was hard enough on a costly habit.

The concrete staircase felt cold and damp, despite being open to the wind and, for once, washed by dilute sun. I hadn't been there for months, hadn't paid much attention when I did, but it all still looked the same from the outside. I knocked on the door, called out my name and hers so as not to alarm her, waited a minute. No answer.

Maybe she was out. Maybe she was asleep. Maybe she was ignoring me. Maybe she was dead. You can never tell with some people.

I wasn't about to let it go and come back later, so I fished out a syringe from inside my leather jacket, and went to work on the lock. It didn't take long.

I found her lying, foetal, in a faded maroon windcheater and track pants, on a fetid mattress on the floor of her room. Shelagh's room, I noticed, had been cleared of its tawdry cargo, but otherwise uncleaned. There wouldn't have been much to clear in Caroline's: a battered clock radio, a science fiction paperback, crumpled clothes and a candle, little more. She was awake, and sick.

She stretched a smile when she saw me, unbothered by a stranger's intrusion as only the thirsty can be. I asked questions, gently, permitting monosyllabic replies. Her dole cheque hadn't arrived, she had nought else to spend and nothing left to trade. Saturday's stock was gone. She hurt bad.

'Will you do anything for me, if I ease your pain?' I asked. 'Will you take up your cross and follow?'

Sadness crossed her face. With difficulty, she patted her oily pillow.

'Not that,' I said.

She simply stared at me, wondering what was to come.

'Well?'

She nodded. I brewed up for her, let her drink from the bubbling stream, just a taste. I'd leave more for her, for later, or sooner, but I didn't want her nodding out before I'd told her what I needed her to do.

I waited, not altogether patiently, until clarity came to her eyes, straining to hear above the dull mantra of the traffic, listening for the sound of a car pulling up, counting minutes.

'You growing your beard out?' she asked, vague. 'You need a shave bad.'

'The police will come,' I said.

She jolted, the fear of betrayal in her eyes. I calmed her by raising my hand. It was a gesture of peace, but I don't think she took it that way.

'They will ask about me,' I continued. 'You tell them we met at ten last night, thereabouts, over on Gertrude. I came back with you. I stayed here. *Right* here.' I patted the mattress. It felt gritty. 'I left, nine o'clock today.'

'Why?'

A hint of warning crept into my voice. 'Caroline.'

She nodded. 'Sure, Joe,' she said, and managed a brief, bitter laugh. 'You stayed here all night, all night with sex bomb Caro. We shook the walls, loverboy, we shook the fucking walls.'

'Amen,' I said, and handed her the rest of the deal. 'Hide this. It will be soon.'

What is truth? I find in her no fault at all.

I heard the hiss of tyre against gravel. 'Now,' I said. 'Fire escape.'

She pointed. I heard a knock on the front door as my boot clanged softly on the stairs.

✝

I was dying for a shower and a change of clothes, but all too conscious of the fact that heading to the warehouse would put me back in the enigmatic gaze of my observers.

For the moment I was still free to move about unmonitored, and that had to be worth something. I jumped the fence at the back of Caroline's block, stole down the driveway of the adjoining apartments, and walked into the street. Sticking to the back roads, and meandering as much as possible, I made my way to Brunswick Street and to Bakers, a cafe a few blocks away from Mario's, hopefully far enough from my usual predictable routes to avoid notice. The latte was good, the cigarette mana.

The situation was a mess. As I glanced through the morning broadsheet, I tried a recap.

Shelagh Purdey was dead. Who killed her? Corrigan, Gordon's choice; or her father, my choice; or her mother, maybe Sophia's choice; or another, unknown, party.

Elaine Purdey was missing, possibly dead. Who took her? Me, Gordon's choice; or her husband, *not* my choice but a possibility nevertheless; Sophia's people, to set me up, or to use as a bargaining chip against Graeme Purdey in trying to spring some dirt on his ex; or, again, another, unknown, party.

Beatrice Cowper, formerly Purdey, PhD, was neither missing nor dead. She was, however, the focus of a murky, high level, international investigation into violent, randomly catalytic snuff porn, the imagery in which bore more than a passing resemblance to the icons of Christian martyrology.

She was also, despite her stated wish to be shot of me, going to curious, complex and, I had to admit, disturbing lengths to bedevil me. Her status as Brigid *doppelganger* could only have been coincidental, right down to her little fancy dress display—that was a Jesus joke, a mockery of the afflicted. Even so, I couldn't imagine that if the Mormons were to pay her a repeat visit she'd greet them dressed as the angel Moroni, carrying two rocks in a hat.

Nor could I imagine, for that matter, how she'd known I'd pop up over the fence.

The book, though, was another matter. That was a

hostile act. I suspected it would not be the last. She was hot for me. But why? Because of who she thinks I am, a deluded loop, a drug-addled and unstable stalker? Or because of who I *really* am (How could she know? Is she *really* Brigid?), the living, breathing, stubbornly undead invalidation of the very principles of law, morality and obedience?

Did I excite the mythologocal psychiatrist in her, or the holy avenger? There is no social value to death or pain, after all, unless that death or pain is symbolic.

The thinking among the more philosophical Romans in the first couple of hundred years after my rumoured demise found Pauly's assertions inexplicable. They had long decided that the gods of their own pantheon were, in fact, all reflections of different aspects of the same, ultimate god. Paul's gig they couldn't come at, not because it posited only one supreme being, but two: God and the Devil, never the twain shall meet, never the twain shall part. Paul made evil a myth, gave it a form and a voice. It was he, not the Devil, who made evil undefeatable, because he made it mysterious and blood-filled.

And that meant he also made it profitable, because profit can always be made from the terror of people. And he made Christianity even more profitable, because profit can always be made from the terror of the people seeking safety. It was a brilliant ploy, just brilliant. It only worked, however, as long as people never realised that the evil itself was not transcendent, but immanent, in each of us, and all around us, independent of any god's good graces.

336

And that realisation could only be prevented by indoctrination and control, or, if that didn't work, the wilful commission of horror, preferably on a grand scale. If voters lose faith in a government, watch it start a war. If believers lose faith in a religion, watch it launch a crusade. Fear precludes reason. When the people start to reason, make them afraid: give them horror to witness, and wait for them to thank god it wasn't them on the news last night.

I ordered another latte. There was nothing much in the paper, save a brief item headlined DOG PUZZLE. It noted that police were looking into the apparent thefts of at least three small dogs from the Fitzroy area. Reported missing were a Jack Russell called Jeremy, a Pomeranian called Kwan Yin, and a Chihuahua called Kurt Cobain. There were no leads. Authorities were still bemused, but working up to baffled.

I sighed. One more thing I had to do. One more outbreak of vanity that could lead to the discovery of the Lord.

As far as I could see there was only one certainty in the whole mess: the Melbourne gig was up for Joey-boy. It was time to go awandering again: somewhere new, another name, another fiction, another pointless sojourn at the arse-end of another city; bored with the present, fearful of the revelation of the past, a stranger to the future.

To get out, I needed money. There were several options, none without downsides.

I could set up the priest and trust the mercy of

the cops. I could help Sophia and trust the mercy of the feds. I could warn Beatrice Cowper and trust the mercy of her gratitude. Then again, I could always just toss it all, find the spookier end of the FBI, confess my divinity and ask to be put in the Jehovah's Witness Protection Scheme in return for information received.

After all, I knew where the body wasn't buried. And I knew who didn't dunnit, officer.

The second coffee was finished. I threw a five buck note on the table and headed out. It was time to get things moving, time to kick some ass. It wasn't going to be pleasant, and it wasn't going to win me any friends, but, shit, it wasn't me who said being a messiah was a popularity contest.

I shall be hated of all men for my name's sake: but he that endureth to the end shall be saved. And that, dear blessed, was going to be me.

✝

'Go away, son. There's nothing for you here.'

John the Baptist, as far as I could tell, was leaning against his door. The stairwell reeked of raw meat. I had tried cajoling and threatening, with no result.

I kept talking through the wood, working quietly at the lock with a fit. An African family—mother, father and a boy of perhaps six—squeezed past me, heading down. The child was sniffling, tugging at his mother's dress, nearly dislodging her headscarf. 'But I want Jo-Jo back,' he moaned. 'Mummy, where's Jo-Jo gone? Mummy, I want Jo-Jo.' His mother patted his shoulders, and reassured him they would find Jo-Jo, he couldn't have gone far. The father wrinkled his nostrils, turned to look at me, caught, perhaps, a glint of surgical steel in my hand, and turned away again quickly, having not seen a thing.

A minute later the sounds of their progress had faded. I heard the snick of a falling tumbler. 'One more time, old man,' I called out. 'Open the door.'

'Go away.'

I turned the handle and rammed with my shoulder. Something gave, the door flew open. I stepped inside and closed it behind me.

Immediately, I knew I'd found Jo-Jo. He was the Yorkie terrier lying twisted and snapped near the armchair. I walked slowly around the room, bending low, checking collar tags. Positive IDs were made on poor Jeremy, Kwan Yin and Kurt Cobain, together with Hinky the Maltese, Priscilla the Bishon Frise, Malcolm the Poodle, and Babaji the miniature Schnauzer. There was one other corpse. I picked it up and waved it at John, who was lying where he fell among the carnage, knees up and weeping.

'This one, old man,' I said, 'is a rat.'

'You can't blame me,' he managed, 'not with my eyesight.'

I dropped it again, then bent over and took hold of the old man under his armpits. I lifted him to his feet, dropped him into the chair. He curled into himself, face wet.

'Tell me,' I commanded.

'That's just it, son,' he blubbered. 'I can't tell you. Can't tell you nothing no more. Oh son, I done so much wrong, and now I'm damned for good. I know that. 'Oh god . . .' He dissolved once more.

First things first. 'What's wrong?'

'Dunno, son, honest, and now I'm damned to hell.'

The tears started again. This time I slapped him. He stopped. I saw his tobacco packet on the windowsill, picked it up, and dropped it in his lap. 'Tell me,' I said. 'From the start.'

He was silent while he rolled. I let him be. His fingers were shaking.

'When I done the Shih tzu,' he stammered, lighting up with difficulty, 'when I done the Shih tzu, I done it as usual: blessed it on its way, offered it up, opened my heart, and, you know, I got that vision, whatever you call it, of that woman, the one you're after . . .'

'Theresa Farndale.'

'Yeah, her. Easy. I did that, was doing that, when . . .'

The tears came again, great wracking sobs that, in turn, spawned wheezes and coughing and spittle and phlegm. His body moved like a mountain getting used to a mine.

'Tell me, old man,' I growled. 'I don't have the time for this.'

'That's just *it*, son,' he said, doing his best. 'I *can't* tell you, not any more, never again. I was doing the Shih tzu, got the goods, then, just as her eyes were closing, it happened.'

I sighed. There are times when theatre is a pain in the arse. My teeth gritted. 'What fucking happened?'

'I felt something leave, son, that's what. Don't ask me what, because I don't know. Knowing's your department. Was like, I don't know, a shake, a shiver, something, maybe I passed out a sec, can't remember, but something deep inside, didn't even know it was there, just upped and left. I knew it then, even as it happened, though I didn't think about it until the next day, too scared, couldn't sleep that night.'

I knew what it was. Too well. So did he. He stared at me, his eyes hungry without hope of nourishment.

'Was it God, son? Was it? It was, I know. All these years he's spoke to me. Then he sent me you, son, I reckon, as a sign: keep straight and you'll get home to heaven. That was the sign, and now, now he's gone and left me.' His tone changed, urgent now as he indicated the massacre on his carpet. 'I keep trying, son. See these, I keep trying. I pray and I try, pray and try, not slept hardly at all, but I get them and I take them and I talk to them and I offer them and nothing, son, not nothing's coming back. I'm bound for hell, son, I know it. I'm bound for hell.'

I tried to comfort him. 'There are worse things than hell, old man.'

It didn't work. That one never does.

341

So I tried again. I needed him stable. For a little while yet.

'Listen to me, old man,' I began, investing as much divine weight in my words as I could. 'Listen to me. The same thing happened to me.'

Hope sparked in his eyes. 'What? The other day? Maybe it's a virus.'

Maybe, I thought. Just maybe. 'It happened to me a long time back.'

He was silent a moment, and then he murmured something, half remembered. 'O Lord, why have you abandoned me . . .'

'Yep.'

'On the cross?'

'Yep. The Germans call it *Goetzvroemdunge*: God's withdrawal. Augustine spoke about it. So did Origen, only in a higher voice. They reckoned the feel of God leaving was proof that he loved you. Never bought it myself.'

'Then . . . then . . .' Suddenly his face drained in terror. He pushed himself back against his chair, eyes wide on me, head twitching and shaking.

'Yeah, yeah,' I said, dismissive. 'I'm Satan in a leather jacket, pleased to meet you. It's bullshit, old man. Look into my eyes, see if I am telling the truth.' I squatted in front of him, my face before his, holding his gaze. 'Look in my eyes. Tell me.'

'They're all bloodshot.'

Damn. That one never works either. 'If God's gone, old man, what will you do?'

342

He simply shook his head, too confused to utter.

'The answer—look at me, John the Baptist—is whatever you want, but that's probably a bit too general for you to get your head around. Sudden freedom can be fatal. Now, the way I see it, you've got two choices. You can either hang around in your new-found emptiness and silence, wondering what punishment's awaiting you when you die, or you can follow the Lord into battle. You have no choice between good and evil. That's no choice at all. What you have is a choice between desolation and purpose.'

The silence lingered a few minutes more. I wanted to hurry the old coot up, but he was jumpy as a black cat in Aleister Crowley's playroom. He extended one skinny leg, and nudged the Bishon Frise with his slippered foot. Finally, he took a deep breath.

'I can't bear it on my own. What do you want, son?'

I smiled. 'Bless you,' I said. 'I'll keep you busy. Do you still think I'm the Antichrist?'

He looked around the room, at the skulls on the wall, the corpses on the floor, the gaps in the carpet, the frays in the furniture.

'Does it matter?' he asked, not looking for a reply.

✝

We put the dogs into leftover supermarket carry bags, but the smell lingered like Pan in a woodland church-yard. It wouldn't be long, I figured, until Jo-Jo's family, bereft and tired from fruitless search, returned, wrinkled their nostrils again and put two and two together. A knock on the door, a call to the council or perhaps the police, and John would be a sad-eyed news story. The state he was in, he was likely to offer me up in explanation, real name and all.

The authorities would think him cracked, of course, another shell-shocked pensioner in a lonely world of wishes, but the damage would have been done: one more bit of gruesome weirdness with the Panther touch.

There was nothing else for it. 'Pick up some of the bags and come with me,' I said. 'We'll dump the trash in a skip. You can stay at my place.'

'I don't want to.'

'So?'

After a lengthy detour, and slowed by the old man's hobbling gait, we reached the warehouse an hour or so later.

'Hey, son,' croaked John as he wheezed up the staircase. 'That fat woman in the little car outside kept a beady eye on you.'

'You'll get used to it,' I said. 'There's a few of them. Try not to speak to them.'

He shook his head. 'No grasser me, son. You know that.'

It was almost 1.00pm, which meant I had half an hour to spare. John the Baptist was wandering around the space, wittering on about how he'd always thought I lived in a mansion somewhere, picking up books, squinting at the covers, putting them down. 'Don't even understand the titles, son.' I bade him relax, went for a shower.

Twenty minutes later, clean and changed, all black, I took him over to the Bradford. Corrigan was already there, the remains of a counter lunch in front of him, glass of beer in his hand. I ordered for John and me, told the old man to sit and eat at a table the other end of the bar, leave us alone. The scent of salvation in his nostrils, the taste of amber forgiveness on his tongue, he agreed without fuss.

The priest greeted me with muted cordiality. He was still high on the success of the memorial service.

'You know, Panther,' he said. 'I really feel it did some good. All those people—more people than that church has seen since thanksgiving services at the end of World War II, I'd bet. Ach, what a circus, people everywhere, never seen them before, most of them.'

'You'll never see them again either.' I nodded, sipping on a Jamesons.

'Mysterious ways, man,' he continued, joining the nod. 'It was a groundswell, felt like. Maybe that's the start, man. Maybe that's the beginning of the change, the people standing up, saying no, they won't tolerate a society that produces lost souls like Shelagh's, or people like the monster who killed her. She was a sign, Panther, not that you'd buy that. Maybe the spirit moved within her. Maybe she died for our sins.'

'Sounds like millennialist bullshit, priest. A thousand years comes to a close, and you reckon everything that happens is some kind of spooky message? Get a grip. You'll be siding with the alien-spotters soon.'

'It's all the same, man,' he said, signalling the barmaid for a refill. 'What's a desire to meet an alien but a yearning for the Second Coming in disguise? Or the Rapture, maybe? Delete cloud, insert flying saucer. And why not? Why shouldn't these all be signs, man? The return has always been a promise, after all.'

'In the past couple of months, priest, a woman who claimed to be a prophet abducted her grandson and took him to Tasmania, a move which would seem to invalidate her position pretty thoroughly. A man dressed in drag stole an old trunk that once belonged to Captain Cook—the guy claimed to be the Virgin Mary. An Arab Christian group were having a picnic when a bolt of lightning zapped in and wiped out a husband and wife. A Japanese youth claiming to be the devil hacked the head off a schoolboy, left a note in his mouth. Are these all signs, too?'

'No, but—'

'In Israel some people are getting excited because a red heifer's been born. They see it as a sign of prophesy fulfilled. The Messiah is coming. It could equally well be a sign that the golden calf Moses ordered destroyed is making a comeback. Then again, it could just be a cow. There's a cult in the Philippines called El Shaddai, got 150,000 followers, charismatics all, run by a real estate agent. There's a Yank mob called the Raelians who practise cloning for god.'

'You read too much.' He chuckled. 'There are always false prophets.'

'And you found the real one in your church?'

'I didn't say that.'

He could've done, though. 'Tell me about Scopemi.'

'Ach, more fucking circus. The man's buggered off somewhere, sudden like, last week. Wondered why he wasn't at the service. Didn't think he'd miss the chance to get his picture in the paper.'

'Where's he gone?'

'Buggered if I know. Looks like he's gone AWOL. Asked around, no ideas. Then I spoke to some guy at his church by phone. Arrogant bastard, wouldn't give his name, sounded like his nose was blocked—'

I smiled.

'—and he told me to bugger off. Didn't know when Scopemi'd be back, hung up on me. It's very odd, Panther, very odd and all.'

It was, that. My glass was empty.

'Priest,' I said, serious now. 'Two things. First, go see your lawyer and your bank. Have the documents drawn up, ceding your house, a loan against its value ready to go twenty-four hours after you give the nod. Do it this afternoon.'

He looked at me, hope in his eye. 'You can see a way out of this? You've got some evidence to clear me?'

'Maybe,' I said, and then wondered if I was lying. 'If it goes down, it'll go down fast. Soon. That's the other thing. Stay in plain sight from now on: no mystery, no solitude. You might need alibis.'

He took it in, appropriately solemn. 'No problems, man. I've a lot of people to see, to catch up on. Matter of fact I was looking to spend a while this afternoon with old Mrs Collosi, remember her? I've not seen her since before the service. I'm a bit worried she might be sick.'

Or babbling about the devil come to see her. 'Don't do that,' I said, then whispered, 'she might be involved.'

He stared at me in disbelief. 'Appearances can be deceiving,' I added. 'Trust me on that one.'

On the way out, I paused a moment with John the Baptist, his demeanour much improved as he slurped at his second pot, relieved, perhaps, that he no longer bore responsibility for his own life. I gave him the spare front door key, told him about the sleeping bag he could use on the sofa, and not to worry if he didn't see me for a while.

'Drink only here,' I said. 'Here's some money. Be here or the warehouse. Don't go wandering. Don't baptise anyone. If you don't see me, you'll hear from me. When word comes, obey without question.'

He nodded. I hit the street.

There was a fair whack of smack still hidden at home. I nicked back, picked it up, stuffed the wraps in my pockets. I grabbed the rest of the speed, as well.

The Cardigan was a warm and smoke-filled corner pub,

heavy on the Guinness. It drew most of its clientele from the ranks of the university campus nearby. The atmosphere inside the bar was loud and tendentious, full of the rude confidence of the young, brash, educated, cloistered and pimply.

The hot topic of discussion that night, erupting periodically from clusters of drinkers like pus from a plague victim, was a court case concluded a few days before about a photography exhibition staged at the main art gallery in the city. The Catholic Archbishop had charged that one of the shots—a depiction of a crucifix immersed in urine—was blasphemous and applied to have it banned. The judge had declined to do so. The fundies were furious: they picketed the gallery, tried to remove the photograph bodily and, when that didn't work, destroyed it with a hammer.

'Fucking bastards,' snarled someone.

'Bullshit,' replied a young blond bloke. 'The photograph was an insult to Christians everywhere.'

'You can't censor art,' said someone else.

The blond guy bridled. 'You can't just kick the shit out of people's religious beliefs, mate. How'd *you* like it?'

Sophia Ognenis arrived, slightly out of breath and wide-eyed, at 11.30pm, apologising for being late and demanding a glass of house red, sounding more like a sophomore out for a date than a federal agent engaged in urgent investigation.

She was dressed in loose black trousers, windcheater, and jacket, with a black woollen hat hanging limp from one of the jacket pockets. Accepting the glass of wine with a nod, she hopped prettily onto a bar stool, took a deep draught, paused a moment, and then, *sotto voce*, turned to the business of the day.

'Elaine Purdey. Have you—'

'I heard.'

'How?'

'The cops picked me up when I got home and—'

She tensed, eyes suddenly cold. 'What did you say?'

'Relax. I faked an alibi. A confirmable alibi. Your cover is holding.'

She smiled. 'Good man. I knew I could trust you.'

She knew nothing of the sort. We both knew that.

'Nice day at the office?' I asked.

'Shit, dahl,' she said. 'You should have seen ... What's the job we have to do, Joe, and, like, when are we going to do it?'

'Soon. After midnight. It's traditional in such matters. Tell me about today.'

'Chaos,' she said, after a moment or two. 'Where to start? Okay, Elaine Purdey's gone missing. That's number one, that's why Graeme Purdey wasn't in when you called. I didn't know at the time. He came in about half an hour later, pretty distraught, but, like, seemed to me more pissed off that his day had gone to hell than his wife had been abducted. There was a couple of cops with him. Suits. They sat with him most of the day—he did bog-all, just hung around. They wired the phones in the place—must've done the same at his place—miking them up to tape decks, waiting for a call, like a ransom or whatever.'

'Let me guess: nothing?'

'It's a fucking disgrace!' yelled a young man from across the bar. 'These fucking god-botherers are the forces of the Dark Ages!'

'They're the forces of America!' rejoined a young woman. 'In God we trust! God is a Republican!'

The woman launched into a slurred, half-remembered chorus from Gershwin's 'It Ain't Necessarily So', her friends joining in, a few with pints waving aloft. The blond guy watched, a storm in his eyes.

No one could hear us, even if they tried.

'Not quite nothing,' grinned Sophia. 'Maybe. The boss left at six, still with a cop entourage. I stayed back, told him I'd mind the fort, take care of things so he wouldn't have to go in tomorrow if he didn't feel like it. He was pathetically grateful. Really, I just wanted to get on with my business—our business—which, obviously, I'd had to put on hold while all the fuss was going on.'

'And?'

'In a minute. I left the place at about ten—I've been home to change—but when I went out the back door, you know the one—'

I nodded. She grinned.

'On the back step I found a video cassette. It was wrapped in plain brown paper with a typed label on it, addressed to Purdey. It must have been put there sometime during the evening, because the boy and his escorts also left by the back door earlier—there were a couple of reporters hanging around the front—so it can't have been there then.'

'What's on it? Did you give it to the cops?'

She shook her head, looked at me, all innocent. 'I *am* the cops. It's at the house, and I haven't looked at it yet, you didn't leave me time, Joe. I'll check it later, and then I'll get to work early tomorrow and, you know, find it on the step before Graeme Purdey turns up.'

I nodded.

'Religion is a weapon of politics!' yelled the young man.

'Economics, you mean!' countered his female friend.

'So you reckon it's okay to trample on God? You think it's funny to piss on the Saviour?' The blond guy gulped his beer and moved up close to his adversary, who was trying to ignore him.

'Siddown, mate,' called out another bloke. 'Save it for the church.'

Blondie turned on him. '*You* siddown, sinner!' he barked. 'Siddown and make peace with God. You'd better fucking apologise to him, or you're *fucked.*'

Sophia raised an eyebrow at me, hooking her head towards the racket. I filled her in.

'Fucking bastard Bible-thumpers!' she spat with sudden vehemence. 'Jesus Christ, religion is still about the leading cause of death in this world and it's dangerous and it's fiction and it's got to be stopped. *Jesus!*'

Her last word was a snarl. Blondie looked over at

her, swaying slightly. I didn't buy into it. I'm not qualified to judge.

'Tell me about the rest,' I said, signalling for a whisky and another glass of red.

'Whose investigation *is* this?' smiled Sophia.

Good question, I thought.

'Right,' she said. 'Quick then. Those bits of code, as you put it, on the zip were, like I thought, web addresses. I checked them all.'

'And?'

She shook her head in amazement. 'Kumquats bloody kumquats.'

'That's a U2 song,' winked the barmaid, putting down the drinks.

Sophia didn't hear. 'Each site was just more of the same, more bloody shit about kumquats. Who needs kumquats that bad, I ask you? It's not healthy. Just more crap: lots of geographical stuff, you know, like different regions of the world where kumquats are grown, different tastes, regional varieties, that shit.'

'On all of them?'

'All I could get into, anyway, which was, like, almost all of them—a dozen or so, can't remember exactly, but I've got it all written down. There was only one I couldn't get past its title page, one about, it looked, about kumquats in Egypt. Probably they grow well there. All the sites needed a password or password-phrase to access more than the title, but that was no problem, just so they know how many people are accessing, I guess, how effective the zips are as publicity kits, you know. The passwords were all like, "kumquat" or "fruit is good", obvious shit like that. I couldn't get into the Egyptian one, because, you know, it's probably because I don't know the Egyptian word for kumquat, or maybe I needed the actual Arab alphabet or something, no big deal.'

'So you're saying write off the zip?'

'I reckon.'

'The guy in Naples?'

'Yeah. Don't know. That's the problem.'

Another burst of singing sprayed from across the bar. Soundgarden's 'Jesus Christ Pose', it sounded like, although it was difficult to tell above the table-thumping accompaniment which propelled it. Blondie had ordered another beer. He was leaning hunched against the bar, alternately shaking his head at the revellers and glaring at Sophia.

'What about that other matter?' I asked.

'Is that what we're doing now?'

I nodded.

'Okay,' she said. 'This is what I found. The organisation has a computer database, yeah, and uses a modem, right, so I hacked in, like you asked.'

'What did you find?'

'Elvis has left the building.'

I stared at her, uncomprehending. She noticed and giggled. 'Joke, Joe, you know joke? What I found was this: yes, someone else had hacked in and rooted about. I don't know who or when or where from, and I don't know what they were after, or whether they found whatever it was. But, yes, someone hacked into the sex abuse group's system, so what?'

'Weird, don't you think?'

'Nasty, probably, but what's it got to do with us?'

'Maybe nothing, maybe lots. Shelagh Purdey wasn't a random victim, yeah? She was chosen, which meant she had to be found. Someone knew, I think, knew about her friendship with Corrigan.'

'Friendship?'

'Whatever.'

'It would have been common knowledge, surely.'

'Among the kids on the street, yeah, maybe, but probably no further. Corrigan himself would have kept schtum about it, even if there *wasn't* anything untoward about it. He was a fool once, with Theresa Farndale, never again.'

'I don't follow.'

'Probably because I'm not sure where I'm leading, but try this: for whatever reason, sometime Shelagh sought counselling, or tried to, about her childhood. You know about the incest?'

She nodded. 'No evidence, but I'm swayed by probabilities, yeah.'

'So maybe she also mentioned the priest.'

'I thought you had the father pinned for her murder.'

'What do you think?'

'Never mind what I think. That's classified.'

'So, okay, yes, I'm thinking Graeme Purdey, but the cops don't.'

355

She snorted. I acknowledged her opinion with a nod, kept going. 'The cops think Corrigan. He's the obvious choice, except for the little problem of evidence. Would he have been the obvious choice had Shelagh's body turned up somewhere else?'

She shook her head, getting with the program. 'So,' she began cautiously, 'you're thinking that Purdey, or whoever, needed to point to a suspect, to divert attention.'

'Uh huh.'

'So, like, Shelagh Purdey didn't exactly move in exalted circles. None of her friends, the other junkies, whatever, would be taken seriously, not with that kind of weird death, which needed, like, planning and balls. So whoever it was needed to know if she hung out with any adults, respectable people, and if there was anything hinky about it.'

I picked up the baton. 'Who'd she talk to in life? Apart from the street. The Department of Social Security, yeah, maybe a doctor—she tried the methadone program a couple of times—but they'd be no good. So, who else, official, semi-official, respectable . . .'

'You?'

'I said respectable.'

'The priest.'

'Yeah, but they had to *know* that, so they had to find that out. Whoever it was had to find out who, if anyone, she'd told, then access her secrets. So they go fishing, find out what they can—'

'They'd have to have known about the incest to go

356

this route. Even then it'd be dodgy—there's quite a few groups.'

I concurred. She hadn't finished. 'So Graeme Purdey still, you reckon? Who else? Did the mother know? I know she left when the daughter was a toddler or something.'

I didn't answer. Sometimes doubt is like debt. It can work in your favour, properly handled. Of course Beatrice Cowper knew about the incest, but I couldn't see why she'd want to draw attention to herself—and her business, if Sophia's assumptions held any holy water—by killing her own daughter. It would have been an act of extraordinary stupidity, and Shelagh's mother was a lot of things (maybe more than anyone realised), but stupid was not one of them. I had no doubt there was a connection, but in which direction? Was somebody also setting *her* up?

I theorised. 'The murder could have been the continuation of the child abuse by other means. We don't know. Maybe Shelagh had been in touch, threatening to expose him. Fathers have been jailed for less. Or maybe the contact had never been broken.'

Sophia considered this.

'Christ, I'm pissed!' cried someone. Drunken applause welled. Blondie punched the bar and growled.

Sophia shook her head. 'Starting to annoy me, that bloke,' she said. 'Listen, Joe; I'm not interested in the incest. I'm not interested in Graeme Purdey, either, except inasmuch as he's possibly linked to the porn stuff, even though I reckon he doesn't know it. If your

357

priest is going to get nailed for something he didn't do, then, well, tough, that's nothing to do with me and I'm not going to help.'

'Complicity is a two-way street,' I reminded her.

'Go put it on a bumper sticker,' she rejoined. 'Now tell me this: what's in it for me?'

'Self, self, self,' I chided. 'The bones: Shelagh talks to the sexual abuse group. Somebody knows this, or finds out, whatever, goes hunting. Comes up with Corrigan's name—maybe mentioned just as a friend, a help, you never know—sets up the body in his church, guaranteed to attract attention.'

'Especially if the other woman, Farndale, had also talked to the same group before. Had she?'

'Don't know, good point. The priest said the group *couldn't* supply the info he asked for. Maybe it was *wouldn't* in a pretty frock. Anyway, maybe also whoever it was knew about the porn, and wanted to let Shelagh's mother know that.'

'But Beatrice Cowper's not a suspect, nowhere near it.'

'No, but maybe she's now in debt to someone.'

'A takeover bid? Bad times in the snuff porn business?'

I shrugged. 'By their fruits ye shall know them.'

'Or not, as the case may be.' She drained her glass, eyes sightless to the ceiling. 'Yeah, don't know Joe, but it's worth a try. The connection to the other woman could do it. If the other woman—'

'Theresa Farndale.'

'—had been there, about Corrigan, then maybe, yes, someone hacked in and ran a search on *Corrigan's* name, see if anybody else had complained about him. Bang: up comes little Shelagh, maybe she'd been there, mentioned him in some context, bad *or* good. Yes, Joe, it might. So, let me guess, it's a little late night B&E you're contemplating?'

'Last drinks!' shouted the barmaid.

'Hey, my wine's turned into water!' someone yelled.

'Miracle! Miracle!' called the chorus.

It was too much for Blondie. He let out an anguished wail and howled, 'Repent! God is coming soon!'

Sophia winced. 'Well, he's too late,' she spat, hurling her remark over her shoulder. 'Bar's just shut.'

That did it. He pushed himself upright and lurched over to us. His face was purple with anger as he shoved it in front of Sophia. 'You blasphemous, fucking dyke bitch,' he screamed point-blank.

I didn't even see her arm move. Next thing, the guy is on the floor, arse in the butt-tray, trying to stop blood from pouring out of his nose.

'A couple of shorts before we start?' I asked.

'Sambuca. White,' she said.

We got them on the house.

The abuse group was called, with intentional irony,

Family Values. It was accommodated in a run-down terrace house midway between the university and a major hospital. Like most organisations dedicated to things that really matter, it was run largely by volunteer labour and funded by various little grants from philanthropic foundations and government departments. The money, clearly, had never quite stretched to a burglar alarm or decent locks on the door. We went in through the back, Sophia happy to let me work the magic with the fit.

We found the filing cabinets in a front room, a street light outside casting just enough illumination between the slats of a sagging venetian blind. The cabinets were locked, of course. At first. We took one each, three drawers apiece.

There was an awful lot of manila files in them.

Sophia found the one with Shelagh Purdey's name on it after about ten minutes. 'Bingo,' she whispered.

It contained a single sheet of paper, typed. Contact, it revealed, had been made about a year previously, and only once, re, it said, *poss case against father, retrospective. Subject eventually reluctant to take action. Unstable housing, substance abuse, no real support network. Abuse ended after subject left parental home, two years ago. Is in no immediate danger—official intervention not suggested. Subject claims adult guidance from Fr B.Corrigan, claims nonsexual. No reason to disbelieve but association should be treated with caution in light of TMF (qv). Action: establish monthly contact/monitor/link up with crisis accomm away from area?*

The monthly contact, if it happened, went unrecorded.

'Give it to me,' I said.

'Why should I?' Play-pouting.

'It's of no interest to you. You said so.'

The Fs were in my cabinet, second draw.

'You'll love this,' I whispered.

There were two sheets in Theresa Mary Farndale's file. The first recorded brief details of a single meeting, a decade back. *Subject distraught and unstable*, it said, *intervention essential*. It noted in outline Farndale's relationship with Fr B.Corrigan, her subsequent allegations to the bishops and judgement levelled at her. It seemed Farndale had come to the group soon after, seeking justice. Her case with the church authorities, it noted, had been handled by *advocate Fr D.Scopemi*. An urgent asterisk was penned in at the end of the name, and the handwritten note, *see over*, scribbled next to it.

Overleaf, I found a hasty paragraph. Sophia read it, pushing her head between my arm and side to get a clearer view:

*Important!!! Fr DS reconstructed evidence for Ch inquiry, with subject's cooperation (see enclosed). This is not only inadmissible if anything goes to court, it is also v.v.v.V. dangerous for subject's state of mind, which is unstable already. Request for all such materials from Fr DS turned down—claims he 'destroyed' them, leaving only the one TMF provided (a 'present' at end of case). Subject says Fr DS told her same thing, keeping only the one as 'evidence'—doesn't know whether she believes him or not and doesn't care: defensive apathy, denial? NB NB NB: Fr DS not, repeat not, to be trusted as advocate. Treat any info from him—this or others—as suspect. His methods stink!*

'Who's Scopemi?' whispered Sophia.

'Good question,' I mumbled. ' "Where" is also good.'

'Let's see the rest.'

The other sheet of paper was a colour photograph, eight by ten. Sophia gasped when she saw it. Theresa Farndale stood, facing the lens, her arms stretched out and tied by the wrists to a crude crucifix made from the sort of four-by-two pine lengths available from any hardware store. It leant back slightly, resting against a pale-plastered wall. She was naked, except for a pair of black underpants—a concession, presumably, to the delicate sensibilities of her judges. She dipped slightly at the shoulders, her knees bent perhaps as a theatrical nicety, perhaps because she was having trouble supporting her own weight. Her hair was shit, lank and unruly.

Her head hung forward, but her eyes were on the lens, staring up and out, aware. There was violence in her look, blood-savage and red-disked again by the flash.

Violence to whom, I wondered. I pondered the many shades of meaning inherent in the word *cooperation*. Judas Iscariot cooperated. The boy in the shroud cooperated. I cooperated with Saul. It's easy with the flesh hanging from your back and the promise of more to come breathing slowly just behind you.

'Seen enough?' It was Sophia.

I nodded, put the shot back in the folder and handed it to her. 'Here,' I said. 'Add this to your collection.'

She opened it again, a flash, closed it. 'Joe, do you think she's dead?'

I shook my head. 'Many of them that sleep in the dust of the earth shall awake, some to everlasting life, and some to shame and everlasting contempt.'

'You talk shit, baby. Pretentious shit.'

✝

'See, big numbers,' Sophia said.

'Wouldn't mind one,' I replied, not really listening.

'That wasn't what I meant,' she replied, tilting her head, 'but not a bad idea. You got any hooch?'

I said nothing.

'Oh, come on.' She laughed. 'We just broke into a building together. I'm hardly likely to bust you for a joint, am I? Roll up. I'll help you smoke it. Like you said, complicity is a two-way street.'

I did as I was bid.

'I meant different big numbers, though,' she continued. 'Ones with lots of noughts in them. The big numbers of physics, that's what people need, not some kind of god. This business of deities, it's shit, it falls down. Like, Joe, correct me if I'm wrong but the whole basis of the god thing is, like, the bastard's so

363

big he's even what he isn't, right? He's huge and tiny, everywhere and nowhere, being and nothingness, yeah?'

We were seated on the sofa at the safe-house. It was 1.30am and Portishead was happening again. She'd invited me back. Debriefing, she said, standard operational procedure. But first: time-out. Let the brain play with other things for half an hour. She'd restocked the alcohol supply: red wine for her, Jamesons for me. You looked like a scotch man, she said. I'm Middle Eastern, I'd replied. She didn't get it.

No shop talk, she had said. Not yet. Relax.

God as the prime cause. Father as the prime cause. I didn't know. There are some sides to him I haven't seen yet. Whoever he is. An infinite number of sides, according to that logic, sides which I would never see, could never see, even if my time were to run without end and my wisdom grow oak in its patience. I don't know. I never met him. He never chucked me on the shoulder, offered me a beer on the porch, tossed a fillet on the barby and said, now son, time for the facts of life.

'That's one theory,' I said. 'Quite popular.'

'So big numbers,' she said, as if concluding. 'There's a number called a googolplex. A googol is the number one followed by a hundred zeroes. A googolplex is ten times as big, exponential. You need a super-computer just to hold the idea of it, never mind the actuality. If you tried to write down all the zeroes, one after another, like, even if you wrote them really tiny, microscopic, you'd run out of universe before you ran out of noughts.'

I fired up the joint. 'Never *was* any good at maths.'

'Doesn't matter!' she chirped. 'Leave the adding up to the egg-heads. Just dig the conclusions. The universe is accidental and vast. It's full of mystery and promise.'

'How can something accidental contain promise? What promise?'

'The promise that if we think about it hard enough then, one day, we'll understand it.'

I passed her the smoke. 'The universe feels misunderstood? Poor thing.'

She shifted on the sofa, suddenly peeved. 'Don't be facetious. Go back to the googolplex. The point is, the number is a possibility and human beings conceived it. We *can* conceive something bigger than the universe, we can think outside the square, and in a googolplex lies the potential of every other number we can come up with.'

'Except a googolplex plus one.'

'The possibility of increase exists in anything, Joe. It's there. What I'm saying is this: that number is every bit as paradoxical as the idea of god, but we can, given persistence and time, understand it, and how it works, because it can never, no matter what you do to it, work capriciously. That's the difference. That's the essence of existence. A googolplex, Joe! Think of the possibilities! With it you can measure anything, even *chaos*. Especially chaos. *Understanding* chaos—cop the power of that. If people want something infinitely bigger than they are, to give them meaning, to make them feel dependent, to make them feel humble, whatever, they can have a big fucking number. It's every bit as mystical as some transcendent spook.'

'But they seem to like the spook.'

'Fuck them,' she said. 'Big numbers don't take sides. No one ever died defending a big number.'

I felt unsettled. It was a bit too close to the bone for my liking. Was I just the detritus left after the divine decimal point?

'What's paradoxical about a big number?' I asked, aware of a defensive tone creeping into my voice. 'It's just an exercise in mechanics.'

There was a glint of excitement in her eyes. 'Does infinity start at zero?'

'Of course it does.'

She shook her head. 'Yes, Joe? How can infinity *start*?'

'Okay, no, then.'

'The googolplex does. It starts at zero. It's ours, human. We *make* it start at zero.'

'So?'

'So, Joe, a googolplex plus any other number—one, two, a million trillion—also starts at zero, yeah?'

'Of course.'

'Even unto infinity.'

'So, yes, but—'

'It doesn't.' Her left knee was twitching, like a school girl confiding someone else's secret. 'It can't.'

'Why not?'

'Does infinity start at zero?'

'But we—you—made it.'

'Yes!' She slapped her leg. 'So it's of our nature, Joe. That's the fun of it all. We are not the masters of what we make. Do you understand?'

'I understand that last bit well enough.' And it was starting to depress the hell out of me. 'Change the subject.'

'Okay, then, to business,' she said, stubbing the butt. 'What have we learned, Joe?'

I'd learned one thing, I knew. The Shelagh Purdey file, with its cautionary reference to Farndale, could in itself provide the evidence Gordon needed to hike Corrigan in on something firmer than convenient suspicion. That could be useful, push come to shove.

I didn't mention it. It was none of her business.

'Right,' I said, sloshing another generous measure of scotch in my tumbler. 'Who hacked in, looking for the computer versions of what we've got on paper?'

'Perhaps no one. We don't know for sure if the hack was connected.'

'But—'

'We don't know, Joe. Stick to what we know. Scopemi took kinky photos. That we know.'

'Is there a connection with your lot?'

'Not then, certainly,' she said. 'We don't know how long this thing's been in operation—a decade without discovery's stretching it a bit—and, anyway, the stuff we've found is much better, you know, it has much better production values—lighting, colour, settings,

367

focus—professional stuff. That shit was just enthusiastic amateur.'

'The note said he destroyed the rest of it. Could he have sold it?'

She nodded.

'To whom?'

She shook her head. 'There's the question. Where is he?'

'Gone from his parish.'

'Got a description?'

'I can get one.'

'Give me. First thing tomorrow. I'll get some people on it. Where's his church?'

I told her.

'There, too,' she said. 'Now, think, is there a link between this guy Scopemi and Shelagh Purdey?'

'Don't know. Could be. Corrigan detests him, never wastes an opportunity to drop shit on him in conversation. If she and Corrigan had talked a lot, she may well have heard of him.'

'And known he was a sort of nemesis,' she said, finishing my thought. 'So she might have gone to see him—say she had an argument with Corrigan, went all little girl silly. Or, at least, she would have recognised his name if he'd introduced himself to her?'

'If he did.'

'If he did. What else?'

'Purdey father and daughter hadn't been an item for years.'

'And no mention of Cowper.'

368

'So?'

'So I'm leaning towards the conclusion that you're a clever man, Joe, Joshua Panther,' she smiled. 'If the hack was connected, then Shelagh Purdey was already marked as a victim, and Corrigan came up as a very convenient patsy. Someone wanted to signal to Cowper that her gig was vulnerable somehow. This is a hard-ball business. How better than to off her estranged daughter, imitating the house style? I wish we had a tap on her phone, Jesus do I wish that.'

'But who knew Shelagh had been to Family Values?'

'Who referred her to the place?'

We both said it at the same time: 'Scopemi?'

'What's his angle?' she said.

'Who's he working for?' I wondered.

We didn't know either answer. But I figured his goon might know both.

Mark that one down for tomorrow, I decided. I didn't tell Sophia. Allies of convenience are quite often neither. Many Turks turned Christian during the crusades. The Knights Templar didn't give a shit, not once the blades were swinging and the horses were blowing sputum.

She was up off the sofa, heading across the room. 'Dead end,' she was saying. 'Let's catch the vid. Want to skin another?'

I made with mull. Small one, single paper job. We were working after all.

Lit, she hit the remote. The television screen fuzzed and hissed for a few seconds and then, the static sinking

369

like a curtain, certain wonders revealed themselves unto us.

I had been right about the size of Elaine Purdey's nipples: they were as tiny as I'd imagined them, as peaky as they'd felt.

And there they were, quite visible, about a third of the way up from the bottom of the screen. The image was moving, and well lit, nothing harsh or bright or jerky about it. Real pro job.

Elaine Purdey was naked. She was tied to a contraption I'd seen once before in a prison movie. I had thought at the time how much the Inquisitors would have loved it, had the technology to produce such upholstery existed in those days. It was the perfect blend of comfort and cruelty.

It was the sort of rotating bed they use in certain parts of America where the chosen method of legal execution is lethal injection: a sort of flat, narrow, black padded platform with extensions on which to strap a person's arms, straight out from the shoulder. The one I'd seen in the movie could lie flat, or swing ninety degrees to upright.

The one on the video was horizontal. Elaine Purdey was tightly strapped in, conscious. The camera was held in front of her, just above her head, positioning it, thus, at the bottom of the screen, creating a harsh foreshortened perspective ending with her bare feet, strapped down apart, at the top. As we watched in silence, the lens moved slowly across the top of her, panning along her body, leaving her status in no doubt. Her lips were moving. She was saying the same thing, indistinct, over and over again.

It might have been *help*. It might have been *please*. It might have been *mercy*. There was no sound.

Slowly, the camera panned back up again, lascivious in its intentions, pulled in for a close-up—her eyes were red, florid marks betraying a slap across the cheek—and then the slow fade to black.

The silence hung for quite a while afterwards, both of us staring at a blank screen while Sophia hit rewind.

'A warning to Graeme Purdey,' said Sophia, matter of fact. 'We've got your wife: just imagine what we can do to her.'

That much was pretty clear. 'Who from, though?'

'I've seen the couch-thing before.'

'When?'

'Railway spikes. I'm pretty sure. Only then it was upright.'

I shook my head. 'Doesn't make sense. If Beatrice Cowper's people are behind the snuff porn, and Graeme Purdey is somehow, knowingly or otherwise, helping to move it, why would they threaten their own?'

'Don't know,' she said. 'To entice him to stay silent, maybe? Maybe, yes. Or maybe it's a decoy. Maybe Purdey's in on it. Maybe it's to kybosh the idea that he's involved—make him appear a victim, a sort of victim.'

I thought of those eyes. I'd seen them countless times before: in dungeons, in the torture rooms of the clerical avengers, on the racks, on the eyes of women healers tied to a stake for the crime of prescribing hellebore. 'She looked pretty convincing.'

She shrugged again. 'He appears a victim; she *is* one. Patriarchy rules.'

'Or maybe it *is* a warning. A warning to you.'

'No.' she said, flat. 'My cover's intact. That way lies madness.'

She looked me in the eyes, and held my gaze without flinching. Then she flashed a smile, quickly, and huffled across the sofa until our thighs were touching.

'Have another drink,' she said. 'Let's watch it again.' She hit the button.

'You don't care about her, do you, what happens to her?'

She turned away from the screen, and straightened her spine, bringing her face close to mine.

'Caring gets in the way, Joe,' she said, almost a whisper. 'You have causes and passions, that's fine, that's what shapes us: ideas, notions, memes. You let individuals get in the way, you lose. We live, we die. End of story. How doesn't matter in the particular. It's the general that's important.'

She glanced quickly at the screen, at Elaine Purdey, naked and bound. 'Poky little nips,' she said. She seemed to make her mind up about something.

'Imagine,' she breathed. 'The awesome freedom of the sociopath. You don't have to pick winners. You don't have to judge. You don't have to find a reason.

And you don't have to lie awake at night, wishing for forgiveness or understanding. You just do, because doing is all there is.'

*What happens, happens.*

Then, gently, she kissed me on the lips.

I looked in her eyes, silent. There is a part of me which is my father's son. There is a part of me which is divine. I know that. I've read it often enough. The centurion was cover, good cover. The rest is what's hid. My father is infallible. He cannot make mistakes.

The one thing he cannot feel is remorse.

And I am my father's son.

I returned the kiss.

*What is, is.*

Help, mouthed Elaine Purdey as we offered ourselves. Help please.

Please mercy.

✝

# 11

THAT NIGHT I WENT TO HELL.

It was no hell in particular. It was any hell, Everyhell. I crossed a river coagulating with bloated bodies. There was a ferry, a ferryman. Pan was there, goat-legged and turgid. Satan howled, Cerberus growled. Beelzebub mourned his losses. Witches gathered, hag-faced and bellyfull, cackling in sabbat. Cats screamed. Magma heaved. Men wept, flayed like toadskins. Everything strobed with the monochrome striations of a seventeenth century woodcut. The air was fogged with the stench of rot and fat-seeping roast.

At the heart of Everyhell a plain door waited, Lucifer its guardian. He bowed low, lifting his cassock, scratching his filthy pudenda as I passed, sinewed hand on the handle, pulling it open, bidding me pass.

Through the door was a room. In the room sat a small boy torching a GI Joe. The boy looked at me. He looked familiar.

In hell they play the Spice Girls.

I opened my eyes.

Sophia was leaning over me, turning down the volume on the clock radio. 'Sorry about that,' she said. 'Keep meaning to tune in a decent station, but I'm always too knackered when I hit the bed.'

She righted herself, pulled her knees around, sat back on her heels. She looked smaller and softer in the gentle orange glow of the morning, her hair jutting out at improbable angles from the weight of sleep and the imprint of our sex. Her smile was lopsided and sad as she reached over and idly stroked my face with the back of her hand.

'You sleep like you carry the weight of the world on your shoulders, Joe.'

'Force of habit.' My voice sounded thick and distant.

'We can none of us escape our fates, can we?'

'I don't know.'

I reached for her, placed one hand on her hip, ran it up her side, pulled her down towards me. She flashed me a smile, patted my thigh through the doona, wriggled away.

'Not now.' She chuckled. 'There's work to be doing. It's eight o'clock and I've got to, you know, get my arse into gear, have a shower and get over to South Melbourne. Got to get that video over, wipe our prints off it, wrap it up again, get it on Graeme Purdey's desk before he gets there. Wonder if Elaine's been freed yet.'

We both knew the answer to that one, so said nothing. The silence grew quickly uncomfortable, begging too many questions. With a start, she bent from the waist, pecked me on the cheek and swung backwards off the bed, hop-skipping on the floor, clutching her arms across her tiny breasts in the chill, the light glinting from the circle of steel inserted through her right nipple.

'Shower and go, Joe,' she singsonged. 'Shit and shower and go. Have a nap if you like. You look like a late morning person—'

Going out of the bedroom door now, bundle of clothes held in one arm, clutched to her body.

'—and then ring me when you've got a description of the other priest, the one—'

'Scopemi.'

'Yeah, him, give me a ring with it, then, like, I think maybe you should ring me again later in the day, towards the end of working hours.'

'What about?'

She turned back, framed. She looked a small perfection. I couldn't read her eyes. 'Whatever,' she chirped, and was gone.

I lay in the stranger's bed, in the featureless room, not thinking, listening to the *tic-tic-tic* of the water meter, sometimes imagining her wet, sometimes revisiting the passionless Mrs Purdey, tied down and victim still.

I must have dozed off. My eyes started open to the sound of a muffled explosion, body tensing fast at the feel of the building shaking. The fear passed as I realised the noise and vibration were just the report of the front door slamming below, marking Sophia's departure.

The cold hit me as I swung out of bed and crossed the floor to the window. Pulling back the curtain slightly, I saw the sky was dry but bloated with grey promise. Sophia was walking away down the street at a fair pace, a bulky black woollen coat, collar up against the breeze, revealing only a pair of red-legginged calves and the black Doc Martens beneath.

The Falcon was parked across the street. Its driver, head down, short scarf around his neck, was leaning against the bonnet, having a cigarette. The breath from his mouth and the smoke from his burn were indistinguishable.

Although its function still escaped me, I had decided not to fret about the surveillance. It seemed clear the order was a watching brief, no more. If they were gathering evidence, so be it. They weren't the first. I knew now that it would never get to court. Whatever happened, whoever's purpose I ended up serving, my role would remain unacknowledged, my departure swift and silent, by violent despatch or hurried evacuation.

Typical, I thought. They only call on me when they're in trouble. Same as it ever was.

Well, amen to that. There were things to do. Shower, coffee, things to do.

My jeans and windcheater were getting pretty manky. I smelled of my raiment. Never mind. I tried for a shave but there were no razors in the bathroom. Sophia was a natural woman, softly hirsute, her face untainted by oils and antimony.

I phoned Corrigan during the second cup. He hooted with unpriestly joy when I told him Scopemi was now a focus for me. 'He's a bastard, that one.' He chuckled. 'Stiff the cunt.'

I copied down his description: a tad under six foot, mid-forties, hair dark brown, greying around the temples, worn short but not crew, clean-shaven, brown eyes, ski-jump nose, average weight, no paunch.

'And a tattoo, man,' said Corrigan. 'Priest with a tattoo, would you believe? It's a kind of Celtic cross—you know the type, the cross in the circle—on a forearm, left one, from memory, old and faded. He was in the merchant navy, apparently, before taking his orders, some middling rank or other. He often refers to the damn thing, says it demonstrates his affinity with the common man or somesuch bollocks. What's he done?'

'Sinned. Have you found him yet?'

'No, man. I rang the diocese office, but, ach, it's a fucking circus there. Said he was probably off with the flu, they didn't know. I'll keep looking.'

'Priority, priest. He's your best chance.'

Not to mention, quite possibly, mine.

I rang the description through to Sophia, who was all professional, didn't echo my words, used no endearments, and called me Mr Flynt. I could hear voices in the background, male, strained, a cough. Purdey and cops, horror revealed. She said she'd get right onto it. Full resources, whatever that meant.

Before leaving, I squatted next to the coffee table,

my smack supply spread before me. I put half the stock into the various pockets and linings of my leather jacket. The rest I shoved inside a plastic bag and wedged, out of sight, in the deep crack between the back and base of the sofa. Insurance. One call to the Drug Squad, relayed with suitable verisimilitude and exact information, and the anonymous safe-house would be raped by a squad of armed cynics. The need might yet arise. To everything there is a season: a time to plant, a time to pluck up that which is planted.

The bloke was back in his vehicle when I closed the door behind me and let myself out through the gate. It was about 9.30am and the drizzle had begun.

I thought about heading back to the warehouse for a change of clothes, but decided it could wait. Anyway, I didn't quite feel up to dealing with John the Baptist, hobbling and lost, bored out of his wits, itching for fulfilling purpose. That could wait, too.

Instead, I walked up to the restaurant strip, hailed a cab and pointed it at Clifton Hill. The watcher fell in behind. I got out two blocks from my destination, walked to the church from there, the Falcon circling.

The big wooden double doors of the church were closed but not locked. They creaked mournfully as I pulled them apart and walked into the birth canal of belief. Inside, the place was dark, a wash of reddy-brown diffusion from the stained glass windows muted by the cloud cover. A couple of candles flickered up the front, prayers silent and remote. My image hung above, agonised and empty.

The air was cold as the tomb.

My boots echoed as I walked down the aisle, the drumbeats of funeral, the slow march of the heretic to the pyre.

I hadn't really expected to find the goon in attendance. There might have been something, however, some note, some entry in a journal in an alcove, which might have pointed to his whereabouts. In the shadows behind the altar, the dark places behind the pulpit I prowled, searching for a door. The drizzle made a ratchet on the roof, a fizzing static in the air.

And then a scrape, a squeak of leather on a floorboard, just behind me. I went to turn. Something solid hit the back of my head. Hard in my face an angel appeared, bright as pain, startling radiant gold. She opened her wings. I saw nothing but light in excess, felt her arms lock around my waist, heard the awesome rush of feathers, found the kinetic surge of uplift, closed my eyes and surrendered.

✝

I am blind and I think I am naked.

There is flesh beneath my palms. It trembles and crawls.

My head is captive. I cannot twitch. I cannot speak. The smell of supple leather encases my head. Thin metal jags against my eyes and lips. I cannot open my eyes. My breath whistles from my nostrils.

I am blind.

The metal at my mouth is a zip. I know. I heard it, felt it slide. I was on my back. I couldn't move. I am standing now, I think. I think I stand. I lean forward. I reach out for balance. Warm skin jumps, wet, without fragrance.

The zip slid. Thick fingers forced something liquid into my mouth. The zip slid again. A rough hand hit my throat, once, twice. I swallowed.

I know the demon within. I know its nature. I know its leaden caress. I know its name.

And the name shall be Ketamine. Tranquilliser.

There is flesh beneath my palms. I move my hands in silence. It shudders. It is viscous. It is afraid.

I think I am naked. The soles of my feet sting with cold. If I move them I will fall in blackness.

I feel a breast. I feel a belly. I would not, but I do.

I hear breathing, shallow breathing, teeth breathing, fear breathing, breathing that breathes the word *yip*, the word *hee'ep*, mystic words, the word *god*, the word *please*.

There is flesh against my groin, my leaning groin. I am limp. I am shrivelled.

To whom does the flesh belong? There is wetness, the seeping of fear. Are you St Juthwara, this cheese your offering on high? Are you Brigid back, your spine to move astride the swaying of yews within the wind? Are you Beatrice Cowper stripped, your malice come undone? Are you Sophia, and must I hurt you now at your command? Are you mother back, or Mary quite the other, this moistness your tears to bless?

I would wipe away your tears, lay me down to rest.

How do I sin in blindness, rendered dumb?

My body sags. There is vomit in my throat, again, again, again.

There is flesh beneath my palms. I am naked and blind. The demon is within.

I am falling.

I am falling now. Of man's first disobedience and fall.

My leather head hits chest, a thumping exhalation greets, a thin squeal of terror tired.

My darkness slowly swirls. My lips are wet and acid bathed. My demon lays me, not to want, to sleep between the nameless tits of mystery.

✝

I woke up in the stinking concrete back yard of a Gertrude Street boarding house, propped and bruised against a skip. I didn't notice straight away.

I noticed first that it was daylight.

I noticed second that my head hurt like shit, drumming from something's departure at the front, stinging from a knockout blow behind.

I noticed third the fuzzy, fusing face of the watcherman, the Falcon man, bending low above. He held something black to his mouth. 'He's okay,' he said at it, flat. 'He's alive.' And then he walked away.

I closed my eyes again, just briefly, trying to centre myself. The rain, light and even, felt good. Slowly, the ground stopped swaying, the ambient sounds resolving from a dull, persistent roar to the individual voices of cars, of trucks, of trams, of a seagull squawk above.

When I opened up again I knew immediately where I was. It was the same litter-strewn yard in which— oh, how long ago?—I had found my first dead customer, my first search commission from a bluff priest in a public bar. There was no one else around.

Levering myself towards a more balanced sitting position, my hand slid into sodden paper. I recoiled from the slime. It was the morning broadsheet. The headline said CHURCH ORPHANAGE BABIES USED IN MEDICAL TESTS. I checked the date. It was the same as it had been that morning.

My brain felt like glue. I sat still, tried to slow down my breathing, banish confusion, backtrack. The morning. I had woken in bed with Sophia. Last night I made love with Sophia. She left. I went to Clifton Hill, to the church. I entered the church, literally if not figuratively. Then what?

I remembered pain and blackness. I remembered falling. I remembered shards and shafts of other things, things imagined, things dreamt, things scattered in the fallow of my mind by mighty hand unknown.

And then I was out the back of a dosshouse in Fitzroy, away in a manger, no crib for a bed.

A spear of fright shot through me. It was obvious. I

had been mugged, rolled and dumped. Me, of all people.

Frantically, hands aflap, I checked my pockets and my linings. Whoever had attacked me hadn't stolen my leather jacket. The smack was still snug. My keys were still in the inside breast pocket, along with a stiff buff envelope, whatever that was. There was sixty odd bucks still in my jeans.

Scratch that, then. I hadn't been mugged. Not according to prevailing standards, anyway.

Whatever had happened, I decided, sanity slowly returning, I wasn't going to find out by leaning against a urine-streaked, malodorous rubbish skip. Levering myself upright was difficult—my head kept spinning—but I made it eventually. A minute or so later, adjusted to the altitude and balance, I walked to the corrugated iron back gate, wrenched it open, and headed out into a lane.

Two old men in filthy coats and mittens were squatting against the fence, passing a paper-wrapped bottle between them. One of them held it out to me. I took it, wiped the spittle from its mouth with my sleeve (not too effective, given that it was leather), and took a pull. It was rough-bite port. As I swallowed, I tasted vomit in my throat.

'What about something in return?' the old man wheezed.

I must have given him the look while I was trying to put him into focus. He pushed himself back against the fence, shaking his head. I tried a smile. It didn't help.

'Bless you,' I said, and walked away.

As I walked down Brunswick Street, heading for the warehouse, I was aware that my posture was bad, my gait was a lurch, my clothing was foul and my mind was elsewhere. I wasn't bothered. It was Fitzroy. No one saw a thing.

As I walked, though, one thing buoyed me, one bright spark of understanding pierced the turbulent gloom. Mystery, suddenly, was revealed. I had knowledge. I puffed up.

I had remembered where I'd seen the Falcon man before.

✝

The journey up the stairs required two stops: the first to allow my head to cease spinning, the second to start it off again when I wheeled around suddenly, halfway up, at the sound of something metallic hitting the ground. I caught sight of a frightened cat disappearing under a car, an empty beer can rocking to and fro.

Inside, John the Baptist was sitting on the sofa, struggling to get up to greet me. The television was on, the sound turned down. The stereo receiver drivelled out radio sports talk. I turned it off immediately.

'Afternoon, son,' croaked the old man. 'Out all night, eh? All right for some, isn't it? Wish I was as young as you still.'

'You are,' I mumbled. 'Younger.'

The cacophony of dread inside him seemed to have died down. His eyes were dry—as dry as they ever got, anyway. The acute phase of apostasy is always the worst. The chronic you can live with.

'Anything happened?' I asked him.

'No, son,' he said, with sudden and overplayed officiousness. 'Nothing. No phone calls, no visitors, nothing. Them people with the cars even left.'

'They're back now,' I replied. 'Don't worry about it. Have you been up to much?'

He shook his head amiably enough. 'Nope. Just learning.'

'Learning what?'

'Two things mainly, son. Bit restless last night, what with everything. First thing is that your telly picks up SBS, you know, the station with all them foreign programs?'

'Mmm. What's the second?'

'The upper limit for Saudi Arabian light comedy is one hour and five minutes.'

'He that hath ears to hear, let him hear. He that doth not, let him read the subtitles. I'm going for a shower.'

'Good idea, son,' he ventured, being brave.

'I know. I reek. Put the kettle on, make me a coffee. Roll me a cigarette.'

'You've always smoked tailors, son.'

'Use the green tobacco in the tin on top of the amplifier.'

The stiff envelope fell from my jacket as I undressed.

I'd forgotten about it. It had my name on the front. I recognised the handwriting.

Washed and changed into fresh black jeans, Smashing Pumpkins tee-shirt, jacket back on for warmth, I took a seat at the table, a little refreshed. John carried over a mug of strong brew, handed me a scrawny joint.

'Difficult to roll, that tobacco,' he said. 'I rolled one for meself as well, hope you don't mind.'

The last thing John needed, I thought, was something to spur his anxieties again, send him reeling off inside himself. 'Give it to me, old man,' I said. 'You're not ready for the sacrament yet.'

He didn't complain. Not much, anyway. It gave me an idea, though, for later.

I slit open the envelope. A five-by-seven snapshot slid out. My face, I felt it, set solid. I turned to John, suddenly feeling like an actor who's trodden on a nail in the middle of a soliloquy.

'Old man,' I said, fishing in my pocket. 'Here's, what, twenty bucks and change. Go to the Bradford, indulge yourself for a couple of hours. I need to be alone.'

'But—'

'*Now.*' I felt my eyes flare. It was enough.

He took the money, shuffled to the door. 'Can I put a bet on?' he asked, voice wheedling.

'Whatever. Just don't wander off. You're on permanent stand-by.'

'Righto, boss,' he said, trying an arthritic salute. The door closed behind him. I locked it from the inside, put the Pumpkins' *Gish* album on the system, returned to the obscenity on my table.

The snapshot was old, maybe a couple of decades. It had been taken in a small suburban back garden, the fence brushed with snow. On the grass, in the foreground, sat a young boy, maybe six, maybe seven, strangely familiar. He was smiling at the camera, head tilted, holding a GI Joe. Behind him, relaxed and crouched, were a man and woman, also smiling to camera, also oddly, uncomfortably, familiar.

Looking at it, I felt colder than the weather would explain.

There were two folded sheets of paper in the envelope. I pulled out the first one. It was also very old, long stored, soft, starting to fray along its creases. I opened it up. Part of me looked at it; part of me didn't. The music was swelling very loud.

It was a birth certificate, issued in the city of Toronto in Canada. I think I passed through Toronto once, don't remember.

It recorded the advent of one Josiah Benjamin Panton, son of Benjamin William Panton and Francois Brigitte Panton, nee Denvir. It was dated August 3, thirty-five years before.

The other piece of paper felt like lead as I unfolded it. It was fresh, and written in a familiar hand:

*Josiah, Mr Panton. Your father died in a car crash when you were seven. Your mother began a relationship with another man, a Chris Williams. In the spirit of the times, they never married. You all migrated to Australia when you*

388

*were eight. You lived in Kalgoorlie, then Whyalla, then Ade-laide. Your mother still lives there. Her man, a drunk, is long gone. You were a troubled child. Later you studied theology. You showed promise. You went mad.*

*Seek help, Mr Panton. No good will come of this.*

I threw it away from me violently. It fell to the ground at my feet, ripped. Billy Corgan screamed. I didn't join in, couldn't.

The phone rang. The phone had not rung since the priest found a head in a hatbox. I let it ring.

Shall a trumpet be blown in the city, and the people not be afraid? Shall there be evil in a city, and the Lord hath not done it?

The phone kept ringing.

I went into mantra. I am the Lord, Jesus Christ, blessed and eternal. I am the redeemer. I am the Saviour, the Messiah, come back, never gone. I am Yeshu am Joshua am Jesus, am the son of High Mary and Pantera the soldier, Yahweh the war god, the nameless immensity in and around. I am the lamb and the first-born, the bringer of grace, of man and divine, in nature as one, the father, the son and the spirit, in hope and in judgement, and, lo, I am with you always, even unto the end of the world.

I looked at the shot.

The phone stopped ringing.

I didn't know these people.

And started again.

I picked up the receiver. 'It is I. Be not afraid.'

'You fucking bastard, Panther.'

Corrigan's voice. Angry. I said nothing.

'Speak, you bastard. I know you're there.'

'What?'

'You fucking . . . I thought I'd seen some arsehole acts from the wretched of this parish, man, but I tell you, not even the lowest junkie of the lot, not even the snake-eyed shiftless . . . There is no one would do what you've been . . . You betraying, vicious, hypocritical . . . I had *hope* for you, man, for all your violent . . .'

He sounded apoplectic with fury, tripping over his words, imprecations fighting each other to spill off his tongue. I'd never heard him like that before. And I didn't want to hear him like it now. I guessed he'd gone and talked to Mrs Collosi after all, been told that I was the devil, that I sold smack to his flock by moonlight and cloud, and now his carefully maintained illusion was shattered, me the target of his own destroyed myopia.

It didn't matter. The gig was nearly up anyway.

But no. He was sputtering something about his computer, about e-mail, about going to the cops as fast as the wind would speed him, about hoisting and petards.

I didn't understand the substance of his speech, but I understood its nature.

Trouble. A shit-load of trouble.

'Wait,' I said. 'Wait till I get there. You owe me that much.'

'I owe you fucking nothing after this.' His voice seethed. 'Ten minutes, Panther. Then Armageddon.'

I put down the receiver and ran, a handwritten hell fluttering, torn, in my slipstream.

I had heard of e-mail, of course, but I'd never seen it. I thought it was just for sending letters. I was wrong. You can send anything by e-mail: articles, music, maps, anything. Even photographs.

The one Corrigan had found in his computer's in-tray when he flicked it on about ten minutes before he rang me was very interesting indeed.

I stood at his desk, staring at it. The resolution, composition and lighting were very good. Corrigan stood to one side, his breath low and threatening, looking at me, looking at it.

'Well,' he said, 'that's you. What do you have to say, you bastard?'

The shot showed Elaine Purdey, again head foremost to lens, that head, chin up, grimacing, teeth clenched and bared, a black blindfold over her eyes. If she could have seen at the time, she would have been staring straight down the barrel.

She was still on the execution couch, arms still stretched out, shoulder parallel. She was still naked. Veins and ligaments in her neck stood out like high-tension cable. Her body glistened.

Something was different, however. The end of the couch, where her feet were, had moved. One could assume that for reasons best known to its manufacturers, the contraption was hinged about midway. Thus employed, her legs now pointed to the ground, leaving her buttocks on its horizon, and forcing an arch to the back.

I recognised the technique, updated though it was. It was a favourite of Matthew Hopkins, Britain's Puritan witchfinder-general in the early seventeenth. He would stretch a naked woman thus, arms and legs tied, a pillar at the small of her back, then fill her full of water. Then he would beat her about the stomach until she confessed her love of old trees and wind.

In my name.

In the name of the Lord, anyway.

I saw him do it, while I sat there at a stout wooden table, scratching the confessions with a quill. It was a job. I needed the cash. There was plenty of work in it.

Unless I read it somewhere.

Which I didn't. So I *was* there. Her name was Agnes. Agnes Waterhouse. Her crime was withering butter in a neighbour's churn.

Standing behind, leaning against, the bent-bowed Elaine Purdey was a man. He was naked, save for a tight black leather S&M mask stretched over his head and face, fastened beneath the chin. The zips across the eyes and the mouth were closed, a small raised flap giving vent for the nose.

One of his hands was on her breast, the other was on her belly. He appeared to be raping her.

'Answer me, bastard,' growled Corrigan. 'Confess it: it's you.'

'I don't know,' I said. 'The man has a mask on.'

'Don't insult me, monster!' he shouted, furious.

'Look, man, look! As if I'd need more telling, but look, look, damn you, look at her fucking neck!'

I looked. I hadn't noticed before. Wound tight around her neck was a set of blue plastic rosary beads. My car-thieving rosary beads, they looked like.

They had been in my jacket, in the briefcase. There was a roar in my head. 'Shit,' said my mouth.

I remembered things in a rush. I remembered an angel. I remembered constriction and blindness. I remembered a hand at my throat, rough, urgent. I remembered, what, I identified it, groggy, at the time. Yes, Ketamine, tranks, cat anaesthetic, cut-price raver shit, nasty, slow and dark. I remembered being withered at the altar of Brigid's affection, of something wet, of the cult of St Juthwara. I remembered dizziness and vomit, a child's doll, a frost-nipped foot from getting snow in my rubber boots, a boat, a big boat, dizziness and vomit again, red earth, heat, a woman's voice, Jesus, Chris, will you put down the whisky and go find a job, all you ever do is crosswords and whinge . . .

No.

I remembered some of that. Some of it I made up.

'The truth is what is believed,' I said, jaw tight.

'Oh, I believe it all right, man. I believe it fine, you rapist bastard—'

'That wasn't what I meant. I didn't . . . I wasn't . . . I withered. I meant something else—'

'And I have no doubt that copper, that man Gordon, will believe it as soon as he sees it, which'll be any minute now—'

393

'I didn't. I was drugged.'

'That's never excused the poor bastards on the street, Panther, and it sure as hell won't excuse you now. All this time I trusted you, the best of my flock, the best hope for redemption on the street.' He was flying now, righteous. 'And all the shit I've gone through over Shelagh's death, the cops on my back, convinced it was me when I knew it wasn't and you—*you*, betrayer—pretending to help, when all the time—I see clearly now—it was you, *you* murderer, *you* defiler, *you* blasphemer—'

I had to think of something useful. Fast.

'—*you* liar. I hope you rot in jail for the rest of your life, and when you die I hope it's slow and brutal, and when you call for confession, I hope there'll be no priest strong enough to hear you.'

Push had come to shove.

'To reality, priest—'

'No! Not this ti—'

'*Listen*. One minute. Just give me one minute.'

'I'm counting.'

'That was a set-up, done today, but, fuck you, believe what you will. But believe this also: the commission of one horror does not automatically imply culpability in another. Not on a mortal level, anyway. Elaine Purdey might be related by marriage to Shelagh, but that doesn't mean the two transgressions share a common source. I know that. You know that. Most importantly, the police will believe that.'

From my jacket pocket, where it still sat snug and

folded, I withdrew the sheet from Shelagh's file at Family Values, handed it to him without another word.

He read it, silent.

'Not admissible in court, perhaps,' I said. 'But more than ample for Gordon to haul you in and keep you for a while, more than ample to send him off on a circumstantial evidence hunt.'

He slapped the piece of paper, contemptuously, with the back of his hand. 'But this is—'

'Believable.' I took it back from him, folded it away. 'So this is a threat?'

'Take it how you will.'

'I'll take it how my Lord wills, bastard. These six things doth the Lord hate, yea, seven are an abomination unto him: a proud look, a lying tongue, and hands that shed innocent blood, a heart that deviseth wicked imaginations, feet that be swift in running to mischief, a false witness that speaketh lies, and he that soweth discord among brethren. Proverbs, six something. Let the cops do with me what they will, your betrayal in their hands, Panther, but I'll not go against my God.'

I shook my head. 'Don't then, priest, but keep reading. The way of the fool is right in his own eyes: but he that hearkeneth unto counsel is wise. Proverbs, twelve something. Hearkeneth, priest, for your own sake.'

He snorted. 'I'm listening.'

'Hold your tongue until tomorrow. This is a frame. Give me that long, and I'll forget about my little find. That's all. One day, then do as your conscience bids.'

He thought it over a minute. 'Apart from anything else, my conscience bids save Elaine Purdey.'

'I was blind and drugged, priest. I haven't a clue where she is, or if she's even still alive.'

I did, actually. Quite a good one. It was one of the few bits of certainty I still possessed. It was therefore also pretty much the only card I held.

'Get out of here. Get out of my sight. This time tomorrow, Panther, you're no responsibility of mine.'

'I never was,' I replied, standing up.

I left him. I went outside.

And it was night.

✝

I walked quickly back to the warehouse, collar up and shoulders hunched against the rain. The Daewoo was on duty.

John the Baptist was still at the pub, which was good. I walked straight to the phone, ignoring the photo and the papers lying in taunting wait. It was 6.30pm. I'd have prayed Sophia was still at Image Makers if I thought anybody might be listening and capable of giving a shit.

There wasn't, but she was.

'What's the matter, Joe,' she asked. 'Your voice sounds funny. Are you, you know, frightened?'

'Yes?'

'Of what.'

'Nothing. Me. Or someone else. Doesn't matter.'

'Are you—'

'Listen. There's an e-mail arrived today in the computer of Corrigan the priest. Can you hack into his set-up?'

'Why?'

'Can you?'

'You got his telephone number?'

I gave it to her. She asked if it was the one for the phone or the modem. Both, I said, I think both, also fax machine. No probs, she replied, why?

'He received the e-mail today. You'll know which one, soon as you see it. You'll probably want your own copy, if you can do that sort of thing. See if you can find out where it came from, who sent it. I think I know, but suddenly I'm not too sure about what I think, or what I know. Whatever you do, though, don't let Graeme Purdey see it.'

'No probs, dahl. It's business, then? Good. Purdey's gone for the day, anyway. He's pretty distraught now, which makes me even more certain, like, he's got nothing to do with this.'

'Should you be talking like this on that phone?'

She giggled. 'Sure. I've debugged it. Call it internecine meddling if you like. Anyway, Purdey's gone, left at lunchtime with the suits, said he'd work back late tomorrow night to make up. Make up what, though, I can't see. Image Makers isn't exactly a hive of new clients. I reckon, too much work ethic, some people.'

Pots and kettles came to mind, but I didn't say anything. I wondered whether I had the right to comment,
to criticise, let alone to judge. It all depended, really,
on what was what. I was the only person in the world
who knew for sure, and I wasn't telling me.

'Come by later?' she was asking.

'Maybe,' I said. 'Depends on who I'm feeling. Give
me the number.' And hung up.

There were demons in my brain, unknown and
familiar each. I am a man of determination and drive—
on that point, at least, there's always been consensus—
so I did a pretty good job of not thinking about certain
matters while I walked around and picked up the photograph, the certificate and the note, and shoved them
back in the envelope, out of sight.

That was what I told myself, anyway. I was lying a
bit, so I helped the process along by chopping up the
rest of the speed and shooting two chunky lines right
up my nostrils. That would concentrate things, I
decided. No more dope, though, not right now,
nothing to set my brain inquisitive and loosely leashed,
wandering off behind the bushes, digging at the dirt,
searching for its vomit.

That done, I headed out again. The Daewoo was
still in its spot in the side street. I walked over to the
driver-side window, which, as always, was open a
crack, and hailed the chunky woman. She turned to
me with a start, went to reach for something under the
dash.

I shoved the envelope through the crack. 'Could be

useful for your bosses, whoever they are,' I said. 'I don't want them.'

But I did. Part of me did. A small part. There is nothing so hard as finding something you might once have lost, or thrown away, and not being sure if it's yours.

Somehow I knew the boy had burned the GI Joe, doused in petrol, standing in the snow of the backyard, standing a long time, feet freezing. Something had happened, something bad. Someone had gone, taking certainty as well.

I wondered who he was. I wondered how I knew. I wondered if omniscience was sporadic, like those mediums who claim to know where the missing children lie.

The woman said nothing. I walked on to the Bradford. John was at the bar, cradling a beer, watching greyhound racing. I sat next to him, said nothing for a while. I wanted to wipe my nose, but that's foolish just after speed. I sniffed instead, hard.

He looked at me. 'It's all coming to an end, isn't it, son?'

I nodded, signalled for a scotch and refill.

'That letter,' he said. 'Scuse me asking, son, no business of mine. Bad news?'

'Ruthless news,' I replied. 'Bad is a value judgement.'

Another voice, at my shoulder. 'Excuse me, Joe, sorry.'

It was Judy from the chemist.

'Sorry to bother you,' she said. 'It's just, well, I hope you don't mind, but, see, I'm in here having a drink with my boyfriend, his name's Joe, too.' She indicated a table at the other end of the bar. A young black man, a professional type, waved briefly, embarrassed.

'What?'

'Well, it's silly,' she continued. 'But he's Joe, too, and that's a contraction of Jordan. Oh, I'm sorry about this, but I saw you come in a minute ago and now we've got a bet on about what you're short for. Your name, I mean. He thinks Joseph, and I'm stuck with Joshua. Do you mind?'

I necked most of the Jamesons, then sloshed the remnants around in the glass for a while, staring at them. The silence hung. A greyhound won a race.

'Sorry, Joe, if it's—'

'Josiah,' I said. 'My name is Josiah.'

'Now I'm *really* sorry,' she said. 'Stick to Joe. That's what I tell him, too.' She flushed, smiled and returned to her life.

John had nearly choked on his beer. 'That's not your name,' he whispered, loudly enough to be heard in the pub up the road.

'What they don't know,' I murmured, tipping him a stage wink, 'won't hurt them.'

He nodded, satisfied by my wisdom.

It's not true, actually. It never has been. But it's a comforting fiction.

At least, it was.

✝

Four more whiskies, a plan was developing. Not so much a plan as a series of contingencies. The priest would keep his word about the e-mail, I was sure of that. I was also pretty sure that in the end his delay would turn out to be irrelevant. The stitch-up was in. By that route or another, Gordon's eyes would feast upon the image soon enough.

I gave John Sophia's number, didn't mention her by name, told him to call me if anything went down.

'Like what, son?' he asked.

'Like anything, old man. You are the eyes and the ears of . . . You are my eyes and ears. I'm counting on you.'

He beamed, gap-toothed.

It was nine when I left the pub and hit the streets, not as a god, but fragile, as a man. I tried to look on the bright side. It might be an improvement, after spending two thousand years, all but, imagining myself to be half a man. Or was I half a man who all but imagined himself for two thousand years? What was I, and in the imagination of whom?

I disgust myself sometimes, my shallowness and fraud.

Smith Street was pumping, despite the cold and wet. As I walked along the pavement, head down, casual, the road was clogged with cars prowling for parking, pausing, halting the flow, horns farting in frustration.

There were pedestrians everywhere: groups of suburbans carried wine bottles, peering at menus in restaurant windows; a trio of local men, dull-eyed and unshaven, argued outside a pub, something about money for the pokies; the younger set headed for the wine bars, dressed according to their tastes, seeking house music, lounge music, world.

An untidy queue of young Greek-Australians stamped their feet and waited outside the door of a new club, a first floor venue above the burnt-out and boarded remains of a shish kebab joint. A wide-eyed man with a jaundiced face and a five-day growth loped along, shoulder rubbing against the walls, tattered headband around his grey hair, talking to someone only he could see. A fat, bearded man in a dirt-crusted jumper lay curled on a wooden bench, signalling passers-by for cigarettes and urinating in his jeans. The amusement parlours pumped green-lit rock, full of kids firing bright orange pistols and adults watching on, no mercy in their patient hunters' eyes. Junkies used the gallery—a block of public toilets on a corner—or sat in doorways, waiting, begging half-hearted, or nodding out. In and around, eyebrows arching, hands fast on the switch of exchange, the dealers moved, shifting product, keeping the economy moving.

A young dealer, part of the Romanian network probably, hung around near one of the parlours, his pitch wordless, conducting business with nods of his head, left hand permanently in the pocket of his Miami Dolphins sports jacket. I watched him for a while from across the street, leaning against a shop window near the tram stop, smoking a cigarette, making like I was waiting for transport, knots of people passing in front of me. My watcher, still the Daewoo woman, was also on foot, the car being pointless in the crush. She stood about twenty metres further along the road, arms folded tight in an effort to combat the chill. I was on my second smoke when she couldn't take the weather any longer and stepped inside a coffee shop, compromising her view.

It was what I'd been waiting for. Dodging cars, I crossed the road.

The dealer was older than most who worked that particular stretch of Smith, maybe all of eighteen. That perhaps explained why he was working solo, holding his own gear, instead of with a partner out of sight. He was also new in the area, so he didn't recognise me.

He raised his chin towards me, eyes darting. I nodded back, almost imperceptibly, and flashed five fingers. To the uninitiated, I appeared to be doing no more than shaking some life into a cold hand. He knew I was ordering, and ordering multiple. A new customer, a big buy, his face showed his delight. Despite his years, he was plainly new at the game. He should have been more careful.

I could have been anybody.

I walked past him without breaking stride, round into a side street, and round again into a shadowed alley. It was only twenty metres from the strip, but still too far for pedestrians to venture without reason. He followed me, profit in his mind.

I have learned many things over the years. He didn't have a chance. I handed him a bundle of small notes and change—all I had left—fumbling as I did so. Reflexively, he held out both hands to secure it. It happened fast. My right fist shot out, straight into the bridge of his nose. Before he even dropped the cash, I hit him again, slamming the heel of my palm upwards into the same spot.

I've been told that, done properly, such a combination breaks the nose and then rams a shard of bone hard up into the underside of the front of the brain. I don't know. Whatever, he fell without a sound and lay still, blood seeping across his face. It took me two minutes to find his mobile phone and money—three hundred and fifty bucks. He obviously hadn't been working the gig too long, holding that much on him. I left his stash, dragged him further into the shadows and propped him in a sitting position against a wall. Someone would trip over him by morning if he didn't pull through. Just another dead dealer, victim of free market competition.

I walked away, heading for Gertrude Street, blood on my hand.

In the shadow of the tower block, pink-flashed from the Speakeasy over the road, I waited for the flock. They came, one by one, to be nourished. I put my worries to the back of my mind. I had a job to do, so I hung my problems at the door. Feeney's finger was healing, his hand still visibly swollen. Rashid told me he'd discovered that cat flea collars make excellent tourniquets, although they tasted shit with the end in your mouth. Shazz told me this was her last, tomorrow she goes onto methadone, for real this time. She said that the previous week, too. No one had any information on Farndale. Caroline arrived, steady on her feet for once, said how you going, partner.

I misheard her, thought maybe she said *Panton*, and glared. '*Partner*,' she said. 'Chill out, Joe, or have you forgotten? I saved your arse, dealer-man.'

I nodded apology, asked her how she was feeling.

'Fine,' she said. 'Been being careful. Still got a taste left, just.'

'I have something for you,' I said. 'Wait for me across the road. Here's ten. Buy yourself a drink. I'll be there soon.'

She looked perplexed, but did so, ducking in front of a tram. She wasn't sick; she had nothing better to do.

Half an hour later I joined her. The Speakeasy was full. Many of its customers had been there all day. The place hummed with body odour and stale beer. Laughter turned to argument, then to heartfelt reconciliation throughout. Bon Jovi was on the jukebox, just to add to the hardships.

Scotch in hand, I joined Caroline at a corner table, where she was doing her best to ignore the advances of a red-faced fat man with his hair swept oiled and sparse across his crown. He took one look at me and backed away, palms up.

'Caroline,' I began. 'Do you have a dream?'

'I do.'

'What is it?'

'Mine.'

I did my best with my eyes, with my voice, with my presence. It felt like pulling on a dirty shirt. 'I can make that dream come true, thy dream, and the visions of thy head upon thy bed.'

'It wouldn't be a dream then.'

'Do you believe me?'

She stared at me for a minute, idly stirring her drink with a straw. It was plain lemonade, alcohol and hep not being the best combination. 'Yes,' she said, 'I know you can. You, of all people.'

I couldn't resist a smile. I've still got it, I thought. Whoever I am.

'I need a big favour. It might not come to pass, but it might. It might tomorrow. You'll need to start working on it now. How well do you know the flock?'

'Well enough.'

I pulled out the mobile phone and copied its number down on a half-wet drink coaster, which I folded into my pocket. 'Take this. Do not try to pawn it. Throw it away tomorrow, when it's finished. If it doesn't happen, throw it away anyway.'

'What do you want, Joe?'

I told her. 'And then, when it's done, I'll give you your wish, whatever it is.'

'If you survive,' she commented, a wry smile crossing her pale lips.

'I'll survive,' I replied, affecting far more confidence than I felt.

We left the bar together, parted company at the door.

Into your hands, junkie Caroline, I thought to myself, I deliver my soul.

✝

Walking is bad. Memory is worse. The architecture of the soul is subject to collapse.

Memes are ruthless.

I banged on Sophia's front door, closed fist and rhythmic, calling her name. I banged like a child against a mission gate, seeking escape from a land turned hateful by the zeal of the God's vanguard. I banged like a boy locked out in the snow, like a frightened adolescent in a mining town lock-up, like a tousle-haired madman in a white-walled room.

She let me in. She sat me down. She wiped my brow. She gave me drink.

'The e-mail was routed through an anonymous server in Amsterdam,' she said. 'From there, you know, it could have come from anywhere, but, like, we both know most likely where.'

I hardly heard her. I felt a tiredness like I'd never known before, despite the speed, could hardly lift the glass to my lips, a cigarette out of the question. The cold was in my bones. I had carried my burden, with all of its weight, every moment of my days, asleep and awake. I had borne it well, as only I could, as only I had to, with its movement and loneliness, its blood and its loss. I had borne it with the perseverance of the blessedly damned, the keeper of the knowledge, the disinherited son. I had seen through the illusion, knew of the con, dangerous and pure in that knowing.

Now my burden had been lifted and I wanted it back. Sudden freedom can be fatal, especially for a knock-kneed boy full of fear and introspection, stripped of the glamour of status, alone without divinity, just one, alone, and weakling. Not even my age was right. I felt as nothing, as no one, despised as a day of small things, and wrong.

On a grey-pink sofa in a house built for show, Jesus wept.

Sophia sat beside me, kissed me lightly on my cheek, wiped at my tears. I recoiled from her touch.

'Don't touch me,' I managed. 'I'm filth. I abhor myself.'

She didn't move. 'Why do you cry?' she asked softly.

'For my father. For me.'

'Tell me about it, Joe. You're no good to us like this. I like you, Joe, as a man, but we need you as, well, as more than a man. You have to be strong right now. It's important.'

'A man,' I echoed bitterly. 'A man, one man amongst a thousand.'

'Spit it out, Joe. Let's have it.'

I took a deep breath, sat up straight. She was right: now was not the time to buckle. There would be plenty of time for that later, perhaps somewhere new, perhaps in a cell, perhaps in the silence of what comes after death, resurrection no longer an option.

'I'm sorry,' I said. 'This is difficult and there's no one I can tell.'

'Tell me, Joe. It won't go beyond these walls, I promise, and no, before you ask, we're not being bugged. You're safe here, you know.'

My nose needed wiping. The speed had long settled in. Not thinking, I used the back of my hand.

'There's blood on your hand, Joe.'

'Not mine.'

'That's okay then.' She tried a smile. It died on her lips. 'Come on, lover man, tell me.'

Another breath.

'I've never really known who I was,' I began slowly. 'I mean, I *did*, I thought I did, I was pretty sure I did. The facts fitted well, my memories worked, only now I find they didn't. Today I found out I'm not who I am at all.'

'Yes?' Her voice was cautious, carrying more than ritual sympathy. 'So now you're saying you're not Joshua Ben Panther, is that it? You have this thing with changing names every second time you meet me?'

Her attempt to lighten the moment was as useless as it was transparent. 'Who are you, then?'

'Forgive me,' I blurted, not quite sure to whom. 'I am not who I thought. I am Josiah Benjamin Panton,

409

migrant, mad, drifter, lost, small and now, now . . .' I looked her in the eyes, tears welling in my own again. 'Please don't mock me, Sophia. Anything but that.'

And then my vision clouded again. My head bent, and I rammed my hands into my eyes, pushing hard, making the black turn red with shame.

The next thing I heard was Sophia, her voice more distant. She was standing over the other side of the room, watching me.

'That's one theory, Joe,' she said, calm. 'Want to hear the other one?'

My mind is vast, my understanding broad. I had no idea what she meant.

'I'm afraid, Joe,' she said, 'I've been less than fully frank with you.'

✝

Many are the levels of understanding, and many, too, are the layers of its veils.

In the earthen jar exhumed at Nag Hammadi were found the secret gospels, sealed from decay beneath the sand, the stories spun in gossamer, teachings untaught for nigh on two millennia, the poetry of myth untouched by the evolution of the meme.

In the jar was found the rout of Samuel, the Yahweh, the blind god, the angry god, the foolish god, the visible god who is but the mirror darkly stained, the petty demiurge who hides the flickered glimpses of the mind within us all, within the trees, within the wind.

They have names, these tracts, names known to few, power known to fewer still. They have names like *Gospel of Truth, The Gospel of Mary Magdalene, Thunder: Perfect Mind, The Gospel of Thomas, The Apocalypse of Peter, The Apocryphon of John,* and, bedevilment to lispers, *The Second Treatise of the Great Seth.*

Don't know what happened to the first.

They were suppressed, of course, in the turbulent first centuries, by Antioch and Rome, by the bishops in conference at Constantinople and Nicea, excluded from the Testament, declared heretic by the fathers of the church.

But they exist. And they give the lie to a world's belief.

Gentle are the gospels of the lost and damned. They speak of God as everything, of God, as male and female, here and now, within. They do not sew the herma-phrodite's vulva and claim to create a man; they offer each in both. They speak of a god indescribable, a god of many parts, yet one: the Ineffable, the Silence, the Grace, the Womb of heaven and earth as one, the Mind, the Intelligence, the Wisdom. They speak of peace and poverty, of tolerance, of a world without blood on its earth.

But the God meme is ruthless. And the ruthless survive. All is one with the meme.

The Greek word for wisdom is *Sophia.*

'And so,' she was saying, cross-legged and calm, 'this task force—'

411

It was a task force now.

'—is after not just the porn, this *type* of porn, or rather, this porn and more, you know. This is pornography as articles of faith, you know, the appropriation of icons, porn of the soul. It attracts a certain *type*, you see? There is a connection.

'It's like the Internet. The Internet isn't a computer. Nothing about a computer, seen in isolation, will lead you to deduce the Internet, and neither will millions of computers. The Internet is an *emergent* force, it exists in the *connections*, in the energy, not in the windows at its end. So this, this is kind of the same.'

'I'm not sure where this is going.'

'Have another scotch, you will. So there are two forces, two emergent forces, on our agenda, Joe, because our theory holds they interact, they reinforce, they synthesise. If you like, Joe, this is a search-and-destroy mission, the God meme the target. Its time is nearly up, Joe, there's a meme of reason selecting it out, and it's cornered, dumb like a virus, fighting the white cells of reason, the vaccine of science.'

'Very pretty.'

'Listen. This involves you. So the meme goes one way, shedding its layer of religion and control, creates its blasphemy—the *Larry Flynt* poster, the martyr snuffs—and it goes the other way, reinforcing the religious. The fastest growing denominations today are the apocalyptic ones, Joe, the conservative evangelicals, the Christian Right, all moral probity and bring on the Judgement Day. The extremes—the Wacos, the US survivalists, the devil man Japanese murderer, the Naples psychopath—they're just symptoms of a much larger shift.'

'But—'

'Hush. Looks like we're dealing with opposites—the secular, the sacred—but we aren't, because, you know, paradox is at its heart, in each bit lies its opposite. So the mockery of God enrages the conservatives, the avenging evangelists take over the mainstream through sheer economic clout, and the zealots spur the secular to mock still harder. But God is at the centre of both, the God meme is at the centre of both. It can only profit from the conflict.'

I am a Pharisee and the son of Pharisees, said Pauly.

'So, now we get to it, Joe. Either direction it goes, it causes strife. Its thousand-year rule is nearly over. It's under attack, and it's gearing up for the final conflict. So the porn kills people and the zealots, for whom the appeal of martyrdom is very strong, drink the images like blood. Horror and fight is blood to these people, Joe, the big loser here is mercy.'

'God be merciful to me, a sinner.' I had it, rote. Luke. Paul's mate.

'No chance, Joe. Mercy and survival don't mix. There is no mercy in the universe, no foresight in the meme, yeah? So the passions stir, either way, and the horror meets in the middle. Look at these cults springing up, Joe. Look at Waco, at Heaven's Gate, and Jonestown, look at any of them. Blood-porn and belief intermingle: some abuse children, some abuse adults, some mutilate themselves, turning inwards what others do to others. Most of them are armed to the teeth, their memberships are growing, most of them believe that Armageddon's just a breath away. The frightening thing is that they're nowhere near alone in that belief.'

And so the Anointed One will arrive, the Messiah, the bringer of judgement, the turnkey of Paradise.

'This is a global problem, Joe, and globally linked. A message of holy war can zip around the world in less time than it takes to recite the Lord's Prayer, less time than it takes to say amen. That's a force that works faster than thought, Joe, that puts us behind from the start, unable to catch up, unless . . .'

She let it hang, a smug smile playing across her lips.

'This is where I say: Unless *what*?'

'Good boy, you're learning. There were moves to start something like this task force after Jonestown, but the powers that be thought Jim Jones and his followers were just an anomaly, never to be repeated. We know different now. The link-up between agents and agencies began straight after Waco, already behind the eight-ball. Our mission is threefold: to track down secular nastiness with the potential to feed the fires, to research and infiltrate the sects already in action, and, here it is, Joe, to track down and identify individuals who show signs of forming cults, wherever they may be. This is a pro-active gig, Joe, pro-active, funded, secret, and unaccountable.'

I wasn't really with her. I hadn't been listening very closely, still sunk in the self-pity of revelation that flooded through me in waves of disgust. 'So where does all that leave me?'

'The subject of some fairly robust betting among the agents.'

That caught my attention. 'Explain.'

'Got any grass?'

'Some.'

'Skin up, then, mate. You might need it.'

I tossed her my mull bag. 'I don't. You do it, help yourself.'

She leant over, started crumbling a bud onto the coffee table.

'This is a very high-powered operation, see, and—Jesus, there's enough seeds in here, isn't there?—and we've got people from all over the place, every discipline, not just law enforcement people. We've got physicists, chaoticians, philosophers, ethicists, radical theologians, the lot—people hand-picked because of their conviction that we as a species don't know everything yet, but that which we don't know can eventually be explained and verified by rational means. I'm not just talking dull empiricists here, Joe, I'm talking high-fliers, people prepared to consider any possibility, however seemingly impossible. Impossibility speaks of knowledge, not of actuality—a lot of things are logically impossible, only because we can't find a way to work out how they happen. That doesn't mean the way doesn't really exist, yeah?'

'Hand-picked by whom?'

'That's classified. You've been quite an object of

415

study for some of our people for quite a while, Joe. Well, not *you*, as such, well, maybe you, maybe not, maybe not at all, maybe, though, yes. I don't hold with it myself, but there you go. Cigarette, please, and papers.'

I tossed them over.

'We started sniffing around Melbourne as a possible source for the porn several months ago. Our methods are diverse, Joe, but pretty thorough. One of our ongoing tasks, as I've said, is to try to pinpoint possible cultists, possible mini-messiahs, before they start to attract followers and infrastructure. That way we can take them out of circulation before the trouble starts.'

'What does "take them out of circulation" mean?'

She tossed her head. 'Anything at all, really. Anyway, we're looking around here and we start to get reports of some guy with a beard spouting Bible shit all over the place, living black and dealing drugs. That's you, boy. Now, the drugs bit didn't bother us—you're a chickenshit dealer, Joe, and not very discreet—but the Bible shit did. Most of it starts with Bible shit—that, and unstable life histories.'

'You mean,' I said, 'I'm a man with no invisible means of support?'

'Don't be flippant and toss me that lighter. See, then we found out your name was Joshua Ben Panther, and, ho, Joe, did that stir up some shit.'

'Why?'

'In a minute. So we talked to people, undercover,

416

talked to people who had met you, monitored your increasingly erratic behaviour, watching for the meltdown. We're thorough, Joe, and we knew we were onto something when we found one guy, just a guy, you know, who told of accidentally knocking on your door one night, in search of an artist named Jim. You told him you were Joe, the ineffable love of the Lord made flesh, and then you slammed the door in his face. Then, Joe, we knew you were *serious* about your gig, not just playing. That sparked some interest, I'm telling you.

'We studied, we observed. We even protected you, Joe, by hacking into the state cops' database and flagging your name. We inserted information, you know, that said you were part of a pilot program for petty psychiatric offenders released into the community. No action was to be taken against you for acts of minor, you know, criminality. You were safe, Joe, unless you did something really stupid. Davey Parker, by the way, was borderline stupid. Good job the guy's parents were dead and he didn't have any friends.'

She offered me the joint. I declined. Even in eternity there's a first time for everything.

'So you want to hear the theory? It's kind of a joke, but not really, a kind of a wish, an unlikely explanation, highly improbable, but no less possible for that. Whatever, it provides distraction for the smart guys, if nothing else.'

'The theory?'

'It's got two names, depending on. It's called the Myth Man Theory, or the Pantera Theory.'

I felt the blood drain from my face, chugged the scotch, poured afresh, managed a nod.

'Here's the start,' she said. 'You'd know this: there's a tradition in the Talmud, echoed by the pagan philosopher Celsus, that a man called Jesus was born to a Roman soldier called Pantera, or Pandera, or, hey what a coincidence, *Panthera*. Jesus or Yeshu or Yoshu or, hey, Joshua, ben Pantera. Jesus was a common-as-dirt name, of course, so you can guess where that led.'

I didn't have to.

'Now, the theory goes, among our people—it's a kind of intellectual game, really—that there was, I don't know, something weird about the guy's DNA, something which halted the ageing process and extended the life expectancy like shit, something that was interpreted as the Resurrection. Guy hasn't died yet, that's the notion, just keeps going, fucked up and angry, the name changing a bit each time to suit the prevailing social conditions. It's stupid, of course, but, you know, the historical record might just support . . . well, you can find evidence to fit any theory if you try hard enough, eh?'

'What evidence? Do you have names?'

'Of the researchers? That's—'

'Classified, I know. Other names.'

She walked to the bookcase, threw a Nine Inch Nails album in the player, picked up a file, opened it.

'Okay, one faction reckons Simon Magus, though

how you fake a death by plummet, I don't know. The historical record for that period is an oxymoron, anyway. They've got more ideas from the current millennium. There's Pope Urban IV, for instance, in the thirteenth century, whose real name—if we can use the term here—was Jacques Pantaleon. That's one.

'Then there's, before that, there's Hughes—soft, after Yeshu—de Payens, who founded the Knights Templar—what a bunch of nasties they were—in the eleventh. Then, same century, later, same mob, Hughes de Pairaud, who lent money at interest to finance more crusades. There's another, in the mid-fifteenth—bit of a transliteral shift here—Guillame Bardin, evil bloke, an apologist for witch-burners; or, maybe, a guy called Joachim Benpanicke, previous century, one of the Waldensian community tortured and burned for heresy. Back again, in the thirteenth, there was Joachim of Fiores—that's Joachim del Patrese, who wrote that the Roman Church was the Whore of Babylon, also condemned as a heretic. Want more?'

I didn't, but I nodded anyway.

'The *Compendium Maleficarum*'s a pretty good hunting ground. You'd know it, of course.'

Did I ever. 'Published in 1608, written by Francesco Maria Guazzo of the order of Saint Ambrose,' I intoned. 'Along with its predecessor, the *Malleus Maleficarum*, a witch-hunters' guide, a torture guide, one of the most influential books in the Christian canon, used to justify the brutal deaths of tens of thousands, mostly women.'

'You got it. Well, in there we found references, one way or another, to a Giovanni Porta, a Johann Pistorius, a Giovanni Pontano, a Gianfrancesco Ponzinibio, and a number of witches just named John or Johann. Then, of course, there are references elsewhere, like the one to a guy called Joachim von Pantagruel, rumoured to have been an early influence on the historical Faust. There was a guy called Count Saint-Germain in the eighteenth—no one knows his real name, but we found references to him in archives in France, Germany, Britain and Holland, including secret service reports that he privately admitted being the Wandering Jew.

'Some of them are a bit way out, though, like the theory about Mahatma Koot Hoomi, Madame Blavatsky's spectral, ghostly channelling spirit in the nineteenth—look, here's a picture.'

She held up an ink-wash impression of a vaguely foreign-looking man with a beard, a distinctive nose, weird eyes and perhaps the earliest recorded example of a mullet haircut.

'One guy on the team even goes so far as to claim Proudhon because his middle name was Joseph and the clergy hated him, but I reckon that's just wishful thinking. There's others, but you get the gist. So, Joe, mate, what do you reckon?'

Cold fingers gripped at my chest, confusion fought confusion. *You're not very discreet*, she'd said. The me that was me, might have been me, always used to be me, was disturbed. You sign nothing, I thought, you tread lightly, do your business, move on and never leave a fingerprint, and *still* they find the trail. Five of those names were spot on, ringing in my ears with sudden familiarity. The others weren't.

Me? A pope? Come off it.

The Blavatsky gig was a real worry, though. I'd thought that one was foolproof. Not even the old bat herself thought I was *really* real. (Ever lived in a wardrobe for two years? Don't. Believe me. Don't.)

The me that was not-me, was me, had been me, maybe, maybe was me again, didn't know what to think. You just get over denial, and you start denying it all over again.

She watched me, watching my face, waiting for reaction. I was supposed to be stunned, twice gobsmacked and more. I could have been, but just at that moment my past, whichever past, seemed of secondary importance. I was thinking, what is, is. And, whatever else I am, I is.

Of course it would explain the watcher, I thought, the Falcon man, the one I thought I'd seen before in another context. Another context indeed—*before* all this really got going, clad in tight-fitting gear, riding a bicycle, unseated by Pordelli's panicked driving outside the church on the feast of St James.

That was where. That was him. And that meant I now knew why Shelagh Purdey had been murdered. Exactly why.

Because she knew *me*.

'What are the odds on Josiah Panton?' I asked.

'Evens.'

'And the Pantera Man?'

'You remember the googolplex?'

'Yep.'

'To one.'

'So it's possible?'

'Ain't reason grand, boy!' she hooted.

'Help me my unbelief.'

She coloured and sighed, all maternal, and gently sat down on my lap. 'Oh, Joe,' she whispered, stroking my face. 'You've had a big day, haven't you? Come on, let's go to bed.'

And then she placed her lips gently on mine, silent, warm, like forgiveness.

And I thought, not for the first time, Betrayest thou the son of man with a kiss?

✝

At midnight the phone rang. Sophia answered it on the bedside extension. Too sleepy to be confused, she simply passed it to me. 'It's for you,' she said.

It was John the Baptist, scared so much he could hardly talk through his wheezing and hyperventilating. The police were at the warehouse, tossing it even as he spoke. I could hear heavy feet and swearing behind him. They were looking for me, he said, and looking for drugs, looking for bloody anything useful. Gordon and Pordelli were at the station, roused from slumber, waiting for my arse. They had a photo, said John, some photo delivered that evening to the station sergeant's desk. He didn't know what.

I didn't have to ask.

'Wha's up,' mumbled Sophia.

'Can this number be traced?' I asked her. She shook her head.

I spoke to John. 'Do you know where you're calling?'

'No, son.'

'Good,' I said. 'Stay put, there or the pub. I'll ring you late tomorrow, be ready to move.' And hung up.

Sophia was awake now. 'Joe, what's—'

I wasn't listening. I was dialling again.

'Caroline,' I said. 'It's on. Six in the evening.' I told her where. 'Don't fail me, girl, and I won't fail you.'

'*Joe*,' urged Sophia. 'What's going on?'

'Nothing that can't wait until tomorrow. Just make sure you stay back at Image Makers after work. First we solve a mystery, then we bring on the Apocalypse. Do you have a car?'

'I can get one.'

She wanted to talk more, but I turned my back on her, pulled the doona up around my ears, closed my eyes. The time for talk was over.

Outside, against the window, I heard the splat of heavy raindrops, like thunder coming.

✝

# 12

SOPHIA LEFT IN THE MORNING, usual time. I slept until ten. I figured I should make the best of it while I could.

The day was vintage Melbourne: a stiff wind gusted from the sea, pushing banks of sodden, storm-laden clouds across the city, alternating with short bursts of chill-bright sun. I looked up at it through a gap in the curtained lounge room window, letting it settle in my mind. I wanted to remember it, given that it was possibly the last Melbourne day I'd see.

This century, anyway. Perhaps ever. Depending on.

The following day, I knew, if there was a following day, I would have to leave, to wander again, with whatever means I had at my disposal. At the moment that amounted to roughly three hundred bucks and enough smack to send me down for five years.

Whatever. It was a start.

Sophia had left a spare key before she went. She had

been full of questions in the dawn. There had been no answers.

Trust me, I'd said. Have faith.

Half-eleven, I left the house, waved to the Honda Civic. I had to see a man about a trip.

✟

The trip in question was a small square of white cardboard with a miniature reproduction of Andy Warhol's banana from the first Velvet Underground album on it.

It had been cut from a larger sheet infused with seventy microns LSD per square inch. It was what was known as a disco dose, geared for ravers out primarily for a speedy night. At that dosage, the hallucinogenic effects for the experienced user would be chunky, but controllable—a bit of colour, bit of movement, pretty in the flashing lights of a dance floor, not much more. Enough, though, for my purposes.

It was pretty weak compared to what you used to be able to get, even a decade before. Then, a hundred and forty mics was about the lowest you could find, two hundred, even two-fifty, being pretty common. I tried it for a while. It had no effect on me.

I picked up some more speed too. I had a feeling it was going to be a long night.

Back at Roseberry Street, I put my feet up and enjoyed being temporarily invisible and invulnerable. I watched a movie, some American soap operas, conserving strength, waiting for the dark.

✝

Up close, the casino was enormous, a huge, jagged, almost windowless sprawl that would have been disproportionately large and ugly in a city twice the size. It stood on the south side of the river opposite the city proper, for the length of three blocks, a towered hotel at one end, fountains at the other, and pillars spitting fireballs in the middle. It was so big, in fact, that one of the main road bridges into the CBD had been engulfed by it, running right through the complex, the business of gambling and purchase continuing around it. So above, so below.

As always, it was crowded with the hopeful and the lost, transported by buses and coach, taxi and car, train and tram, to offer to fate, find augur in cards, give votive to cruel gods of randomness with desperate faith of return.

In all temples of worship and Mass, however, there are quiet places, darkened spaces where only the lone and the apostate tread. At five minutes to six I was waiting at the portal of one: a set of glass doors on the riverside walkway, no more than a dandied-up fire exit really, well away from the lights and the sweeping driveways at each end that welcomed the bulk of the gamblers. The doors gave out onto a riverside promenade, concrete and penitent in the biting wind and slashing rain of a storm not yet quite come to arousal. No one lingered. No one but me, hunched in the shadows, breathing through a Dunhill.

I was waiting and hoping, waiting for the flock, testing allegiance, unsure of the loyalty I commanded.

An hour previously I had telephoned the cops and surrendered. Sort of.

I figured that if Gordon and his chubby offsider had been waiting for my capture since midnight, exhaustion would have set in. By contrast I was fine: well rested, committed to purpose, the blessing of St Amphetamine up my nose.

The officer who took the call didn't want to connect me at first, until I told him my name. Then I didn't even have to listen to hold music.

'Where are you?' said Gordon, focused and determined.

'At a call box. Don't try to trace this. It's pointless. Come meet me.'

'Where?' Cautious. The hunter, not believing. A pro.

'In a minute. I've found Theresa Farndale.'

'It's *you* I want, bastard. I've seen the shot, and . . .' He paused. 'Where?'

'The photograph's a fit-up, but you'll discover that. Farndale's working as a croupier at the casino. Assumed name. I've found her and she'll talk. Now.'

'Panther—'

'Deal, Gordon. She's shit-scared of cops, but wants to help. She's still hot for Corrigan's neck, but wants guarantees.'

'No deals, Pan—'

'Be wise for once in your life, Gordon. She'll talk, but only with me present. You do the interview, let her walk, and then I'll let you take me. I'm innocent, and I can prove it. Let's get this finished. I'm tired.'

He was silent for a moment. 'Where?'

'The ground floor gambling area of the casino in ninety minutes. I'll take you to her.'

'The gambling floor's *huge*, Panther. Where specifically?'

'*There* specifically. Jesus, man, the place has got security cameras hanging from the ceiling every couple of feet. Talk to the security people, give them my description, they'll keep an eye on me for you until you meet me, I'm sure. I'll stand out like a gourami in a goldfish bowl, never out of sight.'

Then, in the background, another voice, possibly Pordelli's, calling, 'We've got the location, boss!'

I hung up and ran.

At five past six Caroline led the flock along the promenade. She'd managed to contact the dozen: Spring-Head and Helen and Rashid and Faye, Tessa and Macca and Feeney and Shazz, Peter and Thomas and Simon and James, grinning, bemused, out on adventure.

When she reached me, Caroline made a show of pulling out the mobile phone and hurling it into the darkness of the river. I nodded approval. 'Follow me,' I said to all, 'and I will make you pissers-off of men.'

Through the doors, it was only a short walk past a

429

coffee shop and bistro to the stairs leading down to a dimly lit small foyer which gave out onto a cavernous underground car park. The foyer contained nothing but a couple of public telephones, some service rooms and a toilet block. There was no gambling, and hence no security cameras. The doors to the male and female bogs led from a mutual alcove, out of sight.

I ushered them into the men's: two cubicles, urinal, black walls, brown tiled floor, Julio Iglesias crooning through the speakers. Truly, we were in Dante's basement.

'Lean against the door,' I said to Rashid.

Caroline and the twelve clustered around, close, perplexed, but with the gig. It was something different. If nothing else, the casino was considerably warmer than anywhere along Smith Street. None had ever been in the place before, spare cash not being a regular feature of their lives, and their addictions being other than to the caprice of fate. Smack is not the chasing after chance; it is the pursuit of numbing certainty.

I handed each a deal, a spoon and a clean fit. 'This is my body which is for you; this do in remembrance of me,' I said each time.

'You're full of it, Joe,' muttered Caroline, chancing things a bit. Some of the others smiled, not sure whether to laugh or not.

Next I gave them each twenty dollars. 'Play the pokies or something,' I said. 'This do also in remembrance of me.'

They took the money, nodding, feeling like they

430

were part of something. There's a first time for everything.

I remembered Pauly, Saul as he was at the time, Malchus by cover, back in that shuttered room, the scourging room. His insistent questions, his pedantic note-taking: *Tell me about the meeting, the gathering in the guest-chamber. Not who was there. We know who was there. Tell me about the bread. What did you do with it? Then what? And said? Now the wine, the wine. Think carefully: what were your words?*

I thought little of it at the time, having other things on my mind. Just another trainspotting cop, I figured.

Stupid assumption, it turned out. He knew what he was doing.

I discovered this early in the second century. I was in Rome, casting lots for the gullible, and became quite friendly with the historian Suetonius, an old man by then, wicked sense of humour. There was a mob, he said, full of self-righteous zeal in the name of Chrestus, making trouble for themselves and others.

Chrestus, it turned out, was me, via the Greek. Nero, in particular, had killed a lot of these people, throwing them to wild beasts being his favourite method, something Suet-boy thought to be one of his less atrocious acts. He seemed to regard the Emperor's fondness for singing operas as his worst crime. (This, you understand, was in the days before Julio.)

Anyway, it turned out the central ritual for the Christians was the thing with the wine and the bread, the Eucharist it was called, using my words, what I'd said in that upstairs room in private. That surprised me.

I hadn't meant anything by it at the time. I'd just been tired and maudlin, sunk in self-pity, the show well out of control by then. There were all these people: the man with the pitcher, the man with the donkey, the others, all my life, in there, quiet, helping, disappearing, asking no reward, yet satisfied. Who were they? Whose wishes did they fill?

The words, when I'd said them, didn't mean shit. I'd just been drunk, depressed, and wanting another drink, seeking alcoholic complicity, no more.

Ah well. Amen to that.

'Hit up in here,' I said, 'but don't stay here. Get out there and mingle. See you among the five thousand.'

The door swung shut behind me.

The ground floor gambling area bulged irregular and long through the building, like lymphoma. Groups of people gathered, quiet and serious, around hundreds of tables offering blackjack, stud poker, roulette and sic-bo, their operators roped off from the punters, each watched from behind and above. Other gamblers wandered back and forth, waiting for inspiration. Banks of poker machines flashed and spun throughout. Display stands held cars, motorbikes, four-wheel drives. In between the black-stalk surveillance cameras on the roof hung gaudy installations: stars and globes of flashing lights in blue and yellow and green and red. Men and women in uniforms, bearing badges of rank, prowled the aisles, croupiers yelled and exhorted, repeatedly, obsessively, wiping the palms of their hands.

432

Bad late-eighties disco snaked through the air, finding spaces between the shouts of loss, the coughs of concentration, and the clattering of slot machines spitting coins into trays.

I was standing, idly watching a huge revolving sign bearing the words MIDAS TOUCH and a constantly changing figure that looked like the mileage readout on a rally car when Gordon and Pordelli found me. They came from behind, constrained and tense.

'Got you, motherfucker,' whispered Gordon, his voice dripping venom.

I didn't turn around. 'Move back away,' I murmured through the corner of my mouth. 'If she thinks I'm working with you, she'll do a runner. She's very nervous.'

'You're not working with us, mystery man,' rumbled Pordelli. 'You're about to be fucked by us, but good.'

He laughed at his own wit, such as it was, but I could hear the tiredness in his voice.

'Whatever,' I said, moving off a step or two. 'Just give me a bit of space. Let's end this thing.'

My voice was passive, tired. I wanted to give the impression that the fight was leached from me, the desire for closure all that remained.

Which was true, actually, but not in the way I wanted them to assume.

'Oh my god!' A woman's voice, full of sudden and concentrated loathing. I turned towards the sound. A matron, wearing a sturdy little number she'd obviously run up at home, was backing away from a roulette table. The six or seven other punters clustered around it were still heads down, trying to concentrate, but flicking glances up and left, again, again, to where Macca was leaning against the edge of the baize, eyelids heavy, chin down, unshaven, watching and not watching.

A security guard, silent and efficient, bore down on the boy, one hand on his elbow, a word in his ear. Macca looked up, not quite comprehending, tried a sloppy grin, asked for some change and then vomited all over the playing field.

He'd overdone it, silly boy.

The matron screamed. The croupier started retching. The gamblers leapt back from their stools, spattered and revolted.

'What the?' Gordon, moving away slightly.

Then, from somewhere else, a cry, another chaotic cluster.

A shout from a guard: 'Hey *you*!' Elsewhere again.

And then there were people moving, shifting, talking, shouting everywhere. There were junkies in the temple: nodding wastrels, ragged thieves in track-suits and flannelette, scum, pin-eyed malcontents, wandering, staggering, swaying, contemplating, cadging money, palming chips, stealing drinks, smelling of the street.

In the absence of charity and grace, a vacuum forms, sucking demons from the depths, and the demons were among them, an affront, an insult, a threat. My charges were not controlled users, they were the lost, utterly given to their addictions, their very existences anathema to the city that created them.

'That one's carrying a *syringe*!' yelled someone. 'He might have HIV! Stand back!'

Perhaps we created the gods; certainly we created the demons, our mirror images, the glass smeared with our own infantile shit. The chaos spread, with punters moving every which way, trying to get out of the road, security people cannoning off them, trying to get through, trying, unsuccessfully, to keep things calm. Macca had passed out. I could see Peter and Thomas, running between the pokie banks, staggering a little, laughing, trying to evade capture, knocking over stools. Shazz had her arm around a Chinese man in a raw silk suit, begging change, her yellow-toothed leer an obscene parody of seduction. Feeney was shouting at a croupier, *demanding* to play stud poker, tell him *how*, tell him *how*, mate.

And now the people were moving in tides, in rips, in whirls, trying to stay out of the way, trying to pick up scattered chips, clutching plastic cups of coins to their breasts, spilling their contents on the carpet, bending low to scrabble, sending grown men and women tumbling, leapfrog, over the top.

And the Lord looked upon his creation, and saw it was good.

Time to leave, I decided, and turned.

Gordon and Pordelli hadn't moved. They were right behind me, rocks in the breakers. They shook their heads, moved towards me. I glanced to my left. I was hard by a baccarat table, one of half a dozen tables in a rough circle, its inside roped off. To the right, the crowd was milling thick, shouldering and pushing, panic in its eyes.

'You're *mine*, scumbag,' growled Gordon, moving in, arms rising. Pordelli's hand was on his belt, freeing his cuffs.

I sighed. Some things never change.

With a nice theatrical roar I lunged to my left, took hold of the baccarat table from underneath and heaved it heavy to one side. More people screamed. I ran through the gap, punching and chopping at all in my way. I grabbed handfuls of chips and flung them in the air, planting seeds of covet in very fertile ground. I leapt another roulette table, rolled across a stud game, sending cards and glasses flying, fell to the floor, got up and legged it, tipping tables this way and that, grabbing stools and tossing them over my head, pushing punters and guards in the chest, head-butting others. A giant wishing-wheel toppled to its face, a sic-bo table overturned, pinning two determined gamblers by their legs to the floor. I trod on a face, kept moving, levering and throwing, the veil of the temple ripped in twain.

The cops didn't have a chance. Glancing over my shoulder as I collided and ran, I saw Pordelli trip on a sliding stool, thud fleshily to the ground. Gordon, just behind him, tangled and caught, cracking his head on the side of a poker machine.

And then I was out in the violent air, beneath the

spreading portal of the western entrance, running between parked coaches and moving cabs, running across the clogged and glistening road, with followers none, heading for a building in a side street, just a block away, boots sliding on the wet slime of the tarmac.

✝

The front door to Image Makers was still unlocked, the lights on in the foyer. I shouldered in, took the stairs two at a time, wanting to get out of sight as soon as possible.

I could hear sirens in the distance, heading for the casino, a helicopter buzzing its tower, panic spreading, crowd control now an issue.

Sophia was at her desk, looking tense. Her head shot up when I barged in.

'Purdey's still here,' she said.

'Stiff shit,' I replied, not stopping, heading for the boss's door. 'Time to blow your cover.'

Not having much choice, she swung off her chair, fell in behind me as I breached the sanctuary.

'Jesus Christ!' squealed Purdey, standing up behind his desk, alarmed. 'Sophia—'

His shirt was flaming orange, his suit a dark bottle green, his command without conclusion. I was round the desk before he knew it, using my momentum, grabbing him roughly by the lapels. 'Move!' I grunted, pulling him out.

He tried to resist. Sophia nicked around the other side, swung a boot into his stomach. 'The man said *move*, fat boy,' she said. 'I suggest you do so.'

He brought up phlegm. Bent, thus, and betrayed, we pushed, pulled and dragged him, not giving him time to catch breath, out of his office and into the next one, the one with the larger computer, the one with the zip drive.

I shoved him down into the desk chair, clipped him one across the ear to keep him quiet. Sophia, meanwhile, had grabbed a pair of scissors and was quickly cutting the sash from the blind. We were working like a well-oiled machine, no rehearsals. I looked at her as she quickly bound his wrists to the chair arms, roped his ankles to its central leg.

What a pity, I thought. We could have made quite an item.

He was terrified, frog breathing, stammering uncontrollably, tears in his eyes. 'Serve thee with a quiet mind,' I hissed in his ear. He shut up.

I told Sophia to fire up the machine, whack in the disk, and then find the Egyptian kumquat page on the Internet, the one she hadn't been able to enter.

This was it. This was *my* gamble.

It took ten minutes all up, and there it was, an advert for something called the Kumquat Corporation of Egypt, all very colourful, and a gaping line in the middle of it, with the flashing legend above it: ENTER YOUR PASSWORD HERE.

'Joe, what—'

'Shut up,' I snapped. 'Have patience.'

'Not faith?'

'No need.' I was assuming the business was a phantom. In the contact details for the corporation, at the top of the page, was listed its address. It claimed to be based at Nag Hammadi.

'L-l-look,' stammered Purdey, 'why don't you just—'

Sophia slapped his face. He shut up again.

'What are you doing, Joe? Where do you think this is going to—'

'I'm concentrating,' I said, pulling the computer keyboard around to face me, bending low. 'I'm trying to remember. Be quiet.'

Remember from where, though, I thought to myself. Are my thoughts *my* thoughts?

*I am the whore and the holy one*, Beatrice Cowper had said. The Thunder poem is very long, difficult to store inside the mind. I tried couplets, groups of lines as they came to memory.

*I am shameless; I am ashamed*, I tried, *I am strength and I am fear.*

ACCESS DENIED.

*But I am she who exists in all fears and strength in trembling. I am she who is weak, and I am well in a pleasant place.*

ACCESS DENIED.

'Three tries, then it'll lock up, Joe, they do that,' warned Sophia.

*I am the one whom you have hidden from, and you appear*

439

*to me. But when you hide yourselves, I myself will appear.*

The screen flashed. The image disappeared. 'Clever boy,' she breathed.

The screen was now black and empty, save for a code I didn't recognise, a gnostic phrase in another tongue. It said: KUMQUAT/A7.UNZIP.

'Mean anything to you?' I growled, close to Purdey's head. He shook it, tight and fast.

'I know,' said Sophia, reaching across, sliding the keyboard over to her side. 'The word kumquat's just a general identifier, I'd guess, the A7, I reckon is a specific, it must get changed, maybe month to month, and the "unzip", well, that's a data expansion program.'

'A what?'

'A key, Joe, the key to paradise. You can store data, information, in little bundles, bigger on the inside than the out, like the Dr Who thing, Tardis. Use an unzip and, well, it unzips the bundle, lets it all hang out. I'm going to download it onto the disk, see what happens.'

She started pushing keys, head down, fast.

Fear precludes reason. It is not rational for a man bound hand and foot to an office chair to try to hurl himself from it. Graeme Purdey knew much fear. He tried. His effort lifted the thing onto one of its four radial supports, making it twist with his weight, sending his head crashing onto the desktop, onto the keyboard. Sophia swore. I grabbed him by the throat and hair, hauled him back upright. He tried to scream, but he only managed a growl, a growl which died on his tongue when he saw the screen again.

It was alive. His head must have hit certain keys, sent certain messages. What was up was something already half done, already under way. It was like a video, a very well-produced video. It showed a man, not much more than a boy, really, naked but for a crucifix around his neck. He looked vaguely familiar; perhaps I'd seen him on the street somewhere. His wrists were tied behind his back, attached to a chain perhaps a metre long, bolted to an anonymous wall. He was being savaged by a Rottweiler. His genitals were gone. There was blood oozing from his groin, and from the spaces where his flesh should have been on his torso, his thighs, his buttocks and his back. He was twisting, kicking, trying to stay upright, no cries left in his lungs. The dog kept leaping, lunging at his face.

I recognised the dog.

'Bingo,' said Sophia, eyes glued, voice flat.

Graeme Purdey's jaw was hanging down. He was breathing shallow and fast.

'Elaine,' he whimpered.

'*Fuck* Elaine,' said Sophia, suddenly, violently. 'What do you know of this, Purdey?'

'My god,' he mumbled.

'Answer the woman,' I growled, not that I cared. 'What's your connection? How many—'

'Please,' he said, eyes wide. 'Who are you?'

'Good question,' I replied. 'I can't answer that right now, but you know who she is?' Pointing at Sophia, who glared back.

'I'm a law enforcement officer, Graeme Purdey,' she

said evenly. 'I suggest you answer our questions.'

His head was shaking like Parkinson's disease. 'I want my lawyer,' he managed.

Sophia laughed.

I pulled out a fresh syringe, slowly slipped the plastic sheath from its needle. He let out a gasp, wet himself. I leant over him, my eyes right in his.

'Young people get piercings,' I said, all reasonable. 'It's very much the fashion. Self-mutilation has always been fashionable. Pain and passion, central themes. Even your receptionist has a piercing. Want to see it?'

'Fat chance,' giggled his receptionist.

The Rottweiler took a chunk of cheek. The young man staggered, almost fell to his knees, somehow stayed upright, leaning against the wall. The dog paused, chewing.

'You can get almost anything pierced,' I continued. 'Nose, ears, eyebrows, nips, belly buttons, you know, even lips. What's a lip piercing called, Sophia?'

'A labrette, I think.'

The dog lunged again, biting at the midriff.

'A labrette,' I repeated softly. 'French, I shouldn't wonder. Want to know how a labrette's done?'

His head moved. He tried to say no. His voice wouldn't work.

The dog's paws were leaving deep gashes down the boy's chest.

'Like this,' I said. I grabbed his upper lip in my left hand, and pulled it out. With my right I rammed the needle up through the flesh, up out the other side. His eyes rolled back, leaking. He gasped like a drowner. But he stayed conscious. I held my position.

'Did you know you were dealing in this filth?' I asked softly.

'Nuh, nuh, nuh . . . nuh I dinn.' He was doing his best.

Sophia's turn. 'Fifty grand a year to send these zips out, almost fuck all else, and you didn't *know*?'

'Nuh . . . nuh . . . I wear, I *wear*.'

'Huh?' asked Sophia.

'He means *swear*.' I like to be helpful. I help where I can.

The dog had leapt again. It had the boy's throat, wasn't letting go, back legs bicycling into his torn groin. He was buckling. Suetonius would have understood.

My turn. I lifted the fit slightly. His face was white. 'What did you *think* you had?'

'I . . . I . . . I thaw I ha a sugger,' he said.

'A sucker?'

'A sugger.' He didn't nod. 'Ngore ngunny tha sense. The gnunny kay in cah each gnunth, written istrushuns, oh keshuns arsed. Ih wa juss a good err-er, goog gnunny, wig wucks.'

Big bucks. Blood money. The boy was down, the dog on top, blood all over its snout and chest. The screen faded slowly to black.

Sophia. 'Who from?'

Purdey's voice rose half an octave. 'I unno, I *unno*, I *wear, ease, ease.*'

Mystic words. Words of angel tongue.

The screen lit up again. We all went quiet, all watched.

There was Shelagh Purdey. Naked and bound to the execution couch.

Her arms were pinioned, as if crucified, bound by straps with thick cushioning around the wrists. The ankles apart, ditto. That explains the absence of ligature marks, I thought.

The camera closed in on her face. She seemed only dimly aware of its proximity, her pupils dull and dilated. Sophia noticed too.

'I thought they didn't find substantial drugs in her bloodstream,' she said.

'I doubt they checked for Ketamine. Not very common.'

'*Eelagh! Eeelaghh!*' Graeme Purdey screamed, oblivious now to his pain.

'Jesus, shut *up*!' snapped Sophia. 'Christ, he'll wake the dead at this rate.'

'Gag him,' I suggested.

She looked around the office, the anodyne, usually uninhabited office. 'What with?' she said to herself. 'I know. You, Purdey, turn away.'

I pulled his head around with the syringe. He didn't resist. Sophia hit a button on the keyboard. The image froze. She stepped back and lifted her skirt—'You I don't mind about,' she teased to me—and quickly slipped off her woollen tights and underpants, straightening her outer garment afterwards.

'It's your lucky day, boy,' she said. 'Open wide.'

He needed a prompt, but he did. Roughly, she bundled her knickers into his mouth, and then gagged him with a leg of the tights, tying it behind his head. I pulled out the syringe. His lip didn't bleed much.

She hit the button again. The camera pulled back from that face, that bewildered, calm face with the solitary pimple on its cheek, to take in her whole body. A man walked into the frame, down by her feet, moderate build, naked except for his head, which was enclosed in a black leather S&M mask, zip-eyes open. He carried a tray, small bottles and jars on it, solemn, like a ritual.

Sophia noticed it first. 'Look,' she said. 'The arm.'

Clearly visible on the man's arm was a faded tattoo of a Celtic cross. 'The troublesome priest,' I whispered. She nodded.

Scopemi walked, funereal, once around the couch, the camera following. After a complete circuit, he stood by her head, put the tray down on her belly, picked up a jar and opened it. He dipped his finger in and withdrew it, some whitish goo clumped on the tip. He started to rub it onto her face and neck. She tried to turn away at his touch. He held her easily with his other hand.

As he applied the make-up, the camera went roving, moving around her body, zooming in on that part and this, emphasising purity, emphasising vulnerability. Graeme Purdey was whistling through his nose, in and out, in and out, in and out.

445

'Look at the little, little movie star,' I said.

He made a squealing noise.

The camera went back to Scopemi. Now he was massaging rouge, too much rouge, into Shelagh's cheeks. She had stopped struggling, resigned, half in oblivion.

'For, surely,' I murmured, 'those women sin against God who anoint their faces with creams, stain their cheeks with rouge, or lengthen their eyebrows with antimony.'

'Huh?' Sophia's eyes had not left the screen.

'Tertullian.'

'Who's he?'

'Someone who came to the wrong conclusions.'

Then came the antimony. Some went in her eyes. She blinked rapidly, involuntarily. Her lips parted, teeth clenched.

Scopemi picked up his tray, walked solemnly out. The camera played with her body again, so close in I could see goose pimples forming. Some part of her, somewhere, was aware, and was afraid. Sophia also noticed.

'They need to see fear, these people,' she said. 'Without fear it doesn't mean anything.'

Graeme Purdey was on talking terms with terror.

Scopemi returned, carrying an axe. It was a big axe, ornate, huge curved blade, a medieval axe.

'Christ,' whispered Sophia, even though she knew what was coming.

He paused, poised by her head for a good three

minutes, lifting the weapon, lowering it, slowly, slowly, lifting it again, lining it up. Shelagh was struggling to focus, trying to wake from dream, catching the glints, perhaps, of the blade in the powerful lights which must have been shining, just out of shot.

The axe came down, clean and forceful. One strike. The camera didn't miss a moment, never even shook, even when the blood spurted on the lens.

The screen snapped to black, snapped up again almost immediately. Shelagh Purdey's body was nailed to the cross at St Cuthbert's. The camera explored it in close up, then withdrew for a full shot, then turned, taking in the church interior, one hundred and eighty degrees, and halted, facing the door. A male hand, body out of shot, held Shelagh's head by the hair, slack-jawed and painted, the severed icon. Then blackness, without mercy, descended.

Fathers and light, fathers and light. John hadn't sensed her father after all. He'd sensed mine.

Sophia hit a button. 'Seen enough?' she asked.

'Our mission is righteous,' I replied. 'Where's the car?'

'Out the back. Where to? What next? What do we do with him?' Pointing at Purdey.

'I'll deal with him,' I said. 'You go downstairs, lock up the front. I'll meet you outside, five minutes.'

'Your call,' she said and walked out, never looking back.

The silence held, maybe thirty seconds. It was a heavy thirty seconds, pregnant with pain and the promise of more. Purdey's eyes were wide and bulging. His chest was heaving.

I pulled the gag down to his chin, hooked Sophia's undies from his mouth.

Keep innocency, says Psalm 37, and take heed unto the thing that is right: for that shall bring a man peace at last.

Me, I learn fast.

'You do banking on the Net?'

He nodded.

'Right. I tell you what I want. You tell me the keys to hit. Do that and I walk out, leave you here. You never see me—or her—again.'

It took just five minutes. Then I called up the disk images again, getting the hang of it. I got the first image of Shelagh, then pulled down a menu from the top of the screen. It gave me several options.

'Tell me,' I said, 'why did you sleep with your own daughter?'

He shook his head, terrified. 'I never hurt her. Not this. You don't understand. It was—'

In the divine, forgiveness is a big part of the job description, but judgement lies at the end. In the human, judgement cannot be supported, vain and egocentric, except by conscious choice. Either way, regardless of what might lie later, written in the great book of Peter's at the gates, a decision was demanded. I shoved the baggage back in his mouth, reapplied the gag. I gave my sentence, mortal and frail. The item I hit said REPEAT FILE.

I clicked off the light, closed the door behind me, headed down the stairs, left him to the glowing horror which he started.

✝

The car was a white Ford Capri, a compact little sports car, two-seater, with a tiny back bench. Its exhaust smoke whipped up and away in the wind as it stood idling in the car park, Sophia waiting at the wheel as I closed the back door of the building behind me.

I hopped in the passenger side. She flipped on the lights, started moving immediately, the engine growling and snarling alarmingly.

'Don't panic, this is the kind of car I normally drive. Where to?' she asked, looking left and right as she turned onto the access road.

'Collingwood.'

'We'll have to go the long way. The traffic'll be grid-locked around the casino: jams, roadblocks, the lot.'

'Do so.'

She turned right, heading south, away from the confusion, on the Great Circle route to the north. The going was heavy, even in the side streets. Sophia pushed the car, engine revving, in short bursts of speed, punching it through tiny gaps in the mess, accelerating through roundabouts, shooting lights with inches to spare, other vehicles burning rubber as they hit the brakes to avoid colliding with us.

I realised then why sports cars only have one passenger seat. It's because very few people are stupid enough to accept a lift in one.

'What did you do to Purdey?' she asked, not overly concerned.

'Left him to contemplate his sins.'

'Switch on the heater, will you, Joe? That sliding knob in front of you, that's it. My fanny's bloody freezing.'

I did so, taking note of the mobile phone lodged just beneath it. Sitting back, I lit up a Dunhill, inhaled deeply. It was some kind of government car, I could tell, despite its anonymity, because of the neat little NO SMOKING plaque glued to the dash.

That reminded me. Is the enemy of my enemy my friend? I didn't think so. When the Saracens asked the West for urgent help to defeat the Tartars in the thirteenth, the Bishop of Winchester recommended the dogs be left to devour each other, then for the Christians to slay the stragglers.

'The Falcon that's been following me has a little sign like that one, doesn't it?' I said. 'That's why the guy was out of the car having a smoke outside your place the other day.'

Sophia glanced at me, snap, glanced back at the road, tried to overtake the vehicle in front. 'Don't know what you're talking about, Joe,' she said.

'Time to shelve the crap, Sophia,' I growled. I laid it out, the way I saw it. The Falcon man had been the cyclist outside the church, ergo, he had to be part of the organisation that planned—or, at least, monitored without intervention—the whole sad game. The mysterious task force might be out to stitch Beatrice Cowper's gig, but she was not the only target, Sophia had admitted that.

Thus, why Shelagh Purdey? *Not* because she was Cowper's biological daughter, but because she knew the priest, and the priest knew me. The ploy rested on Corrigan calling me in, getting me hooked in, and then the Feds using me to get to the baddie, setting me up to do the work. From the very start, I said, I hadn't been making decisions; I'd been fulfilling expectations.

'Clever boy,' she whispered, eyes on the road. 'You got there at last.'

The car was crawling, trapped momentarily in the crush. I opened the door.

She reached over, patted my knee. 'Think about this, Joe,' she said. 'What will you do if you get out now? The area's crawling with cops, all looking for *you*. You're wanted for assault, for attempted murder, abduction, rape, dealing in narcotics, heaven knows what else. You're the Antichrist, mate, front page news all round by tomorrow. They've even got your photo. They'll have people at the bus stations, the train stations, the airports, the lot. Escape is impossible. You can't drive. What are you going to do: hitch-hike, head north, hole up in some desert town in the Northern Territory? It won't last, and, anyway, it'll send you round the twist.'

She had a point. 'I *like* the wilderness,' I replied rather lamely.

'No you don't. There's no coffee in the desert.'

I closed the door again.

'Trust me, Joe. Do this for us, we'll see you right.'

I nodded, sat back in the seat. There was nothing else on offer.

'Now,' she said, 'exactly where in Collingwood?'

I grabbed the phone. John answered on the third ring.

'They left half an hour ago, son,' he stammered. 'All ran off to get you, but I reckon they'll be back. They've taken everything, son, your place is empty—your books, your music, your telly, even your coffee, everything.'

'Bradford, half an hour. You are the adjutant to the Lord.' Then I hung up.

'What's the plan?' asked Sophia carefully.

'You tell me,' I replied.

'Oh, don't be absurd, Joe.' Then she giggled, patted my leg again. 'Sorry. I forgot. Maybe you çan't help it.'

'We do it now.'

Her voice tightened. 'But, Joe, no, like, I need time, this is no ... I've got to arrange backup, I've got to, you know, the dog, the fences—'

'Sometimes small numbers are the best. Anyway, we've got backup for the dog. We're just going to pick him up.'

'Who?'

'Bloke called John the Baptist. You'll like him.'

'Jesus.' She shook her head. 'I'll be fucking glad when this century's over.'

452

We got there in twenty minutes, found a parking space outside the pub. John hadn't arrived yet. Corrigan was there though, leant against the bar in his civvies, hitting the scotch, well to the wind. He looked up when we entered, seemed momentarily terrified and then set his face to a sloppy scowl.

'Ach,' he slurred. 'What the fuck are you doing here? Where's the justice in this world? I thought at last I had something to celebrate.'

I ignored him, signalled for a Jamesons for me and a red wine for Sophia. There's always time for a quick one. He kept rambling.

'You should be locked up by now, bastard. Why aren't you fucking locked up? I took that photo to the cops—just like I said I would, man, kept my word, just like I said I would. They were *jubilant*, Panther, jubilant. They already had one copy of it, they were pleased about that, and pleased again when I gave them mine. And they'll be fucking over the moon when they finally catch you, man, betrayer, traitor, over the moon.' He necked his shot, jerked his chin up for a refill. 'I never knew you man, I know that now. Never knew you at all.'

I didn't look at him. 'You will deny me before the cops crow thrice,' I muttered under my breath. Then, to Sophia, 'Hang there, I've got to have a slash.'

It was time to get the local cops out of the picture for a while. There was a public telephone near the toilets. I dialled Crimestoppers, faked a voice. That man, I said, the one you're looking for, he's been holed

453

up for two days in Carlton. I gave them the address. Don't know if he's there at the moment, I added, but I think he's been (pause) *dealing drugs* there. Go in, I reckon, I reckon you'll find some.

When the officer asked my name I told him Mr Augustine, hung up and returned to my stool.

A blast of chill air shot through the bar as the door opened and the old man limped in.

'Aha,' I said. 'Hello John.'

'Hello, son,' he beamed, glad to be on the move. 'And hello, young Sophia. Fancy meeting you here.'

Instead of hitting him, I bought him a beer and floated the trip on its surface. 'Drink it down,' I commanded. 'It's the spirit of the Lord.'

'You've done a dog's act, Panther, blasphemer,' snarled Corrigan, sagging on his seat.

✝

'No grasser me, son, you know that.'

John was wedged along the back seat of the car as we headed to Toorak. He was thus twice confused and panicked, gabbling. Sophia drove in silence, enjoying the show. I was using her driver's licence to chop up a healthy line of speed on the front cover of the street directory. Ketamine attack was a distinct possibility, I figured. I had no idea whether amphetamine would counteract its reaction, but, shit, it couldn't do any harm.

'I'd never grass on you, Joe, son, you know that, never tell no one nothin' that would do you harm, I swear. But young Sophia, well, she's different, no harm in her, such a *nice* young girl, don't do drugs, don't do nothin'. Always got time for an old man, has Sophia, don't find many like that these days.'

It turned out that young Sophia, as he put it, had sidled up to him one afternoon in one of his pubs, three, four weeks back, seeking to chat, laughing at his tired old jokes. No one talks to old men in pungent clothes eating two dollar meals in stale front bars, especially chatty young women with pretty smiles, so lonely John fell hook, line and sinker, happy, by their third meeting, to tell tall tales of his best friend, Jesus.

'Such a nice young lady,' he repeated. 'She your girlfriend, Joe, or what?'

'She's a cop, old man.'

She giggled.

'Oh, fuck,' he said, then added in a tiny voice, 'Sorry, son. Stuffed up there, didn't I?'

'Never mind,' I replied, rolling a twenty buck note into a straw. 'You'll have your chance to atone.'

I outlined the plan, such as it was. The car was to be parked a block away from Beatrice Cowper's fortress, well out of sight. I would attempt and gain entry, nobble the gate, and then try somehow to entertain the woman. Sophia would come in twenty minutes later, John hopefully having won over Cerberus with whatever remained of his facility with dogs, and then finish the job.

455

It wasn't much, but it would have to do.

I inhaled the speed, then, like Saul, breathed out threatenings and slaughter against the disciples of the Lord.

Ten minutes later we pulled to a halt. I got out.

'Trust me, Joe,' said Sophia.

'Like smallpox trusts a vaccine,' I said, hunched into my jacket against the rain, and walked away.

As I approached Cowper's front gate, I pulled from my pocket the little clear plastic snap-lock bag which had held the trip. Into it I put a few tiny leaves, ripped from the hedge. The camera, I remembered, had moved *after* I pressed the intercom button. Before I did so, therefore, I slipped the bag over the lens. The scuffed plastic would blur its view, the leaves more so, giving the impression, I hoped, that a swatch of wet hedge had been blown across it by the wind.

I hit the button. The camera moved, lens zooming in and out, in and out, and in and out again. After a few seconds it stopped, pointing above my head.

'Who is it?' crackled a familiar voice, sounding distinctly piqued.

I tried to sound penitent and weepy. 'Josiah, small Josiah.'

Laughter, the laughter of victory. 'You have come, small Josiah. You know it's for the best. Stick to the path.'

The gate lock clicked. I pushed it open. Cerberus, one with the night, was waiting, growling, tense, on duty. As I walked between the posts I pretended to get my jacket caught on something, fool that I am, turned to free it. It gave me just enough time to hold Sophia's driver's licence across the lock. The gate swung closed, not with a clang, but a *schick*.

So far, so good.

Beatrice Cowper stood waiting on the porch. She was dressed in a flowing white gown, like King Arthur's lady in samite or some type of vestal virgin, its folds billowing in the wind, now caressing her body, now trying to flee. She looked more like Brigid than ever.

'Come in, small Josiah,' she called against the breeze. 'You've come to your senses, you are ready at last. Your salvation awaits.' She turned and walked through the door. I followed right behind. 'First,' she said, 'let me show you around. It's livelier by night.'

She halted in the hallway. There were people now, in the house, silent people. In the first of the rooms to the left, in among the chesterfields, I saw three men of varying age, all with crop-cut hair, all wearing white robes. One stood, two sat, all staring blank and dim. To the right, in the opposite room, four women in similar poses, clad also in white.

'Follow me,' she said, and strode gracefully through the men's room to the door at its opposite end.

It led into the wing. Inside the light was bright. Bunk beds stood regiment against the walls. There were people here, too, all men. Some lay on the beds, clad in white, hands clasped across their chests, staring at the ceiling. A couple stood naked in one corner, pawing at each other as if playing a game they couldn't quite

457

remember. Another stood behind a small table, on which were tiny plastic jelly cups, each containing a small measure of coloured liquid.

'Aren't you going to offer me a drink?' I asked.

'Remiss of me,' she said, picked up one of the cups and handed it to me. 'Enjoy.'

I necked it, nearly choked. It tasted foul. Addiction is a terrible thing.

A silent queue of five advanced towards the table, each handed a cup by the automaton behind it, eyes dilated, moving on.

'The residents, Josiah,' she said. 'The time is right.'

She turned around, retraced her steps. I followed, saying nothing. The drink was a mistake. Already I could feel tremors through my brain as its narcotic infusion went to work. I couldn't immediately identify it. We recrossed the hallway, past the waiting women, and on, again, to the opposite wing. There the sight was identical, only the occupants were female.

There were straps on some of the bunks.

'Let me show you upstairs.' The train of her gown looked like a river of grace as we ascended. There were many doors at the top.

Through the first was the security room. Another man in white sat before a console of buttons and tiny screens. The property clearly boasted cameras front and back. One screen showed a murky view right up the back lane, which explained, I realised, her nunnish presence in the back garden before. She must have read my thoughts.

458

'I am a private person, Mr Panther, and value that privacy immensely,' she said. 'I don't like surprises. I'm rarely surprised. To be surprised is to be a victim, and that is not in my nature, as you know. I am the saviour of victims. There are cameras at every boundary junction, Mr Panther, top of the range, three hundred and sixty degree turns, precision milled lenses. I saw you as you entered the lane. You skulk and lurk and loiter with intent very nicely, if I may so.'

As she spoke, I noted the screen for the front gate. It showed only translucent haze and green smudge. The man at the console was drugged, his movements sluggish. He'd been programmed to be alert to movement, clearly, not its blurry absence. I had to close my eyes for a second. When I opened them, all the screens had gone blurry.

Still so far, so good, I thought to myself. Then tried to remember what was so far, so, whatever, good.

'What was in that drink?' I asked, not quite recognising my own voice.

'Did you like it?' she asked, suddenly the hostess. 'Penobarbital, actually. It used to be used as anaesthetic, until people discovered it could cause coma and brain damage. More recently, it was the drug of choice for members of the Aum Shinrikyo sect in Japan. It—'

I vagued out on the rest of her reply. It ended in 'good for you'.

In the second room the air was chill and the walls were sanitary white. It contained a very large computer, half a dozen monitors, other electronic boxes, lots of tiny winking lights and cables like the knotted sinews of a dragon, breathing, heaving, coiled to strike.

'The interface, Josiah,' explained Beatrice, not without pride. 'Here, some of it goes out, most to clients on shielded lines, some at random into cyber-space. Nothing like a bit of randomness, is there? Here, too, we put our best pieces down onto disk for our very best, our most discreet, customers. Name your perversion, name your desire, name your god, and we'll put together the package, no questions asked. What do you think?'

I was thinking, trying to think. Where were Sophia and John? They should have arrived. Maybe they had, maybe they were detained downstairs, but somehow I couldn't see the drugged-out followers below presenting much of a problem to a black belt sociopath on a mission.

I couldn't say that, though. Instead, I said, thickly, 'It is better to dwell in a corner of the housetop, than with a brawling woman in a wide house.'

'Old habits die hard, eh, Josiah, but I understand. Thank god for the Bible. It's a constant source of inspiration for me. And for my clients. Come see.'

In the next room a naked woman was strapped to a copy of a medieval rack. A man dressed as Torquemada was operating the wheel. She was silent, near death, moaning. Another man was operating a camera. In the next, a naked man, painted blue, was held to a crude wooden chair. Two others held his legs apart, a third was castrating him, while a fourth, of course, recorded it all.

In the next, naked men and women writhed on the floor among a harvest of fruit; more hung by wrists in chains and leather while others still walked by with flicking whips and paddles; and then there were scenes of burning and dunking, hands forced to grasp red hot irons, women stuffed with water, men with crippled feet, serpents twisting, monsters rising, demons prowling, toads, children flung on fires and roasting, bodies hung from gibbets, torsos drawn, white eyes rolling, muddied hags with goats a-suckle, walls bulging, breathing, the floors whirlpool sucking sinners to damnation, torment everywhere, trumpets sounding, teeth gnashing, virgins wailing, limbs flailing, mists descending, flames rising, roaring, roaring, roaring.

I saw that. I think I saw that.

'Finish up, people,' Beatrice was calling, noble and controlled. 'To your places now. The day is done.'

And then we were back again, in the upstairs passageway. The floor was shifting, like the sea of Galilee beneath my feet.

'Impressed?' she asked. She sounded like Brigid again.

'I've seen it all before,' I said.

'Of course you have.'

I felt I should try to establish dialogue, waste time, wait for the reinforcements. My brain was tumult, the jelly cup demons mating with the speed. I kept her in focus, well as I could, sought refuge in learning. Keep her busy.

'In the fifteenth century there was a story of Beatrice the virgin, a nun, not Saint Beatrice, different one, who was seduced by a cleric, left the convent, became a whore for years. When she returned to the nuns she found the Virgin Mary had been living there in disguise the whole time, keeping her place warm. Was that you?'

Her laugh was robust, familiar. 'Perhaps it was. Were you the cleric, Josiah? Were you the evil cloaked in forgiveness?'

I shook my head, fought to stay upright as dizziness swamped. 'Wrong messiah.'

'Not that it matters, Josiah. Messiahs don't bring change, they reinforce slavery.' And then she smiled. I felt the fear again. 'The time has come. The time for false messiahs is over. We'll do it right this time, you and me.'

And then I saw her eyes flick, just once, over my shoulder. I turned, tried to turn, as something thin and sharp pierced my neck and the light shone and the earth moved and the angel took me once more within its wings.

✝

I woke up naked, strapped to the execution couch, crucified, upright. I was moving forwards, down a wide passageway, rolling slow, by what means I did not know.

Against the walls on either side, the crop-haired devotees stood, innocence-robed, hands clasped, silent, eyes cast down.

Beatrice Cowper walked in front of me, backwards. She was dressed in black patent leather shoes, military trousers and a severe shirt, epaulettes on the shoulders, buttoned tight to the neck, both fashioned from thin black rubber. Her footsteps echoed like ribs cracking.

At the end of the passageway were solid double doors, closed, the colour of spilt blood. Something, air conditioning perhaps, hummed Gregorian, low and devout.

'All right, people,' she barked, clapping her hands, sharp, twice. 'That's enough. It's not as if you've never seen a naked, bearded man on a cross before. To your beds now, and make sure you take your medication. *Move!*'

The devotees shuffled and grunted, turned, one by one, and filed past me, away, slippered feet Chinese whispering along the floor. Some looked up, met my eyes with eyes like mine, looked away again. Others remained downcast, mumbling.

'You talking to me?' I heard myself slur.

She smiled. 'Ahh,' she said. 'Welcome back, welcome back, Mr ... Now, tell me, what do I call you, little Josiah: Mr Panton or Mr Panther, Jesus or Joe? Are you man or god tonight?'

I fought for focus. Without a name, I knew, I was lost. 'I don't know. Panther. I'm used to it.' I think it was my voice. It used to be my voice.

Must become my voice again, I knew. The doors were growing larger.

'Mr Panther it will be, then, Mr Panther,' she cooed. 'It matters little in the end. It never did.'

'Some might disagree.' I turned my head, as well as I could. My wrists were bound by buckled leather.

'Of course they would,' she laughed. 'That was the point of it all, but we know better don't we, Lord?'

The chanting surged loud, reverberating against the walls and the ceiling. I could see her lips moving, morphing, fuzzing. I tried to follow.

'All we ever needed was your name, your reputation, your death and your icon,' she was saying. Her rubber shirt seemed to be breathing by itself. 'Nothing more, nothing more. You yourself were utterly unimportant. But then you had to bugger it up by resurrecting, Yeshu. You weren't meant to do that. That was never in the plan. That was a real problem for us, has been ever since.'

I tried to remember something, something important. Help. Sophia, the federal girl. Old John the Baptist, my cousin. Not my cousin, an old man. Where were they? 'What problem?'

She sneered. 'You are not stupid, Mr Panther, whatever else you might be. You *know* what problem. You rose again, and disappeared. The patsy was up and about, which meant he could blow the whole gig if he ever decided to go public. Can you imagine what would have happened, what would have come out about JFK's Cuban plans, Marilyn Monroe's murder or

J. Edgar Hoover's alien abduction if Jack Ruby hadn't finished off Lee Harvey Oswald?'

'Who was your Jack Ruby? Or should I say Paul's Jack Ruby?'

'Joseph of Arimathea,' she spat. 'Bastard cooled on us at the last moment, went freelance, picked up a cup from your tomb, called it the Holy Grail and fucked off to Glastonbury with it. Never rely on volunteers, Mr Panther, never. By the time we realised what had happened you had the jump on us. We didn't know where to look. Paul almost had you on the road to Damascus, but you hit him in the groin and fled.'

'Kicking against the pricks,' I mumbled. The doors were starting to loom and bend. 'I've often felt that people were watching me.'

'Oh, we *tried*, Mr Panther, we tried, but you're a slippery one. Vicious, too. Sometimes it took decades, lifetimes, before we got a scent of you. We'd move in, start to circle—'

'Whose we?'

'That's classified. People have been trying to identify us for centuries. Take your pick, Mr Panther, who do you want us to be? The Jesuits? The Jacobins? How about the Bavarian Illuminati, the Freemasons, the Rosicrucians, the United Nations, the World Bank, maybe the Club of Rome? They've all been suggested before now. You see, a *real* secret society has to *remain* secret, especially one as old as ours. Anyway, we'd move in, but something always happened. You'd run off again, or you'd get yourself arrested by some other

465

group, the Inquisition, whatever, get yourself where we couldn't get to you without raising suspicion. Some secrets, Mr Panther, must remain occult, top level occult. That Irish bitch was supposed to hold on to you until we got there, but she went and fucking fell in love with you, let you go. Two more days, we would have had you.'

I smiled. I'd always figured Brigid was cool. I realised I was dribbling.

Beatrice Cowper was smiling again. 'But no matter,' she was saying. 'We've got you now.'

'I might be a madman,' I said. 'You think I am.'

'Man or god, it doesn't matter. It never did. Man would be better. Men stay dead. This time. We had the campaign, all we needed was a plausible mascot. The time was perfect then, and, hey, it's perfect now. Maybe there *is* a god, after all.'

Her back was now against the doors. She pressed her shoulders into the wood, hips forward, arms folded, triumphant, across her breasts.

'Why now?' I asked.

'Everything gets tired, Mr Panther, every campaign. It is the nature of things. We need a boost. Oh, we've still got the United States under control, going well there, South America too, but the rest of the world, that's a problem. We're losing the rest of the world to godless reason, Mr Panther, and that will never do. If the people lose the fear, then we lose the power.'

'Whose power?'

'*Our* power, Mr Panther, so it's time for a revamp,

a relaunch. Even Pepsi has to do it from time to time, and this is no different. We still just need your name— what you think of as your *real* name, real or not—your image, your icon, and your death. We're going to give the logo a makeover, Mr Panther, with you: the original and the best.'

She turned and bent to the handles of the door. The blackness of hell caressed her buttocks, inches from my withered crotch. A lock snapped. She stood upright, pushed open the doors and stood to one side.

'And this time,' she said, 'we're going to do it properly.'

And, lo, abandoned and lost, I beheld the new Golgotha.

✝

# 13

IT WAS A LARGE AND WINDOWLESS room, well lit, with cameras positioned, mounted on wall brackets, in all four corners. It contained two film sets.

I saw first, to the left, a mock-up of a witch-burning scene, sans witch. A rough-hewn oak stake extended from a large wooden barrel of oil, beneath which lay a hefty pile of faggoted kindling.

That was not to be my destiny.

'This time, Lord, we won't have to rely on writers,' said Beatrice, pointing to the cameras. 'This time we get it on film, shove it out, post-production, right across the globe. The world is waiting for the Second Coming. You and me, we're going to give them the Second Leaving. Much better.'

The other set-up was mine. My upholstered cross turned on its axis, started rolling towards it. On the far wall was a massive photograph of a woman's bikini-clad belly and thighs, dwarfing me. Written across it,

468

just below the navel, was the phrase CRUCIFIXION II. Next to that was the logo of a major multinational manufacturer of sports shoes and the phrase PROUDLY SPONSORED BY. On the ground in front of it lay a spear, three railway spikes, a large hammer and a coil of barbed wire.

She saw me staring. 'We've updated,' she said. 'There's been enormous interest. Negotiations have been going on for quite some time now—in strict secrecy, of course. There was a soft drink manufacturer wanted in, but only if you wore a tee-shirt with their logo on it. I turned them down, told them that sort of product placement was tawdry, but maybe we'd talk about licensing some images for advertising a little further down the line.'

I fought for clarity above the narcotic tempest in my brain. 'Isn't this all a bit crass?'

She wasn't listening. 'They'll have to pay big, though. I've already pre-sold excerpt rights on the video to two upcoming TV specials—*Doomsday: Is There Anything We Can Do?* and *Armageddon: Fact or Fiction?* We've also promised bits to a program called *World's Whackiest Saviours*, which'll be good for the kiddy market, but, you know, they'll only want three minutes, max. Cable rights have gone for a bundle, as have the licences for the computer game, the board game, the card game, the diaries, the calendars, the baseball caps, the swap cards, the Third Testament— that'll be huge, nothing like getting your product into institutional reading lists—the posters, the cartoons, the tribute album, even the postage stamps. The stills images have been pre-sold all over the place, and the vinegar maker, well the vinegar maker is over the moon. Talk about endorsement. Then there's the burger chain: Salvation Burgers—eat them once, wait for them to rise again—what a concept. You're going to be famous, Mr Panther. We're doing it afresh, O Lord, and this time we've got the copyrights locked down.'

I said something I never thought I'd hear myself say—not since the first century anyway. 'Isn't this all rather immoral?'

She shook her head firmly.

'No, Mr Panther,' she said. 'It's business. The promotion of mystery involves a paradox. If it's to be of any use, it has to be extremely pragmatic. It should also be profitable. I don't need to tell you that the Second Coming has been the most keenly anticipated event of the past two thousand years. Right now, Mr Panther, the number of people who believe in a literal interpetation of the gospels is growing at an astronomical rate—not just among powerless fools, but also among the ranks of the rich and influential. There are people out there who affect the fate of nations, of major corporations, of history itself, who firmly believe that Jesus is going to spook back down and bring on Judgement Day, the Rapture, heaven-on-earth, whatever you want to call it, within their lifetimes.'

'They're wrong,' I said.

'Who cares?' she replied. 'They've got money,

they've got desires, and I'm in a position to take a lot of the former through meeting the latter. I, and the people I represent, are not alone in this, as you can see. Marketed properly, what we're about to do here will make Princess Diana's funeral, Elton John's song and the global welter of magazines and merchandising which followed look like a piss in the ocean. It doesn't take an Einstein to figure that, surely. You've noticed the way major corporations and media companies fight like piranhas to get the rights to be associated with something big like the Olympic Games. Why? Because ultimately there's a shit-load of money in it. Can you imagine the payback in being one of the sponsors of the biggest event ever known, remade for today's consumer?'

I was having trouble with this. 'But surely,' I ventured, 'aren't I supposed to *survive* the second time around?'

'What,' she laughed, tossing back her head, 'and spoil all the fun? The Messiah comes back, the Messiah is the ultimate authority. No, there's quite a few CEOs, shareholders, generals, pedagogues and preachers who wouldn't like that at all. Not a bit. The elite have never served the interests of Christ, Mr P—you of all people should know that. It's always been the other way around. No, better by far to bring you back and knock you off again: keep the fear and the faith and the anticipation going for another thousand years.'

Great, I thought to myself. Countless lifetimes wandering lost and disregarded, trying hard to keep my paranoias in check, and then, right at what could well be the end, what do I discover? Christianity is a conspiracy theory.

'It's all a bit tacky, isn't it?' I managed.

'I prefer the term post-modern ironic,' she said. 'I've done surveys and everything.'

My head spun, equally from revelation and revolution, as my cross was wheeled to position before the giant crotch and then turned one hundred and eighty degrees to face back towards the doors, now closed again. There was movement either side of me, and into my vision came the engines of my journey down the new Via Dolorosa.

To my right I saw the goon, which didn't really surprise me. He was wearing a new pair of spectacles. He was also wearing the costume of a Roman centurion, helmet and all.

'Hi, Dad,' I mumbled.

To my left stood Elaine Purdey, vague-eyed and wobbly. She was clad, like the others, in a white gown. Taped to the back of her head was a halo made from silver tinsel. Unsteadily, following orders, she knelt before me, just to the side.

'Mother, I presume,' I managed.

'Very good, Mr Panther,' mocked Beatrice, walking towards me. 'Very good indeed. Hit the switches.'

This last was to the goon. He nodded, walked to the far wall, cape aflutter, and pressed some buttons on a control panel. A high whirring sound snaked through the room, cutting through the aircon chants, *Miserere*

472

via Gary Numan. Little red lights came on above the camera lenses.

'Fired up, rolling,' he said, returning to his place.

'So it begins,' she purred with evident satisfaction. 'Many that are first shall be last; and the last shall be the first.'

Summoning my strength, trying hard to concentrate, I flexed my muscles against my bonds, jerking, pushing, tugging my arms and ankles. Nothing moved. Fury welled in me like pus in a bubo.

'For the lips of a strange woman drop as an honey-comb!' I yelled, pulling on Proverbs. 'And her mouth is smoother than oil. But her end is bitter as worm-wood, sharp as a two-edged sword! Her feet go down to death; her steps take hold on hell!'

Beatrice Cowper stepped closer, her honeycomb lips pale and thin with disapproval. 'If there's one thing that really pisses me off, Mr Panther,' she said, bending down and picking up the coil of barbed wire, 'it's a misogynist.'

She lifted the coil above my head, its weave shining in the light, and pulled it down over my crown. The barbs bit deep, painful even with the deadening chem-icals rampant beneath my skin, but I did not give her the satisfaction of crying out. My vision blurred still more, tinged red, my cheeks itchy and wet.

She stepped back.

'Now,' she said to the goon. 'Do it.' And then, to Elaine Purdey, 'Remember, you bitch, cry and weep, make like you mean it. Do it right and maybe we won't do the witch-burning tomorrow.'

Elaine Purdey, jaw slack and eyes all over the place, wept fit to win an Oscar.

The goon grinned, bent, steadied his helmet, picked up the hammer and the first of the spikes. I noticed as he raised it that the head of the nail was neatly embossed with the logo of a leading brand of painkiller.

Its tip was cold as it rested lightly against the pale underside of my wrist, just to one side of the buckle, right on a vein. The goon stood behind it, raised the hammer, pulled it back.

'Still want to enter the church?' he asked, grinning.

I closed my eyes.

The doors burst open. 'Shit, sorry,' said a familiar female voice.

I opened my eyes again. There stood Sophia in the doorway, legs placed and solid, the diminutive avenger. Beatrice Cowper said nothing, just stared. The goon, staring over his shoulder, lowered the spike. Elaine Purdey lowered her head and whimpered for real.

And I wondered. I wondered, am I Christ, or am I not? If I *am* Christ, what would I say in such a situation? Two millennia of learning and suffering informed my decision.

'Where the fuck have you been?' I said.

Sophia rolled her eyes heavenwards, lifted her arms, palms up, in a gesture of futility. 'I'm sorry,' she repeated. 'What could I do? Your man John wanted to go to the pub. He was, you know, very insistent about it. Said he got a shiver down his spine, said it was God

474

giving him a mission. What could I do? The old boy's gaga. There's not too many pubs round Toorak, Joe, and those that are run to the posh end of the market. The first two wouldn't let him in and, like, the third one, well, the third one would but I couldn't get a park for *ages*.'

All my life, I reflected, not without regret, good help has been impossible to find.

'Where is the old coot?' I asked.

'What old man?' demanded Beatrice. 'How did you get in? Where's the bloody dog?'

'Just behind me,' she said, then flicked her head around quickly, flicked it back, perplexed. 'Both of them. At least he was, but I think he was finding the stairs a bit hard going. You were right, Joe: he's got a real thing with dogs.'

I nodded. 'Loves them to death.'

And then he entered, hobbling as fast as he could, a look of wild anger and bemusement on his face. He was holding a pub glass of water. Cerberus loped in behind him, gazing up in love, a changed beast, tail stump wagging.

Almost stumbling over as he fought for breath, John the Baptist looked around him aghast, figured out the politics with admirable clarity and advanced on Beatrice, holding forth his holy water like a cross towards a vampire.

'Mercifully hear our prayers, O Lord,' he croaked, scared and furious both. 'And graciously accept this oblation which we thy servants make to thee. You are

475

the Source and the Silence, the Mind and the Truth, the Logos and the Life. Your cruelty is our glory, for ever and ever. Amen.'

With that, he flung the contents of the glass into the face of my tormentor. She screamed, screamed like a banshee, screamed like a god brought low and forced to wander in the woods for mocked eternity. Her hands flew to her face, her knuckles pushed into her eyes, wiping frantically at them as if they burned with fire.

The rest of us watched. Gobsmacked, frankly.

And then she stopped, dropped her hands and raised her head, a sardonic grin on her face. 'Like that?' she asked no one in particular, and then turned to old John, ravens in her eyes. He stayed silent, his lips unconsciously forming the word 'whoops'.

She turned to me, a schoolyard snarl on her lips. 'Who *is* this pill?'

I replied in truth. 'John the Baptist.'

'Jesus,' she growled. I don't think she was talking to me.

And then she hit him, a single right-arm punch, straight in his stomach. He went down like the sack of bones he was, fighting for breath, wheezing, gasping, trying to apologise to me all in one go. Cerberus moved to him, sat on his legs, gazing into his face with goofy admiration and concern. The old man put his arms around the beast's head, started to weep.

'Now,' said Beatrice, reasserting the moment, 'let's get on with it.'

The goon positioned the spike again.

'Sophia,' I said, as calmly as I could. 'Now would be a good time to do something.'

Beatrice Cowper laughed. 'Sophia?' she echoed. 'Ha! Sophia works for me, you poor fool. I've had her tracking you for days, reeling you in, playing good guy to my bad.'

Shit, I thought. Not that it surprised me. Betrayal never does. It is the way of the world. Always has been. The unbelievers want me dead; the believers need me so. I have always been a hit and myth attraction.

The goon also laughed.

Sophia did not. 'Wrong, Cowper,' she said calmly. 'You've been working for *me*. I'm a federal agent.'

The rubber-woman's eyes flashed with ire. 'Under orders from whom?' she demanded.

'That's classified. We deal with power mongers and porn merchants, one and the same. We've had you marked for ages. I just let you think I wanted the madman Joe Panther out of the way. I lied to you.'

Cowper glared in rigid fury. The goon held his pose. Elaine Purdey kept whimpering. John the Baptist kept wheezing. The Rottweiler licked his face.

'So*phia*,' I urged, flexing at a strap.

'Sorry Joe,' she said. 'I lied to you too. You're both too dangerous to have on the loose.' She turned back to Beatrice. 'I fulfilled my part of the deal and delivered him to you. Do what you have to do.' Her right hand snaked inside her jacket. 'And then I'll finish *my* job.'

She pulled out a handgun, aimed it.

I stared. I don't know what sort of gun it was. I

don't know from guns. I've never used one. Knowing the difference between one gun and another is as pointless as the plebs knowing the difference between one sin and the next. Pointed at you in accusation by skilful hands informed by mission, most of them can kill you.

Sophia's gun was chunky, but not massive, maybe extramarital sex.

The goon dropped the spike and spun. From the folds of his cape he produced a gun of his own, much bigger. It was as big as buggering a goat in a bishop's parlour. Assuming you weren't the bishop.

Using two hands he pointed it straight at Sophia. 'Drop it!' he barked.

Sophia swung towards him, expert, pointing her own weapon straight down his sights. 'Sergeant Randall!' she barked. 'Game's over. Break your cover!'

The goon blinked, once, nodded. They both swung their guns towards Beatrice. She was on the move, however, striding fast the short distance towards me, ripping open the top buttons of her shirt. From between her breasts she too pulled a gun, a small one, pearl handled, perhaps coveting thy neighbour's ox, but gun enough. She rammed the barrel up into my throat.

'One more step,' she yelled, 'and the Messiah gets it!'

Randall and Sophia froze, exchanged glances, looked back at her, calm. 'So?' they chorused.

'Joe! My god!'

Everyone stopped. The voice was John the Baptist's, not in fear but in awe. He was still where he had fallen, still with his arms around Cerberus. He was quivering, possessed.

I stared at him. His eyes were all over the place, wandering stars, his jaw tight. It takes about an hour to come on, the average trip. In a body such as John's, old, frail and unused to hallucinogenic rushes, it was having a real party.

The old man was jubilant, clutching the head of the dog. 'He's back, son,' he stammered. 'He's back. I thought I felt him earlier, but now I know, son. The spirit of God is back inside me. I *knew*, son, I *knew* he'd not abandon me for good.'

His skinny arms tightened around the head of Cerberus, trying to twist its neck. The dog didn't look so comfortable any more.

'What can you see, old man?' I asked.

'I can see . . . I can see . . .' His arms locked, his right shoulder moving back. 'I can see . . . I don't *know* what I can see. It's moving, changing, like, red and yellow and blue, there's a lizard in it, angels swooping, there's light in the dog's eyes, son. I can see the light! I can see the light! The light of the father, he's comin' down to get me, son, comin' down to get old John . . .'

The dog's eyes were starting to bulge. I could see a vein thrusting out of its steel-black neck. No Shih tzu this, no Chinese contemplation, just sheer Teutonic force.

The old man inhaled, ecstatic, clutching the dog's twisted head to his skinny chest. 'Come and get me, Father!' he cried, right in its ear.

That did it. With a growl and a snarl, Cerberus spun and rose, anger and fear in his brain, and clamped his huge and slathering jaws across his torturer's throat, biting down. There was a strangled groan, another growl, and then lots and lots of rhythmic chewing, cracking and bubbling.

'Oh god,' murmured Elaine Purdey, and vomited on the gown of Mary.

The sound and smell jolted the rest of us back into the moment, Beatrice a fraction of a second ahead. In a flash, she pulled her gun from my neck and aimed it at the goon. There was a sharp report and the Roman centurion fell silent, blood oozing from a neat little hole in his forehead.

'Father!' I yelled, and then wondered why.

'Fuck,' breathed Sophia, momentarily lost. By the time she'd taken a bead again on Beatrice Cowper, the woman had moved once more. She was crouched down behind the shuddering, haloed, spew-covered Elaine Purdey, using her as a shield, the gun aimed at my lover and betrayer both. She fired.

Sophia winced.

The gun went click. Just click.

Coveting thy neighbour's ox was never really a consistent sin. Bit of a theological grey area, really.

Sophia chuckled, perhaps from relief, perhaps in triumph, and moved forward, her own gun staying level with Cowper's head.

'It's simple, Cowper,' she was saying, quite calm. 'You can still finish your job if you want. If you don't, well, no matter. He's not going anywhere, I can finish him myself.'

The pair were only about a metre apart.

Beatrice tossed her gun away. It clattered on the floor, skidded to halt. 'Lower your weapon,' she said, voice calm. 'I have to finish what's been started.'

Slowly, without stepping back, Sophia did so. She turned to look at me. There might have been tears welling in her eyes. Might have been.

I will never know. The moment she took her eyes from her quarry, Cowper snatched up the spear from where it lay near my feet and rammed the point out and up, straight between Sophia's rightside ribs.

The scream left her throat without voice, just the wind rushing on the wings of a swarm of incubi. Reflexively, as her body swayed in ever-increasing orbits, her left hand scrabbled at her wound, wrenching out the spear tip, blood cascading over her fingers, soaking her clothes, spattering to the floor like sinners cast to Hades. Her eyes were wide and wild, her mouth full of angel words and drool.

Her right hand held on to her gun.

She fell to the floor at my feet, curled, conscious, looking up into the eyes of the Lord.

'Help me,' she whispered wetly. 'Help me.'

Beatrice Cowper laughed, hard and hearty, one arm wrapped tightly around Elaine Purdey's neck. 'All that can save you now, girlie, is a miracle,' she chortled.

With a roar of pain, anger and denial, the small body of Sophia rolled onto its back, over its bending spine,

481

towards the taunting sound of the rubber proconsul. Its right arm extended, its right finger squeezed. Beatrice Cowper threw herself flat to the floor. There was a flash, an explosion, and the left side of Elaine Purdey's blameless, sinless head disappeared, her life force joining mine, spattering across my face and chest.

In the silence and smoke, little bits of tinsel fluttered to the ground. Her shirt flayed ragged by the blast, Beatrice Cowper shook her head, levered herself back upright. She looked down at the mess that had been the wife of her ex-husband. 'Oh well,' she said, and shrugged. 'Shit happens.'

'Help me . . . please.'

Sophia, still going, staring straight at me.

Beatrice Cowper chuckled, getting to her feet. 'What a development,' she said to herself, getting an idea. 'Now we can find out, Mr Panther. Now *you* can find out, at last, just who you are. Your little friend needs a miracle, small Josiah, and maybe the world needs proof. Here, now, live on camera, heal the broken-hearted, bring deliverance to the captive.'

'Joe,' whispered Sophia, blood now flecking her lips, her breathing shallow. 'I'm sorry. I promise . . .'

I looked down on her broken form, this stranger, this lover of mine, this treacherous cop, and I wondered. I remembered other times, way back, raising the child, raising Lazarus, times when I let the blind receive their sight, and the lame walk, the lepers cleanse, the dead raise up, and the poor have the gospel preached.

And I wondered. It was a long time ago. I hadn't

done it since, not after the abandonment. Why heal the sick and miserable when all that lay waiting for them was more of the same?

But still. She showed me kindness once, wiped away my tears.

'*Please*,' she said.

I turned to Beatrice. 'I will do it,' I said. 'I must lay my hands upon her, now.'

She got to her feet, took a step towards me, still proud and forceful even in the ripped mess of her costume, still in control. Now more than ever. She reached over, slipped the buckle on the strap around my left wrist. 'Just one hand,' she said. 'I've halved your sentence.'

I bent from the waist as well as I could, bent at the knees, pain searing along my right arm as it stretched with the force. With my free hand, I wiped the blood from my eyes. My sight stayed clear. Even the Lord must coagulate.

Sophia stared up at me. I stared down.

'I don't know whether I want to do this,' I said.

She caught her breath, tried to catch her breath, her small perfect chest heaving. 'Do this, Joe,' she hushed, 'and I swear I'll renounce reason. I will follow you anywhere, worship you forever, be your . . .'

I stretched as far as I could, asked inside me, for the first time in countless lifetimes, asking for forgiveness, just once, just this once, from the father, asking absolution, asking for help to save this good woman here beneath me.

Beatrice Cowper watched, silent, unmoving.

I pressed my fingers into her wound. She did not flinch.

'Concentrate, Sophia,' I said, doing my best voice, doing my best. 'He that receiveth you receiveth me, and he that receiveth me receiveth him that sent me.'

She reached her right hand up to me, soft fingers seeking my face.

And then she died.

Maybe I didn't want to do it, after all. I stood up again, my eyes dry.

Beatrice Cowper shrugged. 'Well, what do you know?' she asked rhetorically. 'Shit still happens. Well, Mr Panther, now it's just you, me, and the world.'

I took a deep breath. 'One question first, grant me that.'

She nodded.

'Why your daughter?'

She shook her head. 'Why not? No, actually Mr Panther, Shelagh was a mistake. I would have had it otherwise, but there you go.'

'A mistake? Drugging, torturing, painting and beheading your own daughter was a mistake?'

'Yes. Some years ago I took into my employ a certain priest, a weak man like most priests. His name was—'

'Dominic Scopemi.'

'Correct. Sick boy, that priest. He'd taken some shots, religious porn shots, of a young girl who'd been involved with that priest of yours, Mr Panther, and I got wind of them. I have many sources. The priest thought he was taking them in the name of God, in the name of justice, but I knew better. I found him, I bought them from him. They sold well. They also gave me a handle over him, in case I ever needed it. It never hurts to have the clergy in your pocket, as you'd know.'

I nodded agreement. That's the way it's always worked. That was part of the plan, I'm sure.

'So then the business with you came up. A mad messiah in our midst, Mr Panther, just when the people who know these things were casting around for a new image, a new burst of glorious martyrdom. Trouble was, you're smart in some ways, street smart, pariah smart. I had to find a way to get you in, get you off balance.' She paused, smiled. 'Get you *here*.'

'So?'

'So I called on the priest, offered him a deal. He's in South America now, by the way, lay-preaching in some godforsaken village in the Andes. I told him I needed a sacrificial lamb. I knew about you and Corrigan, so I told him we needed to frame the priest, knowing he'd turn to you for help, poor sod. Scopemi knew the first woman had seen a sex abuse help group. I asked him to see if any other poor maidens had been so badly used by the man and gone to the same place, laying a trail. He did some hacking, said there was. One. I told him to coax her, play on her desire for revenge, or justice, whatever, get her here and prep her up.'

485

I guessed the rest. 'And Scopemi found Shelagh. You have different surnames, he didn't know shit.'

'By the time I found out, she was already here and had seen my face. I had no option. Anyway, I realised, what better alibi? What sort of a monster would murder her own daughter?'

'You already did, Beatrice Cowper, when you left her to your ex.'

Her eyes flared. 'Do *not* presume to judge me, you pathetic little boy!' she spat. 'You're in no position to judge.' She bent over and picked up the bloody spear at rest beside the corpse of Wisdom. Point towards me, dripping, she took a deep breath. 'Enough talk. Now we continue,' she hissed.

I played for time, trying to think. 'And what about the others? What about the others you've killed? What about the zombies down below?'

She shook her head, a teacher to her slow-witted charge. 'You've never understood, have you? I give people what they want, nothing more, at both ends of the process. Members of the Purdey family aside, Mr Panther, no one has ever entered this house by other than free will.'

'I saw straps on some of the beds.'

'Restraint is part of the gig for some. It costs them extra, of course, but I'm happy to oblige. I am but a servant. In sadomasochism, it is the masochist who really has the power, whatever the appearance may suggest. Atonement is a powerful drive, Mr Panther, you should know that. I merely facilitate the means.

486

Strength only comes through surrender and abasement. I exist to serve my penitents.'

I think that was the word she used.

She stared at my spattered chest, ran her lascivious tongue along her upper lip, tested the heft of the shaft in her hand.

'And you take responsibility for your actions?'

She puffed her chest out, ragged and proud. 'I don't care if you're the real Christ or not, Mr Panther. I've enjoyed testing and tormenting you, though, because when it comes down to it, whatever else I might be, I'm a right bitch. At this moment, however, I am merely following orders.'

I shook my head. 'Not good enough.'

She took a step forward. 'It's all there is, Mr Panther. It's always been this way and—'

'Spare me.'

She laughed at that, placed the cold flat of the blade against my breast, and smeared a line of Sophia's gore across it. 'No chance,' she whispered.

I looked around in what seemed to be my final moments, mortal me. The room was a mess. There was blood and flesh splattered all over the floor, in great curved streaks up the wall. Smoke hung heavy in the air. The goon, Sophia and Elaine Purdey lay at my feet, in various stages of disintegration. John the Baptist lay in pieces, dismembered and disembowelled, over near the door, the great hulk of Cerberus now lying Schubert beside the remains, blood all over its snout, jowls and chest.

Beatrice breathed deep and hungry, aroused, teasing with the spear, murder in her eyes. I looked at the dog. The dog looked at Beatrice.

And then I realised something. When Cerberus had begun his meal, John's veins had been coursing with the mystic wonder of Andy Warhol's banana. The beast had since absorbed an awful lot of blood, down its throat, through its skin. Canine metabolisms are different from those of humans, more fragile, more sensitive. Its black eyes were limpid pools.

The dog was tripping off its dial.

The dog was open to suggestion.

'Cerberus!' I called.

The dog swung its great head, stared at me.

'*Cerberus*,' warned Beatrice.

The dog kept staring at me.

In the beginning was the word, and it pays, Beatrice had said, not to make the word too obvious. I had one chance, I knew, one chance to utter the name of the composer that would rouse the dog to violent action. One chance to escape a destiny I neither knew nor craved. One chance in a thousand.

I glanced down at the body of Sophia, remembered her passions. It was worth a try, at least, I reflected, divine intervention having failed once already. I resolved to reason. If Mozart stilled and Schubert sedated, what name would unleash murderous fury? Tchaikovsky? Stravinsky?

And there, all of a sudden, I saw into the well of possibilities: there, amidst the carnage of betrayal; there, under sentence; there, naked and crowned with barbed wire; there, painted with the blood of the innocent; there, bound before the holy crotch of commerce; there, endorsed; there, an object of entertainment, an instrument of subjugation; there, an affirmation of what I was, what I once was, perhaps never was; there, drugged and restrained; there, amidst the horror of my long lost lover's twin; there, a glimmer of the googolplex.

And there, then, I *knew*.

With my free hand I pointed at Beatrice.

'Andrew Lloyd Webber!' I yelled.

Cerberus leapt, bedevilled with acid and rage, teeth bared and roaring.

She didn't have a chance. She died within minutes.

I slipped the buckles on my right wrist with my left, freed my feet before I fell, spent a moment getting my breath back. My mind felt surprisingly clear in the silence that descended, adrenalin having flushed my system well.

It *is* all is theatre, in the end. I turned to the nearest camera and bowed low. Then I turned to the next and, on a sudden whim I know not from whence, turned my back, bent over and flashed a brown-eye.

I stood up again and thought a moment. The immediate threat had been nullified, I concluded, which left only the small problems of a house full of drugged white-robed cultists, probably a fair contingent of watchers and other federal agents waiting outside (Sophia probably having called them before entering), joined no doubt by local cops attracted by the gunshots and, quite possibly by now, Gordon and Pordelli pissed off and fresh from a house in Carlton, the interior of which would have raised far more questions than it answered.

Ah well, back to the real world.

I patted my pockets for a Dunhill, and then remembered I was naked, location of clothes unknown. I walked over to the goon and rifled around beneath his cape. Sure enough, he was wearing a shirt beneath it, a packet of smokes in its pocket. Stuyvesants, not bad. I knocked one out, found his lighter, lit it.

As I opened the door, Cerberus trotted past me, too full of flesh and fug to be bothered, and disappeared along the passage. I paused a moment, considering options. I took a drag. It was harsh on my throat.

I held the cigarette before my face, and thought, Filthy habit. I had to be honest with myself. I had to at least face the possibility that I might be, after all, no more than human, lost and small.

In which case, the smokes could kill me. I was in my thirties, a time of reckoning, a time of future planning. I realised I had no wish to end my days, pained and wracking in a cancer bed. There were many decisions to be made, and I might as well start making them right then.

With a sigh of regret followed by an inhalation of purpose, I tossed the Stuyvo over my shoulder, back into the room.

And straight into the barrel of oil.

490

†

The car, an old Valiant with squeaking suspension and a missing headlight, pulled to a smoky halt outside the huge wooden gates. They were open slightly, the woman waiting silent, hands clasped, head up, proud, between them.

Caroline wrenched on the handbrake. 'I'll wait here, Joe,' she said. 'Don't be long. You'll miss your train if you don't hurry.'

I nodded, opened the door.

Four days had passed. The cuts around my head had healed, mostly, the few remaining scabs well covered by hair.

Caroline had woken to my frantic banging against her door, sometime in the lost hours before dawn that night. She found me naked, filthy, exhausted, barbed wire wrapped around my head. I lay for the next three days and nights on the tragic carpet of Shelagh Purdey's old room, lying low, sleeping, recovering, healing, forgetting. No one had come for me.

The barrel had gone up like the celebrations marking the handover of hell to the red army of heaven. By the time I'd found my way along the passage, through some more, down the stairs and to the conservatory, the whole house had been alight, the fire spreading, the roar and suck of its hunger deafening. I'd only just managed to smash the glass wall with the coffee table and run for the garden fence before the roof collapsed.

There had been people everywhere. Men and women in white, stupored and scared, had been racing around, jumping from windows, smashing down doors, running across the grounds. Cerberus was hurling himself this way and that, mad with panic, snapping at whatever came near. Police officers were tripping over each other, shouting commands which nobody heeded, trying to rescue the runners. Men and women in no known uniform were getting in the way, trying to gain entrance, looking for something, looking for anything. Ambulances raced up, fire engines howled and screamed, blue and red lights needing only Donna Summer to turn the scene into a bad eighties nightclub.

I had scrambled over the back gates, slipping on the grass, falling in the mud, half blinded by the rain, but clear enough in my head to run, run down the lane, and keep running.

And I discovered then my true divinity. I heard lumbering feet and wheezing breath behind me, turned without stopping. There was Pordelli, alone, frantic to catch me, his notebook in one hand, pen in the other, calling questions ancient in their origin.

'Tell me about the safe-house!' he is yelling. 'Not who was there. We know who was there. Tell me about the cheesy biscuit. What did you do with it? Then what? And said? Now the wine, the wine. Think carefully: what were your words?'

I wasn't going to make the same mistake twice. He was fat and clothed and wet and mortal. I was thin and naked and blood-covered and Lord. I out-ran him easily, heard him panting to a halt. Faint in my pounding ears, he called his last request, a desperate plea for understanding. 'At least tell me about the licensing deals.'

And I kept running, many miles, to Caroline's flat by the freeway.

And then silence descended. The story was hushed. The hunt was called off, the cops, no doubt, much happier if I simply vanished. I knew too much to confess.

I have always known too much. I know that now.

Caroline bought me a newspaper the next day. The lead story concerned a disastrous fire at a private psychiatric hospital in Toorak, seven dead, four in one room, including its owner. The cause of the fire, it said, was accidental, a fault in an oil heater.

I discovered, too, that Graeme Purdey was found after more than twenty-four hours, still tied to his chair, watching endlessly the death and resurrection of his violated daughter. He was gibbering mad by then.

And now I stood before the gates of the convent, facing Theresa Mary Farndale, pious and devout. Macca had found her in the end, found the lead. His aunt was a nun, it turned out, and knew the name. Caroline had borrowed a car—someone, somewhere, was still prepared to lend things to junkies—driven me there, and from there destined for the train station, safe now, for the long ride to Sydney, and from there, to . . .

Actually, I'll not tell you that.

Away. A long way away. There was twenty grand

493

in my pocket, not much, but enough to get a fake passport and a ticket. Handy thing, banking on the Internet. The withdrawal I'd made Graeme Purdey make had been waiting at the nominated branch, good as gold, cash, no questions asked.

Theresa Farndale's red hair was not to be seen, hidden and cropped beneath her wimple. I looked at her eyes, no red in them now, cool and strong. She looked a little like Mary, yes, Mary the mother or Mary the other. Which Mary, I knew, would depend on the day.

'You wanted to see me,' she said, her voice even.

'Yes. Do you know who I am?'

'I've been told.'

'I've been looking for you.'

'I know.'

'But I don't think it matters any more.'

'I know.'

She turned to go. 'Wait,' I said. 'I know your background. How did you end up as a nun? Was it just the desire for isolation, for protection?'

She shook her head and looked me straight in the eye.

'No, it wasn't,' she started. 'Far from it. There were men in my life, as you know, men of the cloth who did me great harm. My pain was very great, and I don't mind confessing that I came close to taking my life to make it all end. But there was something that prevented me from doing so: the thought that it was *them*, the men, who had sinned, not me. Despite all of it, I still loved my God. I was caught in a paradox, and decided to seek some answers.

'So I took the orders, and entered a life of study and contemplation. For the past ten years I have lived here, lived mainly in the library here. I have read, read as many works by the thoughtful and the holy as I can. I will continue to read until I die, striving to understand the traditions, open and secret, of the God I love with a passion more insatiable than any lust I ever felt in times gone by.'

I modified a question. 'And *thus* you know who I am?'

She did not smile. 'I know who you are,' she said. 'As I said, I have studied the open and the occult traditions. I have studied and I have prayed for understanding. I know who you are, Yoshu.'

I believed her. 'And will you welcome me? Do you forgive me my sins, which are many?'

'No.'

'But you must. You need me.'

She smiled then, a sad, gentle smile, kept her gaze on my face. 'No, Yoshu, no. I know what you know and I feel your pain, but no. I need your name, your death and your icon. These things I love. But you, you were never essential. Saviour, forgive thyself.'

She turned, walked away. The gates swung shut behind her.

✝

At the train station, Caroline parked. She turned to me, before I could get out.

'Have you forgotten, Joe?' she asked. 'My wish. You said you'd make my wish come true.'

I pulled out a Dunhill, lit it. I'll give up one day, if there's a point to it. 'I'm not sure I can,' I said.

She smiled, a sad smile. 'Oh yes, Joe, you can. You, of all people.'

The moment of reckoning had arrived. 'What?'

She held up her hand, the skin dry, the back of it lightly scabbed, five fingers stretched.

'Oh Caroline,' I said, suddenly sad myself. 'I offer you the world, anything you want, take you to the top of the mountain, and all you want is five pissy deals?'

'It's all I want, Joe. It's all I need.'

I pulled them from my pocket, handed them over. 'Hang on,' I added, patting my new leather jacket. 'I've got some fits somewhere.'

'Just one, Joe,' she said. 'I'll only need the one.'

I stared into her eyes, which stared back, calm. 'Oh Caroline.'

She smiled. 'It's over, Joe. At last.'

A tannoy screeched, said the train was leaving in five minutes.

✝

So here I am, a place unknown.

Here. Anywhere. Everyhell.

I might have a beard. I might not.

I might be that man you saw yesterday, the one down at heel with eyes that didn't blink. The one you moved away from, suddenly nervous, inexplicably shy.

I might be. I might not.

You do not know me. But I know you. Every bit of you. Every thought of you. Every silent, timid, echoing yearn.

I know you when you wake at dawn, frightened, fatherless and alone.

I know you.

For I am the Son of Man.

I have been there. I am always there.

I am in you.

Turn away. You don't need me.

And pray that I don't need you.

Because thus do things reduce.

✝